Totally Bound Publishing books by Maren Jenner

Sweet Nothings
The Cupcake Standard

I0564016

Sweet Nothings

THE CUPCAKE STANDARD

MAREN JENNER

The Cupcake Standard
ISBN # 978-1-80250-558-0
©Copyright Maren Jenner 2023
Cover Art by Erin Dameron-Hill ©Copyright August 2023
Interior text design by Claire Siemaszkiewicz
Totally Bound Publishing

THE CUPCAKE STANDARD

Dedication

To my husband and my kiddo.
I wouldn't be here without your support!

Acknowledgements

First of all, I'd like to thank Totally Bound for helping this story reach its full potential and helping me realize my dream of becoming a published author.

A huge thank-you to my editor, Nicki, for all her assistance and patience with my myriad questions.

I couldn't have done this without my beta readers, specifically Lindsay, Jessica, and Heather. Thank you also to Allison who helped me take the next step from revisions to dipping my toe into the publishing world.

But the biggest thank-you goes to my CP Christine who is always around to toss ideas around or read another revision.

To my friends and family who supported me on this journey, who believed in me, who never let me give up—thank you and I love you.

Lastly, a big thanks to you, my readers, because this wouldn't be possible without you.

Chapter One

I stopped believing in fairy tales the day I caught my mother cheating with her book agent. When I was a little girl, I used to stare at my parents' wedding photos for hours, hoping I would find a love like theirs. But true love was a myth, just like Santa Claus and the Easter Bunny. I still dated, but my heart wasn't up for grabs. It wasn't worth the risk.

Two years had flown by since Mother's first cheating incident, even now I felt her sharp eyes following me. I glanced up from the latte I was making, meeting the cardboard cut-out across the room where it stood sentinel next to a display for her newest self-help book. *Why does it have to be here?* I snapped the lid on to the cup with enough force that whipped cream spattered over me.

Great. Typical Monday.

My apologetic smile at the customer was sincere, but my forthcoming excuse was a lie. "Sorry, I'm a little stressed. I have a big exam coming up."

One of the best parts of working at Not Your Average Joe, the coffee shop across from Southern Michigan University, was blaming a bad day on the stress of college life. Customers were shockingly forgiving when SMU, 'smoo' to us students, was looped into the excuse.

Mother's piercing green eyes stared at me, so similar to my own, and I heard her shrill voice scolding me about my apron. I sighed, rubbing my forehead. Had her gross agent Jack made a deal with Not Your Average Joe, just to torture me? It wasn't enough that I had to accept her paying for college to avoid drowning in debt by graduation, I was forced to look at her overly zealous smile, towering red hair and the super low-cut neckline of her dress every shift, as well? Thanks a lot. No one needed to see that much of their mother.

I grabbed a damp cloth to clean tables in the mostly empty lobby. Somehow, I resisted the urge to throw the dirty rag at my mother's smiling face, the face of the woman who had not only betrayed Daddy but still wouldn't cut him loose. I swallowed the familiar stab of pain that came whenever my thoughts drifted to my parents' façade of a marriage.

It wasn't fair. Mother had written self-help books for most of my childhood. Her success exploded two years ago, her fame growing exponentially. Her YouTube channel instantly went viral, becoming an overnight, trendsetting sensation. Companies all over the globe vied for her to endorse products on her show, flooding her with free samples. We went from upper middle class to filthy rich with the snap of a finger, and Mother reveled in it.

Daddy had supported her through it all, celebrating her successes, encouraging her through low points and was the perfect rock for her to lean on. How did she thank him? The moment he needed her help, she shoved him aside. Even after all Daddy had done for her, the world didn't know he existed. As his illness progressed, Mother grew more adept at keeping him in the shadows, and it became his permanent residence.

The bell on the door jangled. I looked up to find the embodiment of my turbulent thoughts sweeping into the coffee shop. Mabel Milbourne — trendsetter, fashion icon and author of the now infamous self-help book *How to Land a Guy...and Keep Him!* — in the flesh. Otherwise known as my mother.

"Avery, darling." Her always blinding white teeth gleamed in a glaring smile framed by fire truck red lips. The shade matched her most definitely dyed hair, her natural color much closer to my own strawberry blonde. She was shorter than me, around five seven, and slender.

My smile was forced. "Mother." I hurried behind the counter to wash my hands. "What do I owe the pleasure?" It was an effort to keep my tone pleasant.

Her latest boy toy sauntered up to the counter, not much older than me. I'd be twenty-one in just over a month, so at least he was legal. As he gave me an appraising grin, I fought to keep my smile in place. My teeth ground together.

"Avery, why do I need an excuse to see my daughter?" The voice was my mother's, but the delivery had changed over the past couple of years — evidence of her speech coaches. Always trying to fit in with the upper class.

Yet another thing taken from me. I kept silent.

"Have you been getting my gifts?" Her perfectly arched eyebrow lifted ever so slightly.

"Oh, yes." I pressed my teeth together so hard I was sure to chip a tooth.

I was almost six feet tall with curves, two traits I'd hated for most of my teenage years. I'd hunched to appear shorter, worn baggy hoodies despite our humid Michigan summers and avoided high heels at all costs. But Daddy loved me no matter my height or my weight. I'd always been his little girl, the mascot at his poker games, the one by his side watching football every Sunday. Mother, on the other hand, had always been quick to swap my chips for a celery stick or my sandwich for a salad.

Ironically, I had Mother to thank for helping me accept my body. If she hadn't dragged me on that book tour during my senior year of high school, I never would have met Trish, her assistant. Trish taught me the art of embracing my curves, accenting my height and highlighting my best features. Because of her, I fell in love with makeup, my own brand of armor.

Mother cleared her throat, bringing me to the present. "Which gift was your favorite?"

The 'gifts' she spoke of were her castaways. Designers clamored to be promoted on her show or worn by her, so they sent her tokens, samples of their upcoming lines in hopes that something would strike her fancy.

I got the leftovers.

"Oh, the Hermes scarf was very colorful." And the only thing that fit.

As a curvy girl, I was a size sixteen on a good day and I had no problem with it. For most designers, I wasn't even close to fitting in their 'sample-size' range, although a select few included my size in the very upper end of their spectrum. Most of what they sent was meant for Mother or one of her models.

"Yes, dear, that scarf was adorable." She gave me a placating smile.

My taste was yet another thing never quite up to her standards. Even if I wore every article of clothing she gave me, I still wouldn't please her. Instead, I prided myself in not using any of her gifts. I stored them in a rented warehouse, to be used for charity functions or to auction off for a good cause. Occasionally, I dipped into them for my own fun, but never for day-to-day expenses. I was determined to pave my own way, with the exception of her much-needed assistance with tuition.

Mother drummed her nails on the counter, a sign she was gearing up for the real reason for her visit.

"Can I get you something?" I gestured to the menu behind me.

Boy Toy beamed, rattling off his order as well as Mother's standard frappuccino like a well-trained puppy. It took some effort to hold in the words 'Good boy'. I wondered if his butt would wag.

I had to ask now, or I knew I wouldn't get the chance. "How's Daddy? Did you look over those facilities I sent you?" Daddy needed more help than she was willing to give him, and I could only do so much.

Her eyes widened, and she glanced from side to side. "What have I told you about speaking about that in public?"

"But—"

"He's doing just fine. At home." She inhaled deeply. "Now, about my coffee?"

Several minutes later, I handed them their drinks.

Mother took a sip. "Delicious. Your shift is over soon, right?"

I froze, realizing it was one of those nights. She wanted to cash in her 'I pay for your college so you owe me' chip. I swallowed, nodding.

A Cheshire Cat smile slid over her face. "Wonderful." She turned to Boy Toy. "Go tell Jack to keep the car running." She watched him go, taking another sip of her drink before she addressed me once more. "We'll wait outside, and you can join us for dinner. I have several important people for you to meet." Her smile was still in place, but her eyes were hard, telling me just how important this was to her.

My chest tightened. The obligation rested heavily on me as I weighed my options against the old well of anger simmering in my gut. I knew she only wanted me there to show me off. I rounded out her image, softening her persona by showing her maternal side. I avoided high society functions whenever I could, out of spite mostly, but it also wasn't a crowd I wanted to belong to.

Not to mention I'd had a full day of classes and worked a six-hour shift. I had homework to do yet. And I was a mess.

"Mother, tonight's not a great—"

"Avery." Steel wound through the syllables. "I've already told people you're coming. As part of our agreement, you committed to attending functions occasionally. This is one you will be attending." There was no room for argument.

Boy Toy met Mother at the door, shooting me a smirk as he escorted her out.

Only ten minutes before my shift ends. Not much time to finagle my way out of this.

I hurried to finish wiping down the lobby, my brain racing over my options. I'd gotten out of dinners before, but Mother knew my tricks well enough now. After I continually evaded Jack, Mother had started bringing along backup. Hence Boy Toy's presence.

My shift over, I rushed through goodbyes to my coworkers, then peeked outside. I shook my head at the portly agent lingering out front. It was pathetic how Jack followed my mother around, begging for any shred of her attention, despite her moving on from him ages ago. He was still her agent, but nothing more. Boy Toy wasn't in sight, and the Town Car's tinted windows gave nothing away. He could be in there with Mother, but I doubted it.

The back door for employees seemed the best route for escape, so I hurried to it, wishing it had a window. I pushed open the door to find Boy Toy casually leaning against a nearby tree, a sleazy grin sliding across his face.

Panic at being caught flared in me, but I shoved it aside, plastering on a smile and tossing my ponytail over my shoulder. I grabbed the door before it closed, forming a plan on the spot. I kept my cool, sounding casual. "Hey, Mother sent me to get you." Hopefully, Mother's only dating him for his looks.

Boy Toy eyed me. "She did?"

I forced my voice to stay even. "Mm hmm. I'm ready to go," I said sweetly. "Meet you around front?"

He nodded, shoving both hands into his pockets before strolling away.

That was just too easy. I stepped inside, letting the door close until there was only a sliver big enough to watch him walk around the corner as I studied the paths I could take.

In front of me sprawled Southern Michigan University's pristine campus. SMU's maze of buildings and sidewalks teemed with students this time of evening as the dinner hour approached. *Perfect.*

As soon as Boy Toy disappeared from sight, I tightened my grip on my backpack and sprinted toward the street separating me from campus. It wasn't a busy road, and I darted right across it. I heard Jack shout when I reached the middle, but I didn't risk a glance until I was safely on the other side.

Jack wasn't in great shape. To say he ran after me was a gross misrepresentation—lumbered was a better word. Boy Toy still hadn't caught on, buying me time since he had the only chance at catching me. *Game on.*

I headed for the first group of students I saw, weaving around them and ducking behind the nearest building. Unfortunately this led me to a fairly wide-open space. *Dammit.*

My pursuers in sight now, I raced for a gap between two buildings, disappearing between them, then took a sharp right. I glanced over my shoulder, relieved to have lost them for the moment. My steps slowed to a fast walk as I rounded another corner. I scanned the area, my gaze landing on the perfect cover—a tall, dark, and handsome guy leaning against the brick wall of the Franklin building, scrolling on his phone. I yanked the hair tie out of my ponytail, my hair cascading to my waist. My movement caught his eye as I shed my jean jacket and rolled down the waistband of my plaid skirt. His bright blue eyes widened as I approached.

He hasn't seen anything yet.

With a brilliant smile and a seductive toss of my hair, I closed the distance between us. My jean jacket dropped over his bag as I grabbed his blue striped tie, yanking his lips onto mine. He was taller than I'd thought, which was something coming from me.

Before he could pull away, I spun us around, so his firm body pressed me against the brick wall, wrapping my leg around his waist to keep him there. He didn't seem to mind. A deep groan rumbled through his chest, and he kissed me back, hungrily. My stomach flipped as I threaded my fingers through his black hair, just the right length to hold on to.

Footsteps rounded the corner, and I peeked over to see Boy Toy sprint by. *Right, this is supposed to be my cover...* Just then, the hot guy deepened the kiss, slanting his mouth against mine and doing this amazing thing with his tongue. My eyes fluttered shut again, my turn to moan.

Another set of footsteps ran by, accompanied by some huffing and puffing. I managed to catch a glimpse of Jack. It was several moments before I registered that the sound had disappeared and I unwrapped myself from the guy, giving him a gentle push away. He stared at me as we both caught our breath.

Why isn't it illegal to have eyes as brilliant a blue as his? One might drown in them. I blinked a few times to regain my senses, abruptly realizing he was waiting for me to say something. My defenses slid back into place. So did my smile, as I gathered my wits, striving to be the very picture of at ease and flippant.

"Thanks for the diversion," I said, grabbing my jacket. And I hurried off in the opposite direction my pursuers had gone. *Mission accomplished.*

I was almost to the library when I received a text from Mother.

No gifts for you for a month.

I rolled my eyes and went to study.

* * * *

The following day, my morning class wrapped up, and I hurried across campus to Michigan Ave to flag down a taxi. I was going to be late for my weekly lunch date. Every Wednesday, Mother had a weekly spa appointment, and I took advantage of her absence to sneak in one-on-one time with Daddy.

"Where to?"

Shit. Normally, I had the address ready. "Um, just a sec." I fumbled for my phone, heat rising in my face as anxiety coiled in my stomach.

Me and numbers did not get along. I always struggled to keep even the basics like addresses and phone numbers straight in my brain. Since Mother moved last year, hauling Daddy along with her, I wasn't confident enough to rattle it off.

The driver snapped his gum. "You know where you're going or not?"

"Sorry, I…" I stopped. "I forgot my wallet." I rushed out, onto the sidewalk.

The yellow cab drove away, the engine roaring as if it too were huffing at me.

I blinked until the sting of embarrassment dissipated, then pulled up Uber. A few seconds later, I had a response and a much easier ride.

Patty, Mother's cook, waited in the open doorway, tapping her foot. "Cutting it close, hmm?" Patty had been with our family forever. She'd been around before…before my mother became famous, before Mother had cheated on Daddy, before the diagnosis. She was family to me.

My humiliation too fresh for me to hide, I ducked my chin.

"Oh, child, what happened?" She pulled me to her ample bosom, the familiar smell of vanilla and lemon embracing me along with her thick arms.

"Why did Mother have to move? The other house was just fine."

She clicked at me, with a knowing smile. "Still having trouble with the address?" Her warm hand patted my back as I nodded, then she guided me inside. "It'll get better, child. Now get on down there before Kyle gets his knickers in a wad."

My footsteps thudded as I jogged down the marble hallway of the way too big house. It wasn't quite a mansion, with only five bedrooms, but it was definitely more house than the two of them needed. Three if I had to include Boy Toy.

I tapped on Daddy's door, greeting Kyle with a grin. Daddy's caregiver just looked at his watch before arching an eyebrow at me.

"I know, I know. But I'm here!"

A reluctant smile crossed his face. "See you in an hour, Miss Avery."

"Bye, Kyle."

Daddy's eyes stayed fixed on the TV, and I waited by the door, content to watch him. Gone was the robust man, full of life and laughter. The man I used to run to, my arms wide open so he could swing me high above his head in a dizzying circle before crushing me in a bear hug. In his place lay a pale, thin person, frailty evident in every movement. Alzheimer's had stolen so much of him from me.

Patty bustled in with her noisy cart, rumbling and clinking. "All right Steve, time to eat some lunch. I made your favorite." Daddy's eyes met hers, then she looked my way. "And you've got a special guest today. This is Avery."

A smile tipped up his lips. "My daughter's name is Avery."

The small bit of hope that sparked to life every time she introduced me burned out when he returned my smile with a blank stare. I was a stranger to him. I pushed aside the sharp stab of pain and forced my smile wider. "Hi, Steve. I heard you're a big Lions fan."

As we ate, we talked about football — nothing current of course, only the glory days. And he told me stories of poker games past where his daughter had helped him, his little shadow. It was difficult hearing stories about me, his favorite mascot. But knowing he remembered, that he treasured those stories, made it bearable.

I was grateful I'd had that time with him — the poker and whiskey and football, all the things we'd shared when I was growing up. At least those memories were still intact for him. For now.

The hardest part was when he spoke about Mother. His eyes would go tender, a loving light shining through as my heart gained another layer of ice. "Oh my Mabel, she sure is something. This one time…"

As soon as I could, I steered him to another subject. Before I knew it, the hour was up.

I wanted to hug him goodbye, to call him Daddy, but it would only agitate him. So I settled for a handshake. "Thanks for lunch, Steve. I hope we can do it again soon." My voice cracked on the last word, and I cleared my throat.

He nodded. "That'd be nice. I don't get many visitors here. It's been ages since I've seen my daughter. I miss her."

His words stabbed at my heart with an edge sharper than a steak knife, and I blinked at the tears pricking my eyes. "I'm sure she misses you, too." The tightness in my throat intensified.

His head bobbed a few times before he settled back against his pillow, his eyes fixed on the TV as if I weren't even there anymore.

I watched him from the doorway for a moment, feeling as if I'd been turned to cellophane, invisible in every way. Then I spun on my heel and made a quick getaway, not wanting Patty to grill me about my damp cheeks.

Chapter Two

After my business marketing class, I headed to the dingy apartment I shared with my best friend, Gina. Also here on a partial scholarship, she'd had a difficult childhood, bouncing from one foster home to the next. On-campus housing was just too expensive for us scholarship girls, so we'd leapt at the chance to rent an apartment together. The location wasn't bad.

But that was all it had going for it.

I sighed as I stared at the dilapidated building with the patchy shingles. *How is it even legal to rent this place out?* Not that I could afford anything decent unless I accepted more help from my mother or applied for a bigger loan. Or worked another job and lightened my class load. None of the options appealed to me.

As I climbed the rickety stairs, careful to dodge the third one that someone had fallen through just last week, I sighed again. I knew Daddy had set me up with some money from my grandparents when they'd passed away. And I knew his own pension would more than provide for him, even in his current state. If only

Mother would divorce him and leave us to our own devices, but she had an image to maintain, after all — that of the wholesome mother and housewife. I rolled my eyes so hard, I nearly stumbled.

My third-floor apartment wasn't far from the stairway. The musty air always smelled faintly of mold and feet, despite the many air fresheners we used. I had my key out, pausing when I heard voices through our paper-thin walls.

Gina's boyfriend, Josh, was over, and they were arguing. Again.

Josh's voice bounced through the hallway, distorting only a little. "I don't understand why you have to stay. She's a grown woman, Gina."

Gina stomped around, a dangerous thing to do on our ancient floor.

Who knows where a good stomp will put you?

"Avery isn't just my best friend. She's *family*." She stomped again. "I'm not leaving her at the mercy of that witch she has for a mother. I'm all she's got."

"But she comes from money, Gina. Can't she just get her own place?"

A wooden chair screeched across the floor. "You don't know anything!"

Great, now I had a kick in my stomach to go with my stab wound from earlier. I trudged back to the stairs and started blasting Lady Gaga to announce my presence. I turned the key, flinging open the door. With an overly bright smile, I said, "Hey."

Gina leaned against the counter, her arms crossed, glaring daggers at Josh who sat on one of our two dining room chairs.

"Everything okay?" I tossed my bag down on a wobbly end table before perching on the hideous, not second, not third, but fourth-hand couch we'd found for free.

Josh sighed, giving in first. "Yep, everything's fine. You two want to order dinner? My treat?" It was his version of an olive branch, saying sorry for pushing her. Including me always helped soften her up.

And it worked. She melted like butter, walking over to wrap her arms around him from behind and kiss his cheek. "I'm starving. How about Luigi's? I've been dying for some ravioli."

"I'll take the Chicken Alfredo, with a side salad." I could already hear my jeans yelling at me, just from the thought of all that pasta, but no way would I pass up free food.

Gina smiled at me, like she knew what I was thinking. Five foot seven and gorgeous, her frame stayed slender no matter what she ate. Her skin had that all-year tan without setting foot outside, combining with her dark hair and big dark eyes to give her an exotic edge. She was my opposite in every way.

Right down to the fact that she let herself fall in love.

Josh hung up after ordering, turning to pin Gina against the counter and kiss her. Josh was lean, wiry but toned, not at all her usual type. His long brown hair was pulled back in a ponytail, and he wanted to be an actor, majoring in theater. I didn't see the appeal.

Dark, curly hair and a set of amazing blue eyes flashed in my mind. The stranger's firm body as I grabbed his tie and pulled him closer. Heat rushed through me, my stomach flipping at the mere memory.

Great. Now I need a diversion from my diversion.

* * * *

A week later, as I sharply rounded the psychology section in the campus library, I ran smack into the back of someone much taller and sturdier than me. I hit hard enough to tumble gracelessly onto my ass. *Ouch*. I grabbed the hand offering to help me to my feet, my gaze colliding with a hauntingly familiar pair of brilliant blue eyes. I bit back a gasp as he tugged me up, a smirk playing on his lips.

It was *him*, Mr. Tall, Dark and Handsome. The guy I'd daydreamed about fourteen times in the seven days since we'd made out. *Not that I'm counting*.

But I noticed a difference today as I studied his face. *Is that panic in his eyes?*

A demure-looking girl stood next to my mystery man, a frown playing on her lips as she watched him help me up. His gaze hit mine, darting to the girl and back to me.

Yep, definitely desperation.

"There you are." He gave me a look that said I owed him. "You're late."

Willing to play along, I rearranged my expression into my best apologetic smile. "So sorry. Got held up trying to find the right book for my psych class. It was shelved under psychiatry instead of psychology." I rolled my eyes at the petite dark-haired female currently glaring daggers in my direction. "Oh, forgive me. I'm Avery—"

"My girlfriend."

The guy's interruption was so smooth that I didn't even have time to look surprised.

The girl in front of us exchanged her daggers for machine guns. "Derek, you have a girlfriend? When did this happen? Rhonda didn't mention it."

Derek slid a casual arm around my waist, pulling me to his side. I was hardly in a position to argue. I did owe him after last week. To really ham it up, I rested my head on his shoulder and splayed a hand across his firm chest.

Holy muscles!

I wondered what he did to keep in shape. *Running? Swimming? Secret fight club no one could talk about?*

"We haven't wanted to be too public, but it's been going on for a while." He glanced down at me with an adorable smile.

Cue the butterflies. It had been forever since a guy looked at me like that. *If only it were real.*

"Actually, you're the first person we've told." My grin dripped with acid in a clear hands-off message. I actually saw the color drain from her face. "Congratulations…?" I trailed off, waiting for one of them to fill in her name.

Derek choked on what I assumed was laughter, but he hid it with a cough. "Um, Yolanda."

A strangled noise escaped my lips as I choked back my own laughter. *Didn't she say her friend's name is Rhonda? Rhonda and Yolanda? What are the odds?* He gave me a strange look, and I made a motion to continue as I finally got myself under control.

"Could you please not tell my sister about this?" His smile could charm the pants off a used car salesman. "I just want to tell my family myself when we're ready, you know?"

Yolanda looked from Derek to me, then back again, her face falling more with each second. A splash of pity surprised me as I watched her fight for control. She gave a single, tight nod, then fled.

"Well, she must really like you. She brought a whole new level to 'if looks could kill'." I maneuvered out from under Derek's arm, startled at the disappointed expression on his face. *If he wanted that girl to stick around, why did he say I was his girlfriend?*

"Yolanda?" He rolled his eyes. "It's not me. She just doesn't want to disappoint my sister."

I was beyond confused. My questions lined up, waiting to tumble out of my open mouth, only to be thwarted by Derek's warm finger pressed to my lips.

"I haven't had breakfast yet. And since we've done everything else ass backward up to this point, let's save the explanations and introductions until after we have some food. My treat?"

His logic stunned me into silence. Or maybe it was those blue eyes.

I nodded, spellbound, letting him tug me to the checkout desk where I handed over my book. Once it was scanned and stamped, I shoved it into my backpack, turning to follow Derek.

He shocked me further when he casually laced his fingers through mine. And I almost stopped walking when I realized that I really didn't mind. This whole situation should have felt weird, awkward, crazy, but it didn't. There was a rightness to it. As I walked along, hand in hand with a complete stranger whose name I'd just learned, who'd I'd already made out with and who'd called me his girlfriend, I was actually more relaxed than I had been in weeks.

When he let go of my hand to open the cafeteria door, I had to clench my teeth to keep a sound of protest from escaping. But then his hand splayed across my lower back, guiding me inside. A thrill ran through me again at his touch.

This isn't like me. At all.

The thought sent a skitter of fear skipping along my stomach. I knew first-hand the dangers of falling in love, so I had to be on my guard.

A couple of swipes of his card — college chivalry at its finest — and my breakfast was paid for. The tantalizing smell of bacon caressed my nose. I was fairly hungry — our apartment fridge hovered on the empty side at the moment. Gina and I had both been shorted on hours at our jobs this past week, and my curvy fit jeans were actually starting to feel loose.

Derek nudged me. "Go on, get some food. I'll meet you over there." He nodded toward several empty tables before his gaze wandered over my hips. "Those jeans are practically falling off you, and I want my girlfriend to flaunt her curves." With a wink that left my jaw unhinged, he sauntered toward the omelet station.

My stomach growled as if agreeing with Derek, and I grinned. Who was I to look a gift waffle in the mouth? I practically ran to the waffle station, pouring a pre-filled cup of batter into the iron. While I waited for it to cook, I perused my other options, opting for eggs, bacon and fruit. Satisfied I'd covered most of the major food groups, I returned for my perfectly golden, delicious-looking Belgian waffle.

Hands down, my favorite thing about the dining hall was the always open self-serve ice cream station. Instead of syrup, I poured a nice swirl of vanilla ice cream over my waffle and spread it around like butter. *Perfection.*

Derek wrinkled his nose as I sat down, but I shook my head. "Don't knock it till you try it." I sawed off a square filled to the brim with ice cream.

After a brief moment of hesitation, he leaned forward, eating the offered piece of waffle. I waited for his reaction, cutting my waffle into individual squares in the meantime. When I glanced up, he looked surprised.

"See?" I smirked.

"I think I prefer syrup."

I rolled my eyes. "The stuff they have here isn't syrup. It's corn syrup in a bottle." My uncle made real maple syrup every February, so I was a bona fide syrup snob. If they didn't have maple syrup or vanilla ice cream, I wouldn't eat it.

Derek ate a bite of his omelet.

I felt his eyes on me as I finished cutting up my entire waffle. "First thing you should know about me is that I cut up all my food before I eat it. And I only eat one thing at a time. So I'll eat all my waffle, then move on to my eggs. I might have a piece of bacon in between, but I'll eat a whole piece, not just a bite." I shrugged.

He chuckled, a low rumble. "You had a full-on make out session with me last week, then danced away with just a 'thanks for the diversion'." He narrowed those blue eyes. "About this diversion, I'll need to hear that story." But he didn't let me respond, plowing on with his list. "Then I told Yolanda you were my girlfriend, without either of us having been introduced to each other. But your *eating habits* are where we're starting the explanations?"

Well, when he puts it that way… Heat rushed to my cheeks as I scooped a bite of waffle into my mouth. The contrast of the cold ice cream and the warmth of the waffle grounded me. "It's a starting point. Better than, 'hey, want to know why I shoved my tongue down your throat last week?'"

His cheeks tinged pink this time, and he took a sip of his coffee, black by the look of it. "Why did you?"

But I shook my head. "Oh, no. We're doing things backward, remember? I think introductions should probably be next. Then get-to-know-yous. Then possibly explanations." My smart mouth couldn't help throwing one more thing out there. "Maybe we should just sleep together to continue our backward tradition."

Derek sputtered on his coffee, setting the mug down with a clang. The dark liquid sloshed over the side as he coughed and pounded on his chest.

Embarrassment washed over me. That had been too forward, even for me. I wasn't one to go out and sleep with a guy I just met. Sticking my tongue down his throat was one thing, propositioning him was a whole other ballpark. I ducked my head, staring at my plate.

"Avery, it's fine. Just caught me off guard. I was trying to laugh, okay?"

I glanced up at him, saw the earnestness in those deep blue eyes, and relaxed once more. Somehow, I knew he really got me. My hunger returned, fork meeting waffle with a vengeance.

"I'll go first," he continued. "I'm Derek Elgin and I have a twin sister named Rhonda."

I held up a hand, interrupting him from further speech. "Wait, Elgin? As in *the* Elgins? The ones who own that huge shipping company on the Great Lakes?" They were practically royalty around here, with their obscene wealth and community involvement. There was even a hall on campus named after them. I blinked at him, when he nodded. *Holy shit, I kissed a billionaire.*

Taking advantage of my stunned silence, he went on, "I'll be graduating this semester. Go SMU." He pumped a half-hearted fist in the air. "I'm studying the ever-so-exciting subject of mathematics and I live in one of the apartments just off campus."

My eyebrows were probably on top of one another by the time he finished his spiel. I heard what he didn't say — his family legacy spoke for itself. He was rich and didn't have to work. I couldn't quite wrap my head around that level of wealth. The name Rhonda stood out to me. "So Rhonda's your twin…?"

He nodded.

"And that was her friend…?"

Another nod.

"Yo-landa." I emphasized the rhyme and couldn't help my laughter.

Comprehension dawned. "Ah, that's what you were choking on in the library."

I threw my hands in the air. "How many names rhyme with Rhonda? I mean, not many. What are the odds?"

He fought a smile. "That's not the worst part." Leaning in, he lowered his voice. "There's a third one."

I cocked my head, angling forward to hear the secret.

His delivery was perfect. "Fawnda."

My laughter rang out short and loud. So loud I drew a few stares before clamping a hand over my mouth. "You're joking."

"I wish."

The way he stabbed his last bite of omelet made me wonder how serious that statement was. "Let me guess. They call themselves the Three Musketeers?"

He dropped his fork, his gaze rising up to mine in exaggerated slowness. "How did you know?"

I slipped my last bite of waffle into my mouth with a smug smirk. "Didn't I tell you? I'm psychic."

Derek moved on to a bowl I thought contained biscuits and gravy. It looked disgusting, even more so when he mixed it together into a lumpy, gray mush. His lips pressed together in a grim line as he stirred.

I guessed it was my turn to say something. "Do you and your twin have the whole psychic bond thing going on?"

He shook his head, letting out a sigh. "No. Actually, we're not that close, not anymore. And she keeps sending her two friends after me." His pause was underlined by the clinking of his spoon in his bowl. "I'm really not sure what she's thinking. Maybe if I fall for one of them, it'll help bring the two of us closer? If me and one of her friends hang out, she and I will, too?"

I stayed quiet, unsure what to say to that.

"Yolanda had me cornered this morning, so when I saw it was you who ran into me, I took it as a sign." He shrugged. "Plus, I figured you owed me."

That I did. "Yeah, but a girlfriend is a bit more of a commitment than making out against a wall." I tried to keep my tone teasing, but he still didn't smile.

Another sigh escaped his lips. "The truth is that I can't stand my twin. At all. Not even a little bit anymore." A furrow appeared on his brow, and his mouth turned down. "Who says that about their own twin? Having a twin is supposed to be wonderful, practically a built-in extension of yourself, or at the very least a forever best friend."

I looked down to see my fingers entwined with Derek's. *Did I reach for him? Or did he reach for me?* I studied our hands, confused but not begrudging the comfort he so obviously needed.

He stared at our interlocked fingers. "But Rhonda...she doesn't understand anything about me. She doesn't even try. I could never tell her the truth, could never hurt her like that, but I really don't want to be around her."

"Derek, I'm sorry." I gave his fingers a squeeze.

He raised his eyebrows, signaling it was my turn to spill the tea.

I picked up a piece of bacon, the crispiest one. "I'm an only child." The bacon stuck in my throat, so I washed it down with coffee. When the vanilla creamer hit my tongue, I moaned in delight. We ran out just yesterday at my dingy apartment, and it'd be a while before I could get more.

"My parents did everything right. So right, in fact, my mother wrote a book on it." *Here's the hard part.* "I'm Avery Milbourne. My mother is Mabel Milbourne." I waited as recognition flooded Derek's face.

"Wait, I've heard that name."

I nodded. "She wrote *How to Land a Guy and…Keep Him!*, a self-help book on marriage." He'd been more than honest with me and as I studied his kind face, I decided to trust him. "Now for what you don't know. What I can't tell anyone but for some unknown reason, I'm going to tell you." I held his gaze, imagining my forest green eyes crashing into his deep blue ones, and the beautiful color that would explode from their collision.

Tears pushed against my eyes in a constant boxing match, but I won, keeping them contained. The words I'd kept in for so long tumbled out. "My mother's whole image is a lie. All of it. If I out her though," I swallowed hard, "I won't be the only one crushed in the aftermath." It was so much more, but that was the simple version. And it felt good telling him that much.

We sat together in the wake of our truths, the silence between us a comforting barrier against the rest of the world.

He withdrew his hand from mine, moving back to his side of the table. "You still didn't say why you kissed me." His voice held a question, a vulnerability that made me shift in my seat.

"Mother demanded I come to dinner and sent her goons after me. I was running from them—not for the first time. I've found it's best to hide in plain sight."

When his face fell a little, I wanted to tell him I'd almost forgotten to watch for them because I was so lost in his kiss. But that felt like too much on the heels of everything we'd just shared.

"Done that to a lot of guys, huh?" He pushed his spoon around in the gray mush, not meeting my eyes.

I shook my head with a small laugh. "No, that was most definitely a first for me. But your tie was just begging to be grabbed. Not to mention your eyes had glazed over like donuts while you were locked in your doom scroll."

"You got my attention. I'll give you that." A hint of a smile played on his lip as his eyes found mine. Then his face grew pensive as he spun his mug around, pushing the handle from one hand to the other. "Maybe we could help each other."

The very definition of interested, I leaned forward to prop my chin on my palm.

"I've already told Yolanda you're my girlfriend." He spoke slowly, as if thinking aloud. "And having a girlfriend would get Rhonda off my back."

Is he asking me out? Alarm trickled through me.

He met my eyes, then looked right back down at the table. "Not for real. It'd be a fake relationship, just as a front, and it'd benefit you, too. You could use me as an excuse to get out of family dinners and events, or as a buffer at ones you have to attend." One corner of his mouth tipped up. "I'm a great date, and I've got a whole closetful of ties just begging to be grabbed."

I let out a little laugh as I turned his words over in my mind. *Dating Derek Elgin...my mother would kill to have his kind of upper-class panache to lord over her friends.*

"Assuming you don't already have a boyfriend. I mean— I-I just thought... With you kissing me...like that...well, you probably didn't."

Aww, he's cute when he stammers. "No, I don't have a boyfriend." I gave the standard excuse, not wanting to go into the whole 'I don't believe in true love' spiel. "I don't really have the time. I'm a junior with a full class load. I have a scholarship to maintain, plus a part-time job at a coffee shop." I frowned. "Why don't *you* have a girlfriend?"

He snorted. "Well, contrary to my track record with you, random girls aren't lining up to be with me."

When he ducked his head, his black hair nearly obscured his blue eyes, and I realized he hid behind it. On purpose. *The question is, why?*

"Rhonda's the popular one. Most people don't notice me." His tone had an edge to it.

Not quite bitter…maybe wistful?

I studied him, wondering how many times I'd walked by without seeing him. SMU was a small campus, catering to a fairly niche set of students. Part of me wished he'd asked me out for real, wondering what it'd be like to be more than just a cover. I mulled over his words, uneasy at committing to anything.

The pull of using him for cover at Mother's dinners was strong, plus I did want to help him out. Unease hit my gut as I met his assessing gaze. I got the feeling if I agreed to this arrangement, I'd be getting way more than I bargained for. I couldn't remember the last time I'd reacted to a guy like this. Could I agree without putting my heart at risk?

"How about I let you know tomorrow?" The disappointed look that swept over his face sent an arrow through my chest. I slid my phone toward him as a conciliatory gesture. "Put in your number?"

He quickly bounced back with a dazzling grin. His thumbs flew, then he snapped a selfie with an audacious smirk, sliding the phone to me.

I fell in love with the pic. After gawking at the way his tie made his blue eyes even bluer, I mentally kicked myself back into gear. I hurried to send him a text, wanting him to have my number as well.

His phone hooted. Like an owl. And he waited, staring at me expectantly. When I didn't move, he swiped, showed me the camera app then held up his phone to take a pic.

Rolling my eyes, I gave him my snarkiest look as I waited for him to snap the photo. I heard the click, surprised at his self-satisfied grin, then I glanced at the clock. "Crap! I'm going to be late for psych!" I pushed back from the table, frantic to gather up my dishes only to find Derek's hand on mine.

"Go on. I've got this."

"You sure?" He'd already bought me breakfast. I didn't want to make him clean up after me, too.

He nodded. "Just text me tomorrow, okay?"

I smiled my biggest smile. "I will!"

Chapter Three

I lied. I hadn't meant to, and I'd had every intention of texting Derek. But Gina had wanted to try the new Greek joint downtown. Of course, *I* was the one who ended up in the hospital with food poisoning. Not her. I was still there when Derek texted me.

So where are you?

Almost immediately another text came through.

Ignore that. Yolanda stole my phone.

Then another.

Yes I did. We're all wondering where the doting girlfriend is for her boyfriend's birthday party.

It's Derek's birthday? I made a quick note of the date, October eighteenth.

A picture came through of Derek smooshed between three girls, each of them holding up a shot glass. What struck me most were the identical smiles on the girls' faces, as if they were having the time of their lives. Meanwhile, Derek's expression seemed closer to someone who had just eaten a slug but was pretending to enjoy it.

I recognized Yolanda from our brief encounter at the library. The girl to her right wore a tiara with the number twenty-one on top. She looked a lot like Derek—same nose, same cheekbones, same mouth. Although her eyes weren't quite as brilliant blue.

This wasn't just any birthday. I was missing his twenty-first. *Well, this fake relationship is off to an amazing start.* It was time to have some fun with Yolanda.

Sorry, had a little hookup to get out of the way first.

I waited just long enough for Yolanda to start typing a book, then I sent a picture of me connected to my IV and monitors.

I got food poisoning. Spending the night in the hospital. Green, about to puke emoji, for effect.

My phone rang instantly. Derek's deep voice in my ear was like a warm hug I didn't know I needed.

"Hey, Avery, are you okay?"

I shrugged. "Better now that I've stopped emptying my stomach every ten minutes. They've got me on meds, and I have to stay overnight because of the dehydration. Everything hurts after all that throwing up." *Yeah, that's probably TMI, but he asked.*

"What hospital?"

I gave him the name. "They're taking good care of me. I told Gina that gyro smelled funky."

A loud noise echoed through the phone, and Derek sighed. "Hey, I gotta go."

"Okay. Happy birthday."

"Thanks."

And I was left alone with only the sound of my monitors to keep me company.

* * * *

"Hey, sunshine." Derek's voice pulled me out of a light doze not an hour later.

"What?" I squinted up at him. And the gorgeous vase of flowers he held. "What are you doing here?" Self-conscious, I pulled the oversized hospital gown a bit higher on my chest, then shifted to sit upright. I hoped he wouldn't notice my day-old makeup or the state of my hair.

Derek leaned down to kiss my cheek, his voice surprisingly tender. "My girlfriend's in the hospital. Where else would I be?"

I gaped at him. I felt like hell and could only imagine how I looked. *Like a raccoon, probably.* But he'd kissed me anyway.

Yolanda stood in the doorway with her arms folded. "I can't believe you left your own birthday party to come check on her. She said she was fine."

A muscle clenched in his jaw, but Derek kept his blue eyes on me. "I wanted to see for myself."

"Well, now you've seen her. Can we go? It's Rhonda's birthday too, you know."

"I can't believe I missed your birthday." I winked at him, wanting him to relax. I reached out to run a finger lightly over his knuckles, even as I tried to wrap my mind around him being here.

He turned his hand over, catching mine in his. "It's not over yet."

"Yeah, but I'm all out of party tricks." Exhaustion was setting in.

"Excuse me." My nurse pushed past Yolanda. "Visiting hours are almost through."

Derek gave her a brilliant smile. "I'm so sorry. I just found out my best girl here was sick."

The nurse blinked in the blinding light of his sudden charm, and I fought a giggle.

"Julie." I kept my voice low. "Is there anything you can do about that?" I pointed to Yolanda leaning against the doorframe, still glaring at me. "She kind of tagged along when she wasn't supposed to."

Julie looked from me to Derek, knowingly. "You just leave her to me." She escorted Yolanda down the hall despite her screeching protests.

"Can I have your phone?" I asked Derek, feeling mischievous.

He arched an eyebrow, unlocked it, then handed it to me.

I found Yolanda's thread and sent her a quick text, telling her thanks for getting Derek here, but he could find his own way home. And asked her to wish Rhonda a happy birthday. From both of us. Derek chuckled as he read it.

When Julie came back, we both thanked her profusely. She gave Derek an extra half hour to visit, but no more.

Once we were alone, I shot Derek a sheepish smile. "Sorry I didn't give you my answer about being your girlfriend. Got a little sidetracked with everything." I waved a hand at all the gizmos behind me. "I told Gina that gyro tasted funny."

His brows knit together. "Gina? Gina Rossi?"

I nodded, staring at him in confusion. "How do you know Gina?"

"We had a class together last year — economics — and we partnered up for a research project." He smirked. "She is spunky."

That's putting it mildly. I nodded again, this time with a smile. "Yeah, she is. She's also my best friend, food poisoning aside." I studied him for a moment, still amazed he was even here. "Happy birthday. I'm sorry I didn't know."

One corner of Derek's mouth tipped up. "Don't worry about it. I was going to invite you if you texted, but I figured you making it to my party was a long shot." He shrugged. "It was more for Rhonda. Mostly her friends and her scene."

I frowned. *What kind of sibling throws a joint birthday party and only invites her friends? Let alone a twin?*

"But I'd still like to hear your answer." His brilliant blue eyes seared into me.

I played with the rough blanket, feeling a little shy. "Yes, I'll be your fake girlfriend." And he turned that megawatt smile on me. *Seriously, where are my sunglasses?*

"Best birthday present ever." He glanced up at the clock, his smile dimming a little. "My half hour's up. Talk to you tomorrow?"

And even though no one was watching, he leaned down to kiss my cheek. As I watched him walk out the door, a warm feeling spread over me, staying with me through the night.

* * * *

I was getting antsy. Julie promised I'd be released first thing this morning, but it was after eleven, with no sign of my doctor. I understood about emergencies and on-calls. However, I just wanted to go home.

When my door opened, the last person I expected was Derek, but there he was. *Doesn't he have better things to do on a Thursday?* Gina trailed in after him. I gawked at the two of them together...how did they know each other? Then I registered the expression on her face.

"What?" I asked, instantly on edge.

"Told ya she'd know something was up." Gina shot Derek a look before perching on the edge of my bed. "At least you're already sitting."

My fake boyfriend came to stand on my other side, his blue eyes scanning me.

Now I was really worried. "Okay, spit it out."

Gina took a deep breath. "We've been evicted. Our building was condemned last night."

What? Before I could ask any questions, Gina kept talking.

"We managed to get all our stuff out. Derek was a huge help." She flashed him a grateful smile. "He happened to be there when the notice came."

I could handle this. I'd been through worse things before...though I wasn't sure what. *At least I still have Gina.*

"Don't kill me." She grimaced, ducking her head. "You know Josh has been begging me to move in with him, and he *did* help me move all that stuff. I just couldn't say no." She wouldn't meet my eyes, staring at my pillow instead.

That's what she's really worried about. Yeah, the building being condemned sucked, but she was bailing on me. *After everything we've been through together.* And I had no one, no place to go. Except my parents'.

As if reading my thoughts, Derek piped up. "I have a spare bedroom. And I'd love some extra cash for odds and ends if you want to chip in on the rent." He pushed away from the wall he'd been leaning against, laying his offer out there oh so casually. "It'd be good for 'us' too. Make everything seem real."

Gina's eyes drilled into me, and I knew, I just knew I'd been set up. They'd conspired against me, arriving together so I had no choice but to agree. And she chose to tell me now, while I was still bed-ridden so I couldn't get mad, couldn't chase her around the room. I whipped my head around, locking my gaze with hers. "You scheming, meddling, so-called best friend—"

She held up her hands, standing up and backing away.

Derek looked between us. "You were right about her getting mad about that, too."

Gina smiled sadly. "Should have bet on it, huh, Ave?"

Her words hit me hard. Gina was amazing at knowing outcomes of situations, predicting what people would do. And just like that, my anger deflated, hurt and betrayal taking over. Tears pricked my eyes. My best friend was shoving me off with some guy I'd just met so she could move on with her own life. *Oh good, here's a convenient way to tie off that loose end. Perfect.*

Gina and Derek exchanged looks once more, then Gina started to speak but I shook my head, not wanting to hear it.

"Could you give us a minute?" Derek's low voice registered through my misery, and I heard the door open, then close. The mattress dipped as he settled next to me.

"Listen, Avery, I reached out to Gina last night. I still had her number from when we worked on that project together." He sheepishly ran a hand up the back of his head. "I was just trying to help, and I wanted to make sure you had everything you needed when you got home." He grimaced. "She questioned me—actually, interrogated is probably a better word."

Those blue eyes met mine. "She really cares about you. She wanted to know my intentions with this whole fake dating thing, to make sure I'm not out to play you or hurt you. That this isn't just some game to me. And I assure you, it's not."

He paused, as if to let that sink in. "Anyway, I happened to be there when the condemnation notice came. She mentioned this would be the perfect time for her to move in with her boyfriend, but she would never leave you high and dry like that. I told her about my spare room. She had more...questions, but I guess I passed her test, because she told Josh yes."

I stewed despite his sweet words. My whole future had been decided without me even getting a say in it.

He shrugged. "I wanted you to hear the whole story. My offer still stands. I'm willing to give this a try if you are, plus I can just picture Yolanda's face when I tell her." A smirk tipped his mouth, fading when he took in my solemn expression. "But I'll give you some space to think on it, all right?"

His footsteps faded, the door latching behind him, and I let out the breath I'd been holding. Only for the door to swing open once more.

Gina stomped back in, glaring at me.

I glared right back, more pout than anger. "You don't want to live with me anymore. You're just moving me in with some guy I just met so you can be with your boyfriend. Who does that?" I stared at the blanket on my lap, rough and scratchy.

With a sigh, Gina sat on the edge of my bed. "Seriously, Avery, do you know anything about me? Would I really do that to you?"

No, she wouldn't. But I needed her explanation before I was ready to admit it.

"Derek called me last night, after I left here, explaining who he was and the deal he offered you. Which, what the hell, girl? You didn't tell me any of this at breakfast?"

I remained silent. I'd still been thinking over my options, not ready to discuss it until I had a firm decision.

"I think he was hoping I had an answer." She smirked. "But, like I said, he wanted to make sure you had everything you needed when you came home. I gave him a list of your favorite foods for when you're sick, and he showed up with a grocery bag full of them." Her brown eyes stared at me. "Fake boyfriend, my ass. That boy likes you."

My mouth twitched.

"There was a big commotion downstairs. When I went to check it out, a fire marshal was announcing that the place had been condemned." Her face grew pinched. "It was pretty awful, seeing what some of the people came out of there with, girl. We were living on the higher end of things."

I pictured our ratty couch and wobbly table, our bare fridge and thin blankets. I couldn't imagine.

"Anyway, Josh was on his way over, and you know he's been begging me to move in with him…" Her eyes flashed the way they did when she went into planning mode. "When Derek offered his place, I grilled him."

I could just imagine it. I'd seen her interrogations, people reduced to tears when she was done.

She shrugged. "I mean, he'd already gone out of his way to bring you your favorite sick foods. Hell, he left his own birthday party to check on you. That has to count for something."

Her brown eyes searched mine. "I had that economics class with him last year. This guy is crazy smart. He's never mean to anyone, and I've never heard a bad word about him. I asked around, texted friends, looked online. His background check is awesome. Nothing bad. He answered all my questions, straight up and honest." She sighed. "He's the real deal, Avery. You'd be a fool to pass this up."

I stayed silent for a long moment. "You really think so?"

If Gina vetted someone and offered a pass, that was a huge deal. She didn't trust easily. Not with her background. She nodded. "And I'm sorry. There wasn't any good way to warn you. I thought it was better to tell you in person."

Of course, she did. I sighed, still annoyed and hurt. "It's a lot, Gina. My apartment, my best friend, gone. And I didn't get a say in any of it. Then my fake boyfriend steps in with this Hollywood rom-com solution, and you've already agreed to it?"

She bit her lip. "I swear I have your best interests at heart. He's a good guy."

I picked at the blanket again. *If it were anyone but Gina…*

"So, will you do it?" Apprehension laced her tone.

I swallowed. "Anything's better than living with Mother, right?"

Derek stood in the open doorway, an amused expression on his face.

Gina sagged with relief. "Your stuff's already at his place. I knew you'd see it my way." She stood up, leaning over to give me a hug. I stayed stiff, but she persisted, whispering in my ear, "Give him a chance. Maybe he'll turn out to be a fairy tale prince, after all."

"Fairy tales aren't real." But I softened before she left, calling out, "Have fun with Josh, and thanks for moving all my crap." This wasn't over, but at least I didn't have to move in with Mother.

"Let me know how all this goes." Gina nodded to Derek as she walked past him.

"Oh, I will." I glanced at Derek, who smiled tentatively. "So about this spare room."

The doctor walked in not fifteen minutes later, and *poof*, I was discharged. The universe was conspiring against me. Then again, maybe it was for me, because if I had been let out at the crack of dawn, where would I have gone? At least Gina had brought me a change of clothes. I did not want to wear the vomit-covered ones I'd arrived in.

A friendly aide wheeled me to the curb, a ridiculous hospital policy enforced even after I'd insisted I could walk.

Derek opened the door of a sleek black Town Car. "I called in a driver for the day. My usual one had today off. You'll meet him soon enough."

I couldn't imagine having a person on staff whose sole job was to cart me around. My eyes met the driver's in the rearview mirror, and I smiled as I settled against the leather seat. He grinned back, then my attention shifted to Derek who climbed in the backseat next to me.

"I wasn't sure where all we would need to go. Is there anything else you want to pick up?"

I remembered my conversation with Gina. "Evidently we have food." I gave him a pointed look, and he ducked his head.

"Gina gave me a list of all your favorites. Everything's at my place."

If only I could find a real *boyfriend who went to half those lengths.* "That was really sweet."

The driver pulled up in front of a taller, upscale building with a mirrored front.

"Fancy," I muttered, trying to find the door handle.

Derek had my door open before I made any progress. I headed into the building, feeling woefully underdressed in my yoga pants and oversized hoodie.

He greeted the doorman. "Oscar, this is Avery Milbourne. She's living with me now, so don't give her any trouble, you hear?" His words were accompanied by a teasing grin.

Oscar nodded. "Very good, sir."

I let out a big yawn as we crossed the lobby, my body stiff from lack of movement. I wished I had more energy to be excited that Derek's place had a working elevator.

"You look worn out."

"I've never slept well in hospitals," I confided. "Plus they said the medicine would make me tired." My stomach rumbled. "I'm more hungry than anything."

He chuckled. "Chicken noodle soup, coming up."

I followed Derek to his apartment, almost bumping into him when he stopped because I was too busy gawking at the pristine hallway. His delicious citrus and clove scent washed over me before I forced myself to back up. *I wonder what soap he uses?*

The spacious apartment had a large living room and an open kitchen divided by an island. A table nestled under a window against the opposite wall and to the left was a hallway.

He nodded to it. "Your room is the first door on the right. Bathroom is the next door on the right. My

48

room's way down, on the left. I could give you a tour or heat you up some soup?" He raised his eyebrows, those startling blue eyes taking my breath away.

"Um, soup please." I leaned against the island, trying to recover as he pulled out a can of soup and a bowl. "Actually, let me make it?" I had my own water to soup ratio, and I knew just how hot I liked it.

He smiled, handing me a spoon, then stepped aside. "So generic condensed chicken noodle soup, huh?" It was his turn to lean on the island, his arms folded in front of his trim stomach.

I nodded, a wistful smile crossing my lips as I dumped the contents of the can in the bowl. "I was maybe four or five, and I wasn't feeling great. We have a cook, Patty, who took care of me when Mom was writing. Daddy worked full-time heading up the safety design team for a big appliance company. For whatever reason, he took care of me that day." I used the empty can as my measuring cup, filling it half with water then mixed it with the soup. I continued the story as I started the microwave. "He came in for lunch with two trays, saying he had just the thing to make me feel better. Chicken noodle soup and butter sandwiches."

Derek's eyebrows lifted. "Butter sandwiches?"

"That's what he called them." I chuckled. "I'm assuming Gina had you get saltine crackers and spreadable butter?"

Still looking puzzled, he found the items, setting them on the counter in front of me.

"And a butter knife, please."

He handed me one, then returned to his spot against the island.

I opened the pack of crackers. Taking one in my hand, I spread a thin layer of butter over it before stacking another cracker on top. "Voila! Butter sandwich."

Less than impressed, Derek gave me a skeptical look.

"So, Dad and I spent the afternoon eating butter sandwiches, dunked in chicken noodle soup, and watching cartoons." I loved the way the crackers turned soggy as they soaked up the broth. The hint of butter just made everything richer, more delicious.

The microwave dinged, and I brought everything to the island. "The only problem was the next time I got sick, Patty took care of me. I asked for chicken noodle soup and butter sandwiches." I glanced at Derek, one corner of his mouth already turning up in a smile as if he anticipated what I was going to say. "She brought me homemade soup and a legit sandwich, with just butter in it. I was *not* happy."

His chuckle rumbled between us, his dazzling smile full of amusement. "Did you get it straightened out?"

I nodded, swallowing my mouthful of noodles. "I'm not sure she ever forgave me for choosing generic store brand soup over her homemade version, though." We both laughed. I ate in contented silence for a few minutes, tiredness washing over me. The warm soup relaxed me even more, and I yawned.

"Maybe you want to rest after this?"

A nap sounded amazing. "Yeah, the whole not sleeping thing is catching up to me." I finished off my soup, dunking in one more butter sandwich. "How much do I owe you, anyway? For this and the room? This is a really nice place." Anxiety gripped my stomach at the thought of how much this could actually cost. There was no way I could afford to stay here on my own.

"The food's on me, a get-well present." His blue eyes met mine, then darted back to the island. "It was probably a little much, huh? Buying all that for my fake girlfriend."

I reached across the island, running my fingers over his knuckles like I'd done in the hospital. I waited for him to meet my eyes again. "I thought it was sweet." Then I let out another yawn.

He smiled once more. "As for rent, let's talk about it more after you get some sleep, okay? We'll work it out."

The anxiety lessened. *Yeah, he's doing me a favor, but he doesn't seem like the type who'll lord it over me. Not like Mother.* "All right." I moved to take care of my dishes, but he stopped me with a gentle hand on my wrist.

"I've got this. You get some sleep. First door on the right, remember?"

I swallowed, confronted once more with the brilliant blue eyes that made me forget everything. All I could do was nod.

My room was beautiful, fully furnished with better furniture than my old apartment ever dreamed of. My sheets and comforter were there, though, cozy and welcoming, the bed all made up for me. Too tired to look further, I sank onto the mattress, pulling the covers to my chin.

The next thing I knew, I was waking up to a white textured ceiling that definitely wasn't the hospital's or my apartment's. I didn't immediately remember where I was. Then I heard voices — deep, male voices. I relaxed when I recognized Derek's. I'd left my door cracked open, and the voices carried in, one in particular louder than the rest.

"I'm sure she's something, but Derek has carried a torch for Princess forever. You really think he's going to just give that up for some random girl?"

Incoherent murmuring was the answer. I crept across the room, wanting to hear more.

"He dated a princess?"

"No, you idiot. That's just her nickname." There was a pause. A pair of angry footsteps stormed down the hall, followed by a slamming door. "The rest of you were here when he swore his undying love for her. You all witnessed it. It wasn't just some careless fling—it was the real deal."

I ignored the pang in my chest at the proof that Derek's heart belonged to another. *That's a good thing, right? All the more reason this fake relationship is perfect. We can both keep our hearts safely out of it.*

"Dammit, Kevin." Another rumbly voice scolded the first. "Not only is his girlfriend in the next room, you know how Derek gets when *she's* brought up. What the hell? He invites you over to watch football, and you run your mouth? Asshole."

It must have been Derek storming down the hall, slamming the door. I wanted to know more about this mysterious Princess. *What did she do to make him react like that?* We hadn't discussed our pasts yet, and I wondered what other secrets he had. I reminded myself he'd never made me any promises. This was all for show.

"I'm just worried about him, man. Us men of means gotta stick together, watch out for each other." That was definitely Kevin.

I bristled. *Worried about him, my foot. More like worried I'm some gold-digging tramp wanting to rob him blind.* I stalked back over to the bed. An en suite bathroom caught my eye, as did my full closet. A wicked idea slipped into my mind, so I set about putting it into action.

Half an hour later, I stepped out of the bathroom, happy that everyone still seemed to be hanging out. When I heard Derek's voice join theirs, relief pulsed through me. *Good, he's back in time for my show.*

In a slinky gold wrap dress I'd bought for a Halloween costume last year, I really played up the part by teasing my hair high on my head. Since my hair reached my waist, I was able to attain an impressive height. I completed the look with evening makeup and my best costume jewelry. I'd even found a pair of rarely worn heels that had me teetering down the hallway.

Before I rounded the corner, I bit my lower lip to plump it out, squared my shoulders, then I made myself known. There were five guys total in the spacious living room, all jaws dropping as I strutted across the floor to plaster myself against Derek. To his credit, my fake boyfriend recovered quickly, catching my wink and schooling his face to not give anything away.

I pitched my voice to an annoying whine. "Derek, darling, aren't you going to introduce me to your friends?"

"Of course, Avery. I hadn't realized you were up yet." He went around the circle, ending with Kevin.

The triumphant gleam in Kevin's eye was hard to miss. "Ah, the infamous Avery. We've heard so much about you."

I set about exacting my revenge. "All good things, I hope." I batted my fake eyelashes, running a hand down Derek's chest before pushing off him to go after his friend. "I've heard you're sitting on a pretty penny, too." I lowered my voice to a stage whisper, leaning in,

"Maybe if you're lucky, you can find a gold digger of your very own."

Kevin's face blanched.

"But don't worry, I'm not after Derek's fortune. My mother is Mabel Milbourne, author of *How to Land a Guy and...Keep Him!*, YouTube trendsetter, fashion guru." I paused, a cold smile curving my lips as I stared into his pale face. "You might have heard of her. I'm doing well enough on my own that I don't need to be drooling after Derek's money."

I spun on my heel, pausing to give my fake boyfriend a very pointed, slow scan from head to toe. "Besides, he has plenty of other parts to drool over, thank you very much." I moved to press a kiss to Derek's cheek.

Instead, he turned to meet my lips, crushing his mouth against mine. Too surprised to pull away, I gave in as he claimed me, deepening the kiss for several long moments before he broke it off. Wild-eyed, I stared up at him, unsettled at the pride in his gaze and the butterflies in my stomach. It took a minute to regain my confident persona. I swallowed, stepping back. "Now if you'll excuse me, I'll go change into something...normal." And I made my exit.

As soon as I was out of sight, the guys erupted into laughter. They hooted and hollered, with one noticeable exception--I didn't hear Kevin's obnoxious voice once in all the commotion. I'd just made it to my room when there was a tap on my door.

Derek's voice was tentative. "It's just me. Can I come in?"

I cracked it open, coming face to face with him. Uncertain, I stepped back, then shut the door behind him.

"Sorry we woke you. I hope you were able to get some rest." He leaned against the wall near the door. "How are you feeling?"

"Much better, thanks. It felt good to get some sleep." I gave him a small smile. "Hope I wasn't too much out there, but I had to do something."

The grin on his face showed his appreciation. "You were great. Sorry you overheard Kevin being a jerk."

I shrugged. "Gina interrogated you. Your friends think I'm a gold digger. We all have our crosses to bear."

Derek's face darkened. "Kevin is...not exactly a friend."

Confusion hit me, my brow furrowing. "Then what's he doing here?"

"He's Rhonda's fiancé. I guess she heard about you moving in, and she thought she'd get the scoop when I invited the guys over to watch the football game."

My head snapped toward him. "Wait, who's playing?"

With a confused look, he slowly answered, "Detroit Lions versus Green Bay Packers."

"So it's still Thursday?" I did a happy dance. "Help me out of this thing before I miss kickoff." It was hard enough to squeeze myself into the stupid dress, but it was definitely a two-person job getting it off.

"Um, excuse me?" His eyes were wide, gaping as if I'd spoken another language, and his cheeks grew redder by the second. "How do you propose I do that?"

Good question. "You pull up, and I shimmy down?" I lifted my arms while Derek tried to find a good handhold, finally settling on the hem of the dress. I counted then dipped while he yanked it over my head, the dress flying off. "Nice. Thanks."

He stared at me.

I glanced down at my lacy one-piece bodysuit. Everything seemed to be in place. Realizing I still had on my heels, I bent to slip them off, and Derek let out a strangled noise that had me glancing at him in concern.

"I'm just...going to go check on the guys." And he rushed out of the door.

I dug around in my drawers wondering who had put everything away because it was nowhere near how I would have done it. Finally, I found my Lions jersey, a vintage one of Barry Sanders' that used to be my dad's. I paired it with yoga pants, fuzzy socks and a ponytail, then tamed down the makeup on my face before making my entrance once more.

Derek was the only one who noticed, looking up from the oversized armchair to nod at the space beside him. I perched on the arm for the time being. My eyes were drawn to the coffee table, bowing under the weight of an incredible spread of pizza, chips, pretzels, dips, wings.

"I'm starving." I touched my chin to make sure I wasn't drooling.

Concern crossed his face. "You think you can eat any of that?"

"Any of it?" I looked at him, affronted. "I could eat all of it!"

He chuckled. "Help yourself."

So I did, ducking and weaving and trying to stay out of the guys' view of the TV. Except Kevin, of course. I blocked his a little more than necessary.

"Nice jersey."

One of the guys gave me a thumbs-up while another threw a cheese puff at me and booed. The second guy was beefy and muscular, with short, cropped hair and stubbly cheeks. I immediately thought of Gina. He was the very definition of her normal type. Although he wore green and yellow Packers gear, so I hissed at him. Then we grinned at each other before I went to sit with Derek. When I perched on the arm again, Derek gave my shirt a couple tugs until I capitulated, sliding into the space beside him.

"Who's the jerk?" My curves fit perfectly against his lean, narrow body. Two puzzle pieces filling in each other's gaps.

"You'll have to be more specific." He smirked, letting me know he was teasing.

I snorted. "The one in Packers gear."

"Oh, that's Liam. He hates the Lions, owns every jersey except theirs." Derek absent-mindedly stole a chip off my plate. "He's also my best friend."

My eyes shot to the beefy guy in the green, sizing him up. I took in his muscles, the banded tattoo on his right biceps, his easy smile. The way he laughed when he was teased. How he'd thrown a cheese puff at me and grinned when I'd hissed. Liam could be all right. He caught me staring, giving me a pensive look of his own.

The game was close, with good, clean calls by the refs. I cheered and yelled with the rest of them, garnering surprised looks when I knew my terms. "Yeah, that's right. Gold diggers can watch football, too." I couldn't help sticking my tongue out at Kevin.

Derek slung an arm over my shoulder, and I cuddled against his warm side, resting my head in the crook of his neck as if it had been made for me. The Lions managed to eke out a win with a field goal in the last seven seconds, much to Liam's dismay. My victory dance may have dismayed him more.

The guys trickled out, leaving the apartment a quiet mess. Then Derek and I were alone.

"So, how you doing?" He aimed the remote at the screen and shut it off.

I began gathering up leftovers. "Good. The food was amazing, didn't bother me a bit. My sides are still a bit sore if I move just wrong, but otherwise, I think I'm fine."

He grabbed some containers to put food in, packing it up as I brought it over. "I never would have pegged you for a football fan."

With a sideways glance at him, I sniffed in a haughty manner. "I never would have thought you were one either."

"Touché." He snapped the lid down on the container with the pizza. "Want to hang out, chill for a bit?"

"Actually, I should look over my email and start catching up on schoolwork." *Ugh.*

His eyebrows crinkled together. "Didn't Gina say you don't have class on Fridays?"

"Yeah…" *He remembers my schedule?*

"So, want to rest tonight? Watch a movie or something, tackle your stuff tomorrow?"

That sounds really good. My gaze lingered on his oh so kissable lips, drifting down to the firm chest I'd snuggled against for the last hour. *Too good.* Longing filled me, but I had to remember that he was off the table, for both our sakes. We were just friends. *Although, friends could sit and watch movies, right?* "Sure."

"What kind of movie are you in the mood for?" he asked before offering me several beverage choices.

"Something funny."

"Stupid funny or rom-com funny?" He handed me my Gatorade, our fingers brushing.

My stomach flipped. I waved my other hand, trying to act casual, like I wasn't close to drooling over this sweet guy taking care of me. "Whatever."

His gaze drifted down to my yoga pants. "I'm jealous."

My eyes lingered on his lips as he formed the words, my breath catching as I realized I was the focus of his undivided attention. "Of what?"

"You look really comfy." One side of his mouth tilted up. "I think I'll go change." He disappeared down the hall.

I leaned against the back of the couch, feeling unsteady. It was definitely the aftereffects of the food poisoning, not Derek's brief touch. I wandered over to the small set of shelves near the TV. There was an autographed football, Derek's high school diploma, a class photo, along with several other framed photographs, but one picture in particular drew me.

Derek was smiling his megawatt smile, his arm around a girl I assumed to be Rhonda, based on how similar they looked. She was the same one who wore a twenty-one tiara in the birthday picture, but in this photo, her smile was just as brilliant as Derek's. A Ferris wheel lit up the background.

"That's my favorite picture of me and Rhonda. Liam took it." Derek came to stand behind me, peering over my shoulder. "We were all at the fair for a concert, and I told her some joke, just to get her to smile."

I tilted my head back, catching a glimpse of wistfulness on his face. As much as he said he couldn't stand his sister, there was a time when they used to hang out. This picture was proof. Maybe there was hope for them yet.

My phone dinged, and I pulled it out to see a text from Gina, asking how I was doing. I glanced at Derek. "I need to check in with Gina. Give me a sec?"

He nodded.

I headed to my room. Normally I'd call her and not think twice about it, but I was still annoyed. I sent her a text back instead. "He's got a nice place. We just finished watching football, going to watch a movie now."

"Good. Feeling okay?"

My lips tilted up in an amused smile. "Gina, quit hovering. I'm fine. And no, you're not off the hook yet."

She sent back a pouting gif. "Girl, I'm just glad you're feeling good enough to be mad at me. I'll make it up to you soon."

"You better." I had a full smile on my face as I reappeared into the living room.

"Ready for that movie?" Derek pushed off the island when I nodded.

We made our way to the couch. I nearly tripped when I realized Derek had changed into flimsy gray sweatpants, low on his hips. I'd definitely have to watch my drooling tonight.

It took a few minutes to look through his extensive movie collection, but we finally settled on *Robin Hood: Men in Tights*, a comedic movie with rom-com overtones. I stretched out on one end of the couch, and he claimed the other, propping his bare feet on the coffee table. As the movie moved along, my energy flagged. I oozed farther and farther down the arm of the couch until I lay flat on the cushion. He tossed me a pillow for my head, pulling my feet onto his lap. Then he covered me with a blanket.

Chapter Four

I woke up in the morning in my bed with no memory of getting there. *Had Derek carried me?* At nearly six foot, that was no small feat. I was sorry I'd missed it. As I went to the bathroom and stumbled around getting ready, my eye caught on the gold dress from the day before. One question stood out. *Who is this Princess that he'd pledged his love to?* He was obviously still hung up on her, the way he'd stomped off at just the mention of her name. *And what does she have that I don't?* That thought startled me, and I shook my head. I must have been half asleep still, because I definitely didn't care.

Groggily, I made my way into the kitchen to find Derek pouring coffee, shirtless. A towel looped over his neck, his black hair damp and tousled. I decided right then and there this was forevermore a shirtless apartment. He definitely worked out. Those sculpted shoulders, chiseled chest and amazing abs did not just happen with wishful thinking.

He had a laptop next to him which he closed with a grin when he saw me. "Morning."

I was too busy staring to answer.

"Coffee?"

Nodding, I slid onto a barstool.

A mug appeared in my hand. A container of French vanilla creamer next to it.

My brain did what it always did before coffee in the morning, sending my thoughts out of my mouth with no filter. "Why French vanilla?"

He frowned. "That's what Gina said you liked."

I waved at him. "No, not why'd you buy it." Then it was my turn to frown. "Which, thank you again for that. What else did you buy?"

"Um. I don't know what to answer first." He blinked at me.

My lips curled into a smile, and pretty soon I was laughing. "Sorry. I'm sorry. My morning train of thought is kind of a wreck."

He eyed me, perching on the barstool next to mine. "What were you saying about French vanilla?"

"Oh, right." I gestured to the creamer. "Why don't they have plain vanilla coffee creamer? Why does it have to be French? What makes French vanilla so much better than the others?"

He raised his mug to his lips, taking a thoughtful sip. "Hmm. I don't know. I guess that's why I take mine black, then I don't have to worry about it."

We shared a silly grin, comfortable silence resting between us like an old friend.

"What's on the agenda today?" He leaned a scruffy chin on one hand, focusing on me way too intently.

How does one being hold so much intensity? His megawatt smile that had me reaching for my

62

sunglasses. A simple glance that made every thought in my brain melt into a gooey puddle. *Wonderful.* "Um."

"Homework?"

A lifeline, perfect. Maybe he'll give me CPR if I hold my breath? I thought about that first kiss and the brief one last night. He cleared his throat, bringing my daydream to an end. I scrambled to answer his question. "Yeah, I should at least crack open the old laptop." I noticed he was frowning once more. "What?"

"Hmm?"

I gave a little half-laugh at our incoherent conversation. "You were frowning. You do that when you have a question, but don't want to ask. So what's up?"

"I do?"

My nod was succinct. "Yes, and don't avoid the question."

He smirked. "I was trying to remember if you told me your major."

"Oh." I ran through our conversations. "I don't think I did. It's business with a communications minor."

"How does psychology fit into that?" he asked, brow furrowed.

I gave him a sheepish smile. "It doesn't. But I kept hearing really good things about that class and I couldn't resist."

His nod was thoughtful. "Any plans for what to do with your degree?"

"Nothing concrete." I shrugged. "Not work at a coffee shop forever."

He chuckled. "Solid."

I swirled my spoon in my mug. "Gina's always wanted to own a bar, turn it into a hot spot. Me, I'm still looking for my dream."

"That's okay, too." Silence hung between us once more.

I pushed away from the counter. "I'm going to go check my laptop." Derek stood up at the same time, and I ran smack into his bare chest. I nearly toppled over, trying to back up only to trip on the chair behind me, but his hands on my arms steadied me. My palms rested on his smooth pecs. I couldn't look away. My heart raced, and my thumb brushed over his warm skin of its own accord.

Goose bumps appeared on his torso, and he shivered. "I'll just go get dressed."

We awkwardly stepped away from each other. Unable to look at him, I waited until he disappeared before I took my cup of coffee to my room. Thankfully my breathing had returned to normal. *Now if I can focus on my work and not that beautiful, smooth chest, I'll be all set.* After flopping onto my bed, I opened the laptop and managed to scan through my emails.

There was some reading homework with a couple of online quizzes but that was it. *Nice.*

Quickly, I did my work, making sure no big assignments loomed. I meandered into the living room just in time to hear a knock on the door. Derek was nowhere to be seen, and it was technically my apartment, too, so I opened it up. Only for a whirlwind of women to waltz in.

"Is that her?" a well-dressed lady sneered.

Yolanda lowered designer shades to peer down her nose at me. "That's her all right."

Our run-in from the hospital still fresh in my mind, I met her gaze with my chin high and shoulders square. I wouldn't be the one at a disadvantage this time. She was on my turf now.

The first one pinched the bridge of her delicate nose. "I didn't want to believe Kevin. Derek. Where's Derek?" Her voice rose to a shriek as the other girl and Yolanda patted her shoulder.

I shut the door, stepping forward. "Rhonda, I presume?" I looked to the unknown on her right. "And Fawnda. The Three Musketeers. Listen, Derek's a little tied up this morning. Why don't the four of us go get some lunch? My treat?" I shot them a simpering closed-mouthed smile. "Let me just go change."

As soon as I turned the corner, I ran to Derek's room, barely knocking before I burst in. The running water registered several seconds too late. *Oh. He must have been damp from working out, not from showering. Crap.*

"Avery?"

I slapped a hand over my eyes, put another hand on the door jamb to his bathroom, and poked my head in. "The Three Musketeers are here so whatever you do, don't go out there."

His deep chuckle hit me low. "You can look. I'm decent. I was just shaving."

I peeled my hand away, peering into the steam. *Decent is not the word I'd use.* A towel sat low on his hips, underlining that delicious V. Half his jaw was covered in shaving cream, and droplets of water clung to his chest.

He smiled at me. "Thanks for the warning. I'll finish up here and handle them."

Unable to take my eyes off his beautiful body, I shook my head. Then I realized he wouldn't understand. "No. I have to stake my claim. Draw some boundary lines. Pee on the bushes." *Yeah, that was a bit much.* "I told them I'd change, then take them out for lunch. But *I* have to do it. I need the whole shebang, the Town Car, the driver, a fancy lunch place…" *Now the hard part.* "But I don't really have the money."

He scoffed. "That's the easy part." He made short work of the five tiles between us, then grabbed my hand to run a finger across my knuckles.

My knees went weak at the familiar gesture being returned. And maybe this gorgeous man being half-naked so close to me.

"You sure about this? They can be pretty vicious. They eat newcomers like you for breakfast, and it's three to one." His Adam's apple bobbed. "I've had girls break up with me because of them. I know this is why I asked you to be here, but I didn't mean you had to face them alone."

My nod was firm. "If I don't stand up to them now, first thing, they're going to see me as weak and walk all over me. And they all wear stilettos." I winced playfully, but his serious gaze didn't waver. I wondered at the emotion I saw churning in the depths of his blue eyes. I reached up, against my better judgment, to place a hand on his freshly shaven cheek. "Don't worry. I've swum with sharks before, and I've still got all my limbs."

His gaze searched me. He took his time before he answered. "Well, just in case, my driver's name is Greg, and he's more than an employee. He's a good friend. He's been in our family since I was thirteen." His blue eyes drilled into me. "If you need anything, and I mean anything, just ask him."

I nodded, flouncing out of the room to prepare for battle.

Twenty minutes later I was ready to go, but I made them wait ten more while I caught up on Words with Friends. Derek texted me that his driver was ready downstairs with instructions to take us to a restaurant he knew would impress his sister. All I had to do was tell them my name, and everything would be taken care of.

Derek wore his fake grimace of a smile when I reappeared. *If I'd known he was out here, I wouldn't have taken those extra ten minutes.*

When I leaned in to kiss his cheek, I whispered, "You were supposed to be in your room." Loud enough for the girls to hear, I giggled. "Derek! You don't want to smudge my lipstick. Again." I swatted his chest, then offered him my cheek.

He tugged my sassy ponytail as I sashayed out of the apartment. "Have fun, shark bait."

I flipped him off before I shut the door.

The ride in the elevator was a silent, staring affair during which we all sized each other up. I'd worn a navy-blue dress, the top portion a halter-type that left my shoulders and upper back bare. The bottom portion was tight, like a pencil skirt. It was a bit over the top compared to the other ladies' pantsuits, but that was the point. My makeup was flawless, armor firmly in place, and I knew I looked amazing.

I led the way out of the elevator, nodding to Oscar who held the door for us. Instead of a Town Car, a sleek, black limo sprawled in front of the sidewalk, and a friendly-looking chauffeur waited in front of the open door. He was younger than I'd expected, though older than me. And taller, too.

"Good morning, Miss Avery." He tipped his hat, gray eyes flicking behind me to Rhonda and the others.

I noticed Rhonda do a double take when she heard Greg's voice. I greeted the driver like I knew him, with a cheery, "Hi, Greg."

Then I stepped back to let the Three Musketeers in first. Rhonda's gaze lingered on the driver, reluctantly accepting his help into the limo. It was nice to see her off-kilter already.

Once they'd disappeared, I whispered, "Thank you, Greg. I'm glad to have an ally in all this." I grinned at him.

"I knew I'd like you as soon as I laid eyes on you, Miss." He helped me in, tipped his hat and shut the door behind me.

The girls claimed the forward-facing seat, all tucked together, a formidable if overly perfumed wall. Fawnda poured champagne into flutes.

"None for me. Thanks." I pushed a few buttons, finding the one that rolled down the divider. "Greg? Do you have something stronger than champagne back here?"

His eyebrows went up, but he gave me directions for a barrel-aged whiskey, imported directly from Ireland. *Perfect. Liquid courage, as Daddy would say.* I could use about a gallon of that right about now.

"I'll let you know when we're ready for lunch." Once I'd poured myself three fingers and taken a sip in his general direction, I rolled the window back up. "Now, ladies, let's begin."

I'd been through interrogations before. Gina was a pro. But she was small potatoes compared to this lot. If it hadn't been for my mother dragging me on her book tour all across the country, I probably would have cracked. *The only other good thing from that ordeal.* Instead, I sipped my whiskey and answered everything they threw at me, the questions coming rapid fire, one after another. All from Rhonda herself.

"How long have you two been together?"

What did we tell Yolanda? "A couple weeks."

"How'd you two meet?"

I wanted to stick as close to the truth as possible. "He helped me get out of dinner with my mother."

"Why'd you move in with him?"

"My apartment building caught on fire, and he offered." There was no way in hell I was telling her my former apartment was condemned. I made a mental note to fill Derek in on that cover story.

"Your mother is Mabel Milbourne?"

I nodded, sipping my whiskey.

"But you work?"

Another nod, and I resisted the urge to roll my eyes. The silence stretched on, telling me I wasn't getting out of it without giving her something more. "My mother and I aren't on the greatest of terms. I accept her help with schooling but try to support myself in other areas." I thought that was sufficient.

Finally, after all the tap dancing and tiptoeing around, we came to the heart of the matter. Rhonda looked me dead in the eye. "When did you find out about the money?"

Rich people are so paranoid. "Our first date. We went to breakfast, discussing our backgrounds, and he told me flat out." I took a sip of whiskey. "As I'm sure Kevin already told you, I'm not a gold digger. My mom is a minor celebrity in her own right, and we were upper middle class before that." Shrugging wasn't ladylike, but I did it anyway. "I'm not in this for the money."

"So why are you in this?" Her gaze was piercing.

I blinked at her as if she were daft. Which quite possibly she was. "Have you *seen* your brother?" I pictured him. "Tall, dark, handsome. It's a cliché for a reason, honey. And those muscles are absolutely delicious. Him in a towel is one thing, but without?" More whiskey.

"Has a guy ever left his own birthday party to visit you in the hospital?" My question was met with blank stares. "Then he brought me to his home to take care of me. He made sure his place was stocked with all my favorite foods. He's thoughtful, caring and he gets me in a way that no one has before." My voice caught on the last word, the truth causing more pain than any lie ever could. *If I ever do end up dating, how can anyone come close to this fake boyfriend of mine?*

Before they had a chance to say any more, I rolled down the divider. "Greg, I believe I'm ready for lunch."

Derek did not disappoint. The outside of The Gilded Lily was beautiful, all marble and sparkling in the sun. When Greg opened our door, I saw Fawnda's jaw drop for a split second before she caught herself. Yolanda and Rhonda shared a skeptical look as if I were above my station to even think I'd get in. Anxiety skittered across my belly when I approached the podium and clearly stated my name. Any place with this much gold-plating made me want to tuck my tail and run.

But the hostess just smiled, gathered four menus, and said, "Right this way, Miss Milbourne."

The indignant look on the Musketeers' faces made it worth all the hassle. Our food tasted divine, even if the portions were tiny. I marveled at the soft linen tablecloth, the fine cloth napkins and the heft of the silverware. There were three forks. The service was immaculate, and I took care of everyone's lunch with one signature. Relieved to have made it through the meal without any huge fiasco, I led them back to the limo.

Before I climbed in, I murmured to Greg, "One extra block, if you please."

His eyes took on a knowing glint as he assessed my battle-ready face. "Of course, Miss Avery."

The simpering compliments on lunch finally died down.

And I charged. "I'm very glad we finally had a chance to get acquainted and clear the air a bit, so to speak." I deliberately poured another couple of fingers of whiskey. "Each of you has known my boyfriend much longer than I have, and I respect that. I would never ask him to give up his friendships." Sip. "Or his family." Sip. "Even if they are toxic, demanding more of him than humanly possible, and giving nothing in return." Sip, this time I added an extra moment to meet each of their wide-eyed stares.

"I would, however, caution anyone who wants to take advantage of my boyfriend, emotionally, financially, socially." Sip. I glanced pointedly down at my well-manicured nails. "Just one little puff can make a whole house come tumbling down. Especially if it's a house of cards. And I control which way the wind blows now."

Greg pulled up in front of our apartment building, hurrying around to let me out.

The Three Musketeers blinked at me, sitting frozen like little statues.

"Oh, don't worry, girls, Greg will drive you home. Take care now." I brought the fifth of whiskey out of the limo and smiled up at Greg as he shut the door behind me.

The color of his gray eyes reminded me of steel, but his smile was as soft as room-temperature butter.

I could easily see us being friends. "Thanks for everything." I grinned, leaning in and whispering conspiratorially, "Take the bumpy way home, okay?"

"Anything you say, Miss." He tipped his hat one time, his smile thoughtful as he watched me walk into the building.

The doorman greeted me, and I realized I had a very real problem. "So I was straight out of the hospital coming here last time. And I have no idea which floor or room I'm supposed to go to. I'm with Derek Elgin." Not to mention my issue with numbers.

He glanced at my whiskey.

I'd only had a glass. Or three.

"Let me tell Mr. Elgin you're here." *Doorman code for 'let me ask someone for help'.*

A few moments later, the elevator doors slid open, and there was Derek, hands in his jeans' pockets, green long-sleeved shirt clinging to his chest. And a smirk on his lips. "What seems to be the problem?"

I wrinkled my nose at him. "The problem is that I don't know where I live." My feet screamed as I strode over to the elevator, but I kept it off my face until the doors closed behind me. Then I thrust the whiskey into Derek's hands, grabbed his arm for support and shucked off my shoes.

A rough finger ran down my exposed shoulder before I straightened, his husky voice giving me goose bumps. "So much skin. Weren't you cold?"

I tossed my ponytail out of my face as I stood up. "Yeah, but I looked better than the Musketeers, so it was worth it. Now give me back my whiskey."

"Whiskey?" His blue eyes widened as he looked down at the bottle in his hand. He gaped at me a minute as I took it back. "How? Who?"

"Spit it out already." I needed comfy clothes and more whiskey ASAP.

"This is from the private stash." He spoke with an air of awe. "How in the world did you get your hands on a bottle?"

I glanced down at the fifth cradled in the crook of my arm. *Well, that explains why it's so good.* "Someone has taste." After glancing back at Derek, I shrugged. "The other girls were having champagne, and I needed something stronger. So I rolled down the divider and asked for it. I might be inclined to share if you make it worth my while." I waggled my eyebrows, teasing.

His blue eyes darkened like the sea before a storm, and I gulped. More intensity. *Too much.* I retreated, thinking the elevator wall was right behind me. It wasn't. I teetered dangerously until his warm hand splayed across my bare back, steadying me. My stomach flipped as his citrus and clove scent stole my breath.

The elevator dinged, and the door slid open as his hand left my skin. I missed his touch immediately, then cursed myself the whole way. He unlocked the door, muttering about needing to get me keys.

Liam sprawled across the couch. "Hey."

Derek nodded, guiding me past him with a hand at my back once more and his lips at my ear. "Need help with dress removal?"

"Yes, please."

In my room, he shut the door behind us. I dropped my shoes onto the thick carpet, leaning forward on the low dresser to peer at myself in the mirror. The built-in bra of the halter part of the dress really did a decent job perking my ample chest up. When I tossed my hair back, I yelped as a strand got caught in my dangly earring. Derek rushed over.

"I've got it. You just handle the zipper." I'd had a hard enough time pulling it up in the first place. If he unzipped me, I could undo the top part after he left, and I would have a win-win on my hands. *This damn piece of hair is really caught.*

I was so focused on it that I didn't notice Derek unclasping the halter top until my dress fell around my ankles. My first instinct was to yelp again and cover myself, but something in his eyes stopped me. My gaze locked on his face in the mirror. "I wasn't ready."

"Neither was I." His blue eyes took in everything. Every curve, every bump, and his gaze slid slowly over them, fascinated.

Heat bloomed within me, a slow fire starting low inside. I couldn't look away from his piercing gaze.

His warm finger ran along a dent from the fabric digging into my skin. "What's this?"

I shrugged. "The dress isn't quite my size. I'm sure if I lost a few pounds—"

He growled at me. "No. You're perfect. Absolutely perfect the way you are. Any guy would be lucky to call you his girlfriend." He leaned down, pressing his lips to a freckle on the tip of my shoulder. Then he strode out of the room, shutting the door behind him.

Stunned, I stood there for a minute, one thought echoing in my mind.

If fairy tales were real, he'd make a perfect knight in shining armor.

But they aren't. And he isn't.

A couple of minutes later, I made it to the kitchen, lining up three glasses for the whiskey. Derek paced in a circle around the island, on the phone with Greg. As Derek drew closer, I yelled, "Thanks again, Greg. Hope you handled the bumpy road okay!"

Derek shot me a dirty look, but I saw the twinkle in his eye.

Liam just stared at me as I slid a glass his way, seeming puzzled. "You're not anything like I expected."

My tolerance for bullshit had been surpassed hours ago, and I had no energy left to play games. I met his green eyes with a smirk. "Should have said 'assumed'." I took a drink of the whiskey, sighing as the smooth liquid slid down my throat. "Then I could have called you an ass."

He chuckled as Derek got off the phone.

"What'd I miss?"

"Your girlfriend calling me an ass." Liam took a sip, glancing down at the glass in surprise. "This *is* good. Damn."

I shook my head. "I did not call you an ass." Both guys looked up at me, confused, so I explained, "Liam said I wasn't anything like he expected. I said he should have used the word assumed, so I could have called him an ass." My punchline fell flat. Again. "You know what they say when you assume…makes an ass out of 'u and me'." I rolled my eyes when all I got were blank stares.

Liam elbowed Derek. "Fell for her sharp wit, did ya, buddy?"

They both laughed while I crossed my arms and huffed. Deciding they could have the barstools, I made myself at home, because it was, after all, my home, and slid my butt onto the counter.

Derek hopped on the stool closest to me, running a finger over my knuckles. "You going to tell us about it? I see you still have all your limbs."

So I told them all the gory details, hamming it up a bit to show how well I'd handled myself. "I told Rhonda the reason I was staying here so soon was because my apartment caught on fire." As soon as the words were out of my mouth, my eyes darted to Liam then to Derek. *Shit.* I had no idea what Liam knew and what he didn't.

Derek's warm, large hand patted my thigh, sending electricity jolting up higher and making me want to squirm. "It's all right. Liam knows what really happened with your apartment. Though I get why you didn't want to tell my sister that."

I ignored the lightning bolts spearing me, responding to his words instead. "Yeah, doesn't exactly bolster my non-gold-digger status."

Liam's brown eyes narrowed over his glass of whiskey. "If your mom is Mabel Milbourne, why exactly were you living in a dump like that?"

Dick. Derek must have told him all *the details.* I didn't miss a beat. "What exactly is the balance of your checking account at this precise moment?" *Two can play that game.*

He reared back, obviously offended, but Derek laid a hand on his arm before saying, "Pretty sure she means you're getting a bit personal."

A warm, fuzzy feeling spread through me. *Derek gets me already.* I took another sip from my glass, the warmth seeping farther. *Or maybe it's just the whiskey.*

Liam blinked at me. "Oh. Sorry."

I nodded. Words bubbled up, tumbling out of my mouth before I could stop them, the alcohol loosening my tongue. "My dad has Alzheimer's, a very early onset." I swirled the golden liquid in the bottom of my glass, watching the tiny whirlpool spin.

"It's been so long since he's even recognized me. Mother pretends he doesn't exist anymore, going on with her own life. The money for my schooling, the stuff beyond my scholarship, is hers. I'll take that. But I'm not taking a dime from her otherwise." I sniffed, squeezing my eyes shut and willing away the tears.

Liam cleared his throat, setting down his tumbler with a clank. "I'm going to go grab my charger from my apartment." He disappeared through the door.

I stared after him. "I didn't mean to make him leave."

Chuckling, Derek shook his head. "He lives one floor down. Plus, he hates tears, so if you ever want to make him disappear..." His eyes landed on Liam's glass where he'd left it on the end table near the door. "He hasn't finished his drink, though, so he'll be back." Derek grabbed my knee and pulled me across the counter, right onto his lap. "You were saying?"

I stiffened, then tucked my head under his chin and allowed him to hold me. It felt amazing to lean on someone else, the final chink in my crumbling barriers.

"Mother's awful. What she did is unforgivable." Anger surged through me, fresh as that day two years ago. "I've always been a daddy's girl." I smiled against Derek's firm chest. "Dad and I were so proud when

Mom's book took off." I paused, sniffling, remembering the celebratory family dinner we'd all had.

His large hand stroked my hair.

"My senior year, her manager scheduled her a huge book tour, a six-month thing." Resentment hit me, leaving a bitter taste in my mouth. "She demanded I go with her, told my dad, 'You've had her for eleven years. It's my turn.' I didn't get a prom or spring break or graduation." A tear leaked out.

Derek tightened his hold, squeezing me against him. He ran his other hand down my hair, over and over.

"I was excited to go at first, but I didn't realize I'd be constantly judged. I've always been curvy and taller than most people." My lips twisted into a wry smile. I didn't want to be petted, so I sat up, steeling myself against the memories. "The beginning of that tour amplified all my insecurities. It was awful."

I remembered begging to go home, but my mom just said whatever didn't kill me would make me stronger. "Her assistant, Trish, showed me how to dress for my body type, taught me the art of makeup. I survived because of her." I raised my chin. "My makeup, clothes, heels became my armor. I figured out how to push back just right. It was sink or swim out there."

"And you came home with all your limbs intact." Admiration shone in his face as he studied me. "Just like today."

I nodded, a lump appearing in my throat as I geared up for the next part. "But when I got home, so excited to see Daddy after being away for months —" My voice broke, and I swallowed. "He was watching TV, and I called out to him, waiting for his eyes to light up, for him to rush over and sweep me in his arms." I shook my head. "But he didn't know who I was." My words were wobbly, my throat thick. "My own dad had no idea who I was. And it wasn't the hair or the makeup."

That first stare of blankness had been terrifying, but not as scary as the anger that had followed. My voice lowered to little more than a whisper. "He threw a mug at me, screaming at me to get out of his house."

"Avery…" Derek's arms cradled me, pulling me back to his chest. "I'm so sorry."

I sniffed, laying my cheek on his shoulder and gripping his shirt in one hand to ground myself. "I ran to Mother, thinking she'd know what to do." I'd flung open the backseat of the Town Car. "Only to find her agent on top of her in the backseat of the car. She'd been cheating on my dad the whole time. When I told her about Daddy, she brushed me off, saying she'd known." I clenched my jaw, seeing red for a second as the memory washed over me.

Mother stood up from the backseat, straightening her jacket. "Yes, he has a rapid onset of Alzheimer's. Why do you think I insisted you come with me on this tour? I couldn't leave you alone with him."

I let out a shaky breath. "She knew the whole time what she was doing. Not once on that tour did she mention it, not once did she prepare me for what I'd be going home to. She stole that time from me, and I can never get it back." The tears coursed down my cheeks then, thinking how Daddy was lost to me forever.

Derek held me tightly as I sobbed, rocking side to side in a minuscule motion that soothed me.

Mother had started sending her gifts shortly after that, but she'd never apologized. Daddy lived in one little room of her huge house with his caregiver and Patty for socialization. I kept trying to tell Mother about treatment options, specialized facilities, different doctors who were trained in proven techniques, but she had the power to decide since she was his wife. And her image, her career, was more important to her than Daddy's quality of life.

My tears finally quieted.

"Oh, Avery." Derek sighed. "I wish I could do something."

"You are." My cheek rested against his shoulder. My chest was flush against his, each breath pressing my breasts against his firmness. I sat on his lap, his muscular legs beneath me, supporting me. One of his warm, large hands splayed across my back, almost protectively. It was the most intimate moment I'd had in over a year.

So, of course, Liam knocked at the door then, poking his head in. "All clear?"

"I'm fine, Liam," I called. I swiped at my cheeks, moving to stand up, but Derek tightened his grip, keeping me there for an extra beat. I patted his chest, reassuring him I was okay, then hopped off him. "No more tears."

Liam picked up his whiskey and took a sip, then wiped his brow in an overly relieved motion.

Derek came to stand behind me, and I leaned against him. My stomach growled. "What's for dinner?"

"You're hungry? You just came from lunch."

I pushed off him. "Have you seen the size of those portions? Here, have a steak." I held my fingers in a tiny circle. "Mashed potatoes?" The size of a pea.

He chuckled. "All right, all right. How about subs?"

"Perfect." After we'd figured out what we each wanted, I hurried to the living room. An idea had been flitting around in my head, and now was the perfect time to put it into action. Especially since I needed to catch Liam alone. "I need your phone number."

"What? No!"

I gave him my dirtiest look. "Don't flatter yourself. I missed Derek's birthday last week and want to throw him a surprise party. So give me your number. I have questions!"

Light finally dawned in his eyes as I shoved my phone toward him. I snatched it back just as Derek finished ordering.

He plopped down between us on the couch, stretching his arms out across the full length of the back. "Now what?"

I grinned. "Either of you like to play cards?"

Chapter Five

Gina wasn't the only one who liked to gamble. It wasn't surprising since I'd been raised in my dad's poker room, the mascot for his weekly games. How could I not love it after I'd sat on his lap hand after hand, studying the cards and reading his opponents, until I'd learned what to do in almost every situation.

As Liam shuffled, I sipped my whiskey, feeling it burn the whole way down. *Daddy would love this.* If I closed my eyes, I could smell the cigars, hear my dad's rough laughter as his friends told jokes I didn't understand.

Derek jolted me out of my reverie with a nudge, since it was my turn to bet. After a few friendly rounds, playing with chips just for fun while we ate our subs, Liam suggested raising the stakes.

"What did you have in mind?" I asked, all innocence and sweetness. *Fly, meet honey.*

He smirked. "Instead of chips, let's play for clothes."

I shuffled the cards. "Strip poker?" I feigned shyness, nibbling on my lower lip. My eyes flew to Derek, who gave absolutely nothing away. I would've liked at least a little excitement from him. *Of course, he's already had a private show.* I felt my cheeks heat up. "What game?"

Liam and Derek exchanged a look to say they didn't care.

"How about a simple five card draw?" It was my bread and butter. We'd been playing Texas Hold 'Em until this point, which I was okay at. But I'd been holding back, trying to get a read on both of them. Plus, I'd had a feeling Liam was still trying to one-up me. And I'd been right.

"Sure." Derek grinned, clearly happy with my choice.

Liam's mouth tightened, but he couldn't say no after Derek had already agreed.

"Okay, five card draw, one draw, up to three cards. Liam, since you suggested it, how are you envisioning this? We assign a point value to each article of clothing?" I'd done that before, and it was a lot to keep track of, so I was relieved when he shook his head.

"How about we all start each hand with the same amount of chips? Then we play like normal, and whoever wins the round doesn't have to take off anything." His smirk was so cocky. "Socks count as one item."

I looked forward to wiping the smile off his face. It was difficult to maintain my façade of uncertainty. "Is there a penalty for folding?"

He and Derek exchanged a look, then Liam scratched his chin. "You can fold before the draw. Otherwise, it's considered a loss."

Sounded fair to me, so I nodded my agreement. Derek's head bobbed, too.

We were using poker chips, blue ones worth ten, red ones worth five and whites each worth one.

I dealt, making sure to watch as they got their cards. Derek tended to press his lips together briefly if his hand sucked. It had taken me a while to notice, the motion so quick and subtle. When things were good, though, his gaze flicked more to us, trying to figure out how much to bet.

Liam was more obvious. He tapped his thumb on the table if he had a good hand, just a couple of quick celebratory taps. For a bad one, he'd touch his face, rub his nose or play with his lip. *Which he's doing right now.*

Derek wasn't making eye contact, so he didn't have a stellar hand. I peeked at mine, relieved to see a pair of aces and a king.

They all stayed in for the betting, and I raised them up to a blue chip. "All right, boys. How many you want?"

"Three for me." Derek's lips mushed together as he eyed his new cards.

Perfect, and he can't fold now without taking something off. I turned to Liam.

He held up three fingers. I watched him as I dealt myself two. He didn't do either of his tells, so likely a middle-of-the-road hand. It'd be interesting to see where he went with it.

Derek checked. Liam threw in a blue chip, smirking like he held a royal flush. I decided to hem and haw a little, then just called him, tossing in my own blue chip. Derek threw one as well—he was in for clothes whether he liked it or not. He laid his hand first, a pair of fours, queen high.

Liam's grin got bigger. "Pair of kings, queen high."

All eyes were on me as I casually laid down my cards. "Guess I win with two pair, huh, boys?" I let the grin I'd been holding back spread across my face.

Both of them muttered, annoyed, but they shoved away from the table. They glanced at each other, and I knew they were silently making a plan. Sure enough, they both turned to face me as Derek blasted stripper music on his phone. Amidst swiveling hips and a lot of fanfare, they both took off their shirts, probably deciding that was their biggest weapon.

They weren't wrong. Even though I'd seen Derek shirtless already, my brain short-circuited. And Liam's bare torso was nothing to sneeze at. He was all muscle, and I loved his tattoo. It reminded me of flames chasing in an endless circle around the thick biceps of his right arm. I'd be happy to stare at him all day, given the opportunity, but not when he sat next to Derek.

My gaze kept drifting back to my fake boyfriend as he turned off the music, plopped in his chair and began shuffling cards. I didn't just want to look at him. I wanted to run my fingers over every ridge, press myself up against those hard planes —

Liam interrupted my daydream. "You're going down, Avery."

Perhaps. In due time. I tried to hide my smile, doing a poor job which made Liam look even more annoyed.

Derek dealt me two tens. Both he and Liam stay in to bid. We all took three. I practically stopped breathing when I looked at my cards. Another ten and two sevens, a full house.

Liam seemed pretty excited about his hand, but Derek, well, maybe it wasn't his night to play poker. Liam and I bid each other up pretty high, until I'd finally had enough, just calling him. He laid down three kings, triumph showing in his eyes.

I had to play it up. "Man, I only had three tens."

He clapped his hands together, and grinned.

Then I laid down my other two. "Plus these." I bit my lip as his smile fell, and he banged his fist lightly on the table.

Derek laughed. "Oh, man, you should see your face."

"Pay up, boys. What's coming off this time?" I leered at them.

As if choreographed, they both reached down and peeled off their socks. I couldn't help laughing. Liam snatched up the cards, going right into his shuffling routine, as serious as he could be. I glanced at Derek, wanting to share my delight with someone. But when I met his eyes they were filled with more than just amusement—there was laughter, happiness and light. I lost myself for a moment, realizing he seemed more alive than I'd ever seen him. Then he smiled at me.

And I forgot to breathe… Until the cards hit my fingers, jarring me back to reality. *I have to focus.* It was difficult to keep my concentration. So difficult, in fact, I made a mistake. Derek folded right off the bat, and I got cocky, thinking I had three queens. But I only had two and a jack. I bid Liam up. And lost.

I scolded myself as I removed my socks. *Head in the game.* I heard my dad's voice, coaching me. It was my deal again, and they only had their jeans left before the real fun began. We hadn't said how far we were taking this.

It was a nail biter of a round. Derek met my eyes then Liam's right away, so he had a decent hand. Liam's thumb hit the table, which meant he did, too.

And I…nothing matched. I had the five, seven and nine of clubs. With nothing else. Chasing straights and flushes was never a great idea. I could fold, but my gut told me not to.

Derek threw in five, Liam called. I held my breath and tossed in my red chip, hoping my instinct was right. Derek took two, his mouth tightening after looking at his new cards. Liam also took two, eyes narrowing slightly. I followed their lead, taking two and hoping for some luck.

Holy shit, I got it! Not only did I get the six and eight, but they were both clubs.

We went around again, just once, but I knew I had them. I felt bad for Derek when he laid down three queens. There was no pang of guilt when Liam taunted him with his full house.

I stood up, smirked, and said, "Sorry, boys. It's just not your night." And I laid my straight flush on the table.

Both their jaws dropped. Liam was obviously working to control his temper, clenching his jaw and taking deep breaths, but Derek just shook his head. "Damn, girl. Well, Liam, let's give the lady what she wants."

My cheeks hurt from grinning so wide as I watched them shimmy out of their jeans. Liam's thighs were all bulk, gorgeous to some, but he didn't hold a candle to Derek's lean sculpted legs. He was my type all over. Hands down.

Or hands anywhere I could put them on that beautiful body. Damn.

I smirked at each of them in turn. "You boys in for another round? I wouldn't mind making sure I didn't get the short straw, if you catch my drift."

Liam's face turned bright red. "You cheated. There's no way anyone could be that lucky."

I raised one eyebrow at him. "Uh-huh. And who suggested playing strip poker in the first place? Hoping to get material for their spank bank?"

His face grew even redder.

Derek outright laughed. "She's got you there."

Liam pushed away from the table, stomping down the hallway, muttering the whole way.

His blue eyes on me, Derek shook his head. "So you were sandbagging the whole time during Texas Hold 'Em, huh?"

"Not the whole time." I shuffled again, bridging the cards to bring the deck back together. "I was getting a read on my opponents." I lowered my voice to a whisper. "When Liam has a good hand, he taps his thumb against the table. If he has a bad one, he swipes his nose or his lip at least once. It's quick, but it's there."

Derek nodded thoughtfully. He leaned back in his chair, giving me an eye-full of his magnificent abs as he laced his hands behind his head. "I think you lost your room for the night."

I whipped my head toward the hallway, a faint snore reaching my ears. "That jerk."

"To be fair, it was kind of his room first." Amusement danced in his eyes.

Oh. "Doesn't he live like one floor down?"

"Yeah, but even that's too much sometimes." He held up the nearly empty bottle of whiskey. "Like tonight. And Liam's talent is crashing out anywhere. Choosing your bed might be more about revenge than tiredness." Derek upended the bottle so the contents were divided equally between our glasses. Then he stood up, pulling his jeans back on.

I unabashedly watched each movement, telling myself I'd earned it fair and square. My glass in hand, I took a sip of my whiskey.

"I'm not sure what pissed Liam off more," Derek said as we made our way to the big chair, plopping down side by side. "The fact that he didn't get a show or that you didn't care about the one he was putting on."

I spoke the truth, staring at Derek. "He's a good-looking guy, don't get me wrong" — I rested my glass on the arm of the chair — "but he was sitting next to you."

He sipped his whiskey, but not before I saw the absurdly pleased smile on his face.

I envied the glass, touching his lips. "What does he know about our relationship?" I took a drink.

"That it's real."

My gaze flew to his. Those blue eyes grabbed me hook, line and sinker as he backed up the words with the intensity of a sledgehammer that slammed into my gut. I choked on my whiskey. Sputtering and coughing with tears streaming down my cheeks, I finally cleared my airway enough to draw a breath.

"You all right?" At my nod, he frowned. "I mean it's good stuff, but you probably shouldn't inhale it."

We were quiet after that. The combined warmth of Derek's body heat and the whiskey in my belly pulled me to the edge of sleep. Next thing I knew, I was in Derek's arms, nestled against his bare chest. "Did you put me to bed the other night?"

"Maybe."

I knew it was a yes from the teasing tone of his voice. At least I was somewhat awake for it this time. "I can walk, you know. You can put me down."

"What if I don't want to?"

His quiet words had me tightening my grip on his neck as my world threatened to drop out from under me. *Steady girl.* "I'm not too heavy?"

"Avery," he breathed, "no. Not at all."

We passed my room, and I frowned. "Wait. Where are we going? I'm not sleeping with Liam."

There went that delicious rumbling chuckle again, hitting me in places that made me want to moan. "No, you're not." He kicked open his bedroom door to set me down on his bed before disappearing into his bathroom.

Well, now I was wide awake. I stayed put, on the edge of his king-sized bed, my blood humming as I smoothed my fingers across the comforter. Where I'd be sleeping in mere moments. *Just sleeping.*

Derek came out of the bathroom, a soft smile appearing when his gaze met mine.

"Could —?" I stammered the word out, so I stopped to suck in a breath before starting again, pulling on the confident well deep within me. "Could I borrow a shirt to sleep in?"

His eyebrows lifted.

I glanced at the hallway. "It just feels weird going in there with Liam…"

He held up his hand. "No problem." After he slid open his closet doors, he pulled a black T-shirt off the shelf. "How's this?"

When I unfurled it, the hem grazed mid-thigh. I nodded, ducking into the bathroom.

When I came out, he perched on the edge of his bed, peeling off his jeans. His eyes slid over me, throat bobbing as his gaze raked down my bare thighs.

"Good night." I climbed into bed, careful not to touch him.

"Good night." He turned out the light.

We didn't make any rules, but I knew he'd be a gentleman. If I reached for him, ravaged him, sure all bets were off. As long as I stuck to my side, I had nothing to fear from Derek. I tried to make my breathing slow and steady, but it was a long time before I actually went to sleep. My imagination would not shut off.

* * * *

When I woke Saturday morning, I eased back into bed after a quick trip to the bathroom. I wasn't quite ready to get up, but I didn't drift off again like I thought I would.

Derek faced me, his hands tucked under his chin, one sculpted shoulder bare. His smooth chest moved up and down in the steady rhythm of slumber. I studied him, somehow so intense, even in sleep. The fierce line of his mouth. His angular jaw and high cheekbones. I'd kill to have eyelashes that long and full. I shifted closer to get a better look, only to be met by those intense, deep eyes.

"How am I supposed to sleep with you staring at me?" He raised an eyebrow.

I pursed my lips, sheepish at being caught. "At least I was being quiet."

He sighed.

Since he's awake... "Did you know you have two freckles on your right eyelid?"

His drawn-out silence spoke volumes. "I don't exactly study my eyelids in the mirror, Avery."

I giggled, picturing him closing one eye, trying to see the lid of the other. "Well, that's what fake girlfriends are for. To tell you important information like that." I stared at him another long moment until he flopped onto his back and closed his eyes once more. *Fine. I can take a hint.*

But my eyes wouldn't stay shut. The ceiling was a textured plaster, and not just a uniformed swirl either. It was full of lumps and bumps. Pretty soon I was picking out shapes, like finding pictures in the clouds. *That one looks like a bunny. And that one looks like...ew.*

"Avery..."

My name was a groan. "What? I was just finding shapes in the ceiling."

Another sigh, this one laced with exasperation. "You must have found something disturbing because you yelped."

Oh. "Yeah. That one looks like a—"

Derek rolled over and covered my lips with his, kissing me deeply. He stole my breath. I softened beneath him, kissing him right back. My fingers threaded through his hair, and he groaned into my mouth. As he rolled off me, he brought me with him, tucking me against his side.

Stunned, I curled into him. *That certainly hadn't felt fake. And no one was here to witness it.* Confusion threatened to overwhelm me, but I'd kissed guys before. Plenty of them, and without getting my heart involved. I could do it again. I shoved aside the whisper of doubt, along with everything else except replaying that kiss over and over. Somewhere between the fifth and eighth repeat, I drifted off to sleep once more.

When I woke again, Derek's side of the bed was empty. I stuffed my hair in a wad on top of my head, then searched for something to secure it with. I came up empty. Awkwardly dashing to my room, I was thankful to see the door open and no Liam in sight. I snatched a hair tie from my end table, made the messiest bun ever and called it good. While I was in there, I pulled on yoga pants and a different top, then headed into the hall.

Liam was speaking. "Have you told her about Princess yet?"

Almost around the corner, I nearly skidded to a stop.

Silence met his question. *If Derek comes stalking past, he'll run into me, and the jig will be up.*

"Derek, seriously, she has a right to know."

"Liam." The name had an edge to it, all threat and growl. Derek was done with that conversation.

I hoped he never used that tone with me. My nose twitched, my only warning before I sneezed. There was no use pretending not to be there after that, so I stepped around the corner.

"Morning, Avery." Liam spoke first. "And bless you."

"Morning, Avery." Derek's gritted tone sounded a little forced, as was his smile.

I smiled at both of them, my gaze lingering on Derek. His jaw loosened the longer our eyes met, and finally, he relaxed. *Good.*

Derek lifted an empty coffee cup, asking if I wanted some. When I nodded, he poured. "Sleep well?"

I went right to the fridge for my creamer. "Yep." I added the perfect amount to my mug then took a sip. *Hot, but delicious.*

"Me too." His eyes took on a teasing glint. "After someone finally stopped talking."

My eyes narrowed as several pieces fell into place, the caffeine jolting my brain into action. "Wait, you kissed me to shut me up?"

A slow grin spread across Derek's face. "It worked, didn't it?"

I slammed my mug onto the counter, coffee sloshing over the side. "Dammit, Derek, that's not right. You can't just go around kissing people to get them to stop—"

Suddenly, he was in front of me, his mouth covering mine once more.

What was I mad about? I moaned and leaned into him.

His teeth tugged on my bottom lip. "Mmm, French vanilla."

Liam started laughing. "Looks like you're onto something there, Derek."

I opened my mouth to yell at him. Then I just laughed. "I guess I can't complain."

"And if you did, I'd just kiss you again." Derek winked at me.

My hand on my chin, I pretended to think about his words. "Hmm, well in that case…"

Liam threw his hands in the air and stalked over to the door. "It's too early for this shit. I'm out."

A startled squeak came from the hallway as he strode out. Gina edged her way in, grinning at me. Her smile faded as she took in my confused expression. "I texted you I was coming. Last night. You said okay!"

I glanced at Derek for confirmation, he just shrugged. I wasn't even sure where my phone was. "Not that I'm not happy to see you—" My brain registered what she was carrying. "You brought Sweetwaters?"

It was Derek's turn to look confused.

With a delighted squeal, I raced over to her.

She held the box away from me, a teasing glint in her eye. "I bring you apology donuts, and you don't even have the decency to say hi to me?"

"Hi, Gina."

My friend looked slightly mollified but still didn't offer me a donut.

"I was planning on calling you anyway today." I sauntered back over to the counter and picked up my coffee mug, both Derek and Gina watching me with narrowed eyes. "I have to go by the storage room, and I was going to ask you to come along." More than a peace offering, it was Gina's favorite place.

An ear-splitting scream tore the air as she registered my words. In her excitement, the box of Sweetwaters' donuts tottered dangerously in her hands. I rescued them, opening the box to snatch out my preferred bear claw before anyone else could even think of it.

"What's the storage room?" Derek asked, trying to follow our power struggle.

I mimed zipping my lips and shook my head at him. "You're not quite there yet."

"When do we leave?" Gina bounced up and down with all the energy of a month-old puppy.

"Eat a donut, drink some coffee. I still have to shower." I frowned as she showed no signs of chilling. "Maybe Derek should kiss you."

Derek's eyes widened to the size of dinner plates.

Gina froze. "Why would he do that?"

I laughed to myself as I walked to my bedroom, leaving Derek to explain my comment. I felt his glare on my back the entire time. But I didn't stop grinning while I got ready.

The beginnings of a plan had been circling in my head since my lunch with Rhonda. Derek's birthday had been a disaster, on his end anyway, and I was working on a way to make it up to him. I thought I might be able to pull off a surprise party—if I could scrounge up the funds. Which necessitated a trip to the storage room to see what I had to sell. Before I left my room, I put a key on a long chain over my head, then tucked it into my blouse.

Gina met me in the hall, a seriousness in her face. "Are we good, Avery?"

I smiled at her. There wasn't a trace of anger left in me. "Yeah, G. We're good."

She beamed, throwing her arms around me. We hugged for a good minute, then she pulled away. "Good. I can't stand it when we fight." We headed to the dining room, where she grabbed her purse. "Should I get Aunt Tasha lined up?" she asked, already digging out her phone.

"I don't even know what I have for her yet." I glanced through my purse, making sure I had everything. I hadn't really looked in it since my hospital trip.

"I know. But if we text now, maybe she'll throw in lunch." She waggled her eyebrows suggestively.

"Why didn't you lead with that?"

Gina grinned and started texting.

I turned to Derek.

He stared at me, a mixture of intrigue and disappointment on his face. "So I take it you won't be around much this afternoon?"

Aw, poor baby. "Nope. Think you can hold down the fort?"

He smirked. "I do have some experience. You gonna fill me in later?"

As I stepped closer to him, I shot him a saucy grin. "Filling you in requires talking. Probably a decent amount of talking. And we all know how you feel about me running my mouth—"

His lips crashed down on mine once more. I sank into him, his hands gripping my waist, steadying me. He ended the kiss on a soft note, my head spinning as I came back down to earth.

I hated feeling so off balance. "Dammit, Derek." I realized I had shoes on, so I kicked him in the shin and gave him a shove for good measure. Then I stomped out of the kitchen, grabbing a laughing Gina as I walked past.

He frowned at my less than playful reaction. "Avery, wait."

But I pretended not to hear, ignoring my racing heart and my flipping stomach as I ran to the hallway to dash for the elevator. Luckily it was waiting for us, the doors sliding shut just as Derek's head appeared from his apartment. As soon as I was out of view, I sank to the floor to bury my head in my hands.

Gina *tsked*. "You are so fucked, girl."

"I know. You haven't even heard the worst of it." We were in the lobby before I finished spilling my guts. "You know how I feel about serious relationships."

They scared the shit out of me. *Look what happened to my parents. How can I ever risk giving my heart to someone and ending up like my dad, forgotten and alone?* I shivered, just thinking about it.

Her snort was anything but ladylike, Gina through and through. "And I keep saying most people aren't like your mom and dad. Shit happens. You're going to have to get over that. Derek's perfect for you." She eyed me. "Why do you think I let him take you home?"

I elbowed her.

When we emerged into the lobby, Greg waited for us. His cheery smile and gray eyes twinkled as he swooped off his hat in a semi-bow.

I stopped, stammering "What are you doing here?"

He grinned at my obvious surprise. "Derek thought you ladies might enjoy some time to chat while you go from point A to point B."

My eyebrow shot up, evidence of my concern about Derek's motives. "Did he ask you to tell him about point B? And its location?"

To his credit, Greg looked confused as we all stepped outside.

Gina lost her mind at seeing a limo with our figurative name on it for the day. She hopped in before Greg could open the door for her, refusing to even consider another mode of transportation. "You need to sort your shit out." She pulled the door shut behind her.

So I pretended to walk away.

Which she countered by popping up through the sunroof. "Please, Avery! I *never* get to do anything like this. You know that." She had no qualms about begging at the top of her lungs.

To salvage what little dignity we had left, I turned to Greg. "The errands I have to do today are of a personal nature. I might, at some point in the future, decide to tell Derek about said errands, but that is to be at my discretion. If we go with you today, you are sworn to secrecy." I stuck out my little finger. "Pinky swear. I'll even throw in an autographed copy of *How to Land a Guy and…Keep Him!*"

Greg extended his pinky, mouth twitching. "I swear I shall not discuss the location or the contents of the places we visit today with anyone other than yourself or the woman stubbornly yelling from my limo."

I cracked a smile at that. "That's Gina. She's my best friend."

Gina waved from the sunroof.

"Gina, meet Greg. He has amazing whiskey." I glanced at him, hoping he'd take a hint.

He tipped his hat and gave me a wink. "Don't worry, Miss, I came prepared."

Clapping my hands, I waited for him to open the door then clambered in and went straight for the hidden compartment with the brand new fifth of whiskey. "Thank you, Greg!" I called when he was in the driver's seat. "We definitely have some catching up to do. So if you can take us here, we'll leave you to it." I rattled off the address, poured us each a glass of whiskey then told Gina how Derek was absolutely perfect. And how terrifying that was for me. I even filled her in on the whole Princess mystery and the way he shut down. The limo pulled to a stop in front of my storage unit just as I drained my glass.

"And you have no idea who this Princess is?" Gina spat out the word.

"Nothing. Nada. Zero. Zilch." *How am I supposed to compete with a ghost?*

Gina stayed silent for a second, then smirked. "What about the kiss this morning?"

I waved her off with a *pssh*. "He's just teasing, a game he started, to make us look more real for when Liam's there. Liam doesn't know we're fake."

She looked at me like I was insane. "Uh-huh, keep telling yourself that." Then she tipped up her glass, licking up the last few drops. "All right, let's do this."

Greg was waiting, and I tapped on the window signaling we were ready.

I pulled my key out from under my shirt, fiddling with it as I approached the door. "C'mon, Greg. You'll want to see this."

He hesitated. "Miss?"

"Sure, why not? But call me Avery, okay?" I waited until they flanked me before I turned the key, opened the door, and flicked on the lights. It didn't look like much outside, a long skinny building like any other storage unit, but I owned half of it. And it was filled to the brim.

Gina clapped her hands. "What's our ballpark?"

Good question. "Um, I don't usually throw parties like this. I want to impress his family and friends, so ten? Fifteen? How many copies do you think I should start with?" I was glad to have Gina with me.

"Girl, you know those sell by the box-load. A couple boxes would make a decent dent in that figure." She tugged on Greg's sleeve. "C'mon, Jeeves, let's put those muscles to use."

They went off in search of the right shelves while I went down another aisle.

She called over her shoulder, "Avery, don't you start without me!"

"I'm just looking!" But I smiled. I pulled back a few tarps and stepped into the main room, the one that got Gina all hot and bothered.

Greg whistled as he came through the door. "Holy shit. Oh uh, pardon me, Miss."

I waved him off. "Enough with the 'Miss'. Call me Avery."

It was a pirate's hoard of goodies of the rich and famous, the residence of the gifts Mother sent me. When that first parcel had arrived, my anger at her was still so raw and new, but when I'd opened the box, a treasure trove of designer trinkets and clothes nestled inside. My rage had softened at the edges, warmed by the idea of her thoughtfulness.

As I'd gone through the goodies though, it became clear that she hadn't thought of me. Nothing was in my size or taste. These were her leftovers, and the hot fury turned to cold embers as I'd resigned myself to the realization that this woman was no longer Mom.

That's when Mabel Milbourne became Mother.

I had one rule—to never use these things for anything but charity or frivolity. Mother's money paid for my college education, but that was as far as I'd let her into my life. These trinkets would only be used to make a difference or for fun, not the day-to-day necessities I supplied myself with from my coffee shop job.

Gina appeared, and her eyes grew wide with delight as she walked down the aisles. She nearly cried when she saw a whole box stamped with the Hermes logo. Her head swiveled to me, asking for permission.

I nodded. "That's perfect. And yes, you can pick something from it." I knew I ran the risk of something going out of fashion or being out of season, but if I waited long enough, it'd be vintage right?

"What is all this?" Greg asked.

Gina explained while I kept looking for more things to fund this party. I found a box of Calvin Klein scents, then some Jimmy Choo shoes that might fit my big toe.

Several pairs of Oakleys came next. There was a Gucci clutch I knew Gina would kill to have, so I set it aside to give to her later. Treasure hunting was tiring and, after a couple hours of sorting, I decided I'd had enough. "Text Aunt Tasha. I'm famished."

Aunt Tasha ran a pawn store and had connections all over town. She was also a shrewd businesswoman. For a commission, she made sure we got top dollar for our loot. She wasn't related to Gina by blood, but they'd become close after Gina turned sixteen. From what I'd gathered, Aunt Tasha would have happily adopted Gina, her husband David onboard with the idea as well. But Gina wouldn't hear of it. She settled for calling them her aunt and uncle.

Before we climbed back into the limo, I held a copy of my mother's book out for Greg, but he shook his head. "No, thank you. Derek's a lucky man. I think I have all the inspiration I need right in front of me."

The kind words hit me unexpectedly. *I'll have to hire a cleaning crew to take care of the dust in that place; my allergies are really getting to me.* Or so I told myself as I swiped at my watery eyes before climbing into the backseat. It had been a while since I'd felt so seen.

Chapter Six

After lunch at the best barbecue joint in town, Aunt Tasha assured me she'd take care of everything, despite it being a rush job. We snuck Greg a pulled pork sandwich, which he ate leaning against the limo.

Between bites, he said, "Where to next?"

I glanced at Gina. "You up for some party planning?"

Greg looked curious.

So I explained, "I missed Derek's birthday last week since I was sick with food poisoning." A pinprick of guilt hit me, but I brushed it aside. I hadn't known about his birthday, and technically we weren't even going out yet.

Fake going out, I corrected myself.

Greg snorted, narrowly avoiding a piece of pork falling onto his shirt. "From what I hear, you didn't miss much."

"Exactly. I'd like to throw a party tailored to him. I get the feeling that doesn't happen very often." *If ever.*

"Is there a coffee shop near Derek's?" I needed some caffeine, and I hadn't had much chance to explore the area near the apartment yet.

Mouth full, Greg nodded.

I sent a quick text to Liam asking what he was up to.

He replied, *Nothing much.*

Good, come meet me for coffee and scheming, but don't let Derek know.

As we exited the limo outside the Starbucks, I paused, eyeing the driver. "Greg, how long have you known Derek again?"

"Since he was thirteen. I was hired on with his family when I was nineteen." His smile twisted. "We've been through a lot together."

I exchanged a triumphant glance with Gina, then we each linked an arm through one of his. "Perfect. You're coming with us."

Coffees in hand, we staked out a table near the window to watch for Liam.

"Greg, why do you keep top-shelf whiskey in the limo? It's Derek's favorite, isn't it?"

He nodded, sipping his coffee.

I exchanged an excited glance with Gina. "So maybe a whiskey tasting." My uncle who made maple syrup was also a whiskey connoisseur. He'd always supplied Daddy from his best, most private stash. He owned a distillery and had a liquor license so he could carry top-shelf liquor from around the world at his little shop. Gina and I had hung out with him often enough that he knew her. If I sent him a text saying what I needed, I knew she could handle the rest. "Could you figure that out?"

Gina agreed.

"Hopefully, Liam can help with the food and music. And the guest list. Derek had a bunch of guys over the other day for football. I'm assuming he'd want most of them." I pictured an intimate gathering, maybe playing poker after. I turned to Greg. "Do you know any place that would be good for around thirty people? On the upscale end?" With his profession and experience, I thought he might have a better idea of the types of places Derek was used to.

Greg thought for a minute. "My cousin manages a hotel with a decent event room. I'd be happy to give him a call. They cater, too."

By the time Liam showed up, my coffee was already half gone. We'd halted our party planning since so many things hinged on him. Frustration swirled within me as he sat down in the empty chair, but I managed to stay calm.

Gina, however, held nothing back. "Gee, so nice of you to grace us with your presence. It's not like we don't have better things to do." She arched an eyebrow in his direction while peering down her nose. She'd perfected the look in high school, one that sent many guys running.

But it just put Liam on the defensive. "Gee, so nice of you to give me some advance notice. I could have come straight from the gym, dripping sweat. I thought someone might appreciate me showering first." He turned to me as if to say 'can you believe this girl?'

Instead of taking sides, I settled for introductions. "Gina, this is Liam, Derek's best friend. Liam, this is Gina, my best friend. So form a truce because you'll be seeing a lot of each other." I glared until they both looked down at the table. Then I got Liam a cup of coffee, and we picked his brain about the party.

"When are you thinking of having it?" Liam turned to me. "Derek's sharp. Rhonda and I've tried to surprise him before with no luck. He always figures it out."

"Actually," I said with a wicked grin, "I think I have a surefire way to prevent that. My birthday is November seventeenth, so he'll expect us to be planning a party, and all the things to go with it. He just won't expect the party to be for him! It's the perfect cover." I beamed, looking around the table for reactions. It only gave us a couple weeks to pull everything together, but I thought we could do it. "It's a little late, but better late than never."

"Not bad," Liam said thoughtfully.

Gina grinned. "Not bad at all."

It was the first thing they'd agreed on.

All of our planning hinged on the place being available, so Greg would get right on that. My phone rang, and I frowned when I saw it was Derek.

"Everyone, be quiet. Well, not you, Gina. It's Derek." I cleared my throat and answered. "Hey, what's up?"

"Where are you?" Tension filled his voice as he skipped the greeting.

"Um." My eyes darted around as if he might somehow appear. "Getting coffee with Gina."

"So, my sister told my parents that I have a girlfriend. And they want to meet you. Tonight."

I blinked. "Oh."

A loud sigh came through the phone. "I tried to push it back, but my mother insisted, and Rhonda was available so…"

"Right." I started to panic as I moved the mouthpiece away from my lips. "Dinner. With his parents. Tonight."

Gina's eyes widened, and Liam hid his face in his hands.

"Do you have anything to wear?"

A dress flashed through my mind.

"It would be best to have something designer to up your odds of surviving the night."

"Would Armani work?" My eyes darted to Gina's, gauging her reaction.

Gina slapped a hand over her mouth to cover a squeal. I nodded to her. My stomach tangled in knots as anxiety wove its way through. *Meeting the parents. Ugh.*

There was a pause from Derek, relief flooding his words. "Yes, that'd work nicely."

My mind raced, trying to work out the details. "What time?"

"Six."

Doable, depending on the answer to my next question. "Where do they live?"

"The Harbor."

I thought fast, working everything out in my head. "Okay, here's the deal, I'll need to meet you there. And Greg will have to drive me, otherwise, I can't make it happen."

"Fine, done, whatever you need. Just…thank you. Thank you so much."

I said a quick goodbye and hung up. Then I stood up. "Everyone to the limo." My eyes locked with Liam, my tone no-nonsense.

He frowned. "But—"

"You're my only intel on his parents, so you're coming with me." I grabbed his sleeve and yanked. After we were all settled, I told Greg, "Back to the storage unit. I have a date with a dress."

There was one thing my mother had sent me that I had never been able to part with. It was perhaps a little formal for dinner, but it would definitely pack a punch. I was on the higher end of Armani's size charts, surprised I fit their range at all. I'd shown it to Gina the day after I'd opened it two Christmases ago.

Her words still echoed in my head. "It looks like it was made for you."

The silky black fabric went down to the floor. The neckline was high in front, then dipped down to mid-back. A slit rose to mid-thigh, and the waist gathered to the left. Gems glittered along the neckline, trailing down to the gather, edging the top of the slit. Hopefully, somewhere in my hoard there were shoes in my size and a clutch to match.

Gina filled Liam in on the warehouse, swearing him to secrecy as well. Then we started quizzing him on Derek's parents. He didn't have a lot to offer. It sounded like they didn't differ much from many of the other stuffed-shirt, rich people I'd met over the years at Mother's various events, so I was confident I could hold my own.

Greg wheeled into the lot, and we made a mad dash for my unit. The dress was easy, I knew right where that was. Greg and Gina searched for purses while Liam and I looked through the shoes. I wore a size eleven, and it seemed no one else did. Finally, finally we found one pair of silver pumps I could squeeze my feet into.

"Gina, you'll have to do my hair on the way. Boys, out. I have to change."

The dress was everything I'd ever dreamed. The only thing I wished I could change was the size, which read XXXL. *No wonder models have self-esteem issues.* It was a little tight, but the fabric stretched enough to hug me just right, and I couldn't wait to waltz into the Elgins' house looking like I belonged. We drove to a local Walgreens where Gina ran in for emergency bobby pins, hair spray and snacks to tide Liam over. Then the backseat became a mobile salon.

As Gina pulled and prodded at my hair, Liam handed her bobby pins.

I eyed him, wondering if I should ask him what was on my mind. Then decided to hell with it. "Liam, who's Princess?"

He jerked, nearly dropping the handful of pins, his eyes locking with mine. "Where'd you hear about her?"

I waved my hand. "That's not important. I need to know more if I'm going to be with Derek, and it seems to be a pretty touchy subject."

Liam glanced to the front of the limo, meeting Greg's eyes in the rearview mirror.

Everyone knows about this mystery woman, except me.

A sigh escaped Liam. "I wish I could help you, but it's Derek's story. And he'll tell you when he's ready."

Disappointment washed over me, but I got it. Liam was Derek's friend first. I'd known it was a long shot when I broached the subject. Gina's jaw tightened as I glanced at her, but I shook my head, telling her to leave it.

We sat at the end of the Elgins' road for a few extra minutes because even Gina couldn't put on runway-worthy makeup in a moving vehicle. Luckily, I never left home without my makeup, so she had decent stuff to work with. The understated look she picked was perfect, polished but flawless.

I sent Derek a quick text letting him know we'd be pulling up in a second. As we headed for the driveway, I grabbed a different bag with handpicked goodies I'd selected for everyone. Gina squealed when I gave her the Gucci clutch, and I hugged her tight, with an extra thank-you for the huge help she'd been.

"Liam, here." I'd found some Oakley sunglasses I thought would look decent on him. "Thanks for letting me kidnap you today."

He grinned, slipping on the shades. "Nice."

Once Greg had parked, I leaned over the divider and handed him his gift, the softest pair of driving gloves I'd ever seen. "Thanks for everything, Greg." And I gave him one of the Hermes scarves, too. "And here's something for your girl, or wife. Or you, if you're into that sort of thing."

He didn't chuckle like I thought he would, instead staring down at the items. Then he shook his head, starting to give them back to me.

But I closed his hand around the objects. "They're only things, Greg. And I picked them out, just for you."

"Thank you." His voice was a little on the rough side.

I patted his shoulder, sitting back down to find Liam staring at me with a thoughtful look on his face. "What?"

"Nothing." He wouldn't meet my gaze.

What's up with the guys in this car? I glanced out of the window and had a mini panic attack when I saw Derek striding down the steps toward the limo. I hadn't planned on him wanting to open the door. *He'll see*

Liam! Frantically, I waved to Liam, who smooshed himself up against the wall nearest the door. Gina practically sat on top of him as I stepped out.

"Hi," I said, smiling up at Derek.

Gina poked her head around the door, effectively blocking his view of the inside of the limo. "Hey, Derek. I'm gonna have Greg run me home before he comes back to pick you up, okay?" With one last emotional smile my way, she said, "Knock 'em dead, girl." And shut the door behind her.

I waved to Greg who tipped his hat, then I turned back to Derek. "Shall we?" He still hadn't said anything, so I started up the steps by myself.

"Wait." He touched my arm, and I paused two steps above him as he took my hand, holding my arm out to take in the full effect of my dress. "I believe Armani made that dress especially for you, Avery. You look stunning." He kissed my hand before tucking it in the crook of his elbow and leading me up the stairs.

'House' was too inadequate a word for the building we approached. Mansion would work. Estate, perhaps. It put my mother's place to shame.

The door opened as we reached the top step, and a butler took my wrap along with my purse before escorting us to a sitting room. We were the last to arrive, but I didn't feel the least bit embarrassed. On the contrary, I held my head high, making an honest to goodness entrance.

My gaze landed on Derek's sister, with her pinched mouth. I smiled, enjoying how she practically seethed with jealousy. "Rhonda, nice to see you again." I nodded to Kevin who sat next to her, watching him try to reconcile his image of me overdone in the gold dress with the perfectly poised image I presented now.

111

"Kevin, is it? I believe we met at Derek's the other day. It's hard to keep track of all his friends."

There was a faint quiver under my hand as Derek stifled his laughter. He steered me toward the two imposing people on the opposite couch. "Mom, Dad, may I present my girlfriend, Miss Avery Milbourne."

I dipped my chin, a polite smile plastered on my face.

"Avery, my father, Malcolm Elgin."

Holding out my hand, I allowed his father to take it, hoping he wouldn't kiss it. *Because ew.*

Luckily, his dad just bowed over it. "A pleasure."

"And my mother, Harriet Elgin."

His mom came in for a fake air kiss, placing her perfectly manicured hands on my shoulders. "You are simply delicious, my dear. Where has Derek been keeping you?"

Thank goodness she didn't require an answer, because how was I supposed to respond to that? Derek guided me to an ornate settee, settling next to me. His arm rested behind my shoulders, fingers playing with a curl that dangled near the nape of my neck.

The butler appeared. "Something to drink, Miss?"

Derek smirked, leaning in to whisper, "Might I suggest the whiskey?"

I nodded.

"We'll each take a whiskey, Alfred." When Derek's dad gave him a surprised look, Derek grinned. "Finally found a woman with taste."

Rhonda sniffed.

Mrs. Elgin politely went through the list of requisite questions about my life, my goals, my parents, my bloodline...oh maybe that last one was in my head.

Then the maid announced dinner was served. *Hallelujah!*

Except when my plate was revealed, it was all I could do not to gag. Escargots, rubbery snails, on a bed of spinach. I didn't care how much garlic or butter you drowned them in, they never got chewed up enough to swallow. And steamed spinach wasn't much better.

I didn't mind spinach in small doses. But spinach as its own thing, especially steamed? It looked like something a cow had already digested once and smelled about as appealing. At least there was a decent-looking chicken and rice mix as well.

So I began cutting my snails into bits, as I did with my food. I carefully kept the chicken and rice away from the snails and spinach. In between bites of the delicious entrée, I cut and rearranged the gross stuff, hoping it would appear I'd eaten some of everything.

The conversation danced from person to person. It started with Mr. Elgin and his shipping business, particularly a deal he'd just closed. Then Mrs. Elgin chimed in, describing how her latest charity ensured all school-aged children had lunch over the weekends or holidays was taking off. Kevin and Rhonda were busy planning their wedding, so the topic stayed there for quite a while.

I waited for Derek's turn, wondering what he would say. To my surprise, it never came. Instead, Mr. Elgin started again, telling some story about lunch at the country club.

Frowning, I leaned over to Derek. "What about you?"

He stared at me in shock. "Me?"

I nodded, keeping my voice to a quiet whisper. "Yeah, when is it your turn?" I glanced around the table once more, before returning my gaze to Derek.

His blue eyes held mine for a long moment. "Math doesn't interest anyone here."

My words were fierce. "Well, it interests me."

Mr. Elgin, who had just finished his boring story, glanced over at us. "Did you say something, Avery?"

A quick look around the table showed all focus was on me. "Oh, I just thought Derek should tell everyone about the fascinating work he's doing at school." I gave him an encouraging nudge, not letting him say no.

He narrowed his eyes at me, then reluctantly turned to his parents. "Actually, I just turned in a major project last week, Dad. I've already got some feedback on it. My professors think I'm onto something, and with a little bit of effort, we could streamline—"

"Mom, did I tell you about the charity idea I had?" Rhonda said, talking right over her brother.

All heads swiveled to her as if Derek weren't even speaking. Except mine. I watched Derek fold into himself, tucking his ideas away into that hidden compartment I'd worked so hard to drag him out of. Ignoring Rhonda's chatter, I racked my brain for some way to distract Derek, bring him back from his retreat. First, I started with the physical, brushing a finger over his knuckles, letting him know I was still focused on him.

He didn't even acknowledge me. No twitch of the lips. No swipe of the thumb.

Hmm, something more drastic. I sat to Derek's right and I was suddenly grateful for that. I shifted in my seat, just so, making my dress ride up my thigh so the slit exposed the top of my lacy, thigh-high stockings.

Then I dropped my napkin, on my right, of course. I scooted my chair out a bit more. After making sure Derek had a view unhindered by the tablecloth, I leaned over to pick up my napkin. I'm not sure how high that slit rose up, but I did hear the gratifying sound of Derek quietly sucking in his breath. When I righted myself, I smirked at him.

The twinkle was back in those blue eyes, but I wasn't done yet.

I leaned over to whisper, "So what was up with your mom's comment earlier?" I slid around some more slimy spinach and snails.

His eyes narrowed. "You'll have to be more specific."

I tried not to snort. "The one about me being delicious. I mean, does she think I look like a dessert or something?"

His mouth tightened ever so slightly, and his eyes crinkled.

So I kept going. "I could see it if I were wearing pink and had ruffles. Then maybe I could be compared to a cupcake. Or if I wore a red bow in my hair, like a cherry on top. But solid black? Which desserts are solid black?"

Derek's lips twitched with barely suppressed laughter, freezing when Mrs. Elgin cleared her throat.

"What is going on down there, Derek? You're being extremely rude to Rhonda."

Under my breath to Derek, I said, "*We're* being rude?" To his mom, I was the picture of innocence. "Oh, Mrs. Elgin, I'm so sorry. I'm afraid that was my fault. I need to use the restroom, and I wasn't sure where the closest is. Could you point me in the right direction?"

Nothing like announcing I need to pee at a fancy dinner party to create an awkward silence.

"Oh, well, Frieda can show you." Mrs. Elgin called for the maid to escort me out of the room.

Once we were out of their line of sight, I said, "I hate to be a bother, but could I trouble you for my purse as well? I'm expecting an important call."

Frieda was quite happy to direct me to my belongings and show me the bathroom. I made quick work of a sketchy plan that paid off when Greg met me at the front door with two signed copies of my mother's book. He gave me a curious glance.

"I'll explain later. I'm just glad you're back, and we still had a few on hand!" I turned to leave, but Greg stopped me.

"While Derek's not around, I wanted to mention that you should talk to Gina soon. I didn't hear all of it, but it sounded like she and Liam really got into it on the way home."

Concerned, I nodded. "Thanks. I'll do that." I waved goodbye, then I sauntered back into the dining room as another maid cleared the plates. *Oh darn, I don't have to finish my snails.*

The conversation paused as I stood behind my chair instead of sitting down. "Oh, I'm sorry. I didn't want to interrupt. It's just, I'm so excited about the gifts I brought you ladies, and I couldn't wait another minute to give them to you." I handed one book to his mom, one to Rhonda. "My mother is the author. And, Mrs. Elgin, I know you've been married for quite some time, but you're not getting any younger, you know. She has a whole chapter in there about how to keep your man interested after things get, well, you know" — I lowered my voice — "stale."

His mom gasped, but I noticed his dad actually seemed intrigued.

"And it's signed by my mother, too! So it'll age well. If nothing else, it'll look great in your collection. A perfect trophy to show off on your shelf." A display of rare books in the sitting room had caught my eye as we came in, so me suggesting my mother's book belonged there was an insult on several levels. But I wasn't finished.

I turned my sickeningly sweet smile on Rhonda then let out a fake-happy sigh. "And I just know you'll be able to get so much use out of it, Rhonda. Between those friends of yours, Kevin's track record and being newly engaged, you have so much to learn. This book can help you grow as a couple, become closer to each other, and spice things up a little." I leaned on Derek's shoulder, trailing my fingers over the back of his neck and grinning at him. "Right, honey?"

Without missing a beat, he grinned back at me. "That's right, Cupcake." He covered my hand with his own, stroking my knuckles and making me shiver. We shared a look, then I sat down.

Glancing around at his family, I said brightly, "So, what's for dessert?"

Mrs. Elgin's lips had almost completely disappeared, she pressed them so hard together: "I'm sorry. We only planned one course tonight."

An obvious dismissal if there ever was one.

Rhonda smirked—eyes cold. "Some of us are watching our weight. The wedding is right around the corner, you know."

I had my hand on Derek's thigh, my nails digging in before he could say the words I knew he wanted to. "What a shame." I stood up gracefully, smiled, meeting each person's eyes in turn. "Well, thank you for a wonderful evening."

Derek didn't leave me hanging. "Mom, Dad. Rhonda, Kevin. Good night." His hand slid to the small of my back, guiding me to the entrance where the butler met us with our things.

As soon as we stepped out of the door, Derek turned to me, a megawatt smile on his face. "You are amazing!"

"What?" I looked at him, playing dumb.

"Marry me?"

I laughed, hoping he was just kidding. "Jumping the gun a bit there, aren't you?"

He shook his head adamantly. "Anyone who can put my mom and my sister in their place like that deserves to be a part of the family. Can you imagine what my holidays would be like if you came to all of them?" He put his hands together. "Please? Pretty please?"

I pushed him away, stuck my nose in the air, and held out my hand. "I never consider proposals after someone tries to feed me snails. Now take me home." His chuckle made me smile.

"Yes, ma'am." He took my hand, helping me down the steps to where Greg waited. As we neared the open door, Derek leaned toward me. His words were heartfelt, warming me to my core. "Thank you."

Chapter Seven

When we climbed in, I chose the rear-facing seat, keeping the divider down. Derek gave me a questioning look, so I said, "I owe Greg an explanation since he's the reason I got the books."

We spent the ride regaling Greg with our awful time. "Oh, and speaking of delicious"—Derek paused to slide an arm around me—"Cupcake, here, didn't get dessert."

I arched my eyebrow at the nickname but ignored it. "Or real food." I put a hand to my stomach, pretending to faint from hunger.

Derek laughed at my antics. "Those snails didn't do it for ya?"

I wrinkled my nose.

A slow smile spread across Derek's face, and he sat on his knees, cupping his hand to whisper to Greg. The chauffeur smiled, too, then made a few quick turns.

The only one left in the dark was me. "Where are we going?"

Derek's fingers played with the slit of my dress, and he smirked. "Well, we can't let that dress go to waste. You deserve to be seen."

My cheeks heated, and I was grateful for the darkness. A few minutes later, we pulled into the parking lot of a quiet but elegant-looking restaurant called Maria's. A frown crossed my face as I watched Greg exit the limo.

"Don't worry," Derek said, mistaking my concern for anxiety. "You'll fit right in."

I was quick to set him straight. "It's not me I'm worried about. I've already tied Greg up for most of the day. What if he's got better things to do on his Saturday night?" Derek's blue eyes drilled into me so long, I squirmed. "What?"

"I have never been out with a girl in my entire life that has shown one ounce of concern for the hired help. Even after realizing he's a friend of mine. Now you *have* to marry me." Thankfully he didn't wait for an answer, disappearing out of the open door.

My heart stuttered at what I hoped was his teasing, and I told myself to calm down. *We're just playing.* Though I may have flashed my lacy stocking while exiting, just for Derek's benefit.

He grinned before turning to our driver. "Greg, I'll leave it up to you. Avery is concerned we may be keeping you from your plans, so I have a few options, any of which work for us. One, we find our own way home. Two, you pick up your hot date and whatever meal you want, provided you're able to be back here within fifteen minutes of my text. Or, three, you hang out here, doing whatever it is you do, and we send you a menu to order from, then you take us home when we're ready."

Greg's surprised gaze flicked to me for a minute before shifting back to Derek. "Option three is more than generous."

I laid a hand on Greg's arm. "Only if you promise to order dessert, too."

His gray eyes twinkled. "For you, Miss Avery, anything."

Derek's hand was warm on my back as he escorted me in, opening doors. The rich, wooden floors gave it a homey feel, but the zigzag molding on the ceiling along with the combination of soft, glowing orbs and sleek white track lighting provided a more modern atmosphere. The dark leather of the booths brought out the dark grain of the floor and the cream chairs around the tables felt chic. I smiled as the hostess led us to a circular booth where Derek slid all the way over so he was next to me.

I raised my eyebrows at him. "Hi."

One corner of his mouth tipped up. "Just wanted to keep an eye on that stocking situation." His gaze darted down to the slit in my dress, safely below my lace line at the moment.

"I see. That's a secret weapon I only use for special occasions." A thrill went through me at his casual flirting.

The waiter chose that moment to appear with our thick menus and cloth wrapped silverware. "I'm Landon, and I'll be your server this evening. Can I start you off with anything to drink?"

Derek's expression changed completely. He was all Elgin now. "Yes, we'll take a bottle of your finest whiskey and two glasses. Please tell the chef that Derek Elgin is here, and I expect to be amazed this time." His tone dripped with superiority.

I blinked at Derek in confusion, at his abrupt shift in demeanor as well as his demanding alcohol. *Drinking on private property is one thing, but in public?* I still wasn't twenty-one. I didn't even have a fake ID. *And what's up with the asshole act?*

The waiter looked uncertain, but, recognizing the air of entitlement, if not the name, hurried to do Derek's bidding. Derek's arm casually rested behind me as the kitchen doors flung open, and an Asian man about our age strode out, anger written in every movement. He looked to be several inches shorter than me.

His white chef's coat was almost pristine, and his dark eyes flashed as he marched up to our table. "You cretin. That chicken was perfect, and you know it!"

The picture of nonchalance, Derek arched an eyebrow. "Bin, this is my girlfriend, Avery. If you try to serve her that subpar chicken you gave me the last time I was here, I'm going to roast you on Instagram and sink this place."

There was a tense moment of silence before both men burst into grins, reaching for each other to clasp forearms.

"It's good to see you."

"How you been, man?"

Unable to keep up with who was speaking, I nodded to the scared waiter who snuck in on the side to deliver our whiskey. Then I poured myself a glass and took a delicious sip.

"Avery, stand up so Bin can get a better look at you."

I gave Derek a stunned look, not too thrilled to be ordered around. "You want me to open my mouth so he can examine my teeth, too?"

Derek chuckled. "Please. I just want to show you off."

A bit mollified, I scooted out to do a few model poses, ending with a twirl that highlighted my Armani gown.

Bin stared, then sat next to me to whisper, "There's another door out the back. Blink twice if you're here against your will."

I threw my head back and laughed, leaning into Derek. "Nope, we're together, a team. But only if I can get some real food. His parents tried to feed me snails and steamed spinach, and they didn't even have the decency to offer dessert."

A knowing look crossed Bin's face, and he glanced at Derek with concern.

Derek waved him off, his gaze settling on me again, tenderness in his eyes. "Remind me to tell you that story after we feed her. What do you want, Cupcake? The sky's the limit."

So I ordered prime rib, mashed potatoes, green beans and cheesecake for dessert.

Once Bin had finished cooking our food, he shut down the kitchen to join us. "My restaurant, my decision." Bin watched fascinated as I carefully cut half my prime rib into bite-sized bits before ever taking a bite. "I've never seen anyone do that before."

Derek grinned. "She does it with just about any main dish, except pizza."

I almost dropped my fork. "Who uses silverware to eat pizza?" My ruse to get the conversation off me failed as Derek nudged Bin and continued.

"She won't eat anything else. She'll eat what she's cut up, or until she's full. Only then will she move on to something else. That's how I knew she wasn't really eating the escargot tonight." His eyes danced with laughter. "She'd take a bite of the chicken and rice then go back to the snails, saw at them a bit, shove them around, take a bite of chicken and rice…"

Of course he saw that. "You're giving away all my secrets." I stared at my plate, annoyed and embarrassed.

"Bin, you should have seen her."

Derek's tone changed so drastically, I had to risk a peek. The amusement faded, a look of intense admiration replacing it. And he launched into the story of me leaving for the bathroom, returning with my mother's books.

I had a feeling the tale would become legend, not that I minded. I'd gladly do it again, if only to keep that light in Derek's eyes. Maybe the next time he sat at their table, and they ignored him, he could think of that memory with a smile. I ate as I listened, savoring every delicious bite. The prime rib practically melted in my mouth, the potatoes were so fluffy they were like air and the green beans had just the right amount of crispness. And the cheesecake was creamy perfection. I made sure to compliment Bin.

Derek had ravioli. His favorite. The whiskey disappeared at an alarming rate. At one point, I had to let Derek out to use the bathroom. He took advantage of my distance by stealing the last bite of my cheesecake.

I protested, "Hey, not cool!"

He just smirked at me. "It was mine anyway." Then he wandered, a bit wobbly, across the room.

I turned to Bin, my frown not only because I was out of dessert. "What did he mean by that?"

Derek nearly walked into another table.

Thank goodness we're the only ones here. Bin shook his head, chuckling. "He's half owner of this place."

I just stared at Derek's friend, needing more of an explanation.

He sighed. "I had typical, demanding parents who expected me to be a doctor or lawyer. So I started college with a doctorate in mathematics in mind, right alongside Derek." A wistful smile came over Bin's face. "He is absolutely brilliant. The way his mind works is really something else. That project he's been working on? Let me be the first to tell you, it's going to change the shipping business as we know it."

Wait, is that the same one he'd tried to tell his dad about today? That Rhonda interrupted?

"Anyway, we quickly discovered I wasn't cut out for math. I wouldn't have made it through the first semester if not for him. But I did have a knack for food and management. He saw my potential, talked me into using the inheritance I got from my grandfather as a down payment on this restaurant with him as a partner, and here we are." He smiled as he looked around the place. "Business is good. We have reservations three months out for peak times on Friday and Saturday nights. And all because your boyfriend believed in me."

I took my time watching Derek as he reappeared. *The white knight is shining through again.*

"He doesn't usually drink like this either."

My attention shifted back to Bin, who watched Derek with a sad smile.

"I can count on one hand the number of times he's drunk more than he should have." Bin's eyes brimmed with sadness. "And they were all after run-ins with his parents."

I thought of the hurt on Derek's face as Rhonda talked over him, the way he'd shut down. I'd hoped my distraction and retaliation were enough, but evidently they hadn't been.

"Oh no." Bin cringed, putting a hand to his forehead. "I know that look."

"What?" I turned to see Derek snapping his fingers to the faint music overhead.

Bin groaned. "He's going to ask me to put on country. He wants to line dance. It's his go-to when he gets drunk enough."

This I have to see. "Is he any good?"

Bin just smiled as Derek yelled for him to change the station. He disappeared with an "I told you so." When the chef reappeared, the music was cranked up, twang filling the air. Then Derek started to move.

Is there anything he's not good at?

All he needed was the outfit, looking a bit out of place in his three-piece suit. But his movements? He was completely at home.

The song switched to one of country legend Piper Kensington's famous hits, called *Heartbreak Canyon*. Derek's head popped up, and he shot us a grin, sliding into the moves like they were second nature. My eyes were glued to his fluid body as he vined across the floor, scuffing his shoe before executing a perfectly timed kick. He looped his thumbs through his belt loops as he did several more complicated box steps.

Bewildered that Derek, who could hardly walk to the bathroom, was able to pull off this dance without a single misstep, I turned to Bin. "Where'd he learn to dance like that?"

Bin sobered. He kept his face away from Derek when he answered. "The Princess." His words were low, quiet. "He was her favorite dance partner. She tried out all the new moves on him." He glanced at

Derek, then faced me once more. "She crushed him when she left. I don't know if he'll ever recover. Usually he switches the station when this song comes on."

Stupid Princess. Anger at this phantom hit me right in the gut, and I went to ask more about her.

But Bin's eyes widened, head swiveling once more in Derek's direction. "Shit." He fumbled in his pocket for his phone.

I frowned. "Are you recording him?"

He shook his head. "Just letting Liam know."

"Why?"

Bin set his phone on the table, giving me a sidelong look. "You haven't seen him drunk before, have you?" At the shake of my head, he said, "Liam needs a heads-up because someone will have to put him to bed tonight, and I doubt you'll be able to do it alone."

I mulled over Bin's words as I watched Derek and listened to the song.

"You found me at the bottom,
Of Heartbreak Canyon where I lay.
You climbed down to rescue me,
From the dark into the light of day.
I learned my lesson this time,
Never again will I run away.
Here is where I want to be,
Safe in your arms I'll stay."

What would it be like to have that kind of love? That kind of security? I stared at Derek, a wave of intense longing welling up inside me. Not only wanting love but wanting to believe it was possible. My throat suddenly felt thick, almost like I was going to cry. I shook my head, pushing down the ridiculous emotions, and sipped some water. I knew better.

Bin was right. He and Greg had to get Derek to the limo. Then Liam met us at the sidewalk to drag Derek inside, him and Greg under each arm. I went ahead to open doors and push buttons.

There was a little tiff in the elevator when Derek insisted he could stand on his own. He put up such a fuss that Liam rolled his eyes and let go. Greg sighed, ducking out from his other arm. Derek looked smug for half a second before crashing against the wall.

"He's like an overtired four-year-old when he's drunk," Liam explained to me.

I arched an eyebrow. "How many four-year-olds do you know?"

"One sister has three kids, the other has two. I'm the favorite uncle."

Not what I expected.

Meanwhile, Greg started arguing with Derek, trying to reason with him. On my tours with my mother, because of my age, I'd been saddled with kids on set, time after time. People had just assumed I was childcare. And I knew reason didn't work on a tired kid.

Distraction, that's the best tactic. "Derek." I spoke in my sultriest voice, leaning against the open door of the elevator.

All three heads snapped up to stare at me.

"Cupcake." Those blue eyes zeroed in on me.

"That's right, Derek. Let's go hang out in our apartment. I need to get out of this dress. Where's the key?" My words were innocent enough, but my tone suggested otherwise.

"Pocket?"

I slid my hand in, coming out with the key ring and jangling it a few times. "We'll get there faster if you let

Liam and Greg help you. It can be like a three-legged race. I bet you're good at that."

Derek frowned a little, looking sideways at the guys. So I stepped out of the elevator, stopping to adjust my shoe and showing off that handy slit with the lacy stocking top he seemed to adore.

Next thing I knew, his arms were looped over the other guys' shoulders, and they all followed me down the hallway.

"What's the number?" I whispered.

Liam gave me a disbelieving look but rattled it off. I still hadn't memorized it yet. In the apartment, I left the guys to get Derek settled, dying to take off my shoes, dress and especially my stockings. Once in comfy PJs, with my hair in a low pony instead of piled with bobby pins, I felt a million times better. Then I heard some commotion from down the hall.

Knocking on the closed door to Derek's room, I went in without waiting for an invitation. This wasn't a time to stand on ceremony, and his friends probably thought I'd seen it all anyway. Liam was practically sitting on Derek, while Greg tried to yank one of his shoes off.

I almost laughed at the ridiculous scene. "What is going on here?"

"Cupcake!" Derek peeked his head around Liam's muscular frame. "They're being mean."

Liam folded his arms, glaring at his drunk friend. "No, you're being a dick."

I couldn't help a giggle then, because he really did sound like a kid. *Not that Liam sounded very mature either.* "Okay, both of you, off."

Derek was in a sorry, disheveled state as the guys stood up. His jacket lay on the floor. Half his shirt was undone. One shoe lay near the door of the bathroom.

His blue eyes landed on me, blinking as he tried to focus. "You're wearing pajamas. I want my pajamamas too." His words were slurred, then his face lit up. "Are you staying in here tonight?"

"Where are your PJs?" With his mumbled directions, I found the right drawer. Both his friends watched me, identical expressions of disbelief on their faces. "Why don't you two wait in the living room? I'll call if I need you."

Giving me an 'it's your funeral' shrug, Liam turned on his heel and disappeared with Greg right behind him.

"All right, Derek. Jammies first, then bed. You do good with this, and I'll sleep here tonight, okay?"

He nodded.

"Lie on your back."

Flopping over, he spread out his arms and stared at the ceiling. "Your dress tonight was so pretty. Wait! I didn't help you take it off. I like helping you take off your dresses."

I started unbuttoning his shirt, pushing down one sleeve then rolling him so I could get the other. "Tonight I get to help you. It's only fair we take turns, right?" He looked like he might pout, so I said, "Don't worry. I'm sure I'll need your help next time." I pulled his undershirt up over his head, my fingers grazing the muscular ridges of his abdomen as I went. *Steady, girl.* "Shirt or no shirt?"

His head flopped side to side in an adamant no.

Oh darn, more time to ogle. Now to tackle the pants. "Okay, shoe off."

I slipped it off, then his socks. It felt weird undoing his pants, so I just steeled myself and did it. It took some effort to slide them down his hips, but he helped me some, and we managed. Then he was in his boxers, staring up at me with all the trust and innocence of a puppy. *Damn, he's hot.*

"Shorts on!" I said with a forced cheerfulness, getting both his legs in the shorts.

He raised his hips, and I let the elastic snap into place as he sat up. "Avery." He reached for me, missed and tried again, this time succeeding in catching my arm. He pulled me to him, resting his face against my stomach and sighed happily. "I'm glad you picked me."

"All right, Derek." I patted his shoulder, trying to break the embrace. "Why don't you lie down? I have to tell Liam and Greg goodbye."

"But then I have to let you go." He sounded so sad.

There was no way I could deal with emotional Derek. Not right now. "Just for a minute. I'll be right back."

With a sigh, he pushed away, scooting up the mattress.

I hurried out to the guys.

"Our turn, now?" Liam glanced at his watch. "You lasted longer than I thought."

What? I shook my head. "No, he's all set. I just wanted to thank you both for your help." I wrapped Liam in a hug before he could stop me. "Not only did you come for coffee earlier, you let me kidnap you this afternoon. And then you came when we needed you just now. Derek's so lucky to have a friend like you." I kissed his cheek as he froze.

After letting him go, I turned to Greg with a big smile. I gave him a hug as well, which he returned with a tight squeeze. "And you, too. Thank you for running me everywhere today. For bringing me those books.

For staying with us at dinner. And helping get Derek up here. You're the best."

Greg shook his head. "Nah, I think that title goes completely to you, Avery. Good night."

Liam paused in the doorway. "You're not half bad, for a Lions fan."

My middle finger shot up of its own accord, but I had a smile on my face. *Is it my imagination, or does his smirk have a hint of fondness?* He shook his head, pulling the door shut behind him.

I locked the door, turned out the lights, then crawled into bed beside Derek who was already snoring softly. After making sure he was covered up, I lay on my back to think over the day.

Derek stirred, rolling over and putting his head on my shoulder with a warm humming sound. "Night, Cupcake," he mumbled.

"Good night, Derek." I wrapped an arm around him, and we drifted off to sleep.

When I woke up in the late morning light, we'd shifted positions. Derek was behind me, one of his biceps under my cheek as I snuggled in the cocoon of his arms, feeling warm, safe and content. It was all I could do not to bolt upright. Instead, I forced myself to ease out of his embrace, slowly replacing the walls around my heart one brick at a time.

This isn't real, after all.

And I'll be sleeping in my own bed tonight.

The too-cozy morning had me feeling antsy, so I shot Gina a text, asking what happened with Liam the night before. She didn't answer. I decided to go on a grocery run, intending to cook breakfast. Of course, when I got back, I ran into the dilemma of still being without a key or remembering the damn apartment number. I doubted Derek was in any shape to be up yet, if his phone was even on. So I called Liam and bribed him with free breakfast if he met me in the lobby to help carry the groceries up.

He grumbled a bit but his mood lightened once I got some coffee in him. I tried asking him what had happened with Gina, but he just grunted from his spot at the island. I made egg bites, a scrambled egg mixture I poured into a mini muffin tin and baked. They came out looking like little muffins but were made completely out of eggs. I added bacon, spinach, mushrooms and Italian cheese to these, then whipped up some cinnamon rolls. *Quick, easy, and delicious.*

My phone dinged. Gina finally responded, but she told me not to worry about it. I frowned, though I didn't have time to wonder much about it because the timer went off. Then Derek emerged. His bed head was adorably messy, his black T-shirt clung in all the right spots and gray sweatpants hung low on his hips.

I set the tray of egg bites down, peeking at his stomach while he stretched and nearly burning myself in the process. "Just in time to eat."

He grinned. "Great. I'm starving."

If I'd drunk that much, my stomach would be turning at the very smell of food. *Some people have all the luck.* I set out plates and silverware, bringing the food to the table, along with the pot of coffee and a mug for Derek.

I plunked down a glass of water in front of him too. "Hydrate, please."

"Yes, mother." He half-rolled his eyes at Liam.

"She's a fricken miracle worker, that one. *She* put you to bed last night. Not a scratch on her!" Liam glared at Derek, making him pause while dishing up food. "You should be thanking her."

"Oh." Derek stayed quiet as he finished putting his egg bites on his plate. "I'm sorry, Avery. I didn't realize it was one of those nights. Thank you." He frowned. "Being around my family...sometimes I get carried away afterwards." He sighed, raking a hand through his crazy hair.

I slid a cinnamon roll onto my plate and waved him off. "You've helped me. I help you. It's this guy and Greg you should be thanking." I jerked my chin at Liam. "You'd be sleeping on a bench at the restaurant if I'd had to get you home on my own."

His voice was quiet, almost gruff. "Thanks, Liam."

Liam was almost too busy inhaling egg bites to answer. "Don't mention it. You've done it for me plenty of times, and I get breakfast out of the deal."

Derek's blue eyes found mine as I sat down. He lifted his fork, almost in a salute. "And thanks for breakfast."

I nodded and happiness coursed through me as everyone enjoyed my food. We ate in the quiet for a few minutes.

Liam surprised me by breaking the silence. "So, what'd you guys do last night? Before I had to haul your drunk ass to bed, that is."

I almost gave everything away by rolling my eyes, but I caught myself just in time. Derek didn't know Liam had been with me in the limo, and we needed to keep it that way. For the sake of the surprise party. I concentrated on eating while Derek filled him in, almost tired of hearing the story already. It was amazing how fast the tale got old.

So I thought about ravioli. Now that I'd found out it was Derek's favorite, we had to have it at the party. And I knew the one person in the world who made the best—Patty. We'd all finished eating, the guys still sipping their coffee, Derek mid-story. I started cleaning up, racking my brain for a way to steal Patty that didn't involve seeing my mother.

The kitchen sparkled, the story ended and Liam looked at me with an expression I'd never seen before. An odd mix of admiration and incredulity. Maybe I was finally passing muster.

Time to change the subject. "All right, so what's Sunday normally look like around here?"

"Football," they chimed.

I grinned. "Do more people usually show up?"

Derek nodded, tentatively.

My grin widened. "Good, 'cause I think I bought enough food to feed an army."

Liam turned to Derek with a pointed glare. "I can vouch for that. I had to lug it all up here because someone was still sleeping. And hasn't given his girlfriend her own key yet." He drained his cup, setting it none too gently down on the table. "All right, you two. I got things to do before kickoff. I'm out."

We said bye, then Derek picked up both his cup and Liam's. He relocated to the island, sliding the empty cup to me and nursing his coffee. "Thanks again for breakfast. It was great. I've never had those before. What do you call them?"

"Egg bites." The silence between us felt awkward, and I didn't know what to do about it. So I started pulling out ingredients for the different foods I wanted to make. "What time do people usually show up?"

"Around two or three." He frowned as I put more food on the counter. "What all are you planning on making?"

"Oh, I've got stuff for spinach artichoke dip, veggie pizza, meatballs and mini pigs in a blanket." I wrinkled my nose. "I might have gone a bit overboard. I like to cook when I'm stressed. Do you have a crockpot?"

He helped me find it. "What are you stressed about?"

It was the perfect opening. "Actually, I need to talk to you about that. I kind of need a favor." Just saying the words made me a nervous, rigid wreck.

Leaning on the counter, he looked at me, every inch relaxed. "What's up?"

My hands twisted together as I bit my lip, wondering how to phrase my request. "This is going to sound awful. I don't even know how to ask it without sounding like I'm using you and your status, because hell, that's exactly what I'm doing."

Something like longing flashed across his face, gone before I could process it. Then his usual disarming grin slid into place. "But that's what this whole relationship is about, right?"

I stilled. *That's what it's supposed to be. That's what I agreed to, and that's all it can ever be.* I stifled my sigh, telling him my situation. "Unfortunately, I need to see my mother tomorrow. I think the best way to get what I want from her is to let her 'kidnap' me for dinner. But I'd like you to be there when I get picked up." I glanced at him. "You're the carrot in this analogy."

One of his dark eyebrows lifted a fraction of an inch. "Technically, it's not an analogy. At least not yet."

Whatever. I rolled my eyes at the grammar police. "Anyways, you, Mr. Carrot, should be waiting with me when whatever goons come to pick me up. Then I arrive alone and wait for the goons to impart the gossip that I was with, gasp, Derek Elgin and didn't bring him along. I tell my mother, the rabbit, what I want. Negotiate how many dinners I have to attend, then bring you in. My trump card."

He frowned. "I thought I was the carrot."

I started to explain again, but I caught the teasing gleam in his eye. I clamped my mouth shut, smacking his hard shoulder instead. "Jerk." His laugh lit up his whole face, and I couldn't look away.

"When did you say this was?"

"Um." I needed a minute to gather my thoughts, which had all disappeared. "Tomorrow, if that works for you."

A thoughtful pause was followed by a nod. "Yeah, shouldn't be a problem. What time will the hijacking take place?"

"Kidnapping." I gave him a stern look. "Get it right. Meet me at the west end of campus near Roosevelt Hall, by the fountain? About five-thirty p.m.?"

"It's a date."

Well, that wasn't as difficult as I anticipated. Somewhat relieved, I smiled to myself as I started putting together the pizza crust. I was just thinking about bringing up rent when Derek spoke again.

"My turn."

Not only were his words short, but his tone was completely different. In the few seconds since I'd last looked at him, his whole body had tensed. *This is serious.*

"I know we didn't set a time limit for this thing. It's only the end of October, and this is really asking a lot, so if it's too far out there or it's too much, I understand.

Feel free to say no. It's just, I don't want to go alone, and my parents are pressuring me to tell them if I'm bringing anyone..."

He was rambling. The nerves were one thing, but to see Derek not know exactly what to say was surprising. My heart went out to him. Before I could think better of it, I moved around the counter. I placed my hands on his stubbly cheeks, pressing my lips to his to stop the flow of words. "Hey, it's just me. Tell me what this big event is, and I'll look at my calendar. If I'm free, I'll be there, okay?" I rubbed a thumb over his chiseled cheek, and he leaned into my hand.

He nodded, collecting himself as I returned to the other side of the island. "There's a big event the weekend after Thanksgiving I have to attend. It's an annual party my parents throw, mostly for their business contacts, and I'd really like you to come with me. It's fancy, a black tie, gala, sort of thing."

I felt my face light up. "A gala? That sounds amazing! What's it for?"

He shrugged. "Networking, mostly. They raise money for one of my mom's charities, recognize some top employees. It's one of those familial obligations we all have to go to."

"What's the date?" I dug my phone out of my pocket as he told me the specifics. Everything looked clear.

"I'd be happy to pay for your dress and all the stuff that goes with it, make sure you can play the part."

I pretended to think about it, tapping my chin for good measure. "So you get to be my fairy godmother and prince charming, all wrapped up in one? Plus I get to go to the ball?" *A pretend fairy tale, emphasis on the pretend.* I glanced at him. "Is there food?"

He looked sidelong at me, trying to decide whether I was teasing or not. "Yes, and it'll be delicious, but probably in bite-sized portions."

"I can live with that." Finally, I grinned. "Yes, I'll go." An image popped into my head of him going to the ball with that infernal Princess, and I shoved it aside. "Even if we're not still together, and you want me to attend, I'll come. Deal?" I stuck out my hand.

A frown passed over his face, but he blinked it away then shook my hand. "Deal."

Instead of releasing my grip, I held on, not letting him pull away. My next words were quiet, but I knew he needed to hear them. "I know you can hold down the fort by yourself, but that doesn't mean you have to." I reached over to cover my hand with his, digging my hole deeper and deeper.

His blue eyes met mine, latching on to me in a way that felt like he was taking a piece of my soul with him. When he broke into his megawatt smile, I felt light once more. And with the hard stuff out of the way, both of us were free to be ourselves again.

Chapter Eight

Nervous butterflies flitted in my stomach when the first guest arrived. I'd only met Derek's friends once, and here I was cooking for them. I hoped they liked it, hoped they liked me. Liam came in with beer, and the rest of their friends trickled in after him. Kevin was absent, which I didn't mind in the least.

The food was ready, which had all the guys exclaiming, but Derek surprised me once again. As they all rushed in, he stuck two fingers in his mouth to let out an ear-splitting whistle. Wincing, everyone turned to look at him.

He slid an arm around my waist. "Avery worked really hard on this all day. I think it's only fair she goes first."

My cheeks were hot as I took the paper plate he offered me.

"And, as her boyfriend, I supervised, so of course I should go second." He winked at me, the guys turning the razzing on him.

I went through the line, piling up my plate, then automatically made my way to the chair.

Derek followed, nudging me over so he could sit next to me. After trying a bite of everything, he glanced at me. "This is all amazing. You should open a catering business, maybe that's your calling. I'd hire you."

His words were nonchalant, and he went right back to watching the game, but they struck a chord with me. *I'll have to think about that.*

Halftime neared, and I had a brilliant idea. After excusing myself to the bathroom, I texted Liam. When I came back, I nestled in next to Derek until there was a break in the game. "Would you mind running to the store? I completely forgot dessert and I need chocolate." I gave him my sweetest smile. "While you're out, maybe you could get a bottle of good whiskey?"

Liam piped in. "And cheese puffs!"

Derek grumbled, but after everything we'd done for him the night before he couldn't very well say no. His friends were here, so of course he stopped to kiss me goodbye. My toes curled in anticipation as he leaned down to brush his lips lightly over mine.

"Thanks for doing this." I stared up at him, trying to remember why I was sending him away. *This is my best opportunity for cuddles and kisses. What am I doing?* I repeated the plan to myself.

He grinned as if sensing my train of thought. "No problem, Cupcake. Be back soon."

As soon as he was gone, I muted the TV. "Okay, guys, here's the deal." I filled them in on the party for Derek. "You all have to come, but it's a secret. And I need ideas on food. The theme is twenty-one, so we want that many of his favorite things to eat. I was thinking of goody bags, too, with silly stuff he likes. Gum, toys, maybe even inside joke type things?"

There was a full minute of blank stares after I finished, then they all started talking at once. I took out my phone, making an email to myself with their suggestions. Liam and I heard the door at the same time.

I hurried to switch gears, speaking loudly while making a quiet-down gesture to everyone. "It's just a cream cheese base, but the real secret is the garlic. Oh hi, Derek."

Liam jumped up to help, taking a bag from him. "Thank goodness you're back. One of our dipshit friends asked a simple question about her veggie pizza, and she wouldn't shut up about it. Make it stop."

Oh, he's good. I stuck my tongue out at him. "Just 'cause you're not interested in delicious food."

He spotted the cheese puffs, snagging the bag and waving it in my face. "I've got all I need right here."

It was all I could do not to crack up as he stalked back to the couch, very deliberately unmuting the TV before he sat down.

"Um, sorry about that?" Derek looked at me with raised eyebrows.

I waved him off before following him to the island where he set down the bags. "Nah, it's fine. I did get a little carried away. Now, tell me you have good news."

He grinned, pulling out a beautiful amber bottle of whiskey and a small round container. "This is a flourless torte from a bakery around the corner. It's amazing, I swear, but you only need a little piece. It's really rich." He kept his voice low so only I could hear it, his body blocking the dessert from the other guys' view. "And don't let them know. I got this for you."

It didn't take long to find a fork. I took a bite, almost having an orgasm right there by the island. "Holy shit," I whispered. "Yep, I'll hide this, just as soon as I have another taste."

"Did you get some chocolate?" one of the guys called from the living room.

Derek's wink made my stomach flip as he produced a bag of mini chocolate bars, ripped it open and dumped them in a bowl. "Here ya go."

Another forkful or two of heaven disappeared before Derek came back. Since he'd done the running, I felt generous and offered him a bite, which he took with a grin, licking his lips afterward. My eyes lingered on his mouth, wanting to taste the remnants of chocolate on his lips. He took a step toward me. My breath caught in my throat, the fork clattering to the counter as he leaned down to grant my unspoken wish.

Several of the guys whistled behind us, and calls of "Go Derek!" made me push away, ducking my head.

"Ignore them." Derek grinned, blue eyes lingering on my lips. "I can't say which I like better, the torte or the taste of it on your tongue." He reached past me, this time clicking the lid in place over the dessert and heading for the fridge, leaving me to sag against the counter.

I'm in so much trouble.

The chair seemed too small after that. And I couldn't take the snuggling, not with my heart nearly beating out of my chest every time he casually brushed his leg against mine or slung his arm behind my head. I grabbed a blanket from my room, wrapping it around myself like a shield. When I returned, I sat on the floor, leaning against one edge of the chair, near his legs.

My plan was foolproof. No snuggles, no pressing into his side, no temptation to rest my head on his shoulder. I sipped on my whiskey and got caught up in the game. Until he started playing with my hair. With one ankle tucked under his opposite knee, he shifted so he was right behind me, then slid my hair tie down, undoing my ponytail.

"So much hair." His voice was filled with awe as his fingers wove through the strands, starting near my face and trailing all the way across my scalp, down to my shoulders.

It was hypnotic. As if he'd cast a spell over me, pulling me into a fantasy world where every movement between us was real and meant something. But I knew better, or so I told myself.

Over and over again.

When only the two of us remained and the apartment sparkled, it was time for bed, but we lingered in the kitchen. I finished my last swallow of whiskey, rinsed the glass then put it in the dishwasher. When I turned, Derek's blue eyes studied me.

"You can stay with me again tonight." His words were soft, his tone vulnerable. "If you want."

But I couldn't say yes because my walls were fragile enough already. I kept the island between us. "Not tonight, Derek." I barely stopped from wincing as hurt flashed across his face. "There's no reason to pretend right now."

His face fell, then went blank. He nodded. "Right. Good night."

When I shut the door to my room, I pushed aside the pang of guilt. If I kept my heart guarded now, I'd never end up like my dad. And when this whole Princess thing came to a head, it wouldn't matter that he was in love with someone else. I was doing the right thing for myself in the long run.

So why the hell does it hurt so much?

* * * *

I was happy to get back into my routine again. Classes were great. Well, other than Classic Literature. *Why do I need to read about Chaucer and Shakespeare? Whatever business I run will have nothing to do with old English.* It was my last class of the day, and all I could do was dread the seconds until I'd face my mother again.

I'd sent Mother another email this morning with links to a nearby specialized facility, somewhere Daddy could socialize if he chose to. I'd read about these facilities tailored to make a person comfortable enough that they were able to regain part of their memory. Some patients could function almost normally, most of the time. I wanted that for my dad.

It wasn't like Mother couldn't afford it. Hell, Daddy had worked most of his life so a decent chunk of that money was his to begin with. She was just afraid it would leak to the press, then her whole image would go down the drain. It surprised me that one of her boyfriends hadn't ratted her out yet. Anger stabbed at me as I glanced at my empty inbox, though I wasn't really expecting a reply.

Someone sat down on the bench beside me, and I turned to tell them the seat was taken, but I realized it was Derek. I was more stressed than I thought. Usually, I sensed Derek before I saw him.

"You okay? You look tense." A little crease appeared between his eyebrows, and his mouth dipped down in the corners.

He's worried about me. "Just thinking about Mother." I shook my head, trying to clear the negative emotions. "Getting it out of the way now because I have to stay in her good graces tonight." I made a mental note to talk with Derek about rent afterward. It was going to happen, dammit, but I was too worked up at the moment.

His arm circled my shoulders, offering comfort. "What exactly is this favor you need from her?"

"Oh, um. It's a surprise." *Great, he'll never suspect anything at this rate.*

His eyebrows shot up. "That's all I get?"

"Yep." I patted his cheek. "Now be a good carrot and dangle nicely for the rabbit." I watched Jack pull up in a sleek black Trans Am. "Hey, Jack." I greeted him with a tight smile.

"Avery." My name came out laced with a mix of surprise and wariness at my almost friendly demeanor.

"I'm starving, ready to go?" I popped up from the bench, slung my bag over my shoulder and gave Derek a proper goodbye kiss. "See you at home, Derek." I blew him another kiss over my shoulder.

"Bye, Cupcake."

Jack's eyes were wide as I walked up to the car.

After climbing into the backseat, I greeted the other goon with a short nod. I didn't even warrant Boy Toy being sent this time. *Interesting.*

"Was that Derek Elgin you were with?" Jack asked, staring hard at Derek before we pulled away.

I nodded, smiling to myself. *Rabbit, meet carrot.* "Where are we eating?"

Turned out Mother wanted a 'quiet' dinner at home. Which meant thirty other people, a live salsa band, and authentic Mexican food. I walked in the door of the villa, handing my backpack to a maid I didn't recognize. Jack and the goon flanked me, leading me straight to Mother.

"Avery, darling!" She was overdone as usual. Her bright red hair towered above her in a high bouffant, her cleavage, which I could see way too much of, practically touched her chin, and her dress had so many sequins she could have been hung from the ceiling in lieu of a disco ball.

"Mother." I forced a smile, patting her back when she hugged me exuberantly.

Her smile dimmed, and she raised her over-plucked eyebrows. "What do you need?" She'd always been good at cutting through other people's bullshit.

I'd learned it was best to spit it out. "Patty. November seventeenth, for the whole night. It's a Friday."

A perfectly manicured hand dropped to her chest as if I'd stabbed her. "My cook? You want to take away my cook? On Friday night of all nights?"

"I'll come for two dinners, on the nights of your choosing. Plus, I'll throw in Christmas." It was a lowball, for sure, and she knew it.

"Hmph."

The muttering under her breath and the evil eye she gave me would have made me shake once, but not anymore.

She waited for me to counter, to back down, or cower. When I didn't, she arched an eyebrow, throwing out an offer of her own. "Five dinners, plus two weekend events, all of my choosing. Christmas and Thanksgiving."

I snorted. "Seven dinners?" I shook my head. "Three dinners, two lunches and Christmas."

The glare was back.

It was time for Mr. Carrot. "And I'll introduce you to my boyfriend."

Jack leaned over to whisper in her ear.

Mother's jaw dropped, her head whipping toward him. Then she turned back to me. "You're dating one of the Elgins? *The* Elgins?"

The nod I gave was one of practiced confidence. "I could text him right now."

Her gaze narrowed. "I'll take three dinners and Christmas if he comes with you, provided he also makes an appearance tonight."

"Done." I got out my phone, then I eyed Mother once more. "But I want a written statement showing Patty is mine from noon to midnight that Friday." When she started to protest, I moved to put my phone away.

"All right, all right. Jack, go find Earl. That lousy lawyer should do something to earn his keep."

I texted Derek the address along with a carrot emoji. He sent back a thumbs-up and a rabbit. "He'll be here shortly."

"Okay, come find me as soon as he gets here." She paused, raking her eyes down my simple outfit, and I braced myself as best I could. "Avery, have you been trying at all? Darling, you're dating an Elgin now. They have standards." She clucked her tongue once, then she was off.

My breath left me in a whoosh as I tried to let the insult slide off me. I didn't care what she thought. I knew I looked good in my fitted black pants and pink top, but a part of me always wished for Mother's approval. I wondered if I'd ever grow out of it.

Surrounded by people I didn't know or care about, I made my way through the crowd to see my dad, pushing the harsh words aside along with the lingering pain they'd caused. Mother wouldn't mind me disappearing as long as I was there to introduce Derek when he arrived. I snuck away from the crowd, winding down the hallway to Daddy's room.

Kyle greeted my tap on the door. "Miss Avery, so good to see you."

I smiled back at him. "How is he?"

"Sleeping, but come on in. I'll give you two some time. I'm about out of coffee anyways." Kyle ducked into the hallway, his footsteps echoing off the cold marble.

I crossed the room to stand beside my dad's bed, not unhappy he was asleep. It gave me time to actually look at him without making him feel uncomfortable. I always had a hard time reconciling the man I'd grown up with, my hero, to the frail, wrinkled man laying here.

I slipped my hand into his, studying it. These hands had taught me how to change my oil. They'd shown me how to throw a football, dribble a basketball, punch something without breaking my thumb. They'd wiped away tears and put on Band-Aids. They'd tucked me in at night, held me when I'd had nightmares.

Him being asleep gave me the opportunity to catch him up on my life too, without confusing him. "I'm sort of dating someone, Daddy. His name is Derek, and he's amazing. He's absolutely who I would choose for myself if I could. We have some complications though."

I thought of Princess and gritted my teeth. "I'll let you know how it turns out." I chatted for a few more minutes, filling him in with school, work, and Gina. Before I left, I leaned down to kiss his cheek.

Kyle returned with his cup of coffee, so I made my way to the kitchen next and found Patty.

"Avery!" She gave me a broad smile, wrapping me in a warm hug.

My smile was just as big. "Patty, I have news for you. I managed to steal you away from Mother next month for a Friday night. I'm surprising my boyfriend —"

"You have a boyfriend? Where is he?" She stalked past me, ready to storm into Mother's party just to meet Derek.

I managed to grab her apron strings and reel her back in. "He's not here yet. I promise I'll bring him in when he is, okay?"

"Darn right you will."

"I missed his birthday because I had food poisoning." I winced, anticipating her reaction.

Patty crossed her arms. "You've been letting Gina pick the restaurants again, haven't you?"

Chastised, I nodded. "Yes, ma'am."

"What have I told you about that?"

I resisted the urge to roll my eyes. "I know. I swear I've learned my lesson. Anyways, Derek's favorite food is ravioli. And since you make the world's best ravioli, I thought maybe you could cook that for the party. Pretty please?"

Her eyebrows shot up. "Child, you know how much work that is?"

Chagrin washed over me, and I hung my head to look at the floor. "Yes, ma'am."

There was a brief silence. "If it were anyone else..."

I beamed and threw my arms around her. "Thank you, Patty!"

She patted my back. "Just ravioli?"

"It's supposed to be a twenty-one-themed party, and I have a list of his top favorite foods. Some of them are junk and store bought, but a few others..." I gave her my most innocent smile.

Those dark eyes narrowed as she tried to glare at me and failed. She swatted at me with her wooden spoon. "Go on with ya. And don't come back in here without that man, you hear?"

"Yes, ma'am." I grinned, happy to have that out of the way. My phone vibrated in my pocket, and I raced to the door before I even looked at the text I knew was from Derek. I met him coming up the sidewalk.

He didn't disappoint. He'd changed clothes since I'd seen him less than an hour ago. His black hair was perfectly waved, the bright blue tie showing off his eyes with the darker blue shirt as the perfect background. The black blazer's one button emphasized his lean midriff as he strode up the steps.

"Hey." I grinned at him.

He lifted his arms and cocked his head, waiting for my approval. "Am I an appealing enough carrot?"

I pursed my lips. "I guess you'll do." I peered behind him. "I don't see any other carrots lining up for the part."

His strong hands grabbed my waist, tickling my ribs.

A squeal escaped my lips. "All right, you look great!"

"That's better." He let me go, flashing me the megawatt smile that made my knees weak.

I was still breathless as I watched him straighten his jacket, his expression growing more distant and poised with each second. He glanced at me, almost a completely different person.

"Hang on." I reached for him. His collar was somehow askew, completely ruining the effect. "There. Much better."

He held out his arm. "May I escort you to the party?"

It wasn't his arm that made me grimace. "Ready or not, here we come." Finding my mother wasn't difficult. I just followed the throng of people and, voilà, there she was. "Mother, this is Derek Elgin. Derek, this is my mother, Mabel Milbourne."

Derek smiled at her. A dazzling smile.

I was secretly pleased to see it wasn't his usual megawatt smile, but how disconcerting to see my mother dazed over my fake boyfriend. *Is that a hint of jealousy I'm feeling? Ew.*

"It's a pleasure to meet you, Mrs. Milbourne."

She tittered as he grabbed her hand. "Oh, the pleasure is all mine. And please, call me Mabel. Mrs. Milbourne makes me feel old."

His grin had a conspiratorial edge to it, then Derek winked. "Well, we can't have that now, can we, Mabel?"

It was like watching a play. Derek performed well, perfect in his role as socialite. He laughed at all the tired jokes, kissed just the right amount of ass, and did it all with his dazzling smile that made the old ladies fan themselves as soon as he took his eyes off them. It made me sick.

But that wasn't the worst part. Not one person, not one single person in that entire room, acknowledged Derek for his own merit. Whenever he was introduced, the conversation jumped to his father's shipping company or his mother's charity work. Sometimes it would go to his twin, either the fact that he had a twin or that his twin was marrying one of the Harrises of the automobile business. Derek served as the bridge. A stepping stone. It didn't matter that he studied mathematics at SMU. Or was graduating soon. His plans for the future were of no consequence to anyone here, and by the time we'd made our way around the room, I was ready to go off on the next person who ignored my boyfriend.

"Mabel, would you excuse us? I think my girlfriend could use a drink. Isn't that one of the rules in your delightful book? Never let your significant other get too thirsty?" He gave her another wink.

She laughed. "No, but it should be. I'll have to make a note."

He chuckled before leading me over to the refreshments. After we'd each taken a margarita, he somehow managed to find his way outside, onto a quiet terrace, away from all the noise. "You all right?"

I set my overly large, sugary drink down on the ledge before leaning both hands on the cool cement. "Probably a good thing you brought me out here. I was about to lose my shit."

The air next to me stirred, and he perched on the ledge. "Why?"

How can he ask me that? I stood there, searching him for a good long moment, but found nothing. No resentment, no anger. "How do you stand it? Not *one* of those people in there values you. Every single person moved the conversation to someone else in your family. You're doing everything right, playing their game perfectly. It makes me sick." I turned away from him, looking out at the dimly lit, well-manicured garden. Several statues scattered about, dotting a winding path. "And I'm the reason you have to put up with it." I crossed my arms over my stomach.

"Avery, hey." A finger ran over the knuckles clamped onto my biceps. "I don't give a rat's ass about any of them. There's only one person in this whole place that matters to me, and I'm talking to her right now."

I glanced over at him, at his finger tracing my knuckles.

"And the reason I can play my part so well, not care about anything they say or think is because *you* see me. You've always seen me. Even when no one else did." He swallowed and looked down at his shoes, his hand dropping to the ledge beside him.

Is that true? I thought about his words — about being the only person he cared about. And suddenly, the one thing I wanted more than anything in the world was to kiss him. Not a fake kiss for the sake of our friends or his sister or my mother. But for me, and for him. My heart raced, and my stomach did a cartwheel. It took a second to gather enough courage to open my mouth to ask when I remembered the stupid Princess he was head over heels for.

The moment passed. I tried a sip of my margarita. The syrupy sweetness nearly made me gag, so I dumped it in the bushes.

"Come on. There's someone here actually worth meeting." And I took him the back way to the kitchen. "Patty!" I called her name from the employee entrance. "There's someone who wants to see you."

Patty came barreling over, practically knocking me backward in her haste to see Derek. "Oh my word, aren't you a fine specimen of a man? I think you might have found a keeper." She winked at me.

Derek's cheeks were bright red as Patty walked a complete circle around him, inspecting him from head to toe.

Ha, now you know how it feels.

I just shook my head. "Derek, this is Patty. Patty, this is my boyfriend, Derek."

"A pleasure to meet you, ma'am." Derek smiled, a real one. "Avery said you were one of the only people here worth meeting."

"That child always did have decent taste." Patty crossed her arms over her ample chest. "Are you taking care of my girl? Making sure she's eating right, getting her exercise, not working too hard?"

I hid my face in my hand and groaned. "Patty!"

Derek chuckled. "Yes, ma'am. I've been taking good care of her."

She grinned, moving her hands to her hips. "That's what I like to hear." To me, she said, "I think he's worth the ravioli."

As if he'd heard a magic word, Derek asked, "Ravioli?"

I groaned again. "That was supposed to be a surprise."

"That's the surprise?" Derek's grin spread from ear to ear. "Ravioli's my favorite. When do I get this surprise?"

This time I clapped a hand over Patty's mouth. "Wouldn't you like to know. But that's why I had to borrow Patty here away from my mom. She makes the best ravioli I've ever had."

The cook shoved me off so she could speak for herself. "Damn straight, I do." Patty grinned. "All right, you two, off with ya. I got work to do."

Derek slung an arm around my waist, pulling me close. "Ravioli, mmm."

"Anything, mmm. I'm starving and, don't kill me, but I hate corn tortillas unless they're hard shell. They smell like dirty gym socks to me. Somehow I just can't get past that." I wrinkled my nose.

A horrified gasp came from Derek, his eyebrows jumping up. "What? You don't eat your dirty gym socks? This relationship is over!" He removed his arm, stalking a few feet ahead of me, then waited for me to catch up. "Have we put in enough time for tonight? Are we free to leave?"

"I think if we say farewell to Mommy dearest we're in the clear." And that's exactly what we did.

On the way home, we ended up arguing over what we should eat and how many parsecs Han Solo actually ran the Kessel Run in. So we ordered Chinese, watched *Star Wars: A New Hope*, and I did a triumphant dance when I was right. I completely forgot about rent until the next morning. But Derek was already gone when I woke up.

Chapter Nine

The week flew by in a flurry of school, work and party planning. I grew more and more frustrated, not only about the rent-free apartment, but because I still didn't have my own key. Plus, Derek and I hardly had a minute to ourselves. Liam or Gina was always there, though never together, and neither one of them filled me in on what their argument was about.

Friday morning dawned with no classes, thank goodness. I'd set my alarm super early, hoping to catch Derek in time to talk. *I need my key, dammit.* After pulling on a pair of yoga pants and a hoodie, I reached the living room just as the door closed.

Yanking it back open, I rushed to the elevator, watching to see what floor he went to. Luckily, it stopped on the basement level, not in the lobby. *Ohhh! Maybe the gym is there, and I can finally see his workout.* Excited enough to not wait for the elevator, I hurried down the stairs.

I'd never been to this level before. My flash of annoyance faded as I reminded myself I'd only lived here a week, and Derek hadn't had much time to play tour guide. Not that it was up to him. There hadn't been much time for me to explore on my own either. I followed my hunch, looking for the signs to the gym. The door started swinging closed. I managed to stick my foot in before it latched, ducking inside without drawing attention to myself.

It was quiet. Derek was the only one here. He sat down at a rowing machine, eyes on a TV mounted high up, earbuds tucked in his ears. His shirtless body had my mouth immediately devoid of all saliva. Then he started moving.

It's poetry. It's fluidity. It's freaking hot.

No wonder he had such an amazing body. Each muscle in his chest tightened as he pulled back on the handle, his biceps standing out. My gaze wandered down his shoulders, his side and settled on his legs — a work of art all of their own. My saliva must have started working again because I was suddenly in danger of drooling. *Damn.*

My brain woke up from its lusty haze to remind me that I was standing in the middle of a gym gawking at my fake boyfriend. Like the creep that I was. I turned around to go, then realized I still didn't know which apartment was mine.

C'mon, brain. Think! Four-two-five? Five-two-four? Two-five-four?

It was no use. My brain could not latch on to the right combination, the numbers trickling through my mind like a sieve. Frustration coursed through me.

I ducked around a partial wall, down a short hallway where they had bathrooms and single-person showers. *Stupid Derek and his white knight complex.* I clenched my fists, annoyed at my own helplessness. If he'd just let me get to the apartment on my own. My shoulders slumped as I realized it wouldn't have mattered anyway. I still didn't have a key.

As I ran through my options, I dismissed them one by one. The doorman would just call Derek. I didn't have my cell, so I couldn't call Liam.

Derek was my only option.

I'd just have to face the music, but I'd wait till he was done. *No point interrupting his workout.* I slid down the wall, tucking my knees up to my chin, mostly hidden from sight by a big plant. I tried to think of what I would say, how I'd explain, but everything sounded stupid. A few tears leaked out despite my best efforts. All too soon, I heard footsteps. I stood up, opening my mouth to blurt out everything, only to see him disappear into one of the showers.

My body moved before I thought about it. I launched myself at the closing door, wiggling through and latching it behind me. When I turned around, I gasped. "Shit." He was already naked. "I'm sorry. I'm so sorry."

"Avery?" He yelped my name.

Chagrin washed over me, as I tried to gear up to admit I'd stalked him down here. I dropped my eyes, quickly realizing that wasn't the best idea as my gaze landed solidly on his package. On full display.

Not that he has anything to be ashamed of. I sucked in a breath. *Wow.*

His tone changed as he stepped closer. "Have you been crying? What's going on?"

Why does he have to be so hot? I tore my gaze away from his body, only to collide with his concerned blue eyes.

"Who did this to you?" He reached out to touch my cheek.

Then I realized, to top everything off, I wasn't wearing makeup. My annoyance became fuel for my anger. "You did." I stamped my foot. "You and Liam and the stupid doorman. If I'm going to live here, I need a key, Derek. I need to push the elevator button for myself. I need to walk to my apartment and know the damn number."

The flare of my temper burned itself out, that quickly. I sighed, pressing a hand to my forehead. "My brain doesn't work right when it comes to numbers. Especially addresses, phone numbers, that kind of thing. They jumble around in my head, and I get all...mixed up. I haven't had a chance to figure things out here." My voice broke on the last word. The frustration was too much, along with the embarrassment of admitting my weakness to Derek. Especially to him, the master of numbers. "I don't feel at home." A tear slid down my cheek, and I looked at the floor.

"Avery, I had no idea." He reached out to run a finger over my knuckles, then grabbed my hand. "I never wanted you to feel like that. Quite the opposite, in fact. I'm sorry." His thumb stroked my hand, then his grip tightened. "I can fix this. C'mon."

He strode forward, only stopping when I placed my hands on his bare, sweaty chest. Surprise crossed his face, and I nearly laughed when I realized he was more concerned about me than with what he was wearing. *Or not wearing.*

160

I locked eyes with him as he waited for an explanation. So I let my hands slide lower, stopping right below his hip bones as I said, "Might be a bit drafty out there."

His eyes darted down as he sucked in a breath, color rising in his cheeks. A sheepish smile spread across his face, and he stepped back.

"Although I appreciate the enthusiasm." I couldn't contain my grin.

"Can you wait while I rinse off quick? I'm gross."

Not quite the word I'd use. My eyes ran over his body of their own accord. When I met his gaze, I found him smirking.

"You're welcome to stay, of course. It's not like you haven't seen it all."

I ducked my head at his teasing, at being caught so blatantly checking him out. I had to live with this guy after all. "Um, no, I'll just, um, wait out here." *If the door would just open.* I fumbled behind me for the handle.

Derek reached around me, close enough that I could feel the warmth radiating off him once more. His face was less than an inch away, those kissable lips right there. I swallowed hard, my gaze latching on to his mouth, my fingers itching to rake down his naked chest.

I heard the click of the lock as the door opened, cool air rushing in and waking me from my trance. I snapped my mouth shut, then fled. After I'd made my not so graceful exit, I found a bench to wait on.

Luckily, his shower didn't take long. Derek emerged wearing athletic pants and a hoodie, his damp hair deliciously tousled. Despite the fact that he was all covered up, all I could see were flashes of skin. His sculpted shoulders and perfect pecs. That ridged abdomen clenching as he pushed back while rowing. Those muscular thighs. And everything in between. His deep chuckle startled me.

"What?" I fell into step beside him as we walked toward the elevator.

"You're picturing me naked, aren't you?"

I felt my eyes widen. "No, I'm not!"

He grinned, the megawatt smile blinding me. "Yeah. Yeah, you are."

My cheeks were on fire as we walked in silence. If I protested any more, it'd be too much, and he wouldn't believe me. *Not that he believes me anyway. Ugh.* I pushed the up arrow at the elevator.

Derek nudged me.

"What?" I glanced at him.

"I'm always naked under my clothes." His eyebrows bobbed up and down above teasing blue eyes.

The elevator doors slid open, and he walked in, wearing a shit-eating grin. *How am I ever supposed to look at him again?* I managed to step into the elevator, glancing at the buttons, surprised to find them not lit.

"You do it." He leaned against the back wall.

I frowned. "Now?" I wasn't prepared. I didn't know where we were going. When I glanced at my options, the six floors seemed like a million. Like they were in a completely different language. And I hated them. Hated Derek who worked with math every day, on purpose. Who *chose* numbers.

"Do you have your phone on you?"

I shook my head. Obviously, I should put the floor and the apartment number in my notes app. Take pictures of it all. But I was also stubborn enough to want to learn to do it on my own. I knew I could, if I did it myself enough times. I stared at the stupid buttons.

Suddenly his warm breath was on my neck, his voice rumbling in my ear, low and soothing. "Stop thinking about the number. Think about my motions. Which button do I always push? Is it on this side or that side?" He pointed as he spoke. "Close your eyes and picture it."

I did as he suggested, leaning into the strong hand he rested on my shoulder. *It's definitely on the left side. Not the bottom row either. Maybe the middle.* I opened my eyes to see what number that was. "Four?"

He nodded. "Do mnemonics work for you?"

I pushed the button, feeling a huge sense of satisfaction. "Sometimes."

"Floor and four rhyme." He stepped back and shrugged. "What floor? Four."

Pathetic, but cute. I wrinkled my nose.

"I see. My rhymes you deplore." He grinned proudly at his awful continuation.

And I groaned.

"I might stop. If you implore."

"Yes, please, please stop." But I was smiling. "At least you're not a bore."

He looked shocked. "Hey, good one."

"It got you out of your rhyming fit."

The elevator came to a halt, and we stepped off. Derek grabbed my hand, placing a small, metal object in it. His key. "Just like the elevator. Don't worry about the numbers. Picture it, how far we walk. What side of the hallway." Maybe I looked tense because he said, "Want some theme music? I bet I could do *Mission: Impossible*." And he tried.

I couldn't even be nervous with him humming the theme song so badly. It was easy to start walking. I led the way, not letting myself think too hard about it. *Maybe a little farther. Definitely on the right.* I stopped and looked back at him.

"Almost." His mouth twitched. "Look at the door, the mat, the surroundings. Is that ours?"

Oh. There was a flowery welcome mat that for sure wasn't his. I walked one more door down, and it felt right. Glancing at him for confirmation, I grinned at his nod. *Four-two-five. Home.* A sense of accomplishment flowed through me as I opened the door all by myself.

Derek followed me inside. "Great job. That was impressive!"

I smiled so wide my cheeks felt like they'd split in half. "Thanks. And thanks for your help." It was only natural to fling my arms around him in a grateful hug. Maybe I held on longer than I should have or breathed a little deeper when my nose was buried in his shoulder, filling my lungs with his citrus and clove scent. He'd just showered, but it still clung to his clothes. *Maybe he's worn the hoodie before?*

I stepped back, holding up his key. "Now I want to go do it again. By myself."

His frown was adorable. *You'd think I'd suggested running over broken glass barefoot while being shot at by angry terrorists.*

"Enough of the white knight routine. If I'm living here, I have to do this. By myself, for myself. And I *will* be paying some rent. You can't keep doing everything for me. It doesn't matter whether you can afford it or not, I need to contribute. Understand?" I put my hands on my hips.

He nodded. "Maybe when you get back, I can take —?" He stopped at my fierce glare, clearing his throat and starting over. This time his words were more of an order, a tone that brooked no room for argument. "Avery, get a move on. Go let yourself in. And when you get back, we're going to figure out a way for you to pull your weight around here. Starting with you taking me out for breakfast." He folded his arms over his chest. "Got it?"

I'd like to hear that voice in the bedroom.

"Avery?" His voice wavered, as if nervous he'd overstepped.

*Holy shit. Where did that come from? Did I really just —? I managed to shut my brain up, smile at Derek and say, "That's exactly what I needed to hear." I ran to get my phone, wishing I had time to go put on some dry underwear. Then I walked out of the apartment door and snapped a pic of the apartment number, just in case. "Okay, do not come looking for me. Do not call the doorman. I will be back." *I hope.*

Derek stepped forward, pulling me into a quick one-armed embrace, and pressed a firm kiss to my forehead. "You got this."

Too shocked to do anything else, I headed for the elevator. *What did the kiss mean? What about the banter earlier, about his nakedness? And how upset he was when he thought I didn't feel at home?*

I pushed the button for the basement, letting my whirlwind train of thought sweep me away until I heard the ding announcing I'd arrived. I stepped off, let the doors close and walked around for five whole minutes. Then I summoned the elevator again.

What floor? Four. 'Cause it rhymes. Dammit, now I'm using his stupid mnemonics. I made it to our floor and strode down the hallway to the apartment after the one with the ridiculous mat. Four-two-five. I turned the knob and opened the door, only to be met by Derek's megawatt smile.

"You did it, Cupcake!" He picked me up, spinning me around until the room became a blur, and we both wobbled when he set me down. "Now I know I said you could buy breakfast..."

"Derek," I said, my voice full of warning.

"But I think I owe you an apology for making you feel so crummy about all of this. Can you let me make it up to you? And we'll go get you your very own key afterward." He paused. "Or that can be your key, and we can go get me one."

A giggle escaped me before I could stop it. "Fine, you can buy me breakfast. But we're still talking about how much rent I owe. Deal?"

"Deal."

The tenderness in his eyes took my breath away, but when I blinked, it was just him and his usual smirk. My stomach growled. "Well, what are we waiting for?" I headed for the door, only to be jerked back by the hood of my sweatshirt.

"Hold it there." He looked down at my clothes, then his own. "I'm not sure what type of breakfast you're thinking about, but I'm not planning on going anywhere until I get some decent clothes on. Why don't you get dolled up? Let me take you somewhere nice. We can celebrate you moving in for real." His eyes ran over me, and he frowned a little. "Now that I think about it, is this the first time I've seen you without makeup?"

My cheeks went hot, and I ducked my head, wishing my hair wasn't pulled back. I'd hoped with everything going on, he wouldn't notice.

He took a step closer, nudging my chin up with his finger. "Please, Avery." His voice was gentle, and I couldn't refuse.

So I lifted my face, not meeting his gaze. And I stood there while he looked at me, feeling naked under his steady stare. Gina was the only other one I felt comfortable enough to be like this around — vulnerable and myself.

A soft touch made me flinch as he grazed the freckles on my cheek. "I've always known you were gorgeous, Cupcake. And you have a real talent for your makeup." His words pulled me in, our gazes colliding. "But this is my favorite look of yours."

His words replayed in my head, echoing over and over as they seared into my heart. My eyes flicked up to meet his, relief coursing through me at the acceptance I found there.

"Still up for breakfast?" he asked gently.

"Yes." Needing the levity of earlier, I reached for my humor. I smirked at him. "Don't think I'm not onto you. You just want me dolled up so you can help me out of my dress again."

He smirked right back, stepping away with a wink. "Seems only fair after the gawking you did today."

My jaw dropped. "And after I kept you from walking out the door without a stitch on. That's gratitude for you." I sniffed, stalking to my bedroom and shutting the door. He didn't need to know that my parting shot brought up images of his delicious body once more.

His footsteps paused outside my room. "You're thinking about me naked again."

"Am not!" I shouted, storming off to the closet to get clothes before I went to drown out his laughter with a shower.

Breakfast was more like brunch by the time we finished getting ready, but Derek was true to his word, taking me to a fairly upscale place. I wore dress pants and a cute jade blouse that highlighted my eyes. My hair was pulled back in a French braid, keeping it out of my face. I kept my makeup to a minimum, remembering his words and smiling to myself. Derek wore slacks and a navy button-down shirt with the sleeves rolled up. He looked delicious, as always.

We sat down, and I opened my mouth to begin negotiations.

But he shook his head. "Order first, then we'll talk. I'm hungry. A full workout will do that to a person."

I could live with that. I settled on eggs, bacon and hash browns. Once we'd put in our order, we set about figuring out rent. His numbers were way too low. After nearly ten minutes of arguing, we finally agreed on a price that included me buying the groceries and doing some of the cooking since he was basically inept at it.

I lifted my coffee cup in the air. "Pleasure doing business with you, sir."

He gently clinked his cup to mine. "The pleasure is all mine." The sincerity in his blue eyes made me pause, my mouth suddenly dry. He really meant it.

Chapter Ten

Once rent was settled and I had my own key, I really felt at home.

Derek and I fell into a routine, one that easily accommodated Liam or Gina dropping in. He and I usually had dinner together. We discovered a mutual love for crossword puzzles. And sometimes, I'd watch him work out, so I could drool over him while he rowed.

I hadn't seen his sister since the family dinner, and she'd been on my mind with Derek's upcoming party. When I got out early from my barista job, I knew I had to find her. Social media said on Thursday nights she was always at The Grotto, a dive bar not far from campus. It was ladies' night. Though I wasn't quite dressed the part, it was still better than taking her to lunch again. I touched up my makeup before I went in, feeling a little better armed.

The tiny place was packed. Of course, Rhonda stood out with her two Musketeers, claiming one of the few high-top tables near the bar. I strode up to her like she was expecting me.

"Rhonda, darling, so good to see you again." I even went for the double-cheek air kiss, which she was too shocked to avoid.

"Avery, what are you doing here?" Her eyes skittered down my outfit, probably finding me oh so lacking.

"I needed to talk to you." I stared at her friends hovering. "Your girls should step off for a few, or you could take a quick walk with me. What's better for you?"

She blinked her pale blue eyes up at me. "Um."

The place wasn't conducive to conversation. It was loud between the karaoke going on and the wall-to-wall people. I glanced at her friends. "I'm just going to borrow her for a few minutes, and chat outside where it's quieter, okay? I'll bring her back when we're done."

"What, no Greg?" Yolanda sneered.

My smile was tight. "Not tonight." I tugged on Rhonda's arm. "Please, Rhonda."

Her sigh was loud and long, letting me know exactly how put out she felt by my request. But she stood up and followed me to the door. The fresh air was cool but welcome after the stifling air rife with stale beer and too many dancing college kids. A bench caught my eye, and I led her to it.

"What's all this about?" She pulled her fashionable, but not exactly made for the cold, coat tighter around her.

"I'm throwing Derek a surprise birthday party."

Her eyebrows pulled together, head tilting, obviously wondering if I were in my right mind.

"I know it's not his birthday. But if you remember, I didn't really get a chance to do anything big for him." Silence met my statement, and I sighed. "Look, I'm going to be honest with you. One of the reasons Derek started looking for a girlfriend was because you kept throwing your friends at him. It's one of the first conversations we had." *The very first actually.*

"I don't know why you're doing that, if it's a desperate attempt to keep him close to you or some twisted way to control him." I shrugged. "If you care about him at all, I'd say your chances at having a good relationship aren't great. And your odds aren't getting any better based on the behavior I've seen from you, or your fiancé."

Her eyes narrowed. "Like you know anything."

I clenched my jaw, frustration coursing through me. I knew a whole hell of a lot more than she gave me credit for, and I was happy to demonstrate. "You talked over him like he was nothing at dinner the other night. I watched him fold himself up, tucking away any hint of the real Derek as soon as you did. Like it was just par for the course." I watched her for any hint of reaction, happy to see her flinch. "*You* don't know a single thing about him, Rhonda. And you don't try. The only person you care about is yourself."

I stared at the bar across the street, looking through the hazy window at the crowds inside. "I don't know why I'm even bothering." As I stood up to go, I almost missed her quiet words.

"I know he's really good at guessing surprises."

I paused, needing more of an olive branch than that.

She cleared her throat. "What's your cover story? For the party?"

My lips curved into a small smile as I shrugged, turning to face her once more. "Well, I'm having it on my birthday, but we're going to celebrate him instead. Pretty sure he won't suspect anything."

Rhonda blinked rapidly — disbelief etched in every feature. "Wait. You're having a party for him on *your* birthday?"

"Yep." I smiled broadly. "Isn't that perfect?"

She stayed silent for another moment. "Why would you give up your birthday?"

"It just worked out." I sat down once more. *What wouldn't I give up for Derek, who's helped me so much?* He was fast becoming one of my favorite people. "The dates lined up. It's on November seventeenth, and we're having a twenty-one-themed party. Twenty-one of his favorite foods. Twenty-one whiskeys. A bunch of his friends are coming. I've been able to get some good suggestions on food and decorations from all of them. Greg scored a great event room at a hotel, and I made sure to get us a room for the night so if Derek actually tastes all the whiskeys, I can put him to bed without driving across town." I beamed at her only to be met with a concerned stare. "What?"

"This is great and all, but why are you telling me?" The snotty tone made her attitude shine through, but her words were underlined with a hint of something that sounded a lot like hope.

I twisted my hands in my lap and took a deep breath. "I want you to come. If you have any chance of being in Derek's life, you're running out of options." I paused, laying down my conditions. "But you have to do this on his terms. Don't bring your friends. Kevin can come, but he needs to be on his best behavior." I glanced up at her, surprised to find her still listening.

"You're his twin, Rhonda. You may not get along perfectly, but that doesn't mean you're not important to him."

It was her turn to study her lap. "He wouldn't want me there. He never invites me to do anything. He's a hard guy to hold on to."

I frowned, her phrasing sounding all off to me until realization dawned. "Well, maybe that's the problem. You're trying to hold on to him." The confusion in her gaze had me scrambling for an analogy. "Okay, think about water running from a faucet. If you close your fist over the stream, how much water do you keep in your hand?"

She frowned. "None."

"Right. But if you cup your hand under it?"

A light dawned in her eyes.

"Maybe stop trying so hard. Let him come to you. Ask him some questions about him next time you see each other. Send him a text when something reminds you of him." And I had to make sure she understood one thing. "I know you guys share a birthday, but I want to make this clear. This one's for him, okay?"

She nodded.

I hesitated, deciding I had to ask. "I saw the pictures of him with you and your friends at your joint party. That really didn't seem like his scene, at all. Did you even try to find something he wanted to do?"

At least she had the decency to look chagrined. "No. But, he's never had a preference before. Eventually, I stopped asking."

"Or," I said gently, "maybe he's had a preference all along, and you just stopped listening. I think he's the one doing all the work in this relationship."

Rhonda sat in silence for long enough that I worried I'd overstepped. Again. Then her head snapped up. "I'll be there."

We smiled at each other before I blurted out, "Can I ask you something?" My words were tentative. I wasn't sure she was the best person to talk to, but Liam hadn't been much help and Derek, well, I'd seen how he reacted. Bin had given me some info, but I was hungry for more. "Who is Princess?"

Rhonda's eyes widened, flicking to mine, then her gaze settled somewhere past me. "She's someone Derek used to date."

Exasperation coursed through me. "Yeah, I got that much. I also heard how Derek declared his undying love for her. I've heard him stomp away or completely shut down any time she's mentioned. And he hasn't brought her up to me yet." I laced my fingers together, clenching them tightly. "I asked Liam. He said to talk to Derek. I just want to know how big the can of worms I'm opening is." I was surprised to feel Rhonda's hand on my shoulder.

"It's big. I won't lie to you." Her blue eyes, only a shade lighter than Derek's, filled with compassion. "Princess was a childhood friend of ours. She grew up with us, and Liam. Derek had a crush on her for as long as I can remember. But she had big dreams. Us three went to SMU, and she…" Her mouth twitched in a ghost of a smile. "She went off to chase those dreams. Derek was upset. Then she came back his freshmen year absolutely broken."

Her pause was lengthy. "Derek helped put her back together. I think he used a lot of himself to do it, and he made her so many promises…" Her gaze flicked to mine, filled with sympathy. "He talked her into enrolling with us, but the day she was supposed to start, she hopped on a bus instead. She left a note saying her dreams were too big, and he was just too small."

Ouch. My heart ached for the pain Derek must have felt at that rejection.

Her intense eyes lingered on me. "I don't know what all he promised her, but I know it wasn't done lightly. After she left, he was a mess. In fact, I haven't seen him anywhere close to himself since that day." She hesitated, studying me. "Until you came along."

It was a pinprick of light in a realm of darkness. I couldn't help wondering if it was best to cling to it, or let it fade? "And when she comes back?"

Rhonda pressed her lips together and shrugged. "I don't know."

I stared back at her, weighing her words, appreciating her candor. "Thank you." And I knew what she needed to hear. "Derek doesn't hate you. He keeps your picture right in the living room, the one of you and him at the fair." I smiled at her. "I love that picture. You both look so happy."

She looked down at her lap again. "I'll come to your party, and I think I know what I want to get him. It's a long shot, but one of his favorite football players volunteered at a few of our charity events. I bet I could convince him to make an appearance. I can't promise anything, but I'll see what I can do. What's your number?" She whipped out her phone as I pulled up my info for her. "Perfect."

I realized what a force she could be when she put her mind to it. She started to walk away, then she stopped. Her blue eyes met mine once more, with a small smile of gratitude before she disappeared back into the club, and I felt like maybe things would be different for them. At least the possibility was there.

* * * *

The following week, I'd just finished my favorite marketing class and was packing up my notes when my phone rang.

It was Derek. "Hey, Liam's parents are out of town, so he's watching their house. He wants us to come over and play pool, hang out, said to invite whoever."

I had to think over my schedule. It was Tuesday, no work tonight. "I have class first thing tomorrow, so I don't want to be out late."

"That's not a problem." He paused. "What do you think about having Greg hang out with us? I could line up another driver to take us home, or we could taxi it."

A smile spread across my face. "That'd be fun. I like Greg, and I'd love to get to know him better. Have you guys ever done anything like that before?"

"Yeah, he's just not into football, which is what we've been doing a lot of lately."

Makes sense. "Should I invite Gina?" It was kind of a touchy subject with the tension between Gina and Liam lingering since the night I'd met Derek's parents.

But Derek didn't even hesitate. "Liam actually mentioned Gina by name when he told me to talk to you about inviting people, so yep, text her. Tell her to bring that boyfriend of hers, so I can actually meet him. What's his name again?"

"Josh." I smiled. Derek was so bad with names.

"Right, Josh. I'll send you the address. And dinner's covered. Liam's ordering a bunch of takeout from a local joint once he knows how many are coming."

"Okay, I'll let you know about Gina."

We said goodbye, and I called her next. She took a little convincing since it was Liam, but she loved pool. Josh was available, and the free food didn't hurt. So I texted her the address.

I made it home in time to change, wanting to be cute, but not over the top. I settled on my favorite jeans, so worn and soft they were like butter, fitting me like a glove. My shirt was long-sleeved and dove gray, with a scooped neck. From the front it looked normal, aside from the lacy sleeves, but the back, well, the back had lace along my shoulder blades, then the lower half was mostly a cut-out. Luckily the built-in bra up front supported things.

Derek waited on the couch when I emerged from my bedroom. He smiled when he saw me. "Ready?" At my nod, he leapt up, handing me my zip-up from the peg near the door.

I managed to put it on while keeping the back hidden from Derek. It would be a fun surprise, and I couldn't wait to see his reaction.

When we hopped in the elevator, he pushed a P button I'd always wondered about. "I thought I'd drive."

Curious, I followed him to an underground parking lot where a sleek black Mercedes waited. He opened my door, ever the gentleman. The drive wasn't a long one, and we caught each other up on our day. It felt so normal chatting with Derek, filling him in on all the mundane details of my life. I glanced at his profile. His sunny smile made my stomach flip, but a clench of anxiety followed it as I realized how comfortable I was getting with everything. With us. As we pulled into the driveway, I pushed the heavier thoughts aside, determined to enjoy tonight.

Greg pulled in next to us, driving a clunky, mismatched SUV. I bit back a laugh, not used to seeing him in anything other than sleek black Town Cars or limos. It was quite the contrast. He grinned as he hopped out, the door creaking when he pushed it shut.

"Hey Avery, Derek." He seemed different out of uniform too, younger. Suddenly the six-year gap between us didn't feel that wide, seeing him in his Henley and ripped jeans.

"Hey, look at you, all casual." I nudged him with my elbow as we followed Derek up the big flight of steps to Liam's parents' estate. The Davenports were another huge founding family in this area, involved in politics and the community. Their house was massive, at least as big as Derek's parents'. *Will I ever get used to this level of wealth? Fake dating a billionaire* and *hanging out at his billionaire best friend's house*. I shook my head. *Talk about rubbing elbows with the upper crust.*

Derek didn't bother knocking, just let himself in. His own parents' house was only one street over, and their properties butted up to one another which accounted for Derek and Liam being friends for so long. He bellowed Liam's name. An answering shout came from the kitchen, and Derek tossed his coat over a dining room chair, glancing to see if I would like to take off my zip-up. But I shook my head, wanting to wait for my reveal. Plus, it was a little on the chilly side.

The smell of delicious food permeated the air, and I inhaled deeply as we rounded the corner into the kitchen. I gaped at the variety of foods, ranging from ribs to dips to potato skins and quesadillas. "Just how many people are coming?"

Liam's shoulders bobbed up sheepishly. "Maybe I overdid it. It's us, Gina and her boyfriend. And maybe Rhonda."

Greg let out a strangled noise at Rhonda's name, but he covered it with a cough. We stared at him for a second, then Liam glanced at Derek for confirmation on his sister. I raised my eyebrows at Derek as well.

Derek nodded. "Yeah, we've been texting some lately. Sounded like she could use a break from her regular group of people, so I invited her."

I grinned at him, happy to hear that she'd taken my advice.

"Wonderful." Greg's mouth looked pinched as he turned to Liam. "Could I use the restroom?"

Liam nodded, giving him directions. As soon as Greg was out of earshot, Liam frowned. "Is it just me, or was that weird?"

I nodded my agreement.

Derek glanced at both of us, taken aback at our eager expressions. "What? There's nothing to tell. Greg was primarily Rhonda's driver growing up, so he worked for her first once we graduated. It didn't work out, and he switched to me."

Yeah, right. I exchanged a disbelieving look with Liam. *Maybe that's what he told Derek, but there's definitely more to that story.*

A horrendous twanging noise echoed throughout the house, so loud we all winced.

Liam sighed. "Who rang the damn doorbell?" He emerged several minutes later looking even more annoyed.

Gina's hands were on her hips as she followed closely after him, Josh right behind them. "How was I supposed to know not to ring the doorbell? There's no sign, and no one told me. I'm not psychic, you know."

Liam ignored her, then he stopped and looked around. "Crap." He disappeared without another word.

Gina let out an exasperated sigh. "Derek, your friend is an arrogant, pig-headed—"

I stepped in. "Gina." My voice held a note of warning.

Her mouth closed with a snap as she turned her glare on me.

"Look at all the delicious food Liam bought. For us. And he's the one with the pool table. Could you just not? Please?" I shot her a tight-lipped smile, mentally telling her all the things I'd do to her if she didn't shut her trap.

She seethed for a minute more, then let out her breath with a whoosh. Just as Liam returned. Her smile seemed a bit forced, but she said, "The food looks amazing. Thanks for inviting us, and I'm sorry about the doorbell."

Liam shrugged, barely acknowledging her words before setting down a stack of plates.

I was grateful Josh put a restraining hand on her arm as she stepped toward Liam. Maybe between the two of us, we could make sure she kept her temper.

Speaking of Josh. "So guys, this is Josh. Josh, this is my boyfriend, Derek. Liam is our host. And that's Greg—most days he's our getaway driver." I pointed him out as he reappeared.

Everyone shook hands, exchanging greetings, and the tension dissipated. *Thank goodness.*

Liam's phone dinged. "Oh good, Rhonda's here." He typed something then shoved the phone in his pocket. "We'll get some food then head downstairs."

Rhonda came in. She looked perfectly put together as always, in a beautiful pantsuit and high heels, her dark hair piled elegantly on her head, a few tendrils curled loosely around her cheeks. The smile on her face was tentative, a far cry from her usual expression of confidence.

I hurried to greet her, going over for a one-armed hug. "So good to see you."

"You too." Her eyes flicked past me to Greg, and she paled.

Yep, definitely a story there. I tried to remember a reaction that day I'd taken the Three Musketeers to lunch. There'd been something. I would need to get to the bottom of this. Maybe not tonight, but at some point.

"Okay everyone, dig in." Liam grinned, his smile dimming a bit when his gaze drifted to Gina.

I hoped she hadn't noticed, but her pursed lips told me otherwise. Josh placed a hand on the small of her back as they got in line, and he leaned down to whisper something in her ear. She scrunched up her nose, fighting a smile. She lost the battle, even giggling as she looked back at him.

Someone came up behind me, and I knew immediately it was Derek. Maybe it was the way my heart sped up, or the hairs on the back of my neck tingled or how I tensed in anticipation of him possibly touching me.

His breath tickled my ear. "Never a dull moment with this crew."

We were with company. It was okay to be in girlfriend mode, so I had no qualms about leaning back against his firm torso, loving how he was just there for me. One warm hand slid to my waist, shooting sparks along its path. I nodded, unable to speak. We walked forward together, only separating when it was my turn to get food. I felt cold, bereft without his heat.

It was like a parade, the line of us following Liam downstairs, plates and drinks carefully balanced. The basement was huge. I couldn't imagine growing up in a place like this—it was every teenager's dream. There was a pool table, a dartboard, a giant TV and gaming setup, complete with surround sound. A mini gym sat in one corner with a boxing bag, a treadmill, stationary bike and a rowing machine. I couldn't help glancing at Derek and biting my lip. He smirked.

We fought over the couches around the TV. I took a spot on the floor, content to lean next to Derek. It was plenty warm down here, so after I set my plate on an end table, I peeled off my zip-up. I heard Derek choke.

I turned around to see his eyes locked on my back, even as he finally managed to suck in air. Everyone stared at us. I shrugged. "I guess I still got it." Then I gave Derek a saucy grin as the room erupted into laughter.

Derek's eyes stayed on me after I sat down, his finger tracing the outline of the cut-out in my shirt.

His gentle touch sent delicious shivers down my spine as he leaned over to whisper in my ear. "That's some shirt. What there is of it."

I grinned at him over my shoulder. "Glad you like it."

We ate our food, the air rife with laughter and ease. Derek's hand drifted over every so often to slide along my bare skin, as if he couldn't help himself. My grin never left my face.

Gina was the first one done. She popped up, jutted out a hip, and declared, "Who's going up against me and Avery?" She worked at a bar. And we'd spent many nights there, perfecting our bank shots.

Liam sneered. "Me and Derek. My house, my pool table." He looked just as cocky as the night I'd kicked his butt playing strip poker. "You're going down."

Derek's soft voice sounded behind me, saying something like, "I wish."

I whipped my head toward him, but he just stared back at me innocently. *Did I hear that right?*

He stood, offering me a hand up off the floor. His muscles went taut against my weight as he pulled me to my feet, not stopping until I was flush against him. "Hearing things, Cupcake?"

Oh, no. He's not getting away with that. I leaned into him, taking full advantage of my ample chest, sliding my hands down to dip my fingers into the front pockets of his jeans. Then I gave him an evil smile that had him stammering.

"What are you doing?"

"Just making sure my opponent is good and riled before we start." I winked. "Plus, it's always smart to check the pockets for stray balls." I strode off to the sound of his choked laughter.

Gina looked from Derek to me as I came up to where she was picking out a cue. "Are you torturing that poor man?"

"Busting his balls a bit. It's good for him." I grinned at her, then called to Derek, "Hey, come help me pick out a stick. I want to make sure I get one with just the right girth."

Derek ground his teeth together. Gina and Liam's laughter drowned out his stomping footsteps. He strode right up to me, fire in his eyes. "There's only one thing to do when you get like this." And his lips crashed down onto mine.

It had been a while since he'd kissed me to shut me up. This was no sweet, playful kiss either. His mouth was brutal, punishing me for teasing him, taking all that I would give and stunning me into silence. My knees gave out halfway through, so I clung to his broad shoulders as his hands wrapped around my waist. He broke the kiss off as abruptly as he'd started it, both of us breathing heavily. I blinked up at him, too dazed to do anything but hope he wouldn't let go.

"That'll teach her, right, Derek?" Liam chuckled.

Derek shook his head as if coming out of a daze, his blue eyes focusing on mine. "Yeah. That'll teach you."

His delivery was so bad, so lacking, that I dissolved into laughter. Chuckles rumbled through him too, the absurdity of our situation striking us both. We stood there laughing at ourselves for several minutes until Gina finally grew impatient.

"All right, you two hyenas. Get your sticks, and let's play some pool."

Gina broke, sinking a solid right off the bat. I looked over to see what the rest of the group was doing. Josh, Rhonda and Greg played darts in the corner. Rhonda laughed at something Josh said, her eyes sparkling, hair tossing. Greg's gaze never left her.

While I looked away, Gina sank another solid. She smiled triumphantly at Liam, who just arched an eyebrow. Unconcerned, she lined up her next shot. And missed.

Liam let out a derisive snort that had all of Gina's hackles up. I didn't understand it. If I had snorted, or Derek had, she'd have rolled her eyes and made some self-deprecating comment. But Liam did it, so it was personal.

I sighed, nudging her. "Calm down. You got two in."

Gina was good, but Liam was better. even though she hadn't left him any easy shots, he didn't seem bothered. He calmly lined up, called his ball in the side pocket and bounced it off two rails to sink it. *We're in trouble. And Derek's smirking at me.*

I could still rile him up, throw him off. My mind racing, I sidled up to him, sliding my hand firmly down my pool cue in an obvious gesture. "Hey." I rested my ass against his hip, making sure he had a decent view of my back.

"Hey." His reply was a bit strangled.

Good. I slid my hand back up the cue, then pressed my ass into him as I circled my fingers and ran them down the wooden length. "Liam's pretty good."

"What?"

Gina was trying not to laugh, and Liam completely missed his shot, glaring at me.

I shrugged. "All's fair in love and pool?" I pushed off Derek, circling the table. My best shot happened to be near where he stood, so I wedged myself in between his hip and the table. "Excuse me." The only fault in my plan was that he pressed back, making me gasp. All I could think about was bending over the table as he took me from behind. *Shit.* I focused on the nine ball I was supposed to be aiming for.

Derek's finger traced the outline of the cut-out of my shirt.

I shivered, nearly miscuing. With gritted teeth, I lined up again, pushing my ass firmly against his side. Ignoring his hands at my hips even as the blood thrummed in my ears, I lined up and took the shot. And missed. *Double shit.*

He chuckled. "Guess I've still got it, too."

I glanced at Gina. "Should've worn a lower cut shirt."

Derek blanched, Liam gulped and Gina threw her head back in a full-on laugh.

With a smirk, I couldn't resist leaning over to Derek. "Now who's picturing who naked?" The darkening in his blue eyes made my breath catch, making me wish I could take back the words. I scurried a safe distance away, searching for a distraction and settling on Liam.

There was a hint of sadness in Liam's eyes. I realized his new girlfriend wasn't around, and he hadn't mentioned her at all. They'd just started seriously dating in the last week. But I'd thought she'd be here.

"Where's Carla? She's missing out on all the fun." I'd met her briefly at the apartment as we were coming and going. And Liam had brought her to get coffee at my shop while I was working, but we hadn't really hung out.

He sighed, watching Derek take his shot. *Dangit, I forgot to distract him.*

"She wanted some girl time." He shook his head, a bewildered expression on his face. "I just don't get her. She says I'm not trying at all, but I am."

I cocked my head at him. "What do you mean by trying? What have you guys done so far?"

Liam leaned against the pool table, staring up at the ceiling before he answered. "I took her to sing karaoke one night at my favorite bar. We've watched football at my place. We had dinner at my favorite diner."

Gina failed to cover her snort. She gave an apologetic shrug when Liam glared at her. "I'm sorry, but that's your definition of trying? Do you know any of her preferences? What she likes to drink? Where she likes to eat? Or do you just go wherever *you* feel like?"

The annoyed, guilty look Liam wore was more than enough evidence for a conviction.

To my surprise, Gina softened. "Look, it's not that hard, but it really does mean a lot." She turned to shout out to her boyfriend. "Josh, what's my favorite drink?"

He glanced over from where he was watching Greg toss darts. "Mai Tais or Fireball." His eyebrow popped up, silently asking what all this was about.

"I'm proving a point." She put her hands on her hips. "How do I like my coffee?"

Josh rolled his eyes. "You like that cinnamon roll thing. Otherwise, lots of cream."

"Favorite donut?" This time she looked at Liam, oozing confidence in her boyfriend's answer.

"Glazed. Preferably from Sweetwaters." When Greg handed him the darts, Josh gestured to the dartboard, wanting to go back to his game.

Gina waved him off. "Thanks, hon. See, Liam?" She turned to Derek. "How about you, hot shot? What do you know about my girl here?"

Derek smirked at me, bumping me with his shoulder. "Top-shelf whiskey, whenever possible." He tapped his chin, trying to remember the other questions. "Coffee has to have French vanilla creamer, and a bear claw is a must. She likes crossword puzzles, funny movies and is a kick-ass poker player. She doesn't mind getting dolled up but prefers yoga pants."

He stared down at me, touching a finger to my cheek. "Her waffles have to have either vanilla ice cream or real maple syrup."

Gina held up a hand. "Okay, now you're just showing off." But she eyed us thoughtfully before turning back to Liam.

I leaned into Derek, reveling in how well he knew me. He pulled me close to kiss my temple.

"So stop strong-arming the girl into whatever you think she wants to do and ask some questions." Gina gave Liam a no-nonsense stare until he nodded, then she finally took her shot.

Not long later, the guys won. Gina gave Liam a run for his money, but Derek started in on me again, distracting himself in the process. In need of a break, I sat the next game out, watching Gina and Josh take on Rhonda and Liam.

Greg stopped by my spot on the couch. "Want to shoot darts with me and Derek?"

I shook my head. "I'd probably stab someone." And I couldn't even blame it on alcohol, since I wasn't drinking tonight. "Thanks anyways." I looked up to find his gaze on Rhonda again. "Why'd you really stop working for her? What didn't you tell Derek?"

He froze, gray eyes locking with mine. "What?"

"Greg, you freaked out when you heard she was coming. Well," I amended, "freaked out for you. And you can't take your eyes off her. What's the story there?" I perched on the edge of the couch, waiting for him to fill me in.

To my surprise, he shuttered down, his walls going up like the barrier in the limo. "Nothing to tell. I just thought Derek and I would be a better fit. Excuse me." And he strode off toward the dartboard.

I frowned. *That was odd.* My eyes sought out Rhonda, but she had no idea what just happened. She looked so at home, leaning on her pool stick, chatting with Liam. Gina laughed at something she said, even smiling at Liam, until she clearly realized what she was doing.

It hit me then. All these people, all these amazing connections were because of one little kiss and me hiding from my mother. Gina was my best friend, but Derek? He was fast becoming my anchor. And Liam…was definitely growing on me. Greg and even Rhonda were an integral part of this. All because of something fake.

Those thoughts hung with me until the car ride home. We said cheerful goodbyes all around, leaving like we were a real couple. Derek was in such a good mood, I decided to take a risk.

"That was fun." I smiled at Derek as I buckled my seatbelt.

"Yeah. It was. I'm so glad you get along with everyone." His blue eyes lingered on me, telling me how important it was to him.

I waited in silence as we drove a few miles. Then I made a blind leap. "I've never had anything like this, Derek. Never done the serious thing, with anyone. Fake or real. This is all new to me." I took a breath, trying to calm my nerves, even as I dug my nails into my palm. "Not that I haven't been with guys. I've had flings, been on dates. But nothing long term. Not since high school." Not since we returned home from the book tour, and Mother burst that particular bubble.

Now, the moment of truth. "What about you?"

Silence met my question. Derek tightened his grip on the steering wheel, and I saw how his jaw clenched in the brief flashes of the streetlights.

"There was one girl. She was my world for a long time. But she left."

I reached out to him, but he pulled away, instead giving me a tight smile. After the closeness we'd shared all evening, it hurt that he shut down, the pain jabbing right in my wide-open heart. We rode the rest of the way in silence, and I spent the time rebuilding my walls, berating myself for letting down my guard so completely. Princess had come between us again, just like I'd known she would.

Chapter Eleven

Sunday morning, Derek and I sprawled across the kitchen table, trying to figure out the paper's crossword puzzle when there was a knock at the door. We both sprang up, saying, "I'll get it."

"Uh-oh," I said, realizing it meant we were both expecting company.

"Is Gina coming over?" He frowned as the thought occurred to him, too.

I nodded. "I told you last night when she texted me. Sweetwaters' donuts, coffee then we're going shopping before my shift. Remember?"

He grimaced. "Liam should be here any minute."

After we'd left the party at Liam's last week, an alcohol-infused Gina had challenged Liam to a round of darts, wanting to beat him at something. Things were fine until they'd come up with different scores at the end, and she'd accused him of cheating. They'd had a huge fight about it, which we'd both heard about the next day. And every day since. Now, it was Sunday morning, and I just wanted a quiet visit with my friend, but instead I had to defuse World War Three.

"What's wrong with you?" Annoyed, I bumped his shoulder, stomping over to the door to yank it open. It was Gina. *Good, I'll get my bear claw first.* "Morning."

She handed over the box of donuts with a smile, then did a double take. "Morning. You okay?"

I found my donut, pulled it out with a napkin, then grabbed Derek's favorite, a chocolate éclair, and brought it to him. "Don't ask me. Ask dumbass, here." I nudged him with my hip for good measure, even as I set his donut in front of him.

He mumbled something incoherent at the same time there was a knock at the door.

Gina frowned. "What?"

"He invited Liam over."

"Oh." Gina huffed as she found a glazed donut and poured herself a cup of coffee. "Whatever. No biggie."

Her strained tone made me wince. It was too early for drama, and I glared at Derek again.

He shrugged as he rushed to open the door. "Hey, man."

Liam slapped his shoulder as he walked by, giving me a grin and a hello. Then he faltered when he saw Gina. "Good morning," he said, stiffly.

She slid the box of donuts a fingernail's width in his direction. "Donut?"

"Thanks." Liam grabbed a chocolate covered one with sprinkles, then shot her a teasing smirk. "What, no coffee?"

Gina gritted her teeth, and I stepped in before she could bite his head off.

"Liam, watch it." I gave him a look that said I wasn't kidding.

He sighed but shut his mouth, his eyes darting to Gina as he made his way over to fill a mug. He cleared his throat. "Actually, Gina, I'm glad you're here."

As one, we all turned to gape at him.

His gaze flicked between us before landing once more on her. He ran a hand up the back of his head. "I talked to Carla, and she likes a wine called Riesling or some shit. Since you work at a bar, maybe you'd have a recommendation of one I could pick up?"

My jaw could not have dropped any further.

Gina glanced at me, as if to make sure she'd heard him right. "Um, yeah. Actually, that's one of my mom's favorites, and a store not far from here sells some decent local ones. Want me to text them to you?"

Relief flooded Liam's face. "That'd be great." They exchanged phone numbers, and his phone dinged when Gina sent the brands through. "Thanks so much."

A small smile played on Gina's lips. "I hope she likes them."

Awkward silence hovered between all of us, until Derek broke it by asking me, "You taking Greg today?"

It always amused me that we talked about Greg like he was a car we shared. "If that's okay. Unless you need him?"

Derek shook his head. "No, he's all yours. And I've got a tab going over at Club Pearl, so if you want to have lunch…"

I pretended to glare at him as I finished my bear claw. "You're supposed to back off on the spoiling." The last few drops of coffee stubbornly lingered in the bottom of the cup as I tipped it up. I stood to put my empty mug in the sink, but Derek wrapped a strong arm around my waist as I walked by pulling me onto his lap. I loved when we had company because we had to play the part of the couple madly in love.

He whispered in my ear as I tried to squirm away. "It's the only way you'll let me spoil you. And if Gina overhears, it practically guarantees you'll have to take advantage of it." With a loud, smacking kiss on my cheek, he released me.

I shot him a dirty look and stuck out my tongue. Surprising me, he put a hand to the back of my head, capturing my tongue with his own. My shock must have shown because he softened the kiss, his tongue retreating.

And I forgot to pretend.

The kiss turned into something beautiful, sweet. The kind of kiss in movies where the music swelled, and the heroine's knees buckled beneath her as the white knight pulled away. I let myself slip into the role of the heroine, allowing Derek to become my fairy tale prince. A breathy moan escaped my lips, and I was just about to fling my arms around his neck, when he ruined it all by whispering, "Don't forget to think about me naked."

Because I need the reminder. I scowled, annoyed I'd let down my guard again, allowing myself to succumb to his spell for even the briefest of moments. It was definitely time to go.

Despite Gina's protests that she hadn't finished her donut, I dragged her out of the apartment, fuming the entire time. When I told her what the rush was all about, she laughed so hard tears came to her eyes.

"That's just hilarious. And the fact he keeps rubbing it in your face? Girl, he wants you. Bad. Everyone commented on how cute you two were after you left that night we played pool."

I wished that were true. *I wish Princess wasn't real, that fairy tales were and that Derek wanted me half as much as I want him.* Hope kept knocking at my door, persistent and tenacious. But I kept sending her away, knowing nothing good could come of letting her in.

Greg dropped me off after shopping in time for my shift at the coffee shop. We were busier than usual, so I got out a bit late, but I managed to pick up enough pizzas to satisfy the hungry guys in my apartment. Sunday night football at our place was becoming a tradition. One that I loved. We got the pizza, they brought the drinks, and everyone brought a bag of chips or some other snack.

The Uber driver dropped me off, and the doorman hit the elevator buttons for me. Then I got to the apartment.

With my hands full, I struggled to open the door. After my attempt at turning the knob failed, and almost sent the pizzas toppling over, I kicked the door with the toe of my tennis shoe instead. "Pizza!"

No answer. No mad rush to the door.

Again, I kicked, the door thudding. "Derek! Liam? Let me in."

Still no answer.

The five boxes of pizza were pretty heavy, and my frustration mounted. I gave the door a sound kick. "Holy crap. What's a girl gotta do to get some help around here?" I spun in a circle, muttering to myself. "When I didn't want any help, there were guys crawling all over the place, pushing buttons, unlocking doors. But now, when I need it? Nope. Not one. I bet if I said I was thinking of Derek naked, *poof*, he'd be right here." I completed my circle to a deep chuckle and an open door.

"Need some help, Cupcake?"

I glared at him. "No, in the time it took you to answer the damn door, I grew a third arm, so I'm all set. Thanks."

He lifted the pizza boxes from my hands, kissing the top of my head. "Glad you're still thinking about me." Curse words had little impact on him, based on his laughter. He called out, "Avery's here with the pizza."

I was met with a chorus of "Hey, Avery" and "Pizza!" then a rush for the counter. Derek handed me two slices of my favorite ham and pineapple before anyone else could touch it. Liam loved it too, and once he got a hold of it, there was hardly any stopping him.

"Thanks." I muttered the word, still annoyed.

Derek's soft smile curled up on one side. "Kevin brought a raspberry ale and a hard cider. He thinks you'll like both of them."

Kevin had started coming again, always on his best behavior. He still wasn't my favorite, but he wasn't nearly as obnoxious as the first couple of times I'd met him. And Rhonda must have sent some of her preferred drinks because he always showed up with fruity beer, ciders and hard sparkling seltzer. To my surprise, I enjoyed most of them. Whiskey was still my favorite, but some of the other choices went better with pizza. I helped myself to a raspberry ale, then claimed our chair.

My other favorite thing about football nights was snuggling with Derek in the overstuffed armchair. The guys would sprawl everywhere else, but the chair was ours. Sometimes I'd perch on the arm, or I'd sit on Derek's lap. Other times I sat on the floor, leaning between his knees. Tonight though, I wanted to press up against his side, his arm around me. And he did not disappoint.

The game wasn't very exciting. Neither team mattered much to me, and it wasn't a very close score. By the end of the third quarter, I grew bored, hardly paying attention to the TV. I did notice that Liam was drinking a lot more than usual.

Derek followed me to the kitchen the next time I got up.

"What's with Liam?" I asked quietly, opening another ale.

He grabbed a light beer for himself. "That girl he's been seeing…Karen, Carole…?"

"Carla," I supplied.

"That's it." He cracked open his beer and took a sip. "You know she's been off lately. That's why he came over this morning, to talk about her. After you left, she called, and they had a really big fight. It wasn't pretty."

I nodded. "Maybe we should do a double date, take the pressure off him a little."

Derek's face lit up. "You'd do that?"

"Sure." His friend was definitely growing on me, and he'd been a huge help with all the party planning. "I mean, I like Liam well enough. It'll be fun."

"I'll talk to him. Maybe set something up for next weekend."

Liam had disappeared when we returned to our chair, and I had a sneaking suspicion that if I checked my bed I'd find him passed out in it. My heart leapt at the thought of spending the night with Derek, even as I scolded myself for the reaction. But it was no use, the game was no longer on my radar. Derek was.

Is the chair smaller? It seemed to have a bad habit of shrinking on me.

My thigh pressed firmly against Derek's, kindling a warmth between us so intense it was nearly a being of its own. His hip bone touched my side as I shifted. My shoulder nestled against his ribs. If I turned a few degrees, I could press my chest to his, and how I ached to do just that. *Screw it. I want to throw my leg over his, straddle him and ride him all the way home.*

I wasn't going to survive the night. My dreams lately had all featured Derek, prominently. And they had not been rated PG. If I slept in his bed tonight, I'd probably wake up screaming his name. *Oh, this is bad.*

The guys started leaving, one by one. I went to clean up the kitchen, Derek escorting his guests out before coming to help. He kept brushing up against me as if the kitchen had shrunk, too. His hand grazed my hip in a familiar way that only stoked the fire within me. *Maybe we should just get it out of our system? A one-time, let-it-all-out orgasm-fest to burn off this tension.* I mulled that over, wondering if it would work.

It wasn't like I was a virgin. *I've slept with other guys, so this shouldn't be any different, right?* I could sleep with Derek, use him for sex and maybe the dreams would calm down. Then we could go back to normal.

When I turned around, I found my body flush with his front. All my softness pressed against his hard angles. And I wanted it, wanted so much more of that delicious friction. *What would he do if I just reached up, grabbed a handful of that silky, black hair, and devoured that delicious mouth of his?*

A loud snore rumbled through the hall, making Derek laugh and snapping me out of my daze. We stepped away from each other.

"Guess Liam's out. Want me to carry you to bed?" His eyes twinkled, teasing me.

I was so far past teasing, I might combust if he looked at me wrong. "Nah, I'll grab my jammies then meet you there. Unless you want me to sleep on the couch."

His eyes narrowed a bit. "My bed's big enough for both of us."

That's settled then. I went to my room, picked out a matching shirt and shorts PJ set, then brushed my teeth and changed in my bathroom. On a whim, I grabbed my book from the end table on my way through. If nothing else, I'd read in the living room, go to bed a bit later, avoiding all the awkwardness.

Derek perched on the end of the bed when I came in, socks discarded. His shirt was next. Then he saw my book. "Whatcha got there?"

"It's called a book." Sarcasm weighed my tone.

His eyelids settled halfway down, giving me a dry look. "No shit. What's the book about?"

"Just a romance." *This was a bad idea.* I hadn't realized he'd be interested. It was one of those old romance novels with the half-naked guys on the cover. I found them a dime a dozen at yard sales and thrift stores. They were so deliciously fun to read, plus I could afford them.

Interest sparked in his eyes.

Crap, I was too nonchalant.

"Let me see it."

I shook my head. "Nah. I thought maybe I'd go read on the couch for a few."

The muscles in his thighs bunched as he stood then slowly stalked toward me. "Why can't I see the book, Cupcake?"

Biting my lip, I glanced behind me, angling for the door. "It's not that you can't see it. It's just really none of your business."

Then he pounced.

I ran. He chased me around the kitchen island. His warm hand brushed my hip, almost getting a handhold, but he came up empty. We circled the couch in the living room, narrowly missing the end table. On our second lap around the kitchen, his long arm stretched farther than mine, plucking the book from my hand.

"Ha hah!" He got a good look at the cover even as I chased him. "Seems like some good bedtime reading."

"Give it back." I couldn't even play dirty and grab his shirt because he wasn't wearing one. *Stinker*.

He darted down the hallway, and I put on a burst of speed, catching him as he turned into the bedroom. We landed on the bed, me on top, pinning his arms above his head.

I breathed heavily. From the running or from the tension between us, I wasn't sure. A thrill tore through me as I looked down at him, his wrists under my hands. "Now, say 'uncle.' And I'll let you go."

Those deep blue eyes locked with mine, my hair forming a strawberry blonde curtain around us. "Why would I want to do that?"

I tightened my grip. "I have you pinned, so I win." *Duh*.

His chuckle rumbled through me, sending shockwaves rippling up my core in a most delicious way. "That's a matter of perspective." He shifted ever so slightly, and suddenly I could feel every solid inch of his hard length against my apex. "Maybe I like the view."

I glanced down at the V-neck sleep shirt. The way I leaned down gave him a full view of my bare chest. My eyes flicked back to his, my breath catching at the intensity there.

"Maybe I like the way you feel, too." His hips rolled, pressing his cock against me, separated only by a few thin layers of cloth. "What about you, Cupcake? Are you going to surrender?"

It wasn't in me to surrender. *Ever.* I shook my head infinitesimally, keeping my eyes locked on his.

He smiled. "Good." Then he closed the gap and kissed me, rolling his hips once more.

As our mouths danced, I got the friction I'd been dreaming of. The hard peaks of my breasts brushed just right against the fabric of my shirt and his chest. Derek set a steady rhythm with his hips, and I met his pace, groaning into his mouth as the pleasure built inside me. I rode him. I was desperate for any scrap of contact, and just this much felt amazing. Soon I was on the edge, then I spiraled over, shuddering and gasping my release. He pulsed under me, both of us coming in our pants like a pair of horny teenagers.

A smile danced on his lips as he breathed my name. "Avery."

I smiled in answer as I stared into those beautiful blue eyes looking up at me in adoration. A warmth bloomed in my chest, setting off the first flickers of panic as I crashed back to Earth. I blinked, inhaling a shaky breath.

What did I just do? I jerked away, rolling off him. Panic hit me full force, waves of it choking out the flutters of pleasant comfort I'd almost allowed myself to feel in Derek's arms.

"I'm going to the bathroom." I bit out the words, rushing to the hall. I hurried through my dark room, fumbling for dry underwear to put on in my bathroom. I'd crossed a line for myself, my heart, for us. *This is fake. All of it.* And here I was tackling him like a sex-starved hound dog. *Maybe I could blame it on the romance novel? Sorry, Derek, I was horny because of the book. Thanks for the dry humping. Let's go back to where we were? Fuck!*

My flight or fight instincts kicked in, my adrenaline pumping as my body assessed the danger creating the ever-increasing panic inside me. The apartment felt too small, my emotions too big. I grabbed a pair of track pants, sliding them on over my pajamas. A hoodie came next, then I stuffed my bare feet into a pair of tennis shoes.

I listened in the hallway for Derek, the light from his room streaming through the partially open door. A toilet flushed, and I knew it was now or never. I shoved my phone and my key into my pocket, then raced out of the apartment door. It clicked shut behind me, and I stared at it for a long second. An image of Derek's blue eyes filled with the pain I knew he'd feel when he discovered my absence hovered before me. I didn't want to hurt him, but I had to protect myself.

Pushing aside the image, I spun away from the door, away from Derek, and rushed down the stairs into the frigid night. A driving energy propelled me. I walked along, hands in my pockets as I desperately tried to rebuild my walls, to put some distance between me and Derek. But the warmth of his touch lingered, the fiery passion of his kiss, the delicious tingles of pleasure radiating —

I shook my head, cutting off the memories. Instead, I thought about my dad. I pictured the day I returned home from the tour, how callous Mother had been about his diagnosis, how she'd just left him to deal with the onset of the mind-stealing disease on his own. I'd ran that day, too. Mother walked into the house, our screen door slamming in my face. I couldn't handle the enormity of what she'd done, so I'd turned around, racing down the driveway, running until my side felt like a knife had been plunged into it and my lungs had a hippo sitting on them.

More images came to me. Daddy in his small room, tucked into his bed, staring at the TV like a mindless automaton. The blank expression on his face, not a trace of recognition in his eyes whenever I was introduced. And Mother, the way she dismissed all my emails, all my research.

My resolve thickened, and I found the strength to pull my walls into place once more. Only then did I turn around. Only then did I allow myself to climb the stairs to our apartment. I shucked off my shoes and the insulating outer layer. The couch was where I should stay, but the warmth of Derek's bed called to me. And I wanted to test the strength of my walls.

My phone lit the way, and I stopped when I realized I had several missed calls, as well as a few messages. I flipped over to them, wondering why I hadn't heard my phone.

They were all from Derek. No voicemails. His first text asked where I was and if I was okay. The second said he was worried about me, that he hoped everything was all right. And the third said he was going to bed, but to wake him if I wanted to talk.

I tiptoed back to his dark room, grateful for the reprieve as I slipped into bed next to him. His breathing was deep and even. A small part of me wondered why he'd given up so easily, why he hadn't tried to find me or wait up for me, but I pushed it aside. That wasn't what I wanted anyway.

My mind still raced, but I curled up on my side, away from Derek, determined to sleep. I focused on his breaths and the rhythm they held as my eyelids grew heavier. At some point, I drifted off.

When I opened my eyes the next morning, I found Derek staring back at me. "Holy shit."

"Good morning to you, too."

My brain scrambled to think of something, anything, but he beat me to it.

"Whoever came up with that phrase anyway? There's nothing holy about poop."

And it was so unexpected, so much like something I'd say, that I couldn't help but laugh.

Derek smiled. "That's better. I'm glad to see you in one piece. What happened last night?"

Panic flared in me, and my eyes darted side to side. I didn't want to tell him too much, how I'd crossed the line I'd drawn for myself. "I just needed to think."

A concerned frown crossed his face. "I get it if you need space, but you don't have to run away to get it. You can just ask." Those blue eyes studied me. He reached out to touch my cheek, a tentative, featherlight brush of his fingertips. "About last night...I liked making you come, that we both did."

Holy shit again. He'd addressed it, just like that. I hadn't been expecting him to be so direct, and it put me even more off balance. My cheeks were hot as I stammered out an explanation. "It's just that stupid book. And I'm always extra horny before my period." *Wait, did I really say that? And my period.* I quickly did the math. *Yeah, that means my pile of shit is growing rapidly.*

Derek stared at me like I'd grown three heads.

Embarrassed beyond belief, I eased out of bed, trying to stay on my side as much as possible. When I peeked under the sheets, I winced to see a quarter-sized red dot. *I cannot catch a break.* "Um, I'm sorry, Derek. It looks like I started last night, and there's a little bit of blood on your sheets." I sighed. "Let me go get cleaned up, then I'll come back and wash them okay?" I started to back out of the room, unsure what state my shorts were in.

"Wait, Avery. It's okay." He paused. "I mean, don't worry about the sheets. Can we talk about last night?"

"Right now?" I clenched my legs together, hoping I wasn't bleeding down them. My first day was always heavy.

He nodded. "C'mon, I just want to talk. Please, let's figure out what happened last night. Then you can run away with whatever excuse you can come up with."

"My period is not an excuse." I snorted. "Look, your sheets have a spot this big on them." I held up my fingers. "That came from me. I have stuff going on down there I need to go tend to, or I'm going to have an even bigger mess. I can't just stop the flow to have a little chat with you. It doesn't work like that." I huffed out of the room, thoroughly in a horrid mood.

To top it all off, Liam was still there, snoring away. I made sure to bump into the side of the bed and slam my drawers, but all he did was snort, then roll onto his back.

Men.

I stomped off to shower.

Chapter Twelve

After my shower, I realized I'd forgotten my pants. I got dressed otherwise and poked my head out of the bathroom door, a towel wrapped around my waist. The hall was clear, and my bed was empty.

Maybe all my stomping around had woken Liam after all.

Pants found, hair in a don't care messy bun, I was beyond ready for breakfast. Maybe I'd get lucky, and Derek would be working out. Or maybe he'd be in the shower. I padded out of my room just in case, breathing a sigh of relief when it was just me.

Then I saw a huge bouquet of flowers on the island. *What?* A folded piece of paper with *Cupcake* scrawled across it sat at the base of the vase, my book next to it. I unfolded the paper.

Avery,

I'm sorry. I'm sorry that I pushed you this morning when you obviously had more pressing things to take care of. And I'm sorry if I was too direct.

I wanted to say thank you for last night. Not just the ending, but the fun and the teasing. It's been a long time since I've had anything close to whatever this is between us, and I really don't want to lose it. If you're interested in pursuing more activities like last night, just know I'm 'up' for it.

There are waffles and bacon in the microwave. And coffee in the pot.

Derek

I set down the note, unable to process what I was seeing. My shower hadn't been that long. *How in the world did he find flowers in that short a time? And waffles?*

When I opened the microwave, there was another note on the dish.

Maple syrup in the fridge or ice cream in the freezer. Thought I'd cover both bases, just in case.

My attitude softened a little because that was the sweetest thing ever. I definitely deserved some ice cream today, slathering it on my waffle. I drowned my coffee with creamer and crunched on my bacon. Then I read his note again, wishing he'd been clearer.

Up for more activities. Could he be any vaguer? I began cutting my waffle as I pondered the meaning. *Friends with benefits, fuck buddies, occasional stress relief? Did I want any of those?* My head really started to hurt by the time breakfast was over. I shoved the note in my purse, took a good whiff of the flowers, and sent a smiley face with a 'thank you for breakfast' text to Derek. I didn't want to be rude after all, and it was truly sweet.

I muddled through my classes, thankful when they were over so I could meet up with Gina. It was a relief to tell her everything.

She rolled her eyes when I told her how I'd run away last night. "Of course you did. That's what you always do."

My glare only made her raise an eyebrow at me. I couldn't protest because she was right. I got to the part about having my period, and she sympathized with me.

"He said what? Like he thought you could turn it off?" She snorted. "Idiot."

I nodded. "And Liam was still in my room." I kept going, telling her what I had found after the shower and handing her the note to read herself.

"You got a real apology, plus breakfast and flowers."

My grumbles cut off when she crossed her arms and widened her eyes.

"Honestly, Avery. Derek's one of the best guys I know. He's not perfect, he's going to screw up. But look." She jabbed a finger at the letter. "He admits it! How many guys do that? And on their own, without prompting or the silent treatment? He was probably just worked up after you ran away last night, thinking you were brushing him off again."

The anger that had lingered in me ebbed as I thought about it from his point of view. "But what about the other thing?"

Gina's eyes skimmed the note again. "Exactly what part of this is supposed to confuse me?"

I jabbed my finger to the line on the page. "It's not like he spells it out. 'I'm up for more activities.' What's that supposed to mean? Golly gee, you're good at getting me off, come do it again sometime?" I dropped my head onto the table, banging it a few times for good measure.

"Avery." Gina waited for me to look at her, and when I didn't, she gave my hair a solid yank.

With a yelp, I sat up, rubbing my scalp.

"You need to pull your head out of your ass and realize what I've been telling you this whole time. That boy is crazy for you. He's trying to talk to you about this but obviously doesn't know how. And you're not helping. He found you a bouquet of flowers, fresh waffles, maple syrup, ice cream and crispy bacon in the time it took you to shower. Plus, he kicked Liam out of there. Look at the big picture, it's so obvious."

My forehead crinkled. I felt it. "What is?"

"You two are made for each other." She frowned, reaching across the table to rest a hand on my arm. The harshness in her eyes eased as she stared at me, sincerity and concern taking a front seat. "I'm not sure what you're waiting for, girl, but I'm afraid you're going to wait too long. You can't avoid him forever, and eventually this fake thing will be over. Derek will only play this game for so long. By then it might be too late for you. If it were me, I wouldn't miss a chance to show him how I really felt."

And risk him laughing in my face, telling me I'm nothing like his Princess? That I'm just a warm body, a placeholder until she's back in his life again? Or give my heart to him, only to have him abandon me when I need him most? An image of my dad hovered in my mind.

But I looked at my friend's earnest expression and I couldn't tell her that. Not again, not with that hopeful look plastered all over her face. Instead, I moved my hand out from under hers to swipe a stray piece of hair behind my ear. "I'll think about it."

Then I changed the subject, asking how she and Josh were doing. Gina took the bait. They'd been having some problems of their own, mostly him complaining that she was too busy with working all the time and juggling a full class load.

I half-listened, my mind still mulling over things with Derek. When she finished venting, I kept her talking. I wasn't ready to go home yet. We ended up staying for a couple more hours, covering all the subjects from school to work to more on boys. It was pretty late when she dropped me off, and the living room was empty when I came in. A weight lifted off my chest.

There was a sticky note on my door.

Double date with Liam on Friday, if that's still okay?

I scribbled 'Yep' with a smiley face and stuck it on his partially open door before tiptoeing back to my room.

Tuesday was so busy I didn't even try to avoid Derek. It just happened. I left while he was working out, went to all my classes, worked my shift at the coffee shop, then met with a study group in the library. I stayed there, working on a few other projects pretty late.

When I came home, he was already asleep, and there was another sticky note on my bedroom door.

Holding down the fort is lonely without you.

My throat was thick as I read it. I had to reply, scrambling for a sticky note.

Super busy couple days. Miss you, too.

I added the last part against my better judgment but couldn't bring myself to redo it.

Wednesday morning was the same. Unfortunately, I forgot my textbook for my afternoon class. I ran home to get it before lunch with my dad so I could go from there straight back to campus. In a foul mood, I rushed in the door.

"Hey," Derek said, as he shut his laptop and stood up from the couch. He flashed me that genuine megawatt smile which I did not have time to be blinded by. "What are you doing? Can we have lunch?"

"Sorry." I shuffled past him, but he followed me to my room, watching me throw things around as I searched for my book. "I already have a date."

"What are you looking for?"

Head half under my bed, ass in the air, I called, "My economics book. I can't find it." Not there either.

"It's on the end table in the living room."

I sat back on my heels, glancing at him as he smirked down at me. "You're enjoying this aren't you?"

"Immensely." He followed me to the living room, pulling on his shoes and grabbing a jacket. A baseball cap pulled low on his head completed the outfit.

"Where are you going?"

"To lunch with you."

The words caught me off guard. My heart thudding in my chest, I stopped with my hand on the doorknob. "I told you I already have a date." *He can't do this to me.* I wasn't prepared for any close proximity to him. *Not yet.*

He arched an eyebrow at me. "Well, it can't be with another guy since we're fake dating. And if you're a lesbian, then I doubt she'll mind your roomie tagging along since it's just lunch." The corners of his mouth turned down as he cocked his head. "Maybe you're bi?"

No way do I have time for this and I'm not in the mood for his teasing. I yanked open the door, narrowly avoiding hitting Derek in the face. He reared back at my forcefulness. A little niggle of guilt tugged at me as I opened my bag and stuffed in my book while hurrying to the elevator.

Derek's phone dinged. "Good. Greg's waiting for us downstairs."

That'll speed things up rather than me waiting for an Uber or a taxi. But ugh, doesn't Greg have anything better to do than be on call for Derek all day?

"Well, that's what I pay him for."

Shit, did I say that out loud? I gritted my teeth together, making sure no more words escaped. The elevator was empty, so I tucked myself into the back corner. Derek followed, finger hovering above the button, looking to me for permission before he pushed it. *Why is he so perfect?* The thought deflated my remaining anger at Derek like a knife to a balloon, and I realized I was actually mad at myself for letting him in at all. My head fell back against the elevator wall with a dull thud. *What a mess.*

He leaned against the wall next to me. Those blue eyes watched me from beneath the brim of his cap as he sighed, then he stuck his hands in his jeans' pockets. "What am I doing wrong, Avery?"

I nearly laughed out loud, catching myself at the last second. Here I was thinking he was perfect, and he asked what he was doing wrong. Luckily, the doors opened just then. We hurried outside. Greg had brought the Town Car this time, thank heavens. I gave him the address, and Derek shot me a funny look. He opened his mouth to ask, but I silenced him with a glare, digging in my bag for my notecards.

"It's a ten-minute ride, and I planned on studying during it. I have a test after lunch that I have to ace. And I'm late because of that dumb book."

There was silence for a minute. "I could quiz you."

I'd be stupid to pass up the offer, no matter how much I wanted to ride in silence on separate sides of the car. "Actually, that'd be amazing. Thank you." I reluctantly handed over the cards, and he spent the ride asking me about various market models, supply and demand trends, scenarios and hypotheticals that would be similar to what was on our test.

As we pulled into my parents' driveway, he checked my last answer. "Not one wrong, great job."

Our fingers brushed as he handed the cards back, electricity jolting through me, right to my very needy core. I pressed my thighs together as I bit out a strained, "Thanks." *Why did he have to come along?* I felt so vulnerable. My walls weren't nearly thick enough for this. Not yet.

"Why are we at your mother's house?"

But I was already out of the door, leaning over to talk to Greg. "I only have forty-five minutes. Can you drop me at campus after? I'm not sure where he's going."

Greg nodded, his eyes flicking over to Derek then back to me. "Of course. Hey, is everything okay with you two?"

I pasted on a bright, forced smile. "Us? Yeah, we're fine. Everything's fine. See you soon." Derek kept up with me as I raced up the steps.

Patty met me at the door, giving me an exuberant hug. "You're running late, child. Kyle was about to have a conniption, and that man never has a feather out of place. Get going." She patted Derek's cheek. "Hello again. Still taking care of our girl?"

He muttered something that sounded a little too much like "when she'll let me" for my taste, but I was already rushing down the hallway. *Maybe I misheard.*

"Kyle, I'm here. I'm so sorry. My boyfriend had a change of plans and came along."

"It's all right, Miss Avery. See you in forty-five." He started out of the door.

Patty came in with a wheeled cart right then. "Kyle, sugar, you take your full hour. I'll sit with him the extra fifteen."

"You sure, Miss Patty?" He grinned his thanks when Patty nodded.

Derek stood off to one side of the room, looking out of place. I ignored him and Patty as she got out a card table from the closet.

I stood next to Daddy, keeping my voice quiet so I didn't startle him. "Hey, Steve."

His eyes fluttered open, and he took me in, scrunching his eyebrows together.

"It's me, Avery." I tried, like I always did.

"Hello there." His voice was the same, but those familiar eyes looked at me the same way one would a stranger. "My daughter's name is Avery."

My throat grew tight, as it did every week. "Can I have lunch with you? I heard we're having meatloaf, mashed potatoes and green beans."

A wobbly smile stretched over his face. "That's my favorite dinner. But only if there's gravy, too."

"Can't have mashed potatoes without gravy." I remembered how he always used to say the words with me, our voices blending together.

"That's right." He gave an assertive nod.

Patty came over with a tray, its legs extended to go over his lap. "Here you go, Steve. You eat up now."

"Oh, thank you. This looks delicious." And he dug right in.

I sat down at the table near his bed, Derek next to me. Patty brought us each a plate.

"Thank you," Derek said to her. "It does look delicious."

"He eats the same thing every Wednesday. It's not on his approved menu, but I've tried to make it a bit healthier. Ground turkey instead of beef, less fat in the gravy. Half-cauliflower mashed potatoes." Patty gave me a soft smile. "It makes sure our girl gets to eat with her daddy."

I returned the smile, reaching out to squeeze her hand. "Thanks, Patty. See you in a bit."

Derek looked around the room. "Your dad's a sports fan, huh?"

Rolling my eyes, I redirected the question to my dad. "Steve, this is my friend Derek. He noticed the stuff on the walls and wants to know if you like football." My dad has Alzheimer's. He's not dumb.

Daddy chuckled. "I'd say that's an understatement. If you asked my wife, she'd say there's only one thing she ever worried about me loving more than her, and that was football."

The tired joke fell a little flat now that I knew who my mother really was. Derek reached over to squeeze my shoulder, and I gave him a tight smile, suddenly grateful he was there.

"But Avery." Dad shook his head. "Every time the Lions played, my girl would scream and shout at the top of her lungs. She loved that team with all her heart. You'd have thought they were her family, she invested so much of herself in them." Daddy's eyes lit up. His whole face brightened as he talked about me. "One year I gave her this old Barry Sanders jersey, and you'd have thought I gave her the moon."

A lump grew in my throat, my voice thick as I said, "I still have that jersey. I wear it every time they play."

Dad's fork dropped as he looked at me, recognition flaring in his eyes. "Avery? Is that you?"

Oh. Oh my, he knows who I am. My heart stopped as it registered. I stood up, nearly knocking over the table in my haste to take advantage of the moment, unsure how long it would last. "Daddy? You know me?"

Tears gathered in the corners of his eyes as he held out his arms. "Of course I know you. My little girl, I always know my little girl. I've missed you, honey. Come here and give me a squeeze."

My cheeks were wet as I wrapped my arms around my father. Disbelief flooded me. *Daddy knows who I am!*

"It's been so long."

My heart broke that he thought I hadn't been there, but I had to seize these few precious moments. I swallowed hard, and my throat was thick with tears. "I know, Daddy. I've just been waiting for the right time."

"Tell me about yourself. What are you up to? How's school?" He scooted over, keeping an arm around me.

So I laid my head on his shoulder, and I did. When I stopped talking, I realized his breathing was deep and steady, his chin drooping on his chest. Patty came in a few minutes later. Derek intercepted her, guiding her back to the hallway.

I kissed my father's forehead. "Thanks for seeing me, Daddy. I love you." His soft snores filled the room as I moved the tray to the table, then I pulled the covers up to his chest. I felt shaky, wrapping my arms around myself as I fought to get my churning emotions under control while I walked into the hall.

Patty took me in her arms. "Oh, child, I'm so glad you had a few minutes with him. I'll see you next week, okay?"

My cheeks were still wet as I swiped at them, nodding. She let go of me, pushing me into Derek's open arms. I didn't resist, not ready to face the world on my own yet. We walked down the hall together until I paused by a bench seat in the foyer. "I just need a minute."

He nodded. "Sure."

I sat down, tugging his arm so he sat with me. Then I leaned into him, laying my head against his broad shoulder. "I'm sorry I was mean to you."

One large hand scooped up my legs and brought them over his, then he cuddled me against his chest. "Oh, Cupcake."

My nose was still stuffy from crying, so I sniffled against his chest, shaking my head. "I need a ridiculous nickname for you. Why'd you pick Cupcake?" I felt him shrug.

"Because of that night at dinner with my parents when my mom said you looked delicious. You were so annoyed, saying you could see it if you were dressed in ruffles, then maybe you could be a cupcake. It just fit." Another shrug lifted his shoulders. "Plus…you taste so sweet when I kiss you?"

It was ridiculous, over the top sappy, but it made me smile. A watery smile, but a smile nonetheless. I peeked up at him. "The only nickname I can think of for you is carrot. And that just doesn't seem appropriate. Or fun."

He snorted. "You can do better."

I sighed as I let my head fall back on his shoulder. "I have to go take a test now."

"Want me to carry you?" His soft words resonated with me.

Yes. "No. I've got this." Reluctantly, I shifted off him, away from his comforting warmth.

He opened the door for me. "I know what'll cheer you up."

"What?" I made my way down the steps.

His voice lowered so his words were just for me. "Picturing me naked."

Chapter Thirteen

I came home that night to an empty apartment, feeling drained. Derek was hanging out with Liam tonight, but he'd told me to text him if I needed anything. I grinned remembering his sweetness. Then I called Gina. We chatted for a while, and I told her about my dad, about those few precious moments of him seeing me. She was so happy for me.

Sprawled on the couch, I flipped on the TV, trying to find something to watch. Nothing sounded good so I switched to my book. Next thing I knew, I was being tucked into bed.

"It's been a while since you did this," I mumbled sleepily. The rumbly chuckle I loved sent a spiral of warmth curling through me.

"Good night, Cupcake."

It seemed like he hovered a moment, but when he didn't say more, I rolled over. He pressed a kiss to my temple, and I hummed happily before drifting off to sleep. My dreams were filled with Derek, even more prominent than before, and I woke up to an empty bed, an empty apartment and an ache in more than one place.

Tonight. We'll talk tonight.

But fate had other ideas. I got through my normal day on campus, having lunch with Gina after insisting I pick the restaurant. *No more food poisoning for me.* Then I went to the coffee shop, where I ended up pulling a double shift. We stayed open until two in the morning Thursday through Saturday, and someone called in sick. Since I didn't have class the next day, I was the logical choice to stay.

By the time I crawled into bed, all thoughts of anything but sleep evaded me. Friday, I woke up to find a note on the island with details about our double date that night. Derek had a meeting with his father for most of the day. He'd be back at four to get cleaned up for the date. Liam and Carla would be over at five for cocktails, so I had the apartment to myself—an unusual occurrence.

It was already noon. I puttered around, grabbing food and coffee, wasting an hour scrolling on my phone. Figuring out my outfit for the night was a battle, and I eyed my shower, wishing I had a tub. An idea hit me. *Derek won't care if I use his.* A soak sounded heavenly, especially since my period was over. *And if I set an alarm on my phone, I'll be out of the way before he's even home.* I gathered up my stuff, including my book. I even found some bubble bath.

First, I showered, shaved and got all the chores out of the way. Then I ran the water, so it was steaming when I sank down into the bubbly goodness. I set the alarm for twenty minutes before Derek was due home, plenty of time to get out of his way. My current romance novel was about a stowaway girl on a pirate ship. Of course, she got caught nearly right away, by the swoon-worthy captain nonetheless. The steam rating on this book was high. *Phew*. I read for quite a while, enjoying the story.

When I put the book down, I laid my head back against the edge of the tub and closed my eyes. Images flashed through my mind, an unbidden fantasy taking over, Derek playing the part of the pirate. Soon I felt overwhelmed and needy. I reached for the handheld shower wand before I knew what I was doing.

Scooting up against the back of the tub so my breasts were out of the water, I guided the warm, pulsing spray between my legs, searching for just the right spot. I imagined Derek kneeling in front of me, Derek pushing my legs open. I rolled a taut nipple between my fingers, pretending my hand was Derek's. A moan escaped my lips.

It didn't take long for an orgasm to build. I could almost hear Derek whisper my name, a low growling sound. "Derek." I tilted my head back, moaning a little louder.

"Avery."

My name sounded so real, and it was just what I needed to push me over the edge. When the spasms faded, I sat up, my eyelids fluttering open. And there stood Derek, shirtless, with one hand on the door handle, not moving. He stared at me, a tempest of emotions swirling in his intense gaze.

He said my name. I came to the sound of his voice. Embarrassment washed over me in a tidal wave. My eyes locked on him as I sank down in the water, hiding under the cover of the bubbles.

His mouth closed with a snap, and he spun on his heel, closing the door firmly behind him.

Why me? That was my first question. My second was, *now what?* After letting out the water, I stood up to rinse off the bubbles, then stepped out onto the thick bath mat, just as my alarm went off. *Perfect timing, thanks a lot.*

The door opened once more as I reached for my towel. I gripped it to my dripping body, a flimsy shield from Derek's intense blue eyes. Every muscle in his body was taut, rigid. I swallowed, wishing I could escape his scrutiny and the feelings welling up in me.

His voice was hoarse as he said, "Avery, I didn't mean to barge in. I heard a noise and I didn't even know you were home. I don't know what just happened. You don't have to explain if you don't want to. But we have a double date with Liam in an hour and a half, and I don't think there's any way I can go like this." He waved a hand in the general area of his hips, so of course my eyes drifted there.

His jeans were definitely straining.

Derek's words sounded rougher under the weight of my gaze. "I'd like to think that what I saw means you want me, even half as much as I want you."

I blinked at him. *He wants me?*

"I dream about you all the time. About touching you, exploring you. Being inside you."

My lips parted as hope burst through my fragile barrier, knocking aside any feeble protests of wanting to protect my heart or questions about the Princess. Need flooded me, and I ached for him to fulfill his words.

"What do you say, Avery?" He hadn't moved, just waited for my answer with his hand still on the door handle as if it were all that were holding him there.

I let the towel drop to the floor. "But I'm all wet." And I bit my lip.

"Avery." My name was a groan—permission had not yet been granted.

Our eyes locked as I took one step off the bath mat. "I was reading my latest romance book, about a pirate. It was very exciting, so I may have gotten carried away in your tub."

"Avery, please." He didn't move.

One more step toward him. "Pirates don't say please."

And that was all he needed. Heedless of my dripping body, he closed the distance between us, taking my face in his hands. Our lips crashed together, needy and desperate.

I slid one finger into the waistband of his jeans, popping the button and adjusting him so his length was set free. It was impressive.

His groan rumbled through us. "I want to take my time. I want to explore every inch of you. I want to make you come over and over again, but I don't think I can wait another second to be inside you right now." He stared at me, all his intensity shining out of those deep blue eyes.

I smirked. "Good thing you already did that."

He narrowed his eyes in confusion.

Jerking my head over to the tub, I said, "The book made me all hot and bothered, but that wasn't what I was thinking of when I...you know." I started to duck my head, but he caught my chin, searching my gaze.

His lips crashed onto mine once more, asking his question around our kiss. "Did you actually come when I said your name?"

I nodded into his mouth.

"Fuck. I need a condom." He broke away from me, turning around to dig through a drawer in the vanity. "Aha." His jeans and boxers hit the floor as he walked back, gloriously naked as he approached me.

"Wait." I stared at him, letting my eyes rove over every delicious inch of his sculpted body.

He paused. "What?"

"Nothing. Just actually thinking of you naked while you're naked. A novelty for me." I reached out to run a hand down his arms, his chest.

His cock jumped as he pushed the condom over the tip. "Sorry if this isn't what you had in mind. We can move to the bed—"

I pressed my lips to his, pulling his body flush against mine. "Beds aren't very pirate-y. Now shut up or start saying 'arr' a lot more."

Desire showed in every inch of his face. He nudged my legs apart, backing me up against the wall. Unable to get the right angle, he cursed, then in a very smooth, sexy move, he picked me up by the thighs, spread me open and shoved his dick inside. I welcomed him, completely ready. My ankles locked around his back, and I dug my nails into his shoulder blades as he kept one hand cupped under my ass to support me. I'd never had sex like this and I loved it. Anticipation coiled within me, rocketing me toward release.

"Shit, Cupcake, I'm not going to last long." He thrust into me, fast and furious, hitting all the right spots.

"Me either," I gasped out, moaning as he hit a particular spot, then I saw stars, clenching around him, over and over.

He joined me, pulsing into me. Our heavy breathing was the only sound for several long seconds before he unhooked my ankles and slid out of me. His hand stayed on my ass though, the rest of my body still pressed against him. "You're not going to run away this time, are you?"

I shook my head, then I giggled.

"What?"

"You said, 'Arrr you'."

He stared at me. I laughed harder, and he finally joined me. He caught me off guard when he captured my bottom lip between his teeth, sucking it in. Then he softened his mouth into a gentle kiss. "I'll play pirate with you any time."

"Hmm, that could be interesting." I shimmied away from him, stepping back into the tub to clean up.

He walked in next to me. "But only if you call me Captain."

Oh, that's perfect. He just gave me his nickname, and he has no idea. I finished wiping down, then dried myself off with a towel as he started up a shower. It felt so…normal. So right. "I'm going to my room to get ready."

"Okay." The shower curtain opened a crack as he peered out. "Need a kiss for the road?"

"Don't you mean the plank?" I leaned in for a kiss, and he turned the spray full blast on my just-dried body. "Jerk! What was that for?"

He kissed my cheek, shutting the shower curtain. "You didn't call me Captain."

I muttered under my breath as I dried off yet again. This time I gathered up my things, then walked by the sink when an idea struck me. I quietly filled a cup with cold water, tiptoeing back to the shower. I threw it at him, the yelp he let out making me laugh as I ran away. "That's what you get, Captain!"

Back in my room, the Princess tried to weasel into my thoughts, but I pushed her aside. I needed to enjoy this time with Derek. It wasn't like I was professing my undying love for him. It was just sex. *Damn, good sex…* I smiled, losing my train of thought to the memory of Derek shoving me up against the wall, the memory of that orgasm bursting through me.

The outfit I'd chosen didn't seem quite right anymore. I wanted to go bolder, sexier. So I raided my closet again, finding a cute forest green dress with a deep V-neckline. It showed off my cleavage with the right bra but had a flared waist that flattered my hips as well. Paired with a cropped three-quarter sleeve black sweater, it would be perfect. *After Derek zips me up, that is.* I did my makeup and left my hair down, putting in a few loose curls around my face. Adding a long necklace to emphasize my cleavage, I stepped back to make sure I wasn't missing anything.

Derek leaned in the doorway just as I was perfecting my lipstick. "I think there's something wrong with that dress." He looked amazing in a dark-gray blazer, with a fitted white shirt and light pants.

I rolled my eyes at him. "Just wanted to see if you're as good at putting dresses on as you are at taking them off."

"Oooh, challenge accepted." He crossed the room to stand behind me.

The zipper was low, starting below my panty line.

"A little sneak peek, I see." His warm fingers held the dress out a bit. He peered down at my backside as I giggled, reaching back to smack him.

"Stop it. You already had some." A thrill went through me at his touch, my heart fluttering with his ridiculous flirtations.

"Ah, that was the main course. Now I want dessert." His blue eyes held mine in the mirror, then his gaze skimmed over my breasts, down my front. "But there's so many delicious parts, I just can't decide what to feast on first."

It was like we'd never even had sex—I was that turned on, again.

He ran a finger up my spine, making me shiver. He bent down to kiss his way along my shoulder, up to my neck.

"Derek." His name was a groan and a plea all wrapped into one. I needed more. I needed him.

A knock at the apartment door jerked me out of my aroused haze.

His lips stayed at the crevice where my neck and shoulder met, his tongue swirling the spot gently as his fingers deftly zipped me up. "Damn Liam and his punctuality."

I turned my head so my lips grazed his. "Shut the door on your way out. I need to change my panties." At least I had the satisfaction of watching his eyes darken and hearing him growl as he stomped out of the door to greet his friend. I wouldn't be the only uncomfortable one tonight.

Dry for the moment, I stepped into the hallway to meet our guests.

"Hey, Cupcake, there you are. What took you so long?" Derek's question was edged with a hint of teasing, obviously enjoying putting me on the spot.

"Just a tiny wardrobe malfunction, *Captain*." *If he wants to tease, I'll give it right back.*

He blanched at the nickname being used in front of his friend, and Liam shot him a curious look.

"Nothing for you to worry your pretty little head over." I grinned up at Derek while he tried to hide his glower.

"Captain?" Liam asked. "That's new. How'd that come about?"

"Well, Derek here walked in while I was —"

"Oh they don't want to hear the story, Cupcake. What did you want to drink?" He pinched my butt as he walked behind me, and I bit the inside of my cheek so I didn't yelp.

That's new. I glared over at him. "Whiskey."

Carla wrinkled her nose at my drink choice.

"What are you having tonight, Carla?" I asked politely, ignoring Derek as he poured us drinks.

"Oh." She smiled at me, her breathy voice a tad on the grating side. "Riesling, from right here in Michigan." It was clear her boyfriend had scored brownie points when she laid her head on his shoulder. "Liam found it for me. Isn't he just the sweetest?"

Liam grinned, and I gave him a thumbs up when she couldn't see it. After grabbing a cheese tray from the fridge, I handed it to Derek, taking the opportunity to say, "What was that pinch all about?"

He whispered back, "Pirates like booty."

I snorted so loud I had to clamp a hand over my face. Derek patted me on the shoulder.

Carla's concerned frown was gratifying as she asked, "Is she okay?"

Derek rubbed my back. "Oh, she's just fine. Took something the wrong way, I imagine."

He got an elbow to the ribs for that one, which I covered by handing him the box of crackers. "So what do we want to do tonight?"

We sipped our drinks, me and Derek leaning next to each other on the counter. The cheese and crackers were perfect to tide us over until dinner, whenever and wherever that would be. Getting Carla and Liam to agree on a place was like getting oil and water to stay together.

Carla wasn't a bad person, but it was clear she wasn't right for Liam. She was a veggie-eating, wine-drinking, prim and proper lady. Liam was much more laid-back than she could stand. He enjoyed his steak while it was still mooing, drank his beer from a tankard and wiped his mouth on his sleeve. He might have been raised upper class, but that didn't mean he wanted to act that way every minute.

Derek managed to come up with a solution, a Hibachi grill that had just opened up on the other side of town. They had the regular Hibachi menu, including sushi, and several vegetarian options.

"Nice job, Captain," I told him on the way out of the door.

"Thanks, Cupcake." He linked his fingers through mine as we waited for the elevator. We took the rear facing seats in the limo, Derek pulling me firmly against him. I clenched my thighs together, wanting more already. Of course, Derek noticed and smirked at my discomfort.

I was a little distracted, so I didn't hear the beginning of the conversation, but somehow the subject of escape rooms came up. Carla had never been to one.

"They're so much fun," I told her. "Clues and puzzles. Six people is a good number for most of the ones around here." I turned to Derek. "Know who's really great at escape rooms? Gina. She's amazing at putting all those clues together."

Liam snorted, while Carla looked confused.

"Who's Gina?" she asked.

"Oh, she's my best friend." I grinned, and Carla returned my smile.

"Well, we should all do that some time. Bring her along. Does she have a boyfriend?"

Crap. I tried to keep my smile from faltering as I nodded. *Liam and Gina in a contained room trying to solve puzzles together for an hour? Sounds like a recipe for disaster.*

Carla beamed. "That's perfect then." She latched on to Liam's arm and squealed. "What about tomorrow or Sunday? We don't have any plans, do we, honey?"

I slowly turned to Derek, blinking up at him, pleading for him to help me.

"I'm free. How about you?" He just grinned, peering down into the hole I'd dug for myself.

When I pulled out my phone, I didn't dare look at Liam. I felt his glare from here. "I'll just see if Gina's free then." I took my time texting her the details, along with an apology that I'd volunteered her unintentionally. Her response was immediate. "She and Josh are available tomorrow."

Carla squealed, already looking at escape rooms on her phone. "There's one not far from here with an availability at eleven-thirty tomorrow morning. Should I book it? Says it's for up to eight people."

Derek and I shared a look, then nodded. I texted Gina to let her know.

Carla was over the moon, but if looks could kill, Liam would be sent to jail for my murder. At least dinner was nice. Hibachi chefs amazed me with their skills, the chopping, sliding, scooping, serving. Although Carla refused to catch a piece of shrimp in her mouth, the rest of us were game. The chef tossed a cooked piece of shrimp from the spatula into the air for each of us to catch. I didn't snag mine on the first try, but I nailed it the second, pride shooting through me as I smiled triumphantly at Derek.

There was a chill in the air that I couldn't quite shake, and Derek offered me his blazer. I accepted happily, letting him drape it over my shoulders. His thigh pressed against mine, the casual touch sending thrills through me, making me wish for more. But once he was done eating, his warm hand rested on my leg, just under my hemline.

He shifted over to whisper in my ear, his lips brushing against my skin. "How arrrre you enjoying dinner?"

I bumped his chest with my shoulder, and he squeezed my leg. I grinned. "It's delicious." As I shrugged out of his blazer, I gave him a sidelong look. "But I think I'm warm enough now, Captain."

His smirk was a little on the self-satisfied side.

When we got back to the apartment, I called out good night to Greg who waved. Derek's hand seared my lower back, and I leaned into him. *I can't wait to get him naked, in an actual bed this time.*

Liam shoved his hands in his pockets as he glanced at Carla. He cleared his throat, addressing Derek. "You guys want to hang out some more? We could play games or watch a movie…"

I gripped Derek's upper arm, and he smirked at me. Then he raised his eyebrows, waiting for my permission. I deflated. As much as I wanted Derek to myself, I couldn't tell Liam no. Not when we'd agreed to do this to help them out. I nodded, and my disappointment disappeared in the wake of Derek's megawatt smile.

He brushed his lips against my forehead, murmuring a quiet, "Thank you." To Liam, he said, "Sure, come on up."

Liam's shoulders dropped as he let out a breath. "Great. We'll stop by my place and be over in a few."

I waved goodbye to Carla, and the moment the doors were closed, Derek's lips found mine. I wrapped my arms around his neck, drinking him in. I'd take every second I could get.

Derek's phone hooted as we got to his apartment. He laughed. "Evidently, Carla's pestering Liam about inviting Gina over tonight. She wants to meet her now, have a real party."

My laughter bounced off the hallway walls. "She must have been relentless for him to text you!" I couldn't picture it, Liam actually typing out the words. "Oh, that must have hurt." We shared another laugh. "I'll text her."

In the apartment, I glanced over my shoulder at Derek and crooked my finger. "I need your assistance, Captain."

He stalked after me, sweeping me into his arms, and I squealed. "Not with walking! I can handle that on my own." *Not that I mind this mode of transportation.* I looped my hands around his neck and snuggled into him. "You have a thing for carrying me, don't you?"

His fingers ran along my bare thigh. "Maybe."

I grinned. In my bedroom, he set me down, running his hands up my full length as he straightened. His blue eyes were twin flames as they drilled into me.

"Why did I invite Liam over again?"

One finger traced my neckline, and I reached up to cup his cheek. "Because you're a good friend. One of your many endearing qualities." I pushed onto my tiptoes to press my lips to his.

He gripped my hips to haul me flush against him with a moan. Our mouths melded together, tongues entwining. My hips pressed into him, wanting more. He ripped his mouth away with a groan.

"Okay, if you want help with this dress, we've gotta do it now. Or our company is gonna be getting a show." He adjusted the evidence of his erection. "Not to mention how uncomfortable I'll be."

I trailed my fingers down his chest, following the buttons of his dress shirt toward that delicious bulge. He growled my name, and I pouted a little, but I turned to give him access to my zipper. The cool air hit my heated skin, and we both sucked in a breath.

"All right." Derek's voice was strangled. "Need anything else from me?"

I spun around, letting my gaze rove over him. "Yes. But not anything we have time for right now."

His blue eyes darkened. "Later." It was more than a word. It was a promise.

Gina and Josh arrived not long after Liam and Carla. Derek played host, grabbing everyone drinks and setting out snacks while Gina dragged me to my room.

"Gina, what?"

She shut the door, staring at me. "What happened? Did you and Derek...?" She waggled her eyebrows at me.

"How?" I threw my hands in the air. "Yes. Once before dinner. But it was really quick."

She squealed. "Tell me everything!"

I told her the short version, leaving a few of the more intimate things for myself.

"I knew it, I knew it! He's head over heels for you."

"It's just sex. Ow." I rubbed my arm where she'd smacked me soundly.

"You need to quit that. He's in love with you and has been from the beginning. Wake up."

"This is real life, not some fairy tale." I shook my head, walking into the hallway. "I need a drink."

Derek had staked out our chair, leaving my space open on it along with a glass of whiskey. Instead of sitting beside him, I sat on the floor between his legs. When I took my drink from him, I ran my hand down his thigh before I settled against the chair.

He leaned forward while the others were deciding what we should do. "Everything good?"

I took a sip from my tumbler. "Just the usual interrogations that come with having Gina as a BFF."

He laughed.

The group decided on charades, guys against girls. Gina had an app on her phone for it, and we tried to get our team to guess as many as we could before the time ran out. Nobody could figure out why Derek blushed when he got pirate. Or why I laughed when I had to act out carrot. Even though there were four other people in the room, it felt like it was just the two of us.

When it wasn't our turn, he'd play with my hair, finding a loose piece to twirl between his fingers. Or he'd massage my shoulders and neck, his thumbs feeling like magic on my skin. As the night flew by, so did the drinks, and it just made sense for everyone to stay.

There was one weird moment as we were all saying good night and Liam kissed Carla a little too long. She pulled away, red-faced as we catcalled.

Liam just shrugged, eyeing Derek. "Well, at least I'm not the only one being blue-balled tonight."

Derek's promise echoed in my head, and my gaze locked with his. He just winked.

"All right, girls with me." I rounded up Gina and Carla, who had both come with extra clothes, just in case. I herded them to my room, while Derek pushed the guys down the hall.

He darted back toward me. "Meet here in fifteen minutes, okay?" Then he was gone.

I looked at the clock in my room, counting down each minute as it passed. I raided the couch for a few extra cushions to make a bed, directing Carla and Gina to mine. *Maybe they won't notice me sneaking out.* They both breathed steadily when I crept into the hallway, only five minutes late.

"Hey, Cupcake," was all the warning I got before his whiskey-scented breath mixed with mine. Then he wrapped a blanket around me and hoisted me over his shoulder, true kidnapper style. But he paused, asking in an almost whisper, "Is this okay?"

"Depends on what you're doing." I trusted him, more curious than anything.

"Kidnapping you, then having my way with you." He paused and added an "Arr."

I couldn't stop my grin. "Carry on then, just try not to bounce too much."

"Don't worry, we're not going far." We ducked into the hallway, down one floor and into Liam's apartment. "I have his spare key, for emergencies. I think this counts."

I tried to keep my giggle quiet. "He's going to kill you when he finds out."

After he shut the door behind us, Derek set me down to spread the blanket on the floor of the living room. Liam's apartment had one thing we didn't, a cozy fireplace, which Derek flicked on. When I nibbled on my lip, Derek touched his thumb to my mouth. "He'll never know. Now stop worrying." His hands edged under the hem of my nightgown.

I smirked up at him. "Make me."

He grinned. "Is that a challenge?"

When I didn't waver, his lips found mine in a kiss that felt different than before. A secret part inside me had unlocked in that bathroom earlier today, and I was scared to look too closely at it.

His warm hands grazed over my ribcage and brushed my breasts before he broke the kiss to tug the nightgown over my head. Those blue eyes raked over my nearly naked length, and my breath caught at his intense perusal. I reached for the bottom of his shirt, slipping my fingers up to touch his flat abdomen. A fire ignited between us.

Derek yanked his shirt over his head, then we collided. We ran our hands over every bit of each other in our frantic need to assuage the hungry yearning. His thumbs dipped into the band of my panties, dropping them to the floor. Our lips met in a fury of passion, not parting as he lowered me onto the blanket. He slipped his fingers into me, and I tore my mouth from his, needing to breathe. I gulped in the air, our eyes locked together. I didn't even try to fight the tidal wave crashing over me, and I came under the heat of Derek's gaze.

The delightful bliss was a mere taste of what it would take to satisfy me. I'd crossed a line today, and there was no going back. I not only wanted him—I needed him with an urgency like nothing I'd ever felt before. He ripped the condom open with his teeth, his movements hurried as if he too were under the same spell. When he finally slid into me, I moaned.

It wasn't enough, and I arched against him as he pounded out a furious rhythm. My fingers dug into his back. His hands gripped my shoulders, each of us anchoring the other. I clenched around him, the only warning I had before reaching that pinnacle. His name slipped from my lips in a rough cry as I shuddered in his arms. Several thrusts more, and he went rigid, pulsing into me. I stared up at him, ripples of bliss washing over me as I stared at Derek. His blue eyes held a tenderness that should have frightened me, but instead I basked in it. There was no room for anything else at the moment. He didn't move right away, simply holding my gaze while our breathing steadied.

When he did pull out, he stood, walking over to grab a tissue from the box on the end table. I missed him immediately, but the view of his chiseled back and firm ass made up for it.

"So?" he asked when he'd disposed of the condom. "Did it work?"

I frowned as I sat up and reached for my panties. "Did what work?"

He chuckled. "I guess that's a pretty good indicator." He slid on his pants, then his shirt before he laughed again at my frustrated stare. "You're not worried anymore."

The light bulb clicked on in my mind as I remembered my challenge, and I laughed. "No, I'm not. You definitely succeeded." I yanked on my nightgown and took the hand he offered to haul me to my feet.

He pulled me to him, my chest grazing his. His fingers slipped under my chin and his thumb grazed my bottom lip. "Avery," he whispered, "what am I going to do with you?"

The intensity was too much. If I let myself, I could drown in it. The walls I'd built were crumbling quickly, and I needed to be cautious. Though the thought didn't terrify me as much as it did before, I was careful to hold back a piece of myself, making sure some part of me would stay intact. For now, I dug for my humor. I glanced at the blanket with a grin. "You can do that anytime you want."

Another chuckle rumbled through him before he touched his lips to mine. "One of these days we'll be able to take our time." His hands slid down to grip my waist through the thin fabric of my nightgown. "I want to memorize every inch of you."

I longed for that as well, but it wasn't happening tonight. "Maybe once we don't have an apartment full of people."

One corner of his mouth tipped up. "I'm free tomorrow afternoon. Say, after the escape room?"

My smile wouldn't dim. "No after-party?" He shook his head and I let out a relieved sigh. "It's a date."

Chapter Fourteen

I woke up on my makeshift couch cushion bed to the alarm blaring on my phone. Bleary-eyed with a dull headache, I trudged to the dresser, grabbed clothes and stumbled to the shower. The hot water revived me. The other girls were stirring when I returned, and they took their turns in the shower.

The smell of fresh coffee greeted me when I walked out of my room. My stomach did a funny little flip when I saw Derek in the kitchen, damp-haired and barefoot. Clips of last night flashed through my mind as a soft smile spread over my lips.

I hurried to kiss his cheek. "Good morning."

His dark blue eyes darkened before he turned his head to claim my lips. "Now that's the proper way to say good morning."

Liam emerged, groaning as he saw us. "Guys, it's too early for that shit."

Gina elbowed him in the gut as she walked by. "I disagree. Josh, where's my good morning kiss?" And she got a decent greeting from her boyfriend.

Carla, on the other hand, crossed her arms, refusing to listen when Liam tried to explain that he meant me and Derek, not them.

"Maybe we could go out for breakfast? Then head over to the escape room?" I murmured to Derek, nibbling on his ear.

"Keep doing that, and we can do anything you want," he growled.

I realized we were the center of attention again, and I ducked my head against his chest, my cheeks hot. Gina stared at me, seeing too much, while the others probably just thought it was par for the course for us.

Derek cleared his throat. "Who wants to go for breakfast?"

Everyone agreed. There was a decent restaurant a few blocks away, so we tumbled out of the door. The crisp walk helped wake everyone up. We found a table big enough for six, though Derek and I somehow got the short end of the stick, ending up across from each other. *How is it possible to physically miss someone when they're a table's length away? At least our feet are touching.* Derek's eyes stayed on me while I ordered, no waffles this morning since they didn't have ice cream and were out of maple syrup. I settled for a scramble—eggs, ham, veggies and potatoes all in one dish. And coffee, of course.

Conversation picked up even more as the caffeine entered our veins, clearing out the fog from our late night. Though Liam seemed extra grumpy.

Derek called him on it. "Looking even bluer than usual there, Liam."

He snorted, gaze flitting to me. "Yeah, it sucks, don't it?" He took a sip of coffee, waiting for Derek to commiserate with him. Eyes narrowing, he looked closely at both of us. "Wait a minute, you guys—?"

My boyfriend's smirk said it all.

"When?" Liam held up a hand. "Never mind. Don't want to know."

Gina grinned, leaning over the table toward Liam. "Looks like you owe me."

He grumbled even more but dug out his wallet and forked over a twenty. She winked at me, mouthing a thanks. Carla's frown deepened. I had a bad feeling about her and Liam.

Things went smoother after that. Gina and Josh drove one car to the escape room, unsure of their plans the rest of the day. Derek drove the Mercedes, he and Liam in front, me and Carla in the back. Carla and I chattered the whole way about what to expect, how much fun she'd had with us last night, and other mundane things. Liam sulked in the corner. I watched Derek in the rearview mirror as he eyed his friend, and I could tell he was annoyed at Liam's attitude. Especially since he was the reason we were doing all this.

I touched Derek's sleeve when we got there, my eyes flicking to Carla, letting him know I'd distract her if he wanted a minute with Liam. He nodded, one side of his lips tilting up.

"Carla, come on. There's this adorable store right next to the escape room, and they always have the cutest window displays." I wasn't lying.

It was a store called Props, and they never disappointed. Their stock was unique, handpicked and local. Today's display was done in traffic light colors.

All reds, greens and yellows, staggered throughout the big window. There were aprons, shaker cups and kitchen items. Then there were cute wispy scarves, berets and fingerless gloves. Sassy coasters and magnets sat off to one side. A metal airplane dangled from the ceiling. A crate display held various abstract art made of metal, contrasting nicely with the rough wood.

His lecture evidently over, Derek slid his hand around my waist, pressing a kiss to my temple. "See anything you like?"

I glanced up at him with a smile, staring at him for a beat. "Oh, you mean in the store."

He rolled his eyes but grinned.

"I like that red sculpture down there." On the bottom right was a twisted pile of metal that somehow flowed in a way that made me think of passion. And Derek. "But it's all neat."

Gina strode up, looking at her watch, with Josh in tow. "Let's go, guys. Don't want to be late."

Liam lingered next to Carla, murmuring to her. Carla's face softened, just a little, and she leaned into him.

Once we'd checked in, our guide led us back to our room, explaining the scenario. I was too busy studying Liam and Carla to pay much attention, figuring the others would fill me in when our time started.

Just before the guide finished, Derek nudged me. "Hey, you okay with this?"

I blinked up at him in confusion.

His face was full of concern. "It's all based on cryptography. Completely numbers."

And I really started to look around. Every surface had numbers on it. I'd been in escape rooms before and had no problem, leaving the number puzzles for the others. But this one was different.

The whole room seemed to taunt me, shoving my weakness in my face. I kept my issue with numbers close to my chest, and if we did this room, everyone would know. They would all see what an idiot I was in that field, how inferior I was compared to them, how lacking. There were even numbers on the floor. I shook my head, involuntarily taking a step toward the exit.

Gina came over. "Avery, is this going to work?"

But I was frozen. Long buried names from my school days reared their head along with the bitter memories of laughter and humiliation. I fled to the hallway before I became completely overwhelmed, Gina following me.

"Girl, I should've paid more attention when we were checking in." She wrapped an arm around my shoulder.

Derek came out with the guide. "I need your discretion here." His words were quiet. "I'll talk to you about it more privately in a minute, and I promise I'll make it worth your while. In the meantime, is there some place where our friends can wait?"

The guide escorted the others down the hall. Gina shielded me from their view, but I felt their curious eyes on me.

Derek stepped up. "It's okay, Gina. I've got her."

Gina tightened her grip for a second, waiting until I nodded. Always the protective one, she couldn't help looking out for my best interests. I gave her a small smile.

Derek waited until we were completely alone before asking, "You all right?"

I nodded, trying to fake it. Then I gave up on pretending and shook my head.

"Aww, come here." He wrapped his arms around me, and I sank into his embrace, letting the safety of him chase away the lingering edges of panic. His chuckle rumbled through me. "You must have really been out of it."

Burying my face in his shoulder, I mumbled, "I was watching Liam and Carla." He was quiet for a second, so I looked up at him.

He smiled. "Hopeless romantic."

I stepped out of his arms, needing some space as the entirety of the situation hit me. I stared at the floor, thankfully number-free. Derek's eyes weighed on me, so I forced out my thoughts. "I ruined it for everyone. Carla's going to hate me." Guilt wracked me, knotting my stomach.

"Oh, Avery." He pulled me back, smooshing me to his chest. "No, she's not going to hate you. I've got it covered, trust me, okay?" After we found the others, he left me with Gina. A few minutes later he came back in with the guide. "I get it. Mistakes happen. Just fix it, all right?" His voice was overly patient.

The guide scurried away, head down.

Derek slid his hands in his pockets, the picture of nonchalance. "Sorry about that guys. I've already done that one, and not too long ago. Want to make sure we have the full experience." He gave me a wink.

And that was it—problem solved without anyone blaming me. Just a simple scheduling error. I ducked my head, this time in relief. Derek sat down on the bench next to me, and I burrowed into his shoulder as he wrapped an arm around me. My muffled thanks hopefully reached his ears.

He kissed the top of my head. "I know how you can make it up to me." He leaned down close to my ear. "Just picture me naked."

I knew it was coming, but I still smiled.

They had another room ready for us five minutes later. Gina casted worried glances my way, but I waved her off. "It's okay. Really."

And it was. This one was all about archaeology, set in ancient Egypt, much more up my alley. We awoke a curse on our expedition and had to figure out the cure before our time was up. After pairing off by couples, we each tackled different sections of the room. Derek and I worked well together, flying through puzzle after puzzle. Gina and Josh made a great team. Unfortunately, this was not Carla's thing and Liam did more explaining, or what I'd call mansplaining, than working. Finally, Gina had had enough. We needed their answer to move on to the next one, so she just shoved them out of the way and took over.

We managed to beat the time by five minutes. Carla wasn't speaking to either Liam or Gina and wanted to go home. Derek ordered her an Uber, per her request. We walked her out. She gave me a hug, saying she'd like to hang out sometime, and thanked Derek. Then she was gone.

"If you'd just let her solve the puzzle instead of telling her what to do, you two would've been fine," Gina yelled as she stepped through the door that Josh held open for her.

Liam stomped after her. "She didn't get it."

Gina crossed her arms. "She might have if you'd given her a chance, instead of mansplaining everything. She's smarter than you give her credit for."

Josh tried to distract her, putting a hand on her shoulder. "Hey, Gina, let's—"

"Back off." She stepped away from him. "This isn't about you."

Derek's phone rang, and he glanced at it with a frown. "I have to answer this." He walked over to our car, one finger in his ear to drown out the arguing.

"Maybe if you paid her the slightest bit of attention, then you wouldn't be in this mess right now!" Gina and Liam were now toe to toe, both red-faced.

Josh stood off to the side, looking defeated.

I moved to stand by him. "Hey, you okay?"

Liam began justifying his behavior, but Gina shut him down again.

Josh shook his head. "I'm done. I can't compete with that, especially now that Carla's out of the picture. Maybe they just need to fuck and get it over with."

My jaw dropped as he walked away. Then I looked back at the two of them, Gina and Liam. There was definitely something between them, volatile and explosive. I wondered if it would ever work in the long run, or if they'd kill each other in the process.

Derek came back. "Where'd Josh go?"

I explained what Josh had said.

He let out a low whistle. "Wow, that actually might work."

"Unfortunately, I thought the same thing." We stared at our two best friends still yelling at each other in the middle of the sidewalk in broad daylight. "If we can get them to calm down first."

"I don't know. I've heard make-up sex can be pretty amazing." The look he gave me heated me to my very core.

Maybe I could find something to get mad about. "Well, what are you waiting for? Pick a fight with me!"

Instead of teasing, Derek sighed and raked his fingers through his hair. "Actually, I have a flight to catch."

"What?" I felt like the wind had been knocked out of me. *He's leaving? What about our private after-party and our time to explore?*

"Yeah." He sighed, staring over at the two maniacs on the sidewalk. "Maybe we should just leave them here. See how long it takes them to realize it's just them?"

I grinned. "They did cock-block us last night. Or tried to."

"Let's do it." We ran for the car, laughing as we drove away.

I waited for Derek to explain why he was leaving which he finally did. "So my dad needs someone in Canada to solidify a business deal."

"Why you?" Frustration made my words clipped. *Is the whole universe against us having decent sex? I mean, quickies are great, but...*

"I speak French."

I blinked. *Surely, I misheard that.* "What?"

He rattled off a sentence in a different language.

Very sexy. I filed that knowledge away for later.

"My parents' shipping business is predominately on the Great Lakes, so French was one of my minors. Sometimes they're short of a translator and they call me."

"When will you be back?" *Next Friday is his party.* Worry gnawed at me, wondering if all my hard work had been for nothing.

Something must have given me away because he laughed and patted my leg. "Don't worry. I told Dad in no uncertain terms I had to be back for your party next week. I'll be there. I promise."

My phone rang, and it was Gina, demanding to know where we all went. I threw out a half-hearted apology, filled her in, then told her about Derek leaving. "So I'll call you after he's gone, okay? To see how everything is."

She agreed, still sounding pissed, and we hung up.

I was quiet in the elevator. *It'll be weird in the apartment without him.* We hadn't even had time to talk about this new level of our relationship or explore each other fully or...anything.

He must have felt it too because he frowned. "Sit with me while I pack?"

So I perched on his bed, watching his suitcase fill up while the apartment grew emptier. There were so many words I wanted to say, but the lump in my throat wouldn't let them through.

"Greg will be here soon." The bed bounced as he plopped down opposite me, his suitcase all zipped up. With a loud sigh, he flopped backward, head landing in the middle of the bed.

I followed suit, our faces inches from each other, gazing into his blue eyes.

"I'm sorry we haven't had more time."

Well, that sounded awful. I frowned. "Yet. This isn't forever."

"Good. I still want to explore." His eyes twinkled. "Us pirates are good at that. And plundering. I think I'd like plundering." His phone chimed. "That'll be Greg. Want to ride with me to the airport? Maybe I could plunder you in the backseat." He waggled his eyebrows.

My nose wrinkled at the thought. "Not sure I could do that to Greg."

"The divider is tinted. And soundproof. He'd never know, and I'd make sure he knew not to roll it down, for any reason." The teasing was gone, replaced with a need so intense I didn't have it in me to say no.

"Give me two seconds. I'll meet you by the door." I raced to my room to put on something more accessible. Rummaging through my closet—and by rummaging I meant flinging, shoving and tearing—I finally found a simple sundress with an elastic off-the-shoulder top and a knee-length hemline. I stripped down, threw the dress on and nothing else, then stuffed some panties in my purse for the way home.

Derek met me in the living room, his suitcase ready to go. His whole face lit up as I sashayed toward him. Those blue eyes roved over my bare skin, lighting a fire in their wake. "I haven't seen that one yet."

I shook my head with a malicious grin. "It's easy access." I snapped the elastic band holding up the bodice. A flash of something I couldn't quite read crossed his face.

His blue eyes bored into me, then he gave a firm nod. I watched, puzzled, as he pulled his phone out of his pocket and dialed. "Yes, listen, something's come up. I'll still be there, but I can't leave for at least three hours. Greg will make the arrangements. Okay. I'll see you then." He hung up and sent a text, then set his phone on the island.

Wait, what just happened? "Derek?"

Derek stepped toward me, cupping my cheeks in his hands and staring down at me. "You deserve so much more than a goodbye quickie in the car on the way to the airport. My father can wait. I have some exploring to do." He paused. "If that's all right."

Hope cascaded through me, a lightness spread through my chest, and a smile sprawled over my face. "Only if there's plundering, too." I stared up at him, unable to comprehend the fact that we actually had time. "What do you want to do first?"

He kissed my lips, softly. "You." His hands slid down to my shoulders, one staying there, the other continuing on to the small of my back to press me against him. "Then maybe I can do you again." He kissed me again, hungrily, our tongues dancing together as I opened for him, groaning into his mouth. "And if there's time, maybe I can finish with you."

"Then I'll be thoroughly explored." I stepped away, grabbing one of his hands and leading him to his bedroom. On my knees, I sat on the bed, waiting for him. I watched him stalk toward me, like a starving man approaching a feast. My thighs clenched together, and his eyes drifted down.

The front of his pants was already straining.

"I'm not sure we should go slow the first time," I said, staring at his zipper.

He chuckled, watching me squirm under his gaze as he ran a finger along the elastic of my dress. "Not feeling very patient?"

"Patience isn't pirate-y." I was done playing. I grabbed the lapels of his blazer, pulling him to me with all the hunger I felt. Passion burned between us, and we kissed with a furious fusion of our mouths. I needed to touch him. Shoving at his jacket, I pushed it from his shoulders as he helped. I fumbled with the buttons of his dress shirt, barely containing my delighted moan when my fingers collided with his bare skin.

A groan rumbled through him. His hands slid to my bodice, tugging it down to my waist, baring my chest to him. He broke off our kiss to stare at me, cupping one full breast in his hand. "Easy access, indeed."

"Derek, please." I would implode if I didn't have him inside me. Now. I moaned as he kneaded my breast, rolling my nipple between his agile fingers.

"Please, what?" He bent down to take my peak into his mouth, sending a jolt of electricity straight to my core.

"I need you." I'd never said those words before, to anyone. But they felt right.

He let go, smirking up at me. "Tell me what you need, Avery."

I'd never been very vocal in the bedroom, but this was Derek. "I need you inside me." I tugged on the waistband of his slacks, undoing the button and drawing out his hard cock.

His eyes stayed on mine as he reached into the drawer of the end table to grab a condom. "Should I go slow and gentle?" He held the condom up, offering to let me put it on as he stepped out of his pants.

I shimmied out of my dress, then snatched the condom from his fingers, staring up at him. "I want to be plundered." I ripped open the package and slid the condom over his thick length. "By you."

"Plundered, huh?" His words came out a bit shaky, and I knew his grasp on his self-control was as tremulous as mine.

His lips devoured mine, then he broke away, turning me so my back was to his front. His mouth trailed down my neck, nipping, tasting, and I groaned, leaning into him. I gasped as his hand found my breast. He let go, and I didn't resist as he bent me forward until I was on all fours with my ass in the air.

He ran a hand over my hip, sucking in a sharp breath. "Avery, you are simply exquisite." I bucked against his touch, aching when his hand cupped my ass and he said, "Is this how you want it?"

I nodded. *Yes, a thousand times, yes.* I couldn't wait much longer.

Both of his hands gripped my hips firmly, his fingers digging in. His cock teased my entrance, and I squirmed against him, even as he tightened his hold on me. He eased into me, filling me completely, then he waited. "Good?"

My 'yes' was mostly a hiss, and I wriggled against him, needing him to move. He didn't disappoint, pulling out then slamming back into me as I cried out at the pressure to my G-spot. Sparks fluttered behind my closed eyelids.

"Harder," I whispered.

My wish was his command, and he pounded into me, powerful and steady. I clenched around him, unable to believe I was so close, so fast. But I held off, wanting to savor it.

His heavy balls slapped against my pussy as he claimed me, every thrust pushing me closer to that peak. Then he let go of my hip, leaning closer to reach my clit. The extra friction shattered my tenuous hold on my self-control, and I jerked under his touch.

"Derek!" One more thrust threw me over the edge of a cliff higher than I'd ever tumbled over before, my muscles clenching with wave after wave of pleasure.

Another thrust, and he joined me, growling out my name.

I collapsed, taking him with me. "Holy shit."

He rolled off me, his face next to mine. "The good kind I hope," he said between breaths.

I nodded, still feeling limp. "That was intense."

"And I haven't even started exploring yet."

Hardly able to move, I couldn't resist teasing him. "Well, what are you waiting for?"

He gave a dirty look. "If I had more energy, I'd come up with something witty to say."

I reached out a hand to rest on his shoulder, needing some connection. We lay there for several long moments before he got up to clean himself off. I closed my eyes, just basking in the afterglow. The mattress dipped behind me, and he pulled me to him, spooning me. He slid one arm under my head and splayed the other across my abdomen.

"What are you going to do while I'm gone?" He pressed a kiss to my shoulder, then snuggled up tighter to me.

"Recover?" We both laughed. "I don't know. I'll have to talk to Gina after you leave, see how things went down with her and Josh. Do you think the guys will still come over for football?" *It would help not to have Sunday all alone.*

He snorted. "They'd probably prefer it that way, with me gone."

I knew he was teasing, but there was a hint of truth in his voice that worried me.

His hand on my belly moved in a slow, wide caress. The motion was neither too low nor too high, just enough to start stoking my fire again, and soon it was hard not to squirm. I felt him growing against my backside. When his hand circled up, I shifted so he grazed my breast, and I arched into him.

"Impatient little thing." He nipped my shoulder.

I rolled onto my back, giving him better access. "I've got a great rack. I don't want it to go to waste."

His lips twitched, but his eyes were intense. "It won't." He started with my mouth, kissing me tenderly while running his hand all over me. Then his lips left mine, beginning the promised exploration, trailing to my collarbone and onto my chest where he made sure to discover every inch of my ample breasts.

The featherlight kisses made me squirm as he continued down my stomach to my hip bone. He nudged my legs apart, then knelt before me. Anticipation fluttered in my stomach as his eyes met mine for the briefest of glances before he licked along my seam.

I threw my head back as his tongue swirled my clit, lapping me up. A new tension built, and every part of me was eager for his ministrations.

"Delicious," he murmured, sliding a finger inside me. "Cupcake, you are amazing." He returned his attention to my sensitive nub, maintaining a steady rhythm with his talented finger.

My breathing grew heavy as the familiar pressure gathered. I let out a moan, reaching out to thread my fingers through his silky black hair. I held his face to me as I writhed under his skilled tongue, small quakes skittering through me, warning me that I was close.

He pulled back enough to say, "That's it. Come for me, Avery."

My name on his lips pushed me over the brink once more, and I quivered beneath him, coming with his mouth on me. He kept his motions steady, continuing until my clenching slowed. When he sat up, he was obviously ready to go again. I twisted to grab another condom, which I offered him with a grin.

He spread my legs with his body after sheathing himself, coming up to kiss me. No words were spoken as he slid inside me. I groaned, arching my hips to meet him and running my hands over his shoulders. His eyes were intense but adoring. He cupped my cheek, holding my gaze as he thrust inside me. I couldn't look away, as if he'd captured me with those blue pools. Desire pulsed between us, but it was more than that. We were really seeing each other, connecting on a level I'd never even dreamt of. As if my soul laid bare before him.

The orgasm caught me off guard, and I gasped, still staring up at him. He kissed me then, thrusting harder, once, twice, then he was done as well. A tear slid down my cheek, but I quickly wiped it away before he saw, not knowing why I was crying. He kissed me again, then his lips brushed my forehead as he pulled out.

I sagged against the bed as he went to the bathroom to clean up. *What happened there?* That was beyond any sex I'd ever had. I wanted to curl up in a ball under the covers until the vulnerability passed. More tears pricked my eyes at the rawness I felt. Every inch of me was fragile, and it scared me.

Derek came back then. We crawled under the covers, and I cuddled up to him, my head on his shoulder, taking comfort in the arms of my anchor, my Captain. I closed my eyes, drifting off to sleep.

He shifted out from under me some time later, making me stir. "It's okay, Cupcake, just time for me to go. You can sleep more if you want."

I blinked up at him, shooting my arms out and pulling him back on top of me. "Nope, sorry, you have to stay."

His smile was sad. "I've already stayed longer than I should have."

Right. I sobered.

He shook his head, then brushed his forehead to mine before our lips met in a tender kiss, full of promise and gratitude. "I'll let you know when we land." He hopped off me to get dressed.

"You better!" I yawned, tugging the covers over my shoulder once more. I didn't close my eyes though, wanting to watch him as long as I was able.

Once fully clothed, he glanced my way again, doing a double take to see me still awake. "Get back to your nap. That's an order." He kissed my forehead and tucked me in.

"Aye, aye, Captain." Then I closed my eyes.

It was late afternoon when I woke up. The first thing I noticed was a red rose on the end table with a note under it. I grabbed it eagerly.

I need to know your favorite flower. It's of the utmost importance. ~Derek

He must have had Greg pick up the rose on his way. I brought the flower up to my nose, inhaling deeply, then I sent Derek a quick text.

Any flower from you is my favorite. Thank you. Xoxo.

I walked around the apartment, feeling more lonely and depressed the longer I stared at the large empty space. So I called my best friend.

Gina answered on the first ring.

"How are you and Josh?"

"We're…okay. He's staying with his parents tonight, but we talked. He said the weirdest thing about me and Liam." She sounded genuinely disturbed about the idea of anything sexual with Derek's best friend, but I couldn't even muster a smile. "How are you?"

"Crappy." The word didn't even touch how low I was feeling.

"Want me to sleepover? You order Chinese, and I'll pick up ice cream?"

This time my lips curled upward. "Yes, please." *She knows me so well.*

I changed into comfier, warmer clothes, then tidied up the kitchen from last night. And I took stock of our drink situation. We had another decent bottle of whiskey. There were still two six packs of light beer, one fifth of vodka and a pack of cider. *More than plenty.*

Chapter Fifteen

A knock on my door had me rushing to answer, grinning when Gina threw her arms around me. "Hey, girl, sorry he ditched you so soon after the main event."

Happy to have my friend with me, I returned her squeeze. "That's not even the half of it." I quickly filled her in on Derek postponing his flight and our mini sex marathon.

"Wow. That sounds serious." She looked at me, eyes now brimming with a different kind of concern.

Because it doesn't seem like some casual fling? "Yeah, I'm still processing. Maybe it's a good thing he's gone? I can sort through whatever the hell just happened." Uncomfortable with the way she studied me, I changed the subject. "And I'm sorry we left you in the parking lot today."

"About that..." She switched to a glare.

I laughed. "Well, you two didn't look like you were stopping any time soon, and Derek had a flight to catch." *At the time.* "Besides, it was a solid twenty minutes before you called me. I mean, it took you that long to notice we were gone."

She chuckled. "You know I love me a good argument."

It was something I'd never understood. Arguing made me cringe, but it was fuel to Gina. "Give me the ice cream before it melts."

We tucked the ice cream into the freezer and looked over the Chinese menu.

"Ooh, I know something that'll make you feel better. Remember how you won the bet that Derek and I would do it last night?" I grinned at her. "Guess *where* we did it?" I had her in stitches, telling her how Derek snuck me downstairs with his spare key to have sex on Liam's floor in front of his fireplace. "We used one of Derek's blankets though, so I don't feel too bad about it."

"I'd love to rub that in Liam's face." She flipped over her menu with a sigh. "So many options. Everything sounds good, and I don't know what to get."

"Ugh, me either." There was a knock at my door, and I glanced at Gina. "Wonder who that could be."

It was Liam, looking a little red around the eyes. As soon as he saw Gina, he deflated even more. "Oh, sorry. I just thought with Derek gone you might be looking for company. I'll go." He turned around.

"Not so fast." I grabbed his forearm, pulling him inside. "What's going on?"

He rubbed his stubbly cheek. "Carla broke up with me."

I shot Gina a look, and she immediately shook her head. *Tough shit, Liam is my friend, too.* I continued glaring at her until she softened just a bit, rolling her eyes but nodding.

Hands on my hips, I looked over Liam's jeans and nice shirt he still wore. "Okay, you can join the rest of us ditched misfits for the night, provided you follow some rules."

He eyed me warily.

"Number one, you go downstairs and find some comfy clothes, preferably ratty ones we can make fun of you about. I'm talking bunny slippers and fluffy pink robes here." I kept my expression stern. "Two, you must consume large amounts of Chinese food and you'll let Derek pay for it."

He opened his mouth, but I cut him off. "Nonnegotiable. He deserted us after all, so it's only fair. Three—this is a biggie, so pay attention. Drinking is the main goal of tonight, and it won't be for the faint of heart. There will be stupid movies, card games and probably some pillow fights, truth or dare, maybe even drunken hugs which you will participate in without complaint. Now if you agree to abide by these rules, you may stay. Do you so swear?"

A hint of his usual teasing spark flared in his eyes as he nodded.

"Good. First order of business, everyone figure out what they want from the Chinese restaurant because dammit, I'm starving." We all piled around the island, jotting down an absurd amount of food. Once we were satisfied with our list, I shoved Liam out of the door. "Item number two is comfy clothes. Don't come back without them!"

I whirled on Gina. "Arguing is off the table tonight. I don't care if he mansplains or gives you dirty looks or whatever. Just pretend that you don't have any beef with him. Better yet, pretend he's one of the girls whose boyfriend just dumped her, got it?"

Gina nodded, eyes wide at my fierce tone. She was usually the ferocious one, but Liam was hurting. I didn't need Gina kicking him while he was down. "Good. Let's pick out the movies while he's gone."

We settled on the *Pitch Perfect* trilogy, lighthearted enough to fit all our moods with comedic relief and, of course, awesome music. Liam returned in a pair of faded blue straight-legged pajama pants that were the softest things I'd ever felt. His hoodie's sleeves frayed around the edges, one side of the pocket hanging down. And he actually had bunny slippers, which made me laugh.

"My little sister got 'em for me. I never wear them, but I figured this was the perfect occasion." His grin was sheepish.

So I went to my closet and dug out some tie-dyed hairy slippers for me and a pair with unicorn horns for Gina. I even made us stick our feet in a circle to take a picture, for posterity's sake. And maybe Derek's.

When the Chinese food came minutes later, we all loaded up our plates and slumped in our respective places as the movie started. I, of course, claimed the chair, though it felt way too big without Derek. Five minutes into the movie, I couldn't stand it anymore, so I marched into the bedroom to grab a couple pillows off his bed. I stuffed them next to me in the chair. *That's a little better.* It helped that they smelled like him, his inviting citrus and clove scent. I nestled into their embrace, wishing he were here.

Liam hadn't seen any of the *Pitch Perfect*s before. And he ended up loving the first one, laughing his way through. Alcohol might have helped a bit.

As the end credits rolled, Gina turned to me, a look in her eyes I knew meant trouble. "Let's play Never Have I Ever."

Oh boy.

Liam latched right on to it. "Yes!" They grabbed their drinks, moving to the table without waiting for my response.

The game was simple. Each person started with the phrase 'Never have I ever' then named something they hadn't done, like broken a bone. Everyone in the group who had broken a bone took a drink. Then the next person said something they'd never done.

Gina started. "Never have I ever had a kid."

No one drank.

She looked relieved. "Phew, no skeletons in the closet there."

I rolled my eyes. "Never have I ever been skinny dipping."

Both of them drank. Gina shook her head as she arched an eyebrow at me. "If it wasn't so cold out, I'd drag you out right now."

"Never have I ever watched *Pitch Perfect 2*." Liam grinned like he was so clever as we both drank.

Gina drummed her fingers on the table. "I've never kissed a member of the same sex."

I ducked my head and took a sip. So did Liam.

"Really? *Both* of you?" Gina looked impressed. "Now I'm feeling left out." The look she gave me had me shifting in my seat.

"I'm not drunk enough for that."

"Yet," she added, with a teasing grin.

Liam looked back and forth between us. "If this goes down, I'm taking pictures. Derek and Josh will be so jealous."

"Moving on." I swirled the amber liquid in my glass. "I've never said 'I love you' to a significant other." The words tumbled out, maybe because of the whiskey, maybe because Derek was gone. Either way, I couldn't take them back now.

Both of my friends paused, then took a drink. Liam was the first to respond. "Really? Not to Derek?"

I shrugged, trying to stay nonchalant. "Not yet."

Liam took his time before he spoke. "Hmm. Never have I ever had sex in a car." Gina opened her mouth, and he pointed a finger at her. "Vehicle. So bus, truck, van, whatever. They all count."

Almost had it in the limo today. I bit back a morose chuckle as I watched Gina take a drink.

We went around a couple more times, Gina getting frustrated when both rounds passed without me taking a sip. She studied me with a wicked gleam in her eye on her next turn. "Never have I ever had sex in front of Liam's fireplace."

My cheeks on fire, I took a sip.

Liam did too, then almost spat his back out. "Wait, what?"

"Gina, you promised not to tell." I glared at her, but she just laughed.

"I didn't tell him. You're the one who drank."

I put my head in my hands. "Derek and I snuck out last night to have sex in front of your fireplace. But we were on a blanket." Then I glared at both of them. "It's your fault anyway, turning a double date into a full-blown overnight party."

Liam looked disgusted. "I'm going to have to hire a cleaning service to come in and scrub my whole apartment."

"Don't you already do that?" Gina asked.

Indignant, I protested, "Hey, we used a blanket!"

"Yeah, but where has that blanket been?" He arched an eyebrow at me, and I was stumped.

"I don't know." I started laughing. "Actually I've never seen that blanket before or since."

Gina caught my giggles, and soon they spilled over to Liam, the three of us laughing hysterically. I got up, offering everyone another round. The whiskey created a fire in my belly, and I was burning up, so I yanked off my sweatshirt.

"Holy shit." Liam's strangled voice had me glancing at him.

"Yeah, she's got great cleavage, doesn't she?" Gina said it in such a matter-of-fact way, I didn't even know how to respond.

Wait, yes I do. "Never have I ever drooled over my cleavage."

They both lifted their glasses, clinking them together and finishing the last few swallows.

"It is hot in here." Gina took off her own hoodie.

I was in a thick-strapped tank top with a built-in bra. My cleavage needed that kind of support, at least around company. Gina on the other hand, could get away in a cute cami with the shelf bra, while still having a decent chest show.

"I don't know why you always knock your knockers. You've got nothing to complain about." I set their full glasses down and went back for mine. "Tell her, Liam."

He studied Gina for a minute, who didn't so much as flinch under his gaze. "She's right. Not too busty. No offense, Ave, but, Gina, you're much more my speed. A solid handful with a lot of perk."

I couldn't remember the last time I'd seen Gina blush. *The only one we haven't ogled is Liam, and we have to even that playing field.* "All right, Liam. Fair is fair. Hoodie off." I'd gotten a good look at strip poker night, but it was worth seeing again.

"What?"

Gina jumped in, chanting his name with me. Finally, the shirt came off to reveal a plain black tank that accented all of his muscles, and that awesome tattoo. I was right. Gina's jaw practically dislocated it dropped so far down.

A faint pink stained Liam's cheeks over his smirk. "Never have I ever drooled over my muscles."

Us girls took a drink, but I elbowed him. "I call bullshit on that. You can't tell me you don't start every day in front of the mirror, talking to yourself and kissing your biceps." I put up my arms, murmuring first to one then then the other, both Gina and Liam cracking up by the time I was done.

The game kind of fell apart after that. It spiraled into me and Gina telling stories about one another, Liam piping in with a tale about Derek every so often. Somehow we circled around to poker.

Gina flung out her hand to rest it on Liam's forearm, him grinning stupidly at her. "Don't ever let her talk you into playing strip poker. Girl won't let you walk away with a stitch on!"

I glared at her. "You deserved it."

Liam glanced between us, waiting.

My scowl deepened, and I jutted my chin in the air. "She stole my crush, so I kicked her ass in poker. Or stripped her ass." I winked at Liam.

She gave me a sassy look. "Well, that boy definitely followed me home after the performance I gave. He got to see *all* the goods."

We all laughed at her smart comment. Then Liam leaned the chair back on two legs and casually threw out there, "We've already played."

"What?" She turned on me. "How did I not hear about this? With who?" Her eyes widened even more, and her voice lowered, though Liam could still hear her. "Did you get to see his junk?"

He slammed forward with a bang, planting all four chair legs on the tile. "I'm right here."

Gina glanced at him, then looked to me for the answer.

I shook my head. "Nah. Besides, Liam suggested it. He was the one hoping for a sneak peek." I smirked.

He glared at me, pointing an accusatory finger in my direction. "You were sandbagging like crazy."

Annoyance flared in me, and I crossed my arms. "In my defense, I *was* getting crap cards, and we *were* playing Texas Hold 'Em."

Gina nodded sympathetically. "Not your game."

"So he suggested strip poker on my deal, and I picked five card draw, to which Derek agreed."

A knowing grin split Gina's face. "That's so your game." When she turned to Liam, a teasing gleam twinkled in her eye. "How far did she get you?"

He propped both elbows up on the table, resting his chin on his hands. "It was me, Derek and her. We were both down to nothing but our boxers. I think she lost her socks."

"And that was completely my fault. I thought I had one card..." I trailed off, realizing that Liam really didn't want to hear it. "Sorry."

Gina looked at me curiously. "How soon was this after you, um, moved in?"

"That weekend?" I glanced at Liam for confirmation, and he nodded. "Talk about trial by fire. Between Rhonda's interrogation luncheon and that poker game, after my apartment being condemned?" I let out a little laugh, startled at how much I'd survived.

Gina's eyes are full of admiration. "Yeah but look at you now."

Liam's eyes held hints of it, too. "Don't forget Kevin's gold digger comment, and you putting him in his place." He shook his head. "None of us could believe it when you came back out and actually knew football. I bet you could have asked any guy in that room to marry you that night, and any one of them would have said yes." He frowned. "Well, except Kevin."

My eyebrows shot up. "Even you?"

The frown deepened. "Yeah, but I would've seen what a handful you are and ran screaming for the hills, so it all worked out."

Tension eased in my chest. I didn't need anyone in Derek's group secretly pining after me, especially his best friend.

A knock at the door broke our silence, and I frowned, not expecting visitors at this hour. "Who is it?"

"Josh."

With a glance back at Gina, I waited for her permission to answer the door.

She stood up from her chair, giving me a tentative nod before she crossed the room, Liam right on her heels.

I cracked the door. "What do you want?"

"Hey." He looked supremely uncomfortable. "I know it's late, but I tried texting Gina and can't get a hold of her. She said she'd be here. Can I talk to her?" He peered behind me.

My eyes narrowed. "I'm sorry, this party is for ditchees only. Since you ditched her —"

Gina put a hand on my shoulder. "It's all right, Avery. I'll talk to him."

So I moved aside, pushing down my overprotective instinct against the guy who'd hurt my friend. I felt a presence behind me. I was so used to Derek being there that I started to lean back, remembering at the last second it wasn't him. Instead, I almost lost my balance, pin-wheeling like an idiot.

Liam planted a hand in the middle of my back, giving me a steadying shove until my feet were firmly on the ground. "You okay there?"

I nodded, keeping it together as Gina poked her head in.

"I'm going to go home with Josh, okay?" She beamed, clasping my hand. "He came for me. Isn't that the sweetest?" Though she tried to whisper, it came out overly loud.

My smile was forced, but it was enough to satisfy her.

After a whirlwind rush to grab her things, she was gone, and I locked up behind her. I sat down at the island, feeling empty, Derek's absence even bigger in the wake of Gina leaving. I crossed my arms, then laid my chin on them.

"That's what I should have done with Carla, isn't it?" Liam came over and took the other chair, assuming a similarly dejected position.

"If you really loved her, yes. Us girls want to be fought for. Definitely." I sighed.

He was quiet for a moment, then he looked at me. "What happened back there? When you almost fell over?"

It was ridiculous, and I didn't want to say it out loud. "I'm so used to having Derek here that I thought you were him. I went to lean on him, share the moment with him. I remembered at the last second." I paused. "Thanks for catching me."

"You're welcome." His answer was gruff.

My thoughts were loud, but our mouths were silent. Until I asked, "Does that make me pathetic?"

"What? Leaning on someone else? Counting on them being there?" He shook his head. "No. I'd say it makes you lucky." He downed the rest of his drink.

I knew he was hurting, but I had to say something. My words came out softly. "Carla wasn't right for you, Liam. She's great, don't get me wrong, but you two didn't work, and it wasn't your fault. It's like trying to use ice skates on a football field. If you want to gain some ground, you'll need a pair of cleats."

His mouth twitched in a ghost of a smile. "Know where I can find any?"

They just walked out that door. But I didn't say that, instead I patted him on the back and stood up. "The way I see it, we have two choices. *Pitch Perfect 2* or cribbage."

He frowned. "How are we going to get drunk doing either of those?"

I scoffed, waving a hand at him for underestimating me yet again. "Drinking cribbage is easy. Every time someone scores a point off you in the opening, you drink. You drink for Muggins and skunks and if you lose. *Pitch Perfect*—you drink whenever anyone says certain words which I'd have to look up."

He gave me a doubtful look.

"I could make a cheat sheet."

This time he smiled. "That sounds Acca-amazing."

And I laughed. "Okay. Let me find some paper."

When the end credits rolled, neither one of us could walk straight. He stumbled to my room, and I careened into Derek's. I noticed an earlier text from Derek saying he'd made it safely to his hotel. Since I had no judgment, I hit his name on my phone.

"Avery? Everything okay?" He yawned.

I lay on my back, looking up at the ceiling. "Aside from you not being here? Yep, everything's just fine."

"Wow, it's really late. I'm surprised you're still up."

The clock finally came into focus, and it was almost two in the morning. "Oh, geez, did I wake you up? I'm sorry."

"No, Cupcake, you're fine." There was a pause. "Are you drunk?"

"Just a bit." I held my fingers a little apart. "Gina's boyfriend ditched her, so she came over, and Liam's girlfriend dumped him, and my boyfriend flew away to Canada. So we had a 'get ditched' party. We drank and watched *Pitch Perfect* and played Never Have I Ever." I hiccuped. "Gina told Liam about us having sex on his floor. He wanted to know where the blanket had been."

Derek chuckled. "I'm sorry I'm missing out."

"Josh came for Gina. It was so sweet." I sighed. "And then I went to lean on you because I'm so used to you being here, and you weren't, and I remembered at the last second." A big, fat tear slid down my cheek.

"Oh, Cupcake." His sigh matched mine. "I'm sorry I wasn't there to catch you this time. Or put you to bed."

I rolled over onto my stomach, swinging my feet in the air. "Hey, that reminds me of the reason I called. There's a guy in my bed. Wanted you to know that I'm already moving on."

"Har har. It's Liam, isn't it?" Then his voice lowered a delicious octave. "Does that mean you're sleeping in my bed?"

My pout could probably be heard through the phone. "Yes."

"Good. It'll make it easier to picture you that way." His voice went even lower, taking on a husky timbre.

"Picture me doing what?" I let out a loud yawn.

His laughter was loud. "Cupcake, do me a favor?"

My eyelids were getting really heavy. "What?"

"Go to the bathroom." He paused, waiting for me to acknowledge I'd done it before giving me the next step. "Get the cup, fill it full of water, and drink all of it. Now go to bed and pretend I'm tucking you in."

I climbed into bed, warmth spreading through me. *He's taking care of me, even though he's not here.* "Good night, Derek," I said softly.

"Good night, Avery."

Chapter Sixteen

"No, she's glaring at me." Liam's loud voice made me groan. "Well, *you* told me to go check on her." He threw his hand up in frustration. "Make up your mind."

"Go away." I hid under a pillow.

"Ave, Derek wants to know—" He sighed. "Yes, I called her Ave. No, I don't know if she likes it. Dude, let me talk to her!"

I peered at him from the edge of the pillow.

"He wants to know if you need anything." Liam held the phone to his chest, and I could still hear Derek speaking.

"Sleep." My mouth was dry, my tongue thick and my head hurt.

"I tried to tell him that. So to recount, no coffee, no flowers, no breakfast?"

My glare might have brought the Pentagon up to DefCon 2, and I leveled my voice. "Liam, if you don't get your ass out of the room, so help me!"

He yelped, darting out of the open door. "Your girlfriend is scary." A pause. "No, I'm not going back in there. No!"

Sleeping through that wouldn't work either. "For fuck's sake, Liam, what is it?"

His crazy bed head peeked around the corner. "I'm supposed to ask if you still want to have Sunday night football."

Oh. I thought about it for a minute, then nodded. The idea of having loud obnoxious guys here to obliterate the stifling silence of the apartment was appealing. *Assuming I get enough sleep and caffeine to cure this hangover.*

He grinned. "I'll get the pizza."

I shooed him away with my hand, falling back asleep with a smile on my face.

It was mid-afternoon when I called Derek. The coffee shop had given me the weekend off after the double I'd pulled, so I had way too much time on my hands. Good for my hangover, bad for my unoccupied mind that kept wandering to the guy I was missing with much more fervor than I'd like to admit. The apartment sparkled. The fridge was stocked, and the guys would eat like kings tonight.

Derek answered on the first ring. "Cupcake! How are you feeling?"

I grinned. "Better than I was when you made Liam interrogate me this morning." I couldn't help teasing him.

"Sorry about that."

"Plus, I'm a little sore from someone missing their flight…" My body ached in odd ways, giving me a twinge every so often. But I wouldn't trade it for the world because it reminded me of all our fun.

"Sounds like a pirate-y thing to do. Miss a flight to have sex." We both laughed.

"How are things in Canada?"

"Making some headway. Lots of wining and dining. We have a big meeting tomorrow, but today's pretty free." He told me a bit about the restaurants they'd been to, the hotel he was at. "So that's all my news, other than missing you. Oh, and Rhonda texted me again. Some goofy math joke that made her think of me."

I smiled to myself. "That's sweet of her!"

"Seems weird talking to her more."

He'll just have to get used to it.

"What's up with you?"

I twirled a lock of hair around my finger. "I want to wear your Lions hoodie today, if you don't mind."

There was another pause. "What about the jersey your dad gave you?"

"It's too cold, and you're not here to keep me warm. So unless you want me snuggling with Liam..."

Derek's laugh echoed through the phone. "I don't think there's any chance of that happening after this morning. Not sure what you said or did, but he's downright terrified of you." His voice dropped, taking on a husky quality that had my breath catching. "Of course you can wear my hoodie. Although I don't think I washed it since I wore it last."

"Even better." *Whose sultry voice is that?*

"It's in my closet, top shelf on the right." A tapping noise sounded on his end. "Someone's at my door. Gotta run, Cupcake. Send me a pic?"

"Will do." And he was gone.

I went right to his closet. His stack of sweatshirts wasn't hard to find, though they all came tumbling down when I pulled on the one I wanted. "Shit." It was like a mini avalanche, and I couldn't help giggling at the mess.

Finally, Derek's closet was back to its original state of order, and I had my prize. Feeling a bit adventurous, with time to kill before everyone else got here, I decided to have a bit of fun with his *"take a pic"* comment. I took several, all of them in his sweatshirt in various poses. On his bed. In nothing else.

It was difficult finding the right mix of good angle and not showing too much. I wanted the pics to be tasteful, although he probably wouldn't mind full nudes either. But that wasn't the point. Satisfied, I flipped through them, sorted out my favorites and sent him a few with an innocent, *Thanks for letting me borrow your shirt.*

I actually got dressed after that, and when I checked my phone again, I still had no response. *Really?* I clicked to make sure the pics had gone through.

There were three dots at the bottom of the screen. I smiled. Then, to my dismay, they disappeared. When they reappeared, so did my smile, and I even laughed out loud. I'd rendered Derek speechless. I decided to tease him even more.

Sorry I didn't pull out the lacy top stockings. I know those are your fav. *winking face*

Just to feel close to him while I waited, I sprawled on his bed, scrolling through my feeds. Finally a text came through.

Damn, Avery. If you had added the stockings, I'd be dialing 911 instead of texting you. You are *flames emoji*.

I grinned, kicking my legs in the air behind me. Another text swooped onto my screen.

Wait, are you wearing underwear?

I laughed out loud.

I'm not telling. Some secrets are meant to be kept. *zipped lips emoji*

Damn, Cupcake.

Two more texts came through, one after the other.

Here's one for you. Thought it could help with your favorite pastime...

I scrolled down, stilling as more and more of my fake boyfriend's phenomenal body came into view. He lay on his back, completely shirtless with one hand tucked behind his head. I sucked in a breath, letting my eyes travel over his muscular abdomen and farther. The view kept going to his delicious V, almost to his 'down there' hair.

Wow. Is it hot in here or just me? What did his text say? I put two and two together, realizing he was teasing me about picturing him naked. Although he hadn't left much for my imagination, which was okay by me. *Damn, Derek.* I had to reply, and I didn't quite know what to say.

He texted first.

You there?

I laughed at myself.

Sorry, was busy drooling over this pic some hot guy sent me. What were you saying?

Lol.

Seriously, Derek, I have to wait till Friday to get my hands on you again? You sure you don't have some top-secret turbo jet at your beck and call...I'll even put on the stockings.

His reply was instantaneous.

Fuck. I wish. I'm gonna have a hard time getting to sleep tonight.

For real. I like your fingers better.

I bit my lip, wondering how he'd take that.

Avery, you're killing me.

I could almost hear his groan as I read his text again.

I miss you, too. XOXO.

And that's enough mooning over him. I stood to leave when a white rectangle caught my eye, peeking out from a corner of the bed. Maybe it had fallen down when his shirts spilled everywhere? I picked it up, turning it over to find a lined piece of notebook paper.

Derek,
Thank you for climbing down into the canyon to rescue me. You showed me the light of day after the worst heartbreak

I've ever known. I know I promised I'd stay with you, but some dreams have to be chased. I'll come back someday. Wait for me?

Yours forever, Princess.

My knees buckled. Luckily, the bed was behind me, and I sank onto it, my fragile world caving in around me. Each flimsy card I'd used to build this delicate house fluttered to the ground. Gina's confident words, Liam's comments and every thoughtful thing Derek had ever done...they all added up to nothing in the end. Not when there wasn't anything to build upon.

It wasn't anyone's fault but my own. This had never been more than a glorified game of pretend. I'd known from the beginning to protect my heart because we were both liars. That old chant kept running through my head, "Liar, liar, pants on fire." *Though "pants" doesn't really fit here. Maybe lips.* I thought of all our kisses, and how many times our lips had lied. How I'd gladly take one more lie right this moment just to soothe the ache in my heart.

This was exactly why I didn't do serious relationships. My parents had been fine one minute, years of perfection under their belt, a real storybook romance, and it had all vanished in a blink. *So what's the point?* There was a reason I didn't surrender, a reason I kept a piece of me locked away. Sex and attraction were one thing, that I could handle. My heart needed to go back into the safe little cave I kept it in for this very reason.

I took a deep breath, looking at the letter once more, wishing I could go back to the lighthearted banter of just a few minutes earlier. But reality had huffed and puffed and blown my house down. A glance at my phone made me realize football would be starting soon, so I needed to pull myself together.

Liam showed up first with the pizza. "Hey." He did a double-take when he saw me in Derek's hoodie — now with pants underneath. "Changing it up a little?"

I nodded from my spot in our overstuffed armchair.

He looked me over again, his easy smile fading to a frown. "You okay?"

Maybe I'm not as good a liar as I thought. I started to tell him I was fine, but I didn't want to lie any more. So I settled for silence.

The slap to his forehead was overly dramatic, even for Liam. "I know something that'll cheer you up." He disappeared down the hallway toward Derek's room. A few minutes later, he returned with a wrapped present in his hands. "Derek wanted me to give this to you before, but I thought you valued your sleep more than me trying to find it. Happy early birthday from him."

Part of me wanted to throw the box at Liam's obtuse forehead. I wasn't one to be cheered up and distracted by shiny gifts, but the other part appreciated him trying. And Derek still wanted to spoil me, even though he was gone. I hesitated when Liam plopped the box on my lap.

"Smile, I have to send a picture to Derek."

I did. I opened the box to find a super soft Detroit Lions blanket just right for snuggling. Liam snapped pictures as I lifted it out of the box. Then I buried my face in it.

He chuckled. "Perfect."

"Maybe I'll go take a nap instead of watching football. If you can't find our box of pizza later, you'll know where it ended up." A bit of my humor sparked, bringing back the warmth inside me like a balm to my soul. Derek was my friend, first and foremost. I knew he cared about me on some level, and that counted for a lot. Our boundaries had gotten skewed, but we could fix that. For now, I'd enjoy the game wrapped up in my cozy new blanket and have fun with our friends.

Bingeing on pizza and junk food won't hurt either.

* * * *

The week passed slowly. Derek was busy with his father's client, so we only had time for texts once in a while. I tried to keep them lighthearted, making him laugh as often as I could, not wanting to add to the pressure he was under. Gina and Josh were busy figuring things out, so she didn't have a lot of time for me. And Liam basically worked around the clock, his little free time spent exercising.

Which left me with a lot of time on my hands. I picked up a couple of extra shifts at the coffee shop, but they only lasted a couple of hours. My romance novels weren't as fun without someone to tease me about them. And my schoolwork was all caught up. By the time Wednesday rolled around, I felt like Derek had been gone for a month.

Lunch with my dad was especially depressing. He didn't even want to eat with me.

When I walked in the door that evening, I stood for a second, hating the greeting of the dark, empty apartment. *What I wouldn't give for a pair of brilliant blue eyes, a megawatt smile and a low, rumbly voice calling me Cupcake.* I sighed, trying to figure out what to do with my desolate evening. Maybe I'd binge a show.

My phone chimed, and I reached for it, thrilled to have someone contacting me. Mother's name flashed across the screen along with a text, killing my happiness instantly. She was calling in one of her dinners, for tomorrow night. *Oh, shit.* I knew Derek was pushing it already, just by leaving in time for the party on Friday. There was no way he'd be able to leave another day early. My fingers hovered over the keyboard, my brain scrambling to come up with something other than giving into the panic pressing in.

Rhonda. She's an Elgin. Surely she'll be as good as her brother in my mother's eyes. I found her number, calling her.

"Hello?"

How to explain this one? "Hey, Rhonda, it's me, Avery. So I have a really weird favor to ask you. I have this arrangement with my mother…" I sighed, pinching the bridge of my nose, and decided to just go for it. "Look, my mother and I don't get along, but her cook makes the best ravioli ever. I had a bargain with my mother to steal her cook for the party on Friday. Part of the deal was that Derek and I would show up for three dinners between now and Christmas, on the night of her choosing. And in her typical, thoughtful style, she chose tomorrow as one of the nights."

"But Derek's still in Canada, right?"

Surprise flashed through me. I was impressed she knew that. "Yeah, he is, and he'll barely be able to make it home Friday. With such short notice, there's no way I'd be able to find someone else to make decent food for the party if I don't hold up my end of the deal. So I was hoping that maybe you weren't busy…"

"Wait, you want me to come to a dinner party with you tomorrow?"

Great, she's going to shoot me down before I even get off the ground. "I know it's really soon but—"

"Sure! When, where and what's the dress code?"

I held the phone away from my ear to stare at it. *Is it really going to be that easy?* "Um, I'll find out and let you know."

"Okay, I look forward to hearing from you. Bye, Ave! And thanks for thinking of me."

Stunned at her exuberant reaction, I stood with the phone clutched in my hand for several long seconds before I realized what I was doing. Then I shot my mother a text explaining the situation. As I knew she would be, she was thrilled with what she called the 'upgrade'. Annoyance shot through me at her choice of words.

After I'd received the details, I forwarded them to Rhonda. On a whim, I asked what she was doing tonight.

Her response was almost immediate.

Nothing.

I'm still not sure what to wear Friday. And then there's the gala the day after Thanksgiving. Derek asked me to go, but we haven't had time to shop.

Girl.

Then nothing else. I waited, my stomach rumbling that it was dinner time. My phone rang just as I stuck my head in the fridge to see what had magically appeared since yesterday. Absolutely nothing.

Rhonda didn't bother to greet me, just started barking orders. "All right, Avery, meet me downtown

282

ASAP. We're going to fix you up. Is Greg around? I already let Kevin have our driver, so I have to hire one to get out there."

"Um, I'll check." I shot a text to Greg, unwrapping a cheese stick. "Have you eaten yet? 'Cause I'm starving."

"We don't have time for food! You have two major events coming in less than two weeks. One of which is in two days. We're in crisis mode here!"

Excuse me! "Greg's available. He'll be here in a few. I guess I'll find some food on the way?"

"Damn straight you will. I'll text you the address, and my personal shoppers will be on standby."

I just polished off my last taco when Greg pulled up to the address Rhonda had texted me. The storefront simply read *Lit* despite the sign being dark. "Are you sure this is it?" Not that I doubted Greg. I was more questioning Rhonda's address than him.

He arched an eyebrow at me in the mirror as he took a bite of his burrito.

"Yeah, sorry. I said it before I thought about it." I sent a quick text to Rhonda just as the shop door flew open.

Rhonda stood in the doorway, waving her arm with a gesture big enough to flag down a 747.

I opened the back door of the Town Car. "Sorry, it's dark. I wasn't sure."

"Shh," she hissed, grabbing my arm and yanking me inside without even giving me time to close the car door.

I glanced over my shoulder to see Greg muttering to himself as he circled around to shut it. I'd have to thank him later because all the store windows were tinted and the lights were off, making it nearly impossible to see. "What's going on?"

"Just shut up and follow me."

Since I didn't have much choice, I did as I was told. She led us down a winding hallway, me tripping over my own feet a few times. I breathed a sigh of relief when light beckoned, becoming brighter and brighter, finally opening into a room. Then I almost wished for the dark. We were surrounded by dresses in all shapes and colors — racks and racks of them.

Designer names shouted their presence from the top of most of the racks, so many I could hardly take them all in. The pressure was almost unbearable as they surrounded me, all these designers, all these beautiful gowns in a rainbow of colors. The majority not my size. *What am I doing here?*

Rhonda tugged me over to three formidable women in pantsuits who stood at perfect attention, one with a measuring tape draped over her neck, thick frames perched on her nose, and an unlit cigarette hanging from her lip.

Nodding at the lady, Rhonda said, "This is Selena, my personal shopper, and her assistants. She will guide you to the right dresses."

I nearly laughed at the introduction, a little too Zen for my usual taste. Then I was glad I'd managed not to laugh as Selena stepped forward with all the seriousness of a heart attack.

"Tell me about the events." She began moving my limbs as if I were a doll, shoving my legs apart, no regard for my balance or personal space.

Rhonda filled her in on the details, which I was grateful for, especially since I knew next to nothing about the gala.

"Walk for me."

There was no question of disobeying her. I was simply walking before I'd even processed her command, finding the clearest space between the racks.

"What will your date be wearing?"

I'd seen one of Derek's nice suits, the one he'd worn for dinner at his parents'. I glanced at Rhonda for help.

She swished a hand in the air. "It's my brother, so whatever we tell him to."

Selena sniffed, in approval I hoped. "Are we doing just the dress? Or the whole kit and caboodle?"

"My brother left very specific instructions that she was to be completely taken care of for both occasions. He also said to remind you of your conversation Sunday? Regarding his favorite article of clothing?" Rhonda arched a narrow eyebrow in my direction, making me bite my lip.

I realized they were waiting for me to tell them what he meant and I stammered out, "He liked these lacy topped stockings I wore. A lot."

Selena gave me an appraising glance. "Perhaps there's more to you after all. Now let me think." She summoned her two assistants, giving them orders that I didn't understand, but they returned with specific dresses or fabric. Selena would eye me, then nod or wave them away.

My anxiety lessened as Selena requested option after option, many from brands I'd never heard of. *She doesn't seem worried, so why should I?* Excitement started trickling in. I'd been around designer labels so much I was practically immune to their status. But the idea of picking out something tailored for me? To shop for an outfit made for me, for my body, with me in mind? A thrill went through me, and I smiled, hardly able to comprehend the notion.

Then it was time for the modeling session. First, I was stripped.

As Selena informed me in her haughty tone, "We must start from the ground up. Can't build a masterpiece on quicksand."

Her fancy way of saying my underwear sucks, evidently. I had to admit though, the bra I was stuffed into was really something. Not only did it make me look amazing, it actually felt comfortable. "Um, can I have a couple of these?"

Rhonda sniffed. "She'll take five, in varying colors."

One of the assistants scampered off to do her bidding as I gaped at Rhonda. I didn't even own five bras now that I truly liked.

"What? Derek's paying. He'll appreciate it, and if he doesn't, say it's part of his Christmas present to you."

Oh, I can just imagine that conversation. My cheeks were hot as I tried to focus on the current dress I was being stuffed into like a doll. Despite Rhonda and Selena's nitpicky taste, they finally approved one dress for the party on Friday. Halfway done with our mission, I was already exhausted. Thank goodness I'd eaten those tacos, or I'd have fainted from lack of fuel. *Who knew finding the perfect dress was such grueling work?*

With no clock to measure the time, I had no idea how long it had been when Selena finally clapped her hands, a slow smile spreading across her face as I spun toward her.

Rhonda practically melted, clasping her hands under her chin. "Ave, it's perfect."

I hardly wanted to look in the mirror. *What if I hate it?* I held my breath and crossed my fingers, spinning around slowly with my eyes squeezed shut. Sneaking a peek, both eyes flew open, and I gasped. *Is that really me?*

"You're going to steal the show," Rhonda said, coming to stand next to me.

One of my hands lay on my chest, and I could feel it against my heart as well as see it in the mirror, otherwise I'd have doubted my own eyes. "Thank you," I whispered to Rhonda, reaching out to squeeze her hand with my free one.

She rested her head on my shoulder. "You're welcome."

The mirror reflected both of us, and I realized it showed me what we were unexpectedly becoming. Friends.

Chapter Seventeen

I wouldn't have made it through dinner Thursday night without Rhonda. She expertly steered the conversation, complimenting those who deserved it and small talking with the best of them. Between the dress hunt the night before and the socialite triathlon tonight, I was nearly dead on my feet. I hoped I'd have enough energy for the party tomorrow.

Somehow Rhonda spun it so my mother was the one telling us to go home and get our rest. *I need to figure out that trick. Immediately.* She made Greg drop me off first, and I stumbled my way bleary-eyed to the apartment, shot a good night text to Derek, then crashed out.

Friday morning I woke to my phone ringing. It was Patty, wondering how soon Greg would be there because my mother was on a rampage. She wanted to get started on the ravioli.

So I called Greg and explained.

"Oh, that's no trouble. The event center is ours for the day, and I'd be happy to pick up Miss Patty right away." He paused. "Let me know if there's anything else I can help with."

"Thanks, Greg," I said, gushing with gratitude before I texted Patty the good news.

One crisis down, I snuggled back under the covers, almost drifting off when the phone rang once more. This time it was my uncle with a question about the whiskey delivery. As soon as I'd hung up with him, another call came in. Then a text. And it didn't stop.

I was on the phone with my mother when the apartment door opened around noon. Figuring it was Liam, I whirled around to beg him for help only to be greeted by Derek's megawatt grin.

"Hi there, Cupcake. Happy birthday!"

My knees gave out, and I dropped the phone. Tears coursed down my cheeks as the flimsy dam I'd used to hold back the frustrations of the day crumbled. My mother's shrill voice echoed through the phone, calling my name.

Derek rushed to my side, kneeling next to me. "What's wrong?"

I pointed to the phone with a loud sniffle. "She demanded I do dinner last night, so I brought Rhonda, which she texted was fine. But now she's saying I didn't live up to my end of the bargain." I buried my face in my hands, unable to handle one more thing.

One strong arm wrapped around me, pulling me to his chest. He used his other hand to pick up the phone. "Mabel, this is Derek Elgin." His tone rang with authority. "Per your contract with your daughter, we were required to come to three dinners on nights of your choosing. I do believe if I was out of town on business, Avery was given a bye. Since I have just returned from Canada, on business for my father, our contract has not been voided. Furthermore, the text messages you sent confirming that Rhonda, my sister, was a valid replacement for me, would be considered a binding agreement if tested in a court of law." He winked at me as I glanced up at him, my tears starting to slow.

"Lastly, if you had one ounce of kindness in you, you'd do well to remember this is your daughter's birthday. However, if you fail to find that kindness, let me remind you that your daughter is very important to me. And if you want to continue being accepted in the current social circles you run in, you'd do well to stay on my good side." He paused, nodding as he rolled his eyes. "I see. Well, if that's all, I'll hand you back to Avery."

I shook my head, wanting nothing more to do with her, but he insisted, holding the phone out. Reluctantly, I took it, holding it up to my ear as Derek's warm hand rubbed circles across my back. "Yes?"

"Darling, I'm so sorry for the confusion. And I just wanted to wish you a happy birthday. Lots of love. Ta-ta!" Then she was gone.

Torn between throwing the phone across the room and laughing maniacally, I decided on neither, focusing on Derek instead. I tilted my head up to meet those blue eyes I'd missed so much, soaking them in. "You're home."

I threw my arms around him, nearly knocking him over with the force of my hug. I clung to his neck, sighing when he wrapped me in his strong embrace. Then my toes were dangling in midair as he stood up.

"What are you doing?" I asked as he carried me down the hall.

He kissed my nose. "You look absolutely exhausted."

What a compliment. "Gee, thanks." My phone started ringing from the living room. "I need to get that."

But he shook his head, continuing in the completely opposite direction. "No, it's your birthday. Let somebody else hold down the fort for once." Gently, he deposited me on the bed, telling me to stay put. I didn't mind watching him stride back out of the door, his ass just never quit. When he returned, he leaned against the door frame while he talked on the phone, gaze never straying from me.

I soaked him in, letting my eyes take in every inch of him, allowing the rumble of his voice wash over me. *So much for keeping my walls intact.*

He hung up. "Okay, I've forwarded your calls to Rhonda. She'll handle everything from here, which she was thrilled to do. What time is the party?"

A yawn escaped me, and I waited for it to end before I answered. "I want to be there just before six."

We worked backward, figuring out how much time I needed to get ready, how much time it took to get there, and everything else to consider. He nodded. "All right, sounds like you've got a good three hours, so let's get to it."

I propped my head up on one hand. "To what?"

"The pampering. Clothes off." He gave me a look that said he wasn't kidding when I didn't immediately start to strip. "Don't worry, I'm not planning on more plundering just yet. I took massage therapy classes a few years ago, and it looks like you could really use one right about now. So undress, get comfy."

A massage sounded heavenly, so I followed instructions, lying face down on the bed. Quiet footsteps on the plush carpet alerted me to his presence. I peeked up, then gaped at him shirtless in my favorite gray sweatpants.

"Ever had one before?"

A hot guy in sweatpants? Not yet, but it's at the top of my list!

He eyed me with amusement when I just stared at him. "A massage."

"Sorry. No, I haven't."

"Most people enjoy them, and I won't go too deep."

Pity. Ugh, he'd only been home for twenty minutes, and I was already making dirty jokes to myself.

First, he rubbed his hands together to warm them up. Then he gathered my hair out of the way and lowered the sheet so my back was exposed. When he touched me next, his hands glided over my shoulders and down, stopping just before my ass.

This is supposed to be relaxing? The tension curling low in my gut had me practically squirming with need. But then he dug his thumbs into my shoulders, and I groaned.

"Does that hurt?"

"No." I started to relax. "Holy shit, that feels amazing."

He worked his way along my shoulders, upper arms, shoulder blades, down my lower back. His strong hands cupped my sides as his thumbs worked their magic along my spine. It was sweet and comfortable, but at the same time, deliciously erotic. All too soon, he was done, covering my back with the sheet.

"Well, that was nice."

His low chuckle made me pause. "Oh, Cupcake, I'm just getting started." The sheet came up past my knees, and he lifted one foot into his hand.

I'd never been one for my feet being touched, but maybe they had never been touched correctly before. *Because this? This is phenomenal*. His deft hands made their way up my calves and hamstrings, first one leg then the other.

"Now, roll over."

He held the sheet up so I didn't tangle in it as I shifted. Directing me so my head was near the edge of the bed, he began working my neck and my shoulders once more. It felt completely different from this angle. Then he massaged my arms to my very fingers, which he kissed, making me smile.

As he leaned over me, he ran his strong hands up my hips, holding the pressure and releasing it slowly. My senses were awakened more with his every touch, even as my body relaxed. When he shifted, my head was very near his cock. *If I turned my face just so…*

"Avery." His voice held all the warning I needed to stay still. He finished my hips, and circled around to my feet, nudging my legs apart a bit as he worked my shin, knee, then up to my thigh.

I didn't think anything of it at first, his movements were so subtle. Gradually his fingers were no longer on top of my legs, but on my inner thighs, edging closer between them. I sucked in a breath. "Derek." I tried to stop him, close my legs, shut him out.

"Please, Avery. This oil is special, good for all types of massage. I've got you." Then his finger circled my clit.

As I arched into his touch, I moaned.

"That's it. I like to hear you." The mattress dipped under his weight as he settled between my legs, his body radiating heat against my bare skin. He slid a finger inside me, and I tightened around him. His finger pumped in and out, establishing a rhythm as his thumb brushed against my clit, making me jump. Then his hot breath hovered over me. "I've been dreaming about tasting you again." His eyes found mine, waiting for permission.

I nodded feverishly, and his mouth was on me. His tongue lavished me, massaging my clit. It wasn't long before I hovered on the brink, then tipped over, calling his name as I quivered around him. My body felt as if it were made of Jell-O when he raised his head to grin at me.

"So sweet, so delicious." He licked his lips before crawling up the mattress to kiss me.

I felt his hard length through his sweatpants even though I could hardly keep my eyes open. "What about you?"

He forced a big glass of water into my hands, making sure I drank it all. "I just had everything I need. You get your sleep." He brushed a knuckle across my cheek and whispered, "I've got plans for you tonight, so you're going to need it."

* * * *

In nothing but his T-shirt, I tiptoed my way out to the hall, feeling energized and refreshed after a two-hour nap. Derek had his back to me, leaning against the island. I still couldn't believe he was home and how thrilled I was to see him. But I'd worry about that later.

Right now, I had a debt to repay.

My sneak attack in the kitchen led to a quickie on the island and a mental note to sanitize the kitchen ASAP. Then we got ready for the party. One of the requirements for my dress was that I could get in and out of it on my own, since I hadn't been sure when Derek was going to arrive. Plus, this way I could show him the finished product.

Everything was perfect an hour later when I stepped out into the living room. Derek looked up from where he sprawled on the couch as I said, "Ta-da," with a huge grin on my face.

The black dress had my favorite V-neckline, the bodice a silky material with a lace overlay that covered my shoulders and ended just above my elbows. The bottom was multilayered, with just enough fluff to give it body without making my hips look blockish. Its hemline brushed the tops of my knees. A wide black sash wound around my middle, bunched into a rose-like shape, the ends fluttering down over my left hip.

When I'd first seen it on the hanger, I'd wrinkled my nose, thinking it looked innocent and childish. But the black lace was sheer and sexy, the wide neckline showed the shape of my shoulders and the deep V combined with that awesome bra to highlight my décolletage. There was no mistaking me for a little girl.

I did a quick twirl as Derek stood up from the couch, stalking over to me. "What do you think?"

"I think it was worth the wait. You look amazing as always." His deep blue eyes trailed over my exposed collarbone, my cleavage and beyond. "Do we have to go to this party? I'm sure we could think of some other way to occupy ourselves." He trailed a warm finger along the edge of my dress, down my shoulder toward my chest, stopping just short of being indecent.

My smirk was coy, hiding all kinds of secrets to come. *I can't wait.* "My birthday, my decision." With a sly wink, I waltzed around him, taking the time to look him over like he deserved. "I guess I can be seen in public with you."

The truth was he looked magnificent as always. The gray sports jacket over his tight black shirt and black pants was the perfect mix of dressy and casual. His long, black hair curved and curled around, framing his perfect face. I brushed a lock back from his eyebrow, wishing he had a tie I could pull on. Instead, I touched my lips to his, letting my fingers drift down to thread through the hair at the nape of his neck.

"Sure I can't convince you to stay home?" His mouth brushed mine with each word.

"I bet you could, but I'd be so incredibly pissed at you later that it wouldn't be worth it. C'mon, Captain. Let's get this show on the road." I reached up to pat his cheek, grabbed my purse and sashayed toward the door.

He sighed, trailing behind me. "At least I can enjoy the view."

Our arrival at the party could not have been timed better. We'd told the rest of the guests to be there by five-thirty p.m., so there wouldn't be any confusion of meeting his friends on the stairs. I sent a quick text to Gina when we were on our way, and she met us just outside the event room.

"Hey, guys! Happy birthday, Avery. You look fabulous!" She gave me a hug, whispering that everything was all set. "Derek, I have a quick question for our girl here, so I'm going to steal her away for a sec. But Josh is coming up with the cake any minute. Would you mind waiting to help him?"

Of course, he was more than happy to do that. Gina rushed me inside, and I beamed as I scanned the room. The banner I'd ordered looked great. Rhonda and Gina had organized photo boards beneath it on the cake table, next to the gifts. I waved to Patty, who grinned as she peeked out from a swinging kitchen door. The counters looked good and sturdy, thankfully, otherwise I'd be worried they'd buckle from the mountains of food.

The bartenders gave me a thumbs-up from behind the bar, which was divided into a whiskey-tasting side and a regular bar. One of Liam's more brilliant suggestions had been to hire a photographer for the night. His cousin had just finished an internship so had affordable rates but did an amazing job. I grinned as she got into place. Waving and smiling at all our friends, I winced as Gina grabbed my arm.

"All right, Josh is on his way." She signaled everyone to take their places.

With one last glance around the room, I frowned when I didn't see Rhonda. Now wasn't the time, though. Quickly, I rearranged my face back into a smile and gripped the captain's hat I'd found for Derek to wear.

Josh came in first with the decoy box, stepping to the side.

As soon as Derek walked in, we all yelled, "Surprise!" Then, as planned, we sang *Happy Birthday*.

I never looked away from his face, my smile growing wider at his stunned expression. Those blue eyes, so sharp, so intelligent, scanned the room, taking in the décor, the details, his friends. When they came back to land on me, my grin grew until my cheeks hurt.

Our song finished with the majority of us ending at the same time, and all eyes fixed on Derek. We waited with bated breath for him to say something, anything. The last thing I expected was for him to blink rapidly, spinning on his heel to rush back out of the door he'd just come through. I met Gina's shocked eyes, then Liam's.

"Um, just give me a second, guys." I hurried after him, the captain's hat dangling from my fingers.

Derek leaned with one hand against the wall in the hallway, his back to me.

"Hey, Derek, you okay?" When there was no response, I edged my way around to see his face.

He didn't look at me. Just uttered one word, a deep, guttural question. "Why?"

The raw emotion caught me off guard. "What do you mean?"

As he straightened up, his gaze zeroed in on me with an intensity that stole my breath away. "Why did you do this, Avery?" He took a step closer, searching every inch of my face. "Why would my fake girlfriend go through the trouble of throwing me a surprise party on her birthday?" Another step, his voice edged with a desperation that cut through all my walls, all my bullshit. "I need to know *why*."

And it was time for me to stop pretending. Our games were done, especially in the face of his rawness. This moment mattered, my reason mattered, and he was asking me if it was real, if we were real. He deserved the truth, no matter how open, how vulnerable it left me. "Because I care about you, Derek. More than I should." It was as much as I could give him.

He let out a breath, his broad shoulders moving down a full inch.

I reached up to touch his cheek. "I know we have a lot to talk about, starting with what's really going on between us. But no matter what else this is, you are first and foremost my friend."

My thumb ran along his strong jaw. "That room in there is full of people who love you, people you have touched and protected and helped. People who see you every day, just like I do. You're not invisible, Derek. Not to us. I wanted to show you that the moment Yolanda sent the picture of you and the Three Musketeers on your birthday." I wrinkled my nose. "You looked like you'd just eaten a snail. And, I thought, no one should have a party that bad."

"So you threw me a birthday party?"

My smile was soft, tentative.

"On *your* birthday." His lips twitched, trying to hide his amusement.

But I could read between the lines, and my smile grew in response. "I was told I had to be cunning because you're way too good at spoiling surprises."

He rested his forehead against mine. "Well, you certainly surprised me."

I pulled the captain's hat from behind my back. "C'mon, Captain. We're celebrating you tonight." Using my worst pirate accent, which wasn't much better than my best, I said, "Or I'll make ya walk the plank."

The look he gave me was tender and full of something I was scared to name. "Avery, promise me we'll talk tonight. I got us a room —"

"Yeah, I told Liam to tell you to do that. Good job for listening." I shot him a patronizing grin.

He stayed serious. "I didn't bring your present here. I wanted to give it to you in private. Promise? We'll talk later?"

I touched my lips to his, ignoring the flutter of worry in my stomach. "I promise. Now, let's go party." Our second entrance garnered just as much attention as the first, so I kept it light. "Sorry about that, guys. He wanted to thank me privately." I tapped the brim of his captain's hat, smirking as the jokes poured in. The tour of the bar was next, explaining the twenty-one theme and giving credit to all my helpers.

We made him start the line for the food, and he thanked Patty for all her hard work, especially the ravioli. We sat down at one of the tables, but everyone kept coming over to say happy birthday, hug him, introduce themselves to me. His smile never dimmed, and his hand never left my waist. Liam kept bringing him small samples of the whiskeys, hoping maybe he'd fit all twenty-one tastes in without getting trashed.

I'd just finished dessert when Rhonda breezed in.

"Hi, Ave." She air-kissed my cheek, then stepped back to look at me. "We did a damn fine job on that dress, didn't we? And happy birthday!"

Derek stared at her skeptically.

She placed a hand on his arm, turning to him with a similar megawatt smile. "Happy birthday to you too, big brother. I'm sorry I'm late."

He rolled his eyes. "Yeah, we all know how you like to make an entrance."

The smirk on her face nearly masked the hurt in her eyes, but I caught its flicker before she hid it completely. "This time it wasn't all my fault. Your gift came with a little something extra." She moved aside, flinging a hand to the wide-open door. "Your birthday present."

A brick wall of a man strode in, a huge grin splitting his face. Derek lit up like a kid at Christmas.

Rhonda chuckled. "Roy Cobalt, meet the birthday boy, Derek Elgin."

Derek said nothing as he stared at his favorite quarterback, just gaped until the man was right in front of him. Then Derek shoved back his chair, standing up to eagerly shake Roy's hand. "What? How?" he stammered.

Rhonda grinned.

Roy clasped Derek's hand and smiled. "Your sister told me what a fan you were and explained she had some making up to do."

"Thanks, sis." Derek turned to wrap Rhonda in a full hug.

She winced. "Don't thank me yet. There's more." She mouthed "I'm sorry" to us before pointing to someone near the door. "Hit it!"

The lights dimmed. A familiar country song started thumping from speakers I didn't even know were there. The door opened, and in danced Piper Kensington, the princess of country music, a portable microphone in her hand. A million emotions played over Derek's face as he took her in—astonishment, trepidation, acceptance, delight.

"Rhonda!" His dazzling smile turned on her. "You brought Princess!"

The word hit me like a herd of elephants, and I blinked.

Relief crossed Rhonda's face, and she smiled back. She leaned down to me. "Her coming was a surprise to me, too, and I wasn't sure what his reaction would be. I hoped it wouldn't ruin the party. I promise I'll explain more later." She grimaced, sympathy in her eyes. "Can't tell Princess Piper no."

I gaped as Piper grinned, throwing her arms around Derek. The combination of her familiarity with my boyfriend and the second use of the name Princess created a pain in my gut so fierce it felt as though I'd been stabbed. Multiple times. With a dull knife that took forever to break through my flesh.

There she was in person. The words 'Wait for me? Yours forever' flashed across my mind. Jealousy mixed with anger to leave a bitter taste in my mouth. I tried to hold it together, reminding myself that Derek was my friend, first and foremost. This party was to show him how much we all cared about him.

The beginning chords of one of her most popular songs started, and a microphone stand appeared. She pulled Derek with her to the makeshift stage area, and they rocked out to the delight of the crowd. Derek never took his eyes off her, never stopped smiling.

No one noticed me slink over to the whiskey side of the bar. My steps were shaky. I felt like my world was tilted, but I had hardly drunk anything yet. *I can fix that.* The smooth leather of the barstool squeaked as I slid onto it, leaning both my elbows on the bar.

The bartender smiled at me. "Great party," he yelled, then he signaled to ask which whiskey I wanted.

I just shrugged, basically telling him to pick, as long as it was a big glass. While he poured, I looked back at the private concert, at the sparks flying between Princess and Derek, dancing a perfectly choreographed line dance to *Heartbreak Canyon*. The words of the chorus rang out, and I smacked my forehead. The note practically contained the lyrics to the damn song. *How could I be so blind?* And after what Bin had told me.

My first sip passed my lips. I waited for the burn, for the warmth, but I felt nothing. Even whiskey couldn't

302

touch me since my heart had been charbroiled to a crisp in a few short minutes, but I drank it anyway.

What happened to keeping my heart out of this? I winced at the ache in my chest as I watched the two of them together, dancing like they were made for each other. It didn't matter. If it didn't happen now, it would've happened someday, so might as well get it over with.

I could never compete with a princess.

Chapter Eighteen

Piper finished the song with a flourish, Derek dipping her low, then pulling her up for a huge hug. They laughed, slung their arms around each other, and I watched Derek look around the room. When his eyes landed on me, they lit up. He tugged Piper in my direction.

Can't he just let me finish my whiskey? I straightened up on the barstool, trying to keep my expression neutral. *Isn't it enough they get to be together, does he have to rub my face in it, too?*

Of course, Derek saw too much, frowning as he approached. "What's wrong? You okay?"

"Nothing." I shook my head. "Introduce me."

He gave me a long look but did as I'd asked. Letting go of Piper, he stood between us. "Princess, this is my girlfriend, Avery."

His eyes lingered on me as I stared up at him, more confused than ever. *Girlfriend.* The word bounced around my head. *Why would he introduce me like that to her?*

"Cupcake, this is my oldest friend, Piper. We call her Princess."

Piper elbowed him, laughing, then stuck her hand out. When she spoke, her voice was full of sweet country twang, though her stare was full of ice. "I don't believe I've ever met one of Derek's gals before. He must really like you. Did you really put all this together for him? And on your birthday, too?"

Somehow, I managed to nod.

"You really are something." The sideways glance she shot me told me she was sizing me up as well.

But she didn't have to worry, I was pulling myself out of the competition. *How am I supposed to compete with her?* The skinny blonde with flawless skin, chocolate eyes, and a pearly smile who broke hearts all over the country. *Where's a white flag when I need one?*

Derek glanced over once more, as if still trying to get a read on me. He turned back to Piper. "How long are you in town?"

"Heading out tomorrow afternoon for another gig. We'll have to do brunch before I leave. Maybe just the old gang." She patted his arm, giving me a pointed stare. "It's so good to see you again, D. It's been too long. I'll let you get back to your guests. I am the entertainment after all!" And she headed to the mic for another song, much to everyone else's delight.

As soon as she was out of earshot, Derek took the stool next to me. "All right, what's going on?" His tone changed from friendly to demanding.

Piper started belting out some song about a cheating man. *She would.* I slammed back the whiskey, eyed

Derek and decided I wasn't going to shout at him, so I stalked my way across the room to the hallway. Again.

He followed.

The door had barely shut when I whirled on him. "That's Princess? *She's* the mystery girl I've been competing against this whole time? Well, I fold." Hurt sliced through me anew, though I slammed it aside and tried to walk past him to the stairs.

But he blocked my way. "What are you talking about?"

I clenched my hands into fists, my nails digging into my palms. One kind of pain to distract from the other. "The first day in your apartment, I heard what Kevin said about you declaring your undying love for Princess." I gestured to where Piper belted her song out in the other room.

"I heard you and Liam that morning when he asked you if you'd told me about Princess yet. Both Bin and Rhonda filled me in about the girl who tore you up, the girl you still weren't over." Despite my best effort to get past him again, I failed miserably, and I fought the urge to scream. "Then I went to get your Lions hoodie out of the closet, and her letter fell out, asking you to wait for her. Signed 'yours forever'."

It was like I stood on the edge of a big black pit, looking down into its swirling depths. I hung my head, ready to step over. "That was the day I knew I'd let this go on for too long. I'm so far gone over you, but you've already given your heart to someone else. I promised myself I'd just be your friend, Derek, but I keep crossing that line." I wrapped my arms around myself. "I just don't know if I can go back. This wasn't supposed to happen. I can't compete with someone like that."

Derek took me in his arms, embracing all of me, crushing me to him. He rested his cheek on top of my head. "Avery, I don't know whether to throttle you or kiss you. For such a smart person, you can be an absolute idiot sometimes."

I pulled back enough to give him a look of utter confusion.

With a tug on my hand, he dragged me back into the party. "Wait here." He left me on the sideline, going to say a quick word to Rhonda and shake Roy Cobalt's hand once more. Then he was back, leading us right up to Piper. His signal to her was quick, and we waited there until she finished the song.

I wasn't even freaking out anymore. The pit still beckoned, and I welcomed the numbness.

Derek took the microphone. "All right, guys, I just wanted to say thank you to everyone for coming."

A chorus of cheers echoed around the room.

"To Piper and Roy Cobalt for making a special trip just for us. To Rhonda for twisting their arms to get here. To Gina and Liam for all their hard work and coordination. And especially to my girlfriend," he said, emphasizing the word, "Avery, who not only gave up her birthday for me but put all this together."

The cheers were even louder this time.

"Since Avery and I have two birthdays to celebrate, as well as plenty of amazing whiskey to help us do it, we're going to duck out a bit early. So you all, enjoy!"

I frowned. *That's unexpected.* Even more unexpected was his next move, which was to throw me over his shoulder. I yelped. Liam ran over with two bottles of whiskey from the bar, Gina right behind him. I peered up at her from Derek's back.

"You okay?" she asked.

Derek turned, talking before I could. "She's dumb, that's what she is. And we're going to set things straight."

Annoyance bristled through me at being called dumb. My world was upside down in more ways than one, and I couldn't do anything about it.

Gina smirked. "Girl, I told you so. I should have bet on it!" were the last words I heard before he carried me out of the door.

"Are you showing my ass off to everyone?" I asked grumpily as I jostled about, bouncing off his too-firm back. I didn't want to touch him, didn't want to notice the way his ass looked amazing from this angle, didn't want to feel his shoulder muscles rippling beneath me. I tried crossing my arms, but I had to give in and grab on if I had any hope of not ricocheting off him with every step. *Jerk*.

"Nope, got my hand nicely over your skirt." He gave my leg a little squeeze, sending a jolt through me and causing my thighs to clench. His chuckle let me know he'd felt my involuntary response. "Too bad my other hand is full of whiskey, otherwise I'd be enjoying myself even more."

I gritted my teeth. We stepped into an elevator, and the sensation of going up was odd while hanging upside down. I squirmed, but that just made friction in all the wrong, or right, places.

Then he was bouncing me along again. "All right, Cupcake, you either get to reach into my back pocket and do the honors of the keycard, or I get to do a few squats, setting the whiskey down, grabbing the card, getting the whiskey…"

I slid my hand into his pocket. He turned so I could insert the card and open the door.

"Thank you."

He set me on my feet, doing a full body slide so I felt every inch of him on my way down. Then he smirked, locking the door and striding past me without a second glance.

When I'd regained my bearings, I stared at the room. It was gorgeous. There was an en suite whirlpool tub, a huge king-sized bed, a full living room, a dining corner with a fridge. Presents sat on the table, along with a bouquet of flowers, a bottle of champagne in a bucket of ice and two champagne flutes.

Derek paced back and forth in front of the couch. "Just what kind of guy do you think I am, Avery?"

I slipped off my shoes because I was done with the heels and flopped down on the end of the bed. "A great one." It was dawning on me that I'd misread the situation. Completely. "But, seriously, Derek, can you blame me? We started this whole thing based on a lie. How am I supposed to know what's truth and what's fiction?"

He stilled. I felt his gaze on me as I turned to meet his eyes, reading the acknowledgment there.

His shoulders sagged, then he came to plop on the bed next to me. "Piper was my first love. I should have told you about her."

I softened. "Everyone has a past, Derek."

One corner of his mouth tipped up. "She never felt the same about me as I felt about her. The four of us were always together, me, her, Rhonda, Liam. They all knew about my crush. It was a part of us, and it became a source of comfort for her, a fallback. Any time she was between guys, I was there to pick her up, set her on her feet, watch her fly away. Then she started getting noticed for her singing, got an offer for her music contract."

I heard how his voice tightened, the pain in his pause. I rested my hand between us, left it there in case he needed to hold on to something.

"She came to visit at first, but I kept noticing the changes. Mostly in her eyes. Piper wasn't the same. There was a magnetism that drew people to her, but something was dulling it. A couple Christmases ago, she came home in shambles. Some record agent had used her for sex, dropped her like yesterday's news, and she was a wreck. She said she'd thought a lot about it, and she wanted me, only me. That this time would be different."

"But it wasn't." His sigh was long, but not despairing. "I was the safe guy for her, not *the* guy. It took a while to find myself again, and Bin really helped with that. I swore off girls for a couple years." His face tilted toward mine, blue eyes landing on me like twin flames burning with the hottest of fires. "Until you."

I scrunched up my nose. "What was with all your friends' comments then?"

He gave a shrug, awkward while lying down. "People watched me carry a torch for her for my entire childhood. What were they supposed to think?"

"…but you seemed so happy to see her."

He grabbed my hand, running his thumb over my knuckles. "Because I have you. She was a huge part of my childhood, and I can't think about growing up without thinking about her. It may have looked like I was excited to see my ex, but"—he swallowed—"that was just a blip in our relationship. I was happy to see an old friend, and I only got to that point because of you." He cleared his throat. "She's been through a lot.

It's been forever since she came home, and I'm happy to see her in one piece."

I sat up, wanting to put some distance between us, but he followed. "Derek, hang on. I just want some space."

But he shook his head. "I can give you anything but that. Every time I give you space, you run away. And when you're not here, I feel like I turn invisible again." His gaze pleaded with me. "Avery, I don't know what I was doing before I met you, but it wasn't living. Then you came along. You strode up to me, like a vision from a dream, grabbed my tie and kissed me like I'd never been kissed. Like I'd lived in the shadows until then, and you brought me into the light for the very first time."

He took both my hands in his, running his thumbs over my knuckles. "I looked for you every day after that kiss. I dreamt of you, of your strawberry hair, your luscious lips, your cupcake taste. When you ran into me at the library, I knew I couldn't let you get away again. And I called you my girlfriend." He smiled as he remembered. "You didn't even flinch, just took it in stride." When I frowned, he tilted his head. "What?"

"You say you liked me, but you looked so disappointed when Yolanda ran away. I never did figure that one out."

Seconds passed as he blinked at me, then he chuckled. "I was disappointed you didn't let me keep my arm around you. You ducked away from me the minute she was gone."

"Oh. So you held my hand." I recalled how right it had felt.

"And you didn't pull away." He looked down, discomfited by whatever he was thinking. "I never should have suggested the fake dating thing. We should have just started out for real." He smiled wryly. "Who knew one word could ruin everything?"

"I don't know about ruin." I thought about our crazy relationship, the connection we had. Underneath it all, I knew I'd never have moved as fast if circumstances hadn't thrown us together. "I'm scared, though." It was time to tell him the truth, the other piece I'd been holding back. "I thought my parents had an amazing relationship, a fairy-tale love that I spent my whole childhood dreaming of. And look where they are now. They started off doing everything right.

"We did everything backward, built on a lie." I asked the question I was most scared of, the one that had my stomach clenching. "How can we trust what we have is enough?"

Derek squeezed my hand. "That's the falling in love part, Avery."

I sucked in a breath at the word love, fear tightening its grip as I fought the urge to run.

"You can't fall without taking the leap." His eyes bored into mine, his breath warm on my cheek. "But I'm ready to leap with you. We can walk this plank together."

Several long moments passed. We stared at each other as I studied Derek, analyzed his words. It was a big word, but it didn't sound so scary when I tried it out in connection to Derek. Finally, I found the courage to swallow my fear, my doubt, to say it out loud. "I'll jump if you promise to catch me. And only if we're honest from here on out."

"Of course I'll catch you. I'll be there to carry you to bed whenever you need it. And get you out of your dresses." We shared a warm smile. "No more secrets."

"Then there's something I need to tell you." There was one secret in all this mess, one thing I'd kept from him.

He raised an eyebrow.

"I have a warehouse full of designer items and signed copies of my mother's books that I used to pay for this party tonight." I watched for his reaction.

He blinked. "Really? That's your big secret?"

I lowered my voice to a whisper, "And sometimes, when nobody's watching, I do cut up my pizza."

His burst of laughter was a wonderful reward.

I ran my hands up his chest, thinking about everything he had told me. Pieces fell into place, and I thought about the raw moments after we'd surprised him. He'd needed to know my motivation, needed the reassurance I wasn't using him like Piper had. We both had scars from our family and our pasts, but I thought we could help each other move beyond them. If we just gave this a real chance.

"Derek?" I stepped back, my emotion roughening my voice. "Remember the second time you helped me out of my dress, how I said I wasn't ready?"

He gave the slightest of nods, as if anything more would break his fragile hold on his self-control.

"Well, I'm ready now." I held his gaze as I turned around and presented him my back, gathering my hair to one side.

He slid his hands to my waist and his breath warmed my cheek. "I think we have some more exploring to do." He unzipped me with an achingly slow pace, his fingers brushing over each inch of my skin as it was bared to him. When the dress finally fell to the floor, he turned me to face him, and his eyes drifted over my length. One finger traced the edge of my bra, over the swell of one breast, into the valley between, then up the swell of the other. "Is this new?"

I grinned, mentally thanking Selena for the new lingerie that fit me perfectly but was still sexy as hell. "You like?"

The darkening of his blue eyes was enough of an answer, but I didn't protest when his lips found mine. His tongue swept in to dance with mine as he tangled his fingers in my hair. I gripped his shoulders, needing to steady myself against the headiness of being with him.

He stepped back and shrugged off his sports jacket. I couldn't tear my eyes away as he yanked the hem of his dress shirt out of his trousers, then undid the buttons one by one. I had to swallow as my mouth went dry at the tantalizing sight of his bare chest. Once the shirt was gone, I launched myself at him, touching, tasting, gripping. He returned the favor and before I knew it, we were both bare.

With his hands on my hips and his erection digging into my stomach, he walked me backward toward the bed. I sat down heavily but resisted when he tried to lean me back.

I shook my head. "I'm on top tonight."

The delighted grin on his face took my breath away as he let me lead him around to the head of the bed. I waited impatiently as he settled against the wall with a pillow behind his back, then I pounced on him. I straddled his muscular legs, grinding my apex on his eager cock. Our kiss was fueled with every bit of hunger building between us, and I arched into his skillful hands when they cupped my breasts.

"Condom," I breathed.

His eyes went wide. "My pants pocket."

I hopped off the bed, returning with the square package which I ripped open and slid down his length. Then I positioned myself over him, waiting until our gazes locked before I sank on to his straining dick. A relieved breath escaped my lips when he filled me, as if I was now complete in a way I hadn't been before.

My hips began moving before I knew what I was doing, my body craving that sweet release. He groaned then leaned forward to take my peaked nipple in his mouth. A thrill zipped down to my core, and I picked up my pace, edged on by the tantalizing sight of him suckling me. He switched to the other breast, giving it just as much attention before he looked up at me. His gaze overflowed with adoration and want, combining to steal my breath.

When he surged up to claim my lips, I was helpless to resist. I cupped his face in my hands, my thumbs tracing over his strong jaw. He slipped a hand between us, resting his thumb on my swollen clit, and I gasped against his lips at the added friction. Lightning began shooting through me, though I tried to hold it off.

I didn't succeed, the wave of pleasure too strong to fight. I shuddered over him, leaning in to rest in his embrace. When I finished, his hands drifted to my hips, then he bucked into me. My breasts bounced against his chest as he impaled me over and over with his powerful thrusts. I closed my eyes, unable to keep them open in the relentless onslaught of bliss that crashed over me with his every movement. His breathing grew heavy as his fingers dug in and I knew he was close.

I bit my lip, waiting for him this time, only allowing the dam to burst when he went rigid under me. I cried out his name, clinging to him as I rode out the crest that had me shuddering over him. We sat like that for several moments as my heart finally slowed to a normal beat. When I leaned back to look at him, he wore a sweet smile, and his eyes were softer than I'd ever seen.

It wasn't just sex anymore. This time, we'd made love, and there were no more walls around my heart.

* * * *

Soft nuzzles on my bare shoulder pulled me from a deep sleep. I groaned. "No. There is not a thing you haven't explored. Go away and let me sleep." I shoved Derek before rolling over with a hmph. But he heard the teasing in my voice.

His fingers trailed down my spine. "I'm sure I can find some place." His voice was deliciously husky as he brushed several strands of hair off my neck. "Like this freckle for example." He placed a stubbly kiss on it, making me squirm. "I'm quite sure I didn't know of its existence until just now." He kept nibbling and nuzzling his way down to the crook of my neck, making me squeal and laugh, begging for him to stop. Finally, he did, but only to capture my mouth with his, stealing my laughter and my breath.

Our phones chimed at the same time, and I let out a sigh of relief. "Saved by the text."

His glare made me laugh. "Don't think this is over."

I lay on my back, staring up at the ceiling. "Who's bothering us now?"

"Liam." A swoosh sound signaled he'd sent his reply. "We've been summoned to brunch with Piper and Rhonda in about an hour. So I guess our wakeup session will have to wait."

Instantly going into panic mode, I bolted upright. "An hour? I have to pack and shower and—"

Maren Jenner

"Relax," Derek said, chuckling. "We have the room another night. I wanted to make sure we had plenty of quality time together." His gaze drifted down my bare body, completely exposed now that I'd sat up. "As soon as I was sent out of town, I extended the reservation." He adjusted himself, the evidence of his attraction showing.

I bit my lip. "How fancy is this brunch?"

"Casual," he bit out between gritted teeth, not taking his eyes off me.

I crawled my way toward him. "And how far away is it?"

"Right here." His voice was practically a growl.

I was nearly purring. "Then I think we have some time." I barely finished my sentence before he pounced.

As it turned out, we were a little late. I blamed Gina for not packing me the right clothes. I had only brought enough for one night, not realizing I'd be here any longer, so she'd added to my bag on Derek's request. But she'd mostly put in things unsuitable for wearing outside the hotel room. Things that made Derek's eyes widen the more I flung out of the bag and made me swear the more I dug.

I'd finally found a pair of jeans at the bottom along with a plain black T-shirt which I paired with one of Derek's button downs, knotted in the front. It would have to do.

We'd rented the event room for today too, anticipating a late night and the need to tear down. Derek's presents sat on the table, all unopened. The staff had done a good job cleaning up almost everything, but there were still some decorations and personal items I had to take care of.

Liam met us at the door.

I gave him a big hug. "Thanks for everything last night. You were a huge help putting it all together, and it turned out great." I beamed up at him, my smile dimming as I walked in, meeting Piper's icy gaze.

She sniffed, shaking her head at me. All the ice melted as her eyes flew to Derek's, then it was full-on charm. "There he is! Hey, D, you didn't open any presents last night. At least, open mine." She latched on to his arm, trying to drag him over to the table of gifts.

His laugh was a little strained. "Piper, chill. I'm starving. Let's eat first, then open gifts." Those blue eyes found mine, and he winked. "Someone kept me up late last night."

"Yeah, we burned some calories, didn't we, Captain?" We shared an intimate laugh as he crossed the room, returning to my side, even pulling out my chair for me.

Liam just rolled his eyes. "Ugh, let me get some food in my stomach, so at least I have something to throw up."

The door opened, and in came Rhonda. "Morning, everyone."

A small buffet was set up against one wall. There were two staff members at our disposal, taking drinks, clearing plates, stocking food.

"So, whose brilliant idea was this?" I asked between bites.

Rhonda beamed. "Oh, it was mine. I didn't have time to get you a birthday present what with hunting Roy down, so ta-da."

"Food for my birthday?" I grinned at her. "You know me well."

Piper snorted into her napkin, trying to disguise it with a cough but failing.

I ignored her attempt at an insult, instead asking Rhonda, "What's up with the two-for-one celebrity deal?"

Piper giggled, beaming at Derek, taking another opportunity to run her hand down my boyfriend's arm. "Oh, I was at Roy's when he got the call. When I heard it was Derek's birthday, I just had to come. For old time's sake." She fluttered her eyelashes at him.

Rhonda rolled her eyes, giving me a look to say she'd tell me more later.

So I turned to Liam. "How'd the rest of the party go? I haven't had a chance to talk to Gina yet."

He grinned after swallowing a mouthful of food. "It was a blast! Everyone ate too much, drank too much. Princess here was the life of the party. Roy signed autographs. It was the bash of the century."

Piper trailed a finger along Derek's exposed wrist. "Too bad you had to leave so early. Not one of those guys danced like you do."

Derek shifted out of her reach with an uncomfortable smile.

The ball was back in my court. "He sure can dance, can't he? Did you teach him that?"

Her smile could have drawn blood. "That and a whole lot more." Her dark eyes went back to him. "Remember the first time we went skinny dipping?" Those eyes flicked to Rhonda and Liam, pretending to include them in the story. "Remember the meteor shower that night?"

I stopped listening and watched Derek. All I could see was the pain in his eyes. She used her words like claws, leaving gouges so deep it was several long seconds before the blood even welled up. *What kind of person does that? And she's supposed to be a friend?*

"Hey," I said, interrupting her. My voice stayed even but was laced with steel. My smile, sickeningly sweet, dripped with poison. "Remember how Derek helped you pick up the pieces after that record label guy tore you to shreds?"

Her jaw dropped. "How dare you —"

"Or how about the day you boarded that bus, choosing your career and yourself over the one and only Derek Elgin?" My grin never wavered, tone as pure as honey.

Piper stared at me, nails digging into the tablecloth. Her teeth clenched and her eyes narrowed as I prepared for an attack.

Then Rhonda started laughing. Full-on, doubled-over, banging-on-the-table laughing. Liam joined her, while Derek just shook his head, patted my leg, and kept eating. I relaxed a little, sitting back in my seat.

Confusion written all over her, Piper looked from one to the other. "Did I miss something?"

Rhonda wiped her eyes, trying to calm down enough to breathe. "Oh, man, it's just…" The laughter hit her again. "It's just hilarious watching someone else go through it." Liam caught her eye, and the fragile hold on her composure broke once more.

Finally, she calmed down enough to talk. "Oh, sorry about that. Avery is…" She trailed off to look at me fondly. "She's very protective of Derek, and she knows him well. You were hurting him just now, Piper, bringing up old memories that caused him pain, so she shut you down. I know all about that." Her smile was small, apologetic and directed at me, then gathered a fierce edge as she turned it on Piper.

"When I first learned about Avery, I was not onboard. Neither were my parents." Guilt shone in her eyes as she glanced at me. "I'd met her the day before, and Avery put me in my place in front of my friends. So I decided to return the favor."

Taking a sip of water, she paused. "But Avery met every challenge we threw at her. Not only did she outshine all of us in her Armani dress, but it was clear she and Derek are made for each other. She won Dad over instantly. Then at dinner, we—" She stopped, swallowing to regain her composure.

My heart went out to her, my new friend. I reached over and patted her hand—thankful she'd realized her behavior was wrong.

Her grateful smile was still tinged with guilt. "We skipped Derek as usual when we went around the table with our updates. But Avery wouldn't have it. When Derek spoke up, I cut him off…" This time, she met Derek's eyes. "I was jealous of the attention or something. Either way, my behavior was inexcusable, and I'm sorry." Her apology was heartfelt.

Derek nodded at her as one corner of his mouth tipped up.

She went on, telling about me giving my mother's book to her and her mom. "Then she sat down and asked about dessert." Rhonda squeezed my hand. "I decided the next day that I couldn't handle someone like you for an enemy, so I damned well better try harder to be your friend."

I put my elbows on the table and buried my face in my hands. "I'm never going to live that one down."

Derek stroked the back of my head. "Nope."

Rhonda pointed her fork at Piper. "Moral of the story is, be nice to Derek, or you gotta deal with her." She popped a bite of eggs into her mouth.

When I met Piper's eyes over the table, I knew things weren't over between us. But she wasn't the first shark I'd swum with. And I hadn't lost a limb yet.

Things were smoother after that, though, with lines clearly drawn. Liam and Rhonda were definitely on board with me and Derek being together. So we spent the rest of the time chatting about what had happened since Piper ditched them. I really wanted to bring up the way she'd left Derek but I managed to keep that impulse under control.

Then they started reminiscing. Of course, a lot of the stories involved Derek crushing on Piper, but that had been a norm for their childhood—I could deal with it. There were a few more moments of gritted teeth and clenched fists when Piper got overly familiar, but she seemed to sense when she overstepped. Rhonda helped steer the conversation back on track. Overall, I felt like I understood a new piece of him after we were done— Liam and Rhonda, too.

Piper had to leave all too soon. *Oh darn*. "Can I have a minute, Derek? For old time's sake?" She shot him her best puppy-dog-eyed look, then sauntered into the hallway.

He stood up, leaning down to brush a kiss against my cheek. "I promise I won't run off with her. I might come back with lipstick on my cheek, but know that it won't be consensual on my part, okay? I'm yours. And I promise to tell you all about it afterwards."

I shot him a quick salute. "Aye, aye, Captain."

He shot me the finger as he walked away, and I laughed.

Rhonda looked bemused. "I never did hear why you call him Captain."

With an evil grin, I began, "Well, I was reading this romance novel about a pirate…"

* * * *

Back in our room, we set down the last load of presents. Derek shook his head. "I can't believe you told them that story."

"I had to tell them something." His friends had enjoyed the tale, all of us standing up to salute him when he returned.

The bright shade of smeared pink lipstick on his cheek still annoyed me, but I believed him when he said she'd just kissed him goodbye. After she'd asked if he was sure about me. Which he was.

"We should probably open some of these." He stared at the stack.

I'd been surprised to find several with my name mixed in as well. "Dive in?" So we did.

There were lots of shot glasses, gag gifts like Pepto Bismol, saltines, Gatorade and Pedialyte. Gina and Liam had bought all the whiskey, a gift to both of us. Several of our mutual friends had snuck in Lions gear gifts for me, a coffee mug, a keychain, even a pair of super-fuzzy socks. "I just need some Lions undies, and I'm set!"

Derek just rolled his eyes. "You are not getting Lions undies because you will insist on showing them to all the guys at the next Sunday football. Not happening."

Valid point.

"Okay, now my presents."

I frowned at him. "I thought the present was the room. And the Lions blanket."

He shook his head. "No, I said your present was in the room."

"But I didn't get you anything." *Other than the captain's hat.*

The look he gave me was priceless. "You threw me the best damn surprise party ever. You got me plenty." Striding to the dining room table, he grabbed three boxes of varying sizes and brought them over. He thrust the biggest one into my hands first.

I shook the box, frowning when it didn't make any noise. After untying the ribbon, the box lid popped off on its own, revealing a teddy bear holding a cupcake. "Oh, it's so cute!" The light brown bear was soft, perfect for cuddling, and I picked it up, giving it a squeeze. "I love it."

He smiled, handing me the next box, smaller, but not tiny.

I untied the ribbon, lifting off the lid. Tissue paper covered the item, so I peeled it away. It was a Lions T-shirt. Not a jersey, but a comfy-looking, fitted tee. Holding it up, I could see it was the perfect size. I grinned at him, telling him thank-you as he passed me the last box. This one was small, oblong and slender. The ribbon fell away. I opened the lid, and sitting inside was a rose-gold tennis bracelet.

"I didn't know what kind of metal you liked. The rose gold reminded me of your hair, and I couldn't resist."

I lifted it out of the box to drape it over my fingers. "Derek, this is too much."

He chuckled. "What's the fun in having a billionaire boyfriend if you don't let him spoil you once in a while?"

I was a sucker for logic. And sparkles. "Put it on me?"

He smiled his megawatt smile. "That's the spirit."

After he'd fastened the clasp around my wrist, I held it up, admiring it for a minute. Then I glanced back over at him, overwhelmed by how lucky I was to claim him as mine. "Any thoughts on how I could possibly thank the giver of these amazing gifts?"

His smile turned into a leering smirk. "I might have some ideas."

Chapter Nineteen

Sunday afternoon, with Greg's help, we got everything back to the apartment. I wasn't as exhausted as I'd thought I'd be after the active weekend Derek and I spent in the hotel. My cheeks hurt because I couldn't stop smiling. Every time I passed Greg in the hall with another armload of presents or decorations or unopened whiskey, he smirked and shook his head.

Finally, it was all in. Greg left with our many thanks and a bottle of whiskey.

Derek wiped the sweat off his forehead, as he'd insisted on doing most of the heavy lifting. "I think I'm going to hit the shower." He leaned in for a kiss, but I stuck my palm out, making a face.

"I'll wait till after you're clean, thank you."

"Fine, but I get double then." And he hurried down the hall.

I looked at the piles of stuff, getting tired just thinking of sorting it all. A knock at the door had me scurrying over. *Maybe Greg forgot something.* To my surprise, it was Liam with a box…of mail?

Frowning, I said, "It is Sunday, right?"

He laughed. "Yeah, but I was getting my mail and one of the managers was there. Evidently you didn't get your mail last week? The mailman had to start piling it up."

Mentally, I smacked my forehead. "Crap. Derek usually grabs it. Between him being gone last week, the party, and everything, I didn't even think about it. Thanks so much!"

Liam looked at the mess sprawling across our kitchen and dining room. "Good thing you canceled Sunday night football. Looks like you've got your work cut out for you." He shook his head. "Good luck.

"Thanks again."

With one last wave, he disappeared into the elevator.

I shut the door with my foot, setting the box on the coffee table. Mail was the priority, so I started sorting. I tried to make piles. Obviously, mine went into one pile, but the majority was Derek's, and he got a lot of junk, so I tried to weed it out.

A postcard stood out from a name I didn't recognize. Curious, and knowing I shouldn't snoop, I read it anyway.

Derek, congratulations on getting your master's in math! I can't believe you're the youngest SMU graduate to ever earn their master's and I used to date you. I read your paper online. I always knew you'd change the world, looks like that day is finally here. If you're still single, or ever want to catch up, my number's still the same. ~Wendy

It wasn't that he had a postcard from some girl that bothered me. *But why am I just finding out now that he's graduating with his master's this semester?* He'd said he was graduating, and that was early for our age group. When he and Bin had mentioned a project, I'd just assumed he meant for Derek's bachelor's degree. *But a master's?*

I put the postcard down, googling Derek's name along with math. A plethora of hits came up. Derek had created an app that was revolutionizing the shipping world as we knew it. His new algorithm provided a better way to make full use of each shipping container, with less margin of error and less manpower, saving the shipping companies money. Everyone was saying he was a genius.

And I'd had to hear about it from an ex-girlfriend. Frustration and hurt whirled in me, but I tried to keep calm. *We're still new. We had a lot going on, him out of town, the party this weekend…*

I tried to push it out of my mind as I kept sorting through the mail. The next to last piece had familiar handwriting that caught my eye, and I frowned at the name and address of my old landlord. *Why would he be contacting Derek?*

Unable to stop myself, I ripped open the envelope and scanned the contents of the letter. As the words sank in, I stood up, reading faster and faster. I lifted my head, took a deep breath, and told myself that it wasn't true. Unfortunately, when I looked down the words hadn't disappeared.

Right there, in black and white, it said that Derek was the one who'd had my apartment condemned. *So much for honesty between us. The manipulative bastard had me in a chess match right from day one.* I thought back to my time in the hospital, how I was supposed to be released first thing, then had magically been let out after Derek had showed up. And how he'd won Gina over so quickly.

I wondered why. *Was it all about the sex? Was it some sort of sick game to him?* Maybe this weekend was the feather in his cap, and from here on out he'd grow more and more distant.

Well, not if I leave first. I heard the shower stop and knew I didn't have any time. I grabbed my phone, my purse and my shoes, then ran for the hall. Anger, hurt and betrayal compounded with each footfall as I headed for Liam's, pounding on his door.

He opened it, a shocked look crossing his face. "Ave! What's wrong? Is everything all right?"

I tried to speak but couldn't.

His strong hands clutched my shoulders. "Is Derek okay? Did something happen?"

"He's fine." The words burned like acid on my tongue. "Precious Derek is fine. His little lies have caught up to him, though, and I'm done. Liam, were you in on it, too? Was it all a game?" I stared at him, needing him to tell me that he, at least, was really my friend.

"What? I—" he stammered, glancing down the hall. "I don't understand."

"If you're my friend at all, you'll help me disappear. Now. Before Derek comes after me. I promise I'll explain, but I didn't know where else to go. Please." I swiped at the silent tears streaming down my cheeks.

Liam shut his mouth, opening the door wider. "Okay, let me put on my shoes. I know just the place."

A few minutes later, we were in his car. He'd taken some extra time when he'd realized how fast I'd left and packed me up a few things of his own. I silenced my phone, then slouched in the front seat, knees against the door.

"All right. Please explain why I'm helping my best friend's girlfriend run away from him, after they just spent the entire weekend banging like rabbits."

It was time for him to know the whole truth. "Derek and I weren't really dating to begin with."

He laughed.

But I kept my tone serious. "It's true. Ask Gina if you like. Ask Derek. I'm not sure why he didn't tell you. I met him one week before I went to the hospital, when I walked up to him and kissed him randomly to get away from my mother's book agent who was trying to drag me to one of my mother's dinner parties."

His laughter faded. "But…"

As I told him about the library and breakfast, I tried to keep my voice steady, but it wobbled. The stupid tears were back. "Yolanda stole his phone at the birthday party, asking where his amazing girlfriend was, and you know the rest." I sniffed. "What you don't know is we weren't officially, truly dating until this weekend." *Stupid leap, stupid Derek. Why had I trusted him?*

Liam's mouth opened and closed a few times before any sound came out. "Holy shit, so many things make sense now."

"Like why we hadn't said 'I love you'? Why we couldn't wait even one night to have sex so used your emergency key?"

His cheeks were pink, but he nodded.

"Yeah." I sighed, hugging my abdomen to soothe the ache. It didn't help. My forehead rested against the cool window, and I watched the trees rush by. "Derek

330

told me about Piper this weekend, too. I thought it explained a lot about why he let his family treat him the way he did, why he let himself become invisible. And I shared some things of my own..." My voice broke.

I curled into a tighter ball. Maybe if I curled tight enough, I could hold the pieces of myself together. "I've never felt closer to anyone than I have to Derek this weekend. When Piper started digging up that old pain, just because she could, I saw red. I protected him." I swallowed hard, but it did nothing to relieve the lump in my throat.

"We promised to be honest with each other." I made my ball tighter still. "But I had to find out on a postcard that he's not only getting his master's, he's the youngest person to earn it. And the app that's changing the world? Had to google that."

Liam frowned.

"I was upset, but I could handle that." Clenching and unclenching my jaw, I spit out the next words. "Until I discovered Derek was the one to condemn my apartment." It took a minute for my vision to clear. "I was supposed to be discharged first thing that morning from the hospital, but I lay there waiting until Derek fucking Elgin came walking in with Gina to tell me that oh gee, somehow my apartment had been condemned and wow, he just happened to have a room available." My breaths were shaky.

"I'm sure it wasn't like that—"

"Then why didn't he tell me!" My angry words bounced around the car like a bullet ricocheting down an alley. "He had time. If there wasn't anything to hide, then why didn't he tell me?" I glanced at Liam, hoping he'd have an answer, hoping he could right my world once more.

A muscle worked in the side of his jaw, and his knuckles were white against the black leather of the steering wheel. "I don't know, Ave. I don't know."

Half an hour of mostly silence later, the car stopped, and I looked around. "Where are we?"

"You can stay here. It's my family's place, but they only use it in the summer."

It was a three-story house, not a mansion by any means, but with a view that took my breath away. The house sat on a bluff overlooking Lake Michigan, a brick wall surrounding the front and two sides of the property. "Holy shit. For real?"

Liam nodded. "I'll send someone out with your stuff as soon as I can. Until we get this straightened out."

I stopped on the step, turning to face him, the wind whipping my hair into my face. "You won't tell Derek I'm here?"

"No, I won't. Not unless you ask me to." Pain twisted his features as he said the words, and I knew what I was asking him to do.

I threw myself at him, holding him tight. "Thank you, Liam. I don't know how I'll ever repay you. I just need some time." I let go and stepped back.

"I'll see what I can find out. He's going to freak, you know." At my nod, he started toward the car, pausing when he'd opened the door. He grabbed a bag from the backseat and brought it back to me. "There's money in here. Plus a few other things I thought you might need. It should last you the week, and if not, I'm just a phone call away, okay?"

With another nod, I went up to the door, unlocking it with the key he'd pressed into my hand. I watched him drive away before I stepped inside, reaching the couch before I allowed myself to completely fall apart.

* * * *

Sunlight streamed in the window, making me wince. I shoved a pillow over my head, but it was no use. I was awake. A headache pounded at my temples from my crying jag last night. I sat up gingerly, still in yesterday's clothes. It took a minute to get my bearings. I wandered till I found the kitchen, then opened cupboards until I stumbled upon the glasses, finally able to get a cool drink of water for my cotton-dry mouth.

The counter supported me as I braced myself and pulled my phone out of my pocket. Twenty-five missed calls, all from Derek. *Wow*. I scrolled through them, a little miffed to not see any from Gina. My finger hovered over her name, but I decided against it at the last minute. I'd spilled my guts to Liam yesterday, and that had been enough for the time being. Now, I needed to process. To distance. Build up the brick wall between Derek and my heart, then go on with my life.

I went to my phone's settings and changed them so only ones from Liam, Gina, Rhonda and Greg would alert me. Then I decided I should eat something, even though I really wasn't hungry. There was a can of soup in the bag Liam had given me.

Half a bowl of soup and a shower later, I remembered I only had the clothes I was wearing. Liam had thoughtfully tucked in some drawstring pants and a hoodie which didn't fit quite right, but they were better than nothing. My phone dinged.

It was Rhonda.

Just picked up some of the things you wanted. Greg will stop by soon to grab them. Heads up, he's not happy with you. I had to twist his arm to drop anything off. I'd come see you myself, but something came up. Let me know if you need anything else.

I sent her back a *Thanks*, but that was all I could manage. Then I stared at the wall. Sometime later my phone dinged again, this time from Greg.

On my way. Need anything else?

Whiskey, whiskey, and more whiskey. Did I mention whiskey?

Eye roll emoji. *It's covered, Rhonda insisted.*

You guys are the best.

I stared at my phone, wondering again why Gina hadn't called. Or been the one to get my things. The doorbell rang, and I hurried to open the door for Greg.

He had a box in his arms, with a backpack thrown over his shoulder. His concerned gaze looked me over before coming in. "Hey."

"Hey."

Once he saw I was in one piece, he shifted under the weight, glancing around the spacious entryway. "Um, where should I...?"

"Oh." I still hadn't explored the house. "By the couch? On the floor is fine. I haven't really settled yet."

He set the things down, taking off his hat and running his fingers through his sandy hair.

A burning question bubbled up before I could stop it. "How...how's Derek?"

Greg wouldn't meet my eyes and his jaw clenched. "I'm going to be honest with you, Avery. I don't know what happened, but I've never seen him more messed up. And I saw him after Piper." He sighed. "I know you well enough that I'm sure you wouldn't just run out on him, but, well, I hope you know what you're doing." He adjusted the brim of his hat, looking like he wanted to say more, then thought better of it. "I'm sorry. I have to go."

And he left me standing in the middle of the living room gaping after him.

I wallowed after that, like a pig in a mud hole. My phone didn't ring once, and I didn't call anyone else. I didn't bother turning on the lights when the sun disappeared behind the clouds, didn't bother moving from the couch to one of the many more than comfortable bedrooms. I just replayed Greg's words and reread the mail in my mind.

When I'd downed more than my share of whiskey, I pulled out my phone, clicking on my voicemail icon. On my side, assuming my curled-up position, I pushed the speaker button and listened to all of Derek's messages. They started off curious, thinking maybe I was playing a joke on him. Then he got worried, wondering if something was wrong. He was nearly frantic by the end.

But it was the last one that had tears spilling down my cheeks.

"Avery? Look, I talked to Liam. He told me about the mail, and I read it myself. Cupcake, I didn't know, I didn't realize you didn't know about the master's and graduation and the paper. I guess why would you, right? But the other one…the apartment. I get it. I didn't want to tell you because I was afraid something like this would happen."

The silence stretched on so long I had to look to make sure the message hadn't ended. "I did what I had to do, Avery. Those apartments weren't safe." Another pause. "Liam told me not to ask where you are, that you asked him not to tell me. So I won't. I won't call again. You deserve your space, and if this is what you need...I can respect that. Just take care of yourself, okay? I'll be here if you need me. Anything at all."

And that was it, his last message.

I put down the phone and the whiskey and cried myself to sleep. Tuesday passed much the same. I wasn't sure I left the couch to do more than pee.

Wednesday, I thought I was dreaming when I heard Gina's voice. "How much do you like this couch, Liam?"

"Do it."

Then cold water poured down over me. I bolted upright, sputtering and coughing while waving my arms. "What the hell?" When I'd cleared enough water from my eyes that I could see, my vision focused on Gina standing above me, arms crossed, a no-nonsense expression on her face.

"You about done?"

I sagged against the soggy couch. "Gina," I began, only to be doused with another bottle of cold water. "Stop!"

"I said, are you about done?"

"Done what?" I shook my arms, wiping off my face again.

"Having this ridiculous pity party for yourself." She shook her head.

My mouth opened to protest again, but I stopped when I caught her look.

"I have another bottle, so choose your words carefully. If they have anything to do with what you think Derek did, I'd shut that mouth until you hear the whole story." Her chin lifted in a clear threat, waiting until I did exactly as she suggested. "Good, now despite the two bottles of water I just dumped on you, you stink. Go rinse off. Find some clean clothes and meet us back here in twenty. We have some talking to do."

Us? I looked around the room, realizing it wasn't just her and Liam. Rhonda was there too, and Greg. Sheepishly, I took in the state of the couch, the several empty whiskey bottles. I winced as I tried to push my greasy hair back, but it was plastered to my forehead. *Point taken.* I nodded, grabbing the bag of clothes off the floor where Greg had left it the other day.

More clear-headed after showering and in different clothes, I also gave my teeth a decent scrubbing. When I came out, the living room was empty, freshly cleaned and smelling a whole lot better than I had left it. *Crap. I owe Liam an apology.* The sound of voices and the smell of food led me to the kitchen. I arrived to find everyone standing around the island, which was piled high with brunch food.

My stomach rumbled. *When's the last time I ate?* "Um, hey."

All heads swiveled toward me.

"Sorry about the mess, guys, Liam." I nodded specifically to him. "I owe you."

Gina shoved a plate into my hands. "Who knows when you ate something of substance, so go ahead, dig in. Then we're getting to the bottom of this mess."

Gratefully, I piled up the food, taking a little of everything, unsure what my stomach could handle. To drink, I grabbed a water, a Coke and an apple juice. I plopped down at the table to wait for the others.

Once everyone had sat down, Gina took the lead again. "Okay, Avery, Liam's given us the rundown, but tell us your side. Start from the party please, what happened with Piper and the Princess thing?"

So I told them everything. I even went back to the beginning like I'd done with Liam and started with the fake dating bit, which Rhonda and Greg could barely wrap their heads around. I opened up about my insecurities about the Princess, how hard it had been to actually meet her, and how Derek had explained everything. How we'd really started dating, how vulnerable I'd become. When I said that, Gina shot Liam a triumphant grin I didn't understand.

Then I explained about the mail. "I felt betrayed after our commitment to being honest. The timing feels very manipulative, being coerced into moving in with him right after saying yes to the fake dating. It seems awfully convenient and made me question everything again. Why would he do that? Was it all just a game?"

Which is when Rhonda started laughing. "Sorry, Avery, it's just that..." She took a minute to compose herself. "You and Derek had us all convinced that you two were the real deal, so much so that we barely believe you when you tell us you were fake dating. Yet you practically have yourself sold on this absurd idea that somehow Derek was pretending?" She snorted. "What planet are you living on?"

I gaped at her. "Excuse me?"

Gina raised her hand to Rhonda, palm up for a high-five. "Thank you."

Rhonda smacked her hand to Gina's, the two of them exchanging grins.

"I've been telling you all along he's crazy about you." Gina rolled her eyes. "And you told us yourself he basically said the same thing after the party. So why'd you go running scared at the first sign of trouble? Haven't you learned anything?"

Greg leaned back in his chair, crossing his arms. "I watched the two of you coming from parties, heard you two talking, listened to his stories about you. I saw you stand up for him like no one ever has. I saw the light in his eyes when you came into view. You can't tell me it was fake on his end. He may not have said it, but he was really feeling it. I know Derek."

Liam nodded. "And I've got evidence to prove it."

What? I frowned as he pulled out his phone, swiped a few times, then slid it over to me.

Derek filled the screen, making my heart ache just seeing him in a video queued up and ready to play. Tentatively, I hit the button.

Liam's voice came from off camera. "I don't know, man. She was pretty upset about you not telling her."

When Derek spoke, his words were slurred. A partial bottle of whiskey sat next to him. "She deserves better, Liam. She always has. I love her with every piece of me, every broken bit, man."

I sucked in a breath at hearing those words.

"But it'll never be enough." He paused to take a swig. "That day she kissed me. I knew it right then." His blue eyes looked over the camera. "I remember loving Piper, the holes she carved into me. But loving Avery is like loving a star. How can I ever be worthy of that?"

Shaking his head, he propped an elbow up on the table, resting a forehead on his palm. "Those stupid apartments. You should have seen them. No one was safe there. There was a hole in the steps someone had already fallen through once, the roof looked like it could cave in any minute, and the floors... I was nervous walking in the place. It was a fucking death trap..."

He let out a breath, wiping his hand over his face. "She deserved so much better than that. They all did. No one should live in those conditions. I got a hold of the landlord immediately, and we worked out a deal. But I made sure everyone had safe, backup housing to tide them over until we could get the place up to code."

Derek rubbed his forehead with his fingers. "Now Avery thinks I did it to manipulate her into my bed when I just wanted her safe. Anywhere was better than that rickety place. The landlord and I got started right away on plans for rebuilding. He's breaking ground next month."

Doubt crept in. *Maybe I misjudged Derek?*

"Avery is the best thing that ever happened to me, Liam. I love coming home and seeing her curled up on the couch, lighting up just for me. I love her smart mouth, sassing me whenever I tease her too much. She gets me in a way no one ever has, like she sees everything in me, and it doesn't bother her. It's not home without her here." And the screen abruptly went black.

A drop of moisture hit my hand, and I touched my cheek, realizing I was crying. "Well, shit." I looked to Gina, needing her take on Derek, knowing she wouldn't hold back.

"Look, Ave. I know you think I pushed you to move in with Derek just so I could be with Josh. But when he showed up on our doorstep just to see how he could make you comfortable when you got home from the hospital, I also saw an opportunity. For you. It was a win-win, and you were never going to take that risk on your own. I could tell that Derek really cared about you. And our apartment *was* shit, you can't deny that."

It's true, I can't.

"I'm sorry for the way I pushed you out of the nest. I'm sorry I couldn't tell you sooner, because I knew you'd run. Like you always do." Her dark eyes flicked to mine.

I had to glance away because she was right.

"But I'm not sorry I did it. I stand by my choice." She paused until I looked back at her, giving me a surprisingly soft smile. "I know he can hurt you now, because you're in deep with him. But we all think he's worth it. We're your friends, but we're his, too. And we don't want to see either of you hurt." She reached over, grabbing my hand hard. "The two of you together are like nothing I've ever seen. Both of you are better with each other."

Rhonda's chin bobbed in agreement. "I actually broke up with Kevin just before Derek's party. He didn't come close to the cupcake standard."

I frowned in confusion. "The cupcake standard?"

"It's what I call the bar you two set for the relationship I want. The two of you are so adorable, him calling you Cupcake, you calling him Captain. All the inside jokes, all the teasing, all the feels. You're perfect for each other, and you seem to be the only one doubting it."

The cupcake standard. I like that. Her words sank in. "Wait, you broke up with Kevin? Are you okay? Are—?"

Rhonda stopped me, holding up her hand. "I'm fine. We're focusing on you and Derek right now. But I need my standard to stay together, so I have something to measure against." She winked.

My feet needed to move as my brain raced. I pushed back from the table, pacing around the room. I pieced together everything they'd told me, the bits from the video, things Derek himself had said. Going over all the little details again, I could finally see it. "The escape room."

Gina started smiling, while Liam looked confused. He began to speak, but she shushed him. "She's starting to figure it out."

"He was the one who saw my panic. He rearranged the whole thing, so I wouldn't feel embarrassed." More things came back to me. *The way he handled me coming into the gym shower, confessing my problem with numbers and wanting to take care of the problem right away, despite his nakedness.* I giggled. *Kissing me to shut me up. Never keeping his hands off me when his friends were around. Using them as an excuse because he wanted to touch me. The flowers, breakfast, and note the day of my period. Crashing lunch with my dad, then holding me after.* A thousand, perfect little moments.

I froze, letting the realization soak into my skin. The numbers finally aligned for me—one equation finally worked out. Everything added up.

Derek Elgin really loves me.

Gina stood up, beaming, coming over to hug me.

"He loves me." I mumbled the words into her shoulder.

"I told you so."

I pulled back, grinning stupidly at her, and I said it again. "He loves me."

She smirked. "Now the question is, what are you going to do about it?"

Chapter Twenty

Despite the next day being Thanksgiving and the gala being on Friday, we managed to come up with a decent plan. I stayed away from Derek until the gala, going for the dramatic reveal approach. It was the most difficult thing I'd ever done in my life.

Dressed to the nines, with the help of Rhonda's beauty team, we arrived together. She took her place on stage, both she and her brother in their seats next to obviously empty chairs, filled only by their parents' disappointment. As we all knew, their parents' priority was high-class showing off. This year was no different.

Several employees were given awards. Rhonda had managed to finally direct her father's attention to Derek's paper and app, which his company had begun using without their father even being aware. Once Mr. Elgin put two and two together, he was thrilled with the impact it was having on the Elgin name, slotting in a part of the ceremony for it as we'd hoped. I waited on the sideline, out of view until that particular time.

When it finally came, I wiped my sweaty hands on the nearest curtain, not wanting to risk staining my gorgeous seafoam-green dress. Making sure my strapless corset bodice was properly adjusted, I strode onto the stage, the floor-length satin skirt swishing as I walked over to where Mr. Elgin was pontificating away about his son's accomplishment in a way that glorified himself, somehow making Derek invisible yet again. Although I'd counted on that as well.

A spotlight found me, courtesy of Liam slipping the stage crew a few extra bucks to help us out. A crew member handed me a cordless mic as Mr. Elgin's was cut off.

"Hello, everyone." Confidence rushed through me. I felt unstoppable, bolstered by my friends and by love.

People glanced around, a murmur moving through the crowd.

"I'm here today as a surprise, to help with the introduction of our honored guest, Derek Elgin."

Mr. Elgin still stood front and center, tapping his mic, a little slow to understand my hostile takeover.

I leaned over, filling him in. "There's been a change of plans. You can talk after Derek gets his turn."

He frowned. "He wasn't—"

"*After* Derek gets his turn." I gave him a firm look wanting no room for argument before I turned back to the audience with a smile. "Let's give Mr. Elgin a hand, shall we?" I politely led the audience in a round of applause as Mr. Elgin took his seat, then I stood behind the podium.

I could see Derek out of the corner of my eye, Rhonda's hand on his arm, keeping him in his seat. It was hard to remain facing the crowd, but I somehow managed it. "Now, most of you know the Elgins. Mr.

Elgin, of course, owns the Great Lakes Shipping Co., a company that has flourished under his expert guidance. Mrs. Elgin is well-known for her charity work. She's started several of her own charities, fundraised for many others and gives generously of her time and efforts. Where there is a need, she sees that it's filled." After giving them both tight smiles, I moved on.

"Their children have made their own mark on the world. Rhonda has followed in her mother's footsteps. She recently started a new charity, working with local schools to make sure children have warm coats, hats and boots each winter. What you may not know is that she's a kind person, fiercely loyal and someone you would be lucky to call your friend." I gave her a genuine smile, careful not to meet Derek's eyes, though I felt them burning a hole in me.

"I believe I have saved the best for last. Many of you have met Derek, though most of you wouldn't be able to pick him out of the crowd. He's charming, thoughtful, witty and generous. Graduating in a few short weeks with his master's from Southern Michigan University, he will be the youngest person to claim that honor from the prestigious university. On top of that, he is recognized here tonight because the thesis he wrote, along with the app he produced, have changed the shipping world forever. He's definitely a person worth knowing. And, if you give him a chance" — I paused, turning to face him, needing to say the next words to him — "you'll grow to love him. I know I do."

Derek's blue eyes grew wide, and Rhonda shoved his shoulder. He stumbled out of his chair as I clicked off the microphone. His megawatt smile lit his face as he raced over, picking me up and swinging me around to the roar of the crowd. "I love you, too."

We clung to each other for a long moment, then he kissed me soundly as I threaded my fingers through his hair. When I pulled back, I grinned up at him. "It's your turn to talk, Derek."

He frowned. "What?"

My hands gave his shoulders an encouraging squeeze. "I told your dad he could talk. After you."

"But, what am I supposed to say?"

I grinned. "Whatever you want. Make it short and simple or talk forever. But it's your time to shine." That was the point of all this, giving Derek the credit he was due and making him step into the spotlight. I handed him the mic and gave him a gentle nudge.

Uncertainty crossed his face, but it was quickly replaced with determination as he strode up to the podium. "Thank you for that wonderful introduction, Avery." He mouthed "I love you" once more to me, then turned to the crowd, telling everyone about the app he'd developed. With a confident ease that won them over.

My heart swelled, watching him from my seat next to Rhonda. We shared an excited grin that my grand gesture had worked.

The gala was still going a few hours later. I had my head on Derek's chest, one hand in his, the other on his shoulder. The night couldn't be any more perfect. I sighed, looking up into his beautiful blue eyes as he gazed back at me. We just stared at each other, lost in the moment of music and swaying, as the final notes hung in the air.

Everyone around us pulled apart and clapped for the chamber orchestra. I reluctantly let go of Derek to applaud for the musicians, too. They stood, announcing a brief intermission.

"Want to find something to drink?"

I nodded, feeling parched. Derek offered his arm, guiding me to the refreshment table, which had become the gathering point since the music had stopped. We made small talk with several people along the way, mostly well-wishers for Derek, congratulating him on his success.

After handing me a cup of champagne punch, Derek steered me out of the crowd, only to be ambushed by his dad.

"There you are, son." His dad clapped him firmly on the shoulder with a proud grin, as he looked at the stuffed shirts behind him. "Walk with us for a few. There's some things we want to discuss."

A frown crossed Derek's face. "Not tonight, Dad. I just want to spend time with Avery, okay?"

My heart soared, listening to him say no, telling his dad just what he wanted. I smiled up at him, all my adoration in my eyes.

His dad, on the other hand, looked less than thrilled. He stepped closer, leaning in so only Derek and I could hear him. "Let's not forget who sent you to school in the first place." He arched an eyebrow. "Just a short word or two."

And I watched Derek cave, just that quickly, forgetting that he was worth fighting for, forgetting everything I'd worked so hard to show him these past couple of months. He turned to me, an apologetic smile on his face, and he shrugged. Like, what else was he supposed to do? I gritted my teeth together, holding back the torrent of words I wanted to scream at him.

Why can't he see? Why does he blindly go along with what everyone else wants?

His dad led him away, and I stood there, annoyed, seething, wondering if he'd ever realize his worth. When I turned around, ready to go get some air, fate had different ideas.

"Hello, Avery," my mother said, smiling. "I see you're already being left behind by the Elgins. Too bad, I enjoyed having them around."

"Mother." The word came out at least partially on the polite spectrum, though I wasn't sure how I managed it. "I didn't realize you'd be here."

Her expression turned almost sympathetic. "Oh, you poor dear, doesn't he tell you anything? Your boyfriend invited me."

The room reeled, even as I knew there was more to the story. Derek would never have invited Mother without a reason. But now I desperately needed that air. I shoved past her, without even saying goodbye. I'd almost made it to the stairway, looking up at the route to my escape, when a firm hand gripped my upper arm.

"Avery, have you seen Rhonda?" Kevin, Rhonda's ex, asked me, unaware of my near-panicked state. He noticed my dress, his eyes lingering as he leered at me. "Don't you look pretty tonight? Gold digging suits you." His gaze looked over my shoulder, seeing what I'd left behind. "Is that your mother? She is something."

The leer in his eyes transferred to her, and I almost gagged as I wrenched my arm out of his grasp. "I haven't seen Rhonda, but I know she wants nothing to do with you. And neither do I." I continued on my path up the stairs. I finally reached the balcony overlooking the gala, pausing while others made their exit.

Raised voices below had me turning to see what all the fuss was about.

Derek stood just inside the entrance of the opposite way I'd come, hands clenched into fists. "I am not just some pawn of yours, Father. You can't push me around however you want. The app is mine, to use how I see fit. When you want to talk to me as an adult, as an equal, *then* I'll do business with you." He spun on his heel, stalking across the floor.

I put a hand to my chest, watching his every movement. It seemed he'd found his voice after all, and my heart nearly burst with pride. *That's my boyfriend.*

Liam intercepted Derek, whispering frantically in his ear, then gesturing to someone near the refreshment table below me. I peered over the railing, wondering who they were talking about. I gasped as Derek strode right up to my mother.

"Mabel."

His voice was perfect, the commanding voice that instantly had me wet and wanting.

"What did you say to Avery?"

I couldn't make out Mother's answer, but I'd never seen her cower before. My grin widened. The whole ballroom stopped to watch, fascinated by the scene.

Derek stayed in her face. "You listen, and you listen good. Avery's the best thing that's ever happened to me, and you are done walking all over her. Any communication you want to have with her from now on will be done through me. Is that clear?"

Mother's towering red hair bobbed as she nodded.

Derek pushed away from her. His head moved from side to side, then he once again spoke to Liam who shrugged. I frowned. *What's he looking for?* He whirled, scanning the ballroom, eyes frantic. When they crashed onto mine, his lips mouthed my name.

Then he yelled it. "Avery, wait!"

As if I have any hope of going anywhere after that scene. I stood frozen on the balcony, my eyes following him as he wove his way through the crowd and up the stairs, finally appearing before me.

"Running away again?" he asked, not quite approaching me.

I shook my head, unable to read him. "I needed some air after…"

"After what, Avery?" He climbed another step.

My words were barely a whisper. "After you left with your dad. After you didn't fight. After I ran into my mom." I watched him close the distance between us, watched him stand in front of me, those brilliant blue eyes looking down at me.

"But I did fight. For you and for us."

I nodded. "I saw."

Anger flickered in the depths of his gaze. "You were running. You gave up on me. Again."

Indignation flared in me. My neck cracked, that was how emphatically I shook my head as I glared up at him. "Never. I'll never give up on you." Sparks crackled between us, and I swallowed. I realized I needed this, I needed him to chase me, needed whatever closure this was giving us, so I followed my gut. "What would you do if I did?"

He frowned. "What?" Panic flared in his gaze, warring inside him with the Derek I knew was in there, the one I so desperately wanted to win.

"I changed my mind." I crossed my arms and jutted out a hip. "I'm leaving." The panic in his eyes faded as anger took over, my hope growing steadily by the second. His glare should have infuriated me, but instead it ignited something inside me. I resisted the urge to rub my thighs together at the sight of Derek fighting. For us.

"Really?" The word came through his clenched teeth. "*Why* are you leaving?" He stepped even closer, challenging me, trying to intimidate me.

And I was having all of it. My response came out soft and breathy. "Because I can." I studied him, watching the war within. The damaged, conditioned part of him wanted to slink off and lick his wounds while the real Derek, the Derek I knew and loved, struggled to make himself heard. "Why shouldn't I?"

He gripped my shoulder. "Because I love you, Avery. You are the light in my life, you make everything better. Home is not the same without you in it. I walk in the door, and I want to see you there, smiling at me from the couch. I want to wake up in the morning to your ridiculous questions. I want to snuggle in our chair and make love to you every night. Is that reason enough to stay?"

I pulled back to search his face, still not quite seeing the resolve I needed. "I don't know, Derek. Should I leave?"

His eyes narrowed, locking with mine, and one word came out. More growl than anything. "No."

I searched him, hope flaring in me so bright it was blinding. "What?" I breathed, grasping the folds of my dress so I didn't grab Derek and drag his lips onto mine. I waited, needing to hear him say it.

As he leaned down, he smirked. "I said no, don't leave."

It was that no-nonsense, all-business tone of his that pushed me over the edge, and the fragile hold on my self-control slipped.

He tilted his head, studying me now. "What?"

I allowed my need to shine through, my voice husky with it. "I fantasize about hearing that voice in bed."

Those blue eyes widened, blinking in shock.

"What are you going to do to stop me?" I lowered my voice to almost a whisper, taking half a step backward.

His grin was predatory. "This." And with one swift motion, he threw me over his shoulder, striding through the door with my ass in the air.

I smiled as I bounced along, happy to be back where I belonged. "Derek?"

"Yeah?" He slowed.

"I love you." I heard his smile when he answered.

"I love you, too."

My fingers played with the waistline of his pants through the split in his suit coat. "Don't take off the tie."

He paused in his steps. "What? Why?"

I grinned. "'Cause I have plans for it."

"Yeah?" He set me down, making sure I slid down every solid inch of him.

Not that I was complaining. I kept my eyes on his the entire time, letting him see how much I enjoyed it. Particularly when I ended up pressed against his thigh, his warm hands around my waist. Then I realized we weren't alone.

Derek was speaking to a chauffeur, not Greg. When the chauffeur left, Derek said, "Greg took Rhonda home. Tony drove me here tonight, so he'll take us home."

I went to get in, but Derek's hand stopped me.

"One more thing, Cupcake." His hand came up to fiddle with his tie, not meeting my gaze. "I hope I'm not overstepping, but I spoke to my lawyers. They think you'd have a pretty good case if you want to build something against your mom. You could go for power of attorney over your dad, and it sounds to me like a lot of her start-up money was his to begin with, so there might be misappropriation of funds, too. Maybe even neglect, given his isolated situation."

I gaped at him, too stunned to speak.

He touched my cheek, searching my face. "Was that too much? Should I have kept my nose out of it?"

Tears gathered in my eyes, spilling down my cheeks as I threw my arms around him. "No, Derek. That's the best possible gift you could have ever given me. Thank you. From the bottom of my heart." I clung to him for a long moment as I regained my composure, then I stepped back, swiping at my cheeks.

His smile was tender as he allowed me time to compose myself. "Okay, I'll give my lawyers the go-ahead to start looking into it first thing tomorrow."

I kissed him, slowly, passionately, putting all the things I couldn't say into that kiss. When I pulled back and Derek turned those burning blue eyes on me, I was suddenly thankful Greg wasn't our driver.

After opening the door, Derek commanded me, "Get in."

"Yes, Captain." My answer was demure, and I made sure to show a bit more leg than necessary climbing in. I knew he'd appreciate the lacy garters. Desire strained within me, a frantic thing needing to be freed. The coolness of the leather seat jarred my skin through my dress, and I could hardly wait the few seconds for Derek to be next to me. At least the barrier was up between us and the front seat.

As soon as he was within reach, I grabbed a hold of the tie, just like the first day. I yanked him to me, burying my other hand in his luscious curls and finally, finally melded my lips to his.

His delicious weight settled on top of me. Somehow even in our frenzy, he was thoughtful, producing something soft to stuff under my head while we devoured one another. His hands were everywhere, running down my bodice, stroking my thighs, cupping my ass. Our teeth clashed as we deepened the kiss.

"How does this thing come off?" he asked, pulling back and looking at my dress like it was his nemesis.

I couldn't help a laugh. "I picked it out just for you."

He waited impatiently, arching an eyebrow. So I gave him a not so subtle shove as he sighed and moved off me. Then I presented him with my back, sweeping my hair to one side.

"I definitely need help getting out of this one." Silence met me, so I glanced over my shoulder. I grinned to see his mouth open as he gaped at my laces. "You didn't notice?"

He shook his head. "I was so busy staring at the rest of you. And your hair hid most of it." One warm finger trailed along my bare shoulder blade, and he pressed a kiss there.

"It seemed like a pirate-y thing to do."

"Nah, a pirate would just take out his sword and slice through all these." He paused, and I felt the top loosen. "But I think I'll enjoy it, taking my time. Especially..." He turned me so I was facing him, then tugged me onto his lap. "Yes, that's better."

Confused, I opened my mouth to ask, but then he pulled another lace, making my bodice loosen even more. His eyes drifted to where my breasts spilled over the top of the gown. The tension grew between us, connected at the apex of my hips and his cock along with his nimble fingers unlacing my gown. It was a tense game, waiting for the moment for my top to fall. I wasn't sure who would win or lose or what the prize would be, but with each string pulled my panties grew damper and his cock hardened beneath me.

Soon I longed to move against him. My nipples were pebbled peaks that ached for his touch. "I'm sorry I ran away."

He paused. "I'm sorry I didn't come after you sooner."

My heart broke a little at his words, and I threw my arms around his neck. "I'm just glad you did. But more than that, I needed you to realize that you...that we...are worth fighting for." I kissed his cheek first, trailing more kisses until I reached his mouth where I poured out all my love for him.

He gripped me tightly. He ran his hands along the bodice so the front fell down, baring my breasts. His lips left mine, making its way to one of my aching nipples. When he took it in his mouth, I cried out, arching against him.

"So beautiful," he murmured, cupping my other breast in his hand, brushing his thumb over my other peaked point. Then he rolled his hips, and I nearly came on the spot. He smirked. "Just like that first night, when you had me pinned."

As he rolled his hips again, I tilted my head back and went with it. I let go of everything else, trusting Derek, as I truly surrendered.

Epilogue

The bells to the coffee shop jangled, and I waved at Rhonda from where I sat with Gina. Rhonda smiled, but it didn't quite meet her eyes. She looked amazing as always, in an immaculate designer pantsuit with her dark hair up in a sleek French twist. And her Louis Vuitton heels were to die for. She hurried to the counter to order.

It was weird sitting out in the café when I was so used to being on the other side of the counter, but Not Your Average Joe was central to all of us. Plus, they had damn good coffee.

As soon as Rhonda had her coffee, she strode over to us. "Hey, ladies, how is everyone?" She gave me a pointed look since we hadn't really spoken since the gala.

Gina glanced at me too, her smirk all knowing.

I set my cup down, and let my joy shine out in my full-blast smile. "I'm amazing. Derek's beyond amazing." Rhonda wrinkled her nose at my innuendo, but I just laughed. "Thank you guys so much for helping me pull that off. I couldn't have done it without you."

They both grinned back at me, but Rhonda's was lacking.

"So what about you? You left kind of early, and I heard Greg gave you a ride home." I was still dying to know the story there, but both of them had been shut tighter than a stubborn oyster not wanting to give up its pearl.

Her blue eyes dropped to her coffee cup as she spun it around in her hands, reminding me of when I first met Derek for breakfast. She sighed. "Ever since I broke up with Kevin, I've felt...off. It's not that I miss him," she was quick to qualify. "I don't, but I don't quite know how I fit in my own life anymore."

The heaviness in her words draped over the table like a coat of cement. There I sat feeling happier than I've ever been, and my friend was hurting. I reached over to grip her fingers. "You'll figure it out. You've got this."

Gina nodded her agreement. "Plus, there's a certain chauffeur who seems like he'd be willing to give you a distraction any time you need it." She waggled her eyebrows.

"Greg?" Rhonda frowned. "No, there's nothing between us." The disappointment in her words and the way her face fell said she wished there was.

I tucked that observation away for later. "So what happened after the gala?"

Her cheeks flushed a pretty pink, and she ducked her head. "He drove me home, nothing unusual there."

My snort came out before I could stop it, both Gina and Rhonda staring at me. I shrugged. "I mean, there had to be something. Greg told Derek he's not working for him anymore, that he's going back to work for you."

Rhonda's blush intensified. "I guess there was a moment." She looked above my head, seemingly lost in a memory. "When I went to get out of the limo, my feet tangled in my dress, and I fell. I thought I was going to smash face first into the pavement, but he caught me." Her words were on the breathless side, tumbling out faster and faster. "He had me brace myself on his shoulders, then he knelt down and untangled my dress."

She was a million miles away and I exchanged a knowing look with Gina. There was definitely something between those two, and I couldn't wait to see where it went.

I turned to Gina, wanting to hear the latest on her and Josh while I kept one eye on the time. Derek had to travel to Canada again this weekend, but this time I was going with him.

After way too much coffee, a heap of well-wishes and a flurry of goodbyes, I made it back to the apartment at precisely two-thirty p.m., just like I'd promised. Derek sat on the couch near our bags, and he looked up as I walked in. His blue eyes sparkled when his gaze landed on me, then he popped to his feet. I strode over to him, tilting my chin up for a kiss. He didn't disappoint, his mouth claiming me like he always did. *My Captain.*

Would it ever be enough? Would I ever get to the point of having stable knees when his lips met mine or when he flashed me that megawatt smile? He pulled away, grinning down at me.

I linked my fingers behind his neck, smiling back at him. I sure as hell hoped not, but I was willing to spend forever finding out.

Want to see more from this author?
Here's a taster for you to enjoy!

Sweet Nothings:
The Jellybean Dilemma
Maren Jenner

Coming December 2023

Excerpt

I tapped the toe of my Jimmy Choo impatiently as I watched for Greg to pull the limo up. At last, his headlights flashed through the glass door, and I hurried into the frigid night. I didn't go far, though, since I promised Greg I'd wait for him to escort me to the car. Snow was my enemy when wearing heels.

Greg jumped out of the front seat as soon as he'd parked, striding toward me. His twinkling gray eyes met mine before he offered me his arm, and his mouth tipped up at one corner. "You actually waited for me."

With my chin high, I looped my arm through his, gripping his forearm as we crossed the short distance. "I didn't want to risk spraining an ankle." Or making a fool of myself by falling into him as I'd done last month after my parents' gala. Though, the few moments in his strong arms were almost worth my embarrassment.

"You're the one choosing to wear death trap shoes."

As if to emphasize his words, one of my heels slipped, but I steadied myself against him. My heart started racing as his peppermint and cedar scent enveloped me. I had to get control of myself. "These are Jimmy Choos," I sniffed. "I'll have you know this particular style isn't even available to the public yet." I looked up, way up, to see what he had to say about that. Even in my heels, he still had four inches on me, and it was more than annoying at times like this.

Greg scoffed. "Just cause they're pretty, doesn't mean they're practical. Michigan doesn't give a damn about the latest fashion trend." He yanked open the back door of the limo with a chiding glare.

I transferred my grip to his gloved hand, feeling like a chastised child as I slid into the back seat. I couldn't do anything on my own, not even a simple walk to the car. A heavy fog of depression crept over me. Christmas was over. Tonight was the last of the parties I had to attend and the week until New Year loomed before me.

My brother, Derek and his fiancée Avery had hosted tonight. Our friends Gina and Liam were there, too, along with their current significant others. Greg and I had been the only singles there.

Not that I minded being single. It was a huge improvement from being engaged to Kevin, my ex-fiancé I broke up with two months ago. But it was difficult to see Derek and Avery snuggled together, stealing touches or kisses every chance they got. My eye caught on Greg coming out with another armload of presents, and I sighed. It was especially hard when the man I wanted was always so close, yet so unattainable.

Greg shut the trunk with a thud as he finished loading the presents, then he took his place in the front seat. The barrier between us was down, as usual. His gaze caught mine in the mirror, looking decidedly less stormy than when he'd put me in the limo. Especially when he smiled. "Did you get your present?"

I frowned. We'd already exchanged gifts inside. My fingers grazed the soft cashmere scarf he'd given me. I'd given him a bottle of cologne, the same kind he always wore. It ensured I could have my fill of his delicious scent.

The light from a streetlamp glinted off a small package to my right. Excitement fluttered through me as I reached for it, a full smile blooming on my face when I felt the familiar weight. I held it up, giddy to see a whole bag of jellybeans wrapped in cellophane and tied with a lopsided red ribbon. I thought he'd forgotten. Warmth flooded me, a welcome change from the depressing bleakness which had cocooned me over the last few weeks.

"Merry Christmas, Jellybean," he said softly.

My throat was tight at all the memories his gift brought to mind, and I had to swallow before I answered, "Merry Christmas, Just Greg." His face transformed with a genuine grin; the kind that made my stomach do all sorts of acrobatics.

"Home?"

I hated that word. It didn't come close to describing the house I lived in. Exhaustion, heavier than a weighted blanket, settled over me once more, but I nodded. As we started off, I pushed aside my bleak thoughts and let my mind drift to the origin of Greg's nickname.

Greg had hired on at nineteen as an apprentice to his uncle Harry, our main driver. Derek and I were thirteen, at the time, with too many activities for one driver to handle. My parents, owners of the vast Great Lakes' Shipping empire, had wanted someone they knew and trusted. When Harry recommended his nephew, that was that.

I smiled, calling to Greg, "How many nicknames did I try out on you?"

One side of his mouth ticked up, finding my eyes again in the mirror. "I didn't keep track."

Oh, how annoyed he'd been. There weren't many nicknames for Greg, so I'd pestered him for his full name, Gregory James Peterson, trying every combination in the book.

"What was so wrong with Greg anyway?"

Absolutely nothing. "I thought it was too formal." I shrugged. "Sorry." We both chuckled.

One day he'd had enough. As I'd exited the limo, he'd stopped me with a gentle, "Miss Rhonda?"

I'd haughtily paused, staring up at his face while also trying to look down my nose at him. Difficult to do with him so much taller than me. His six-foot two frame had seemed even more gigantic back then.

"No more nicknames. It's just Greg."

And I'd smiled brightly. "Fine, Just Greg." Then I'd skipped off to my activity.

As the limo slowed to a stop in front of my too big house, I grabbed my candy and waited for Greg to open the door. I took my time getting out, letting his steady hand guide me. At least my steps were clear so he wouldn't need to walk me all the way up.

I couldn't help glancing at his handsome face, a wave of longing crashing over me as I cradled my precious bag of jellybeans. Greg became my brother's driver after I turned nineteen, just over two years ago. I didn't like to analyze why Greg had jumped ship. One specific incident stood out, but I shoved that aside, like always.

Lately though, Greg had drifted back to me, but I wasn't sure why. It seemed like he had a good thing going with Derek and Avery, crossing over from mere employee to good friends with both of them. Since the gala though, I'd seen more and more of him.

I turned to make my way up the steps, dreading the emptiness of my huge, dark house.

"What should I do with the presents?"

The question halted me in my tracks, and I had to stop myself from wrinkling my nose. Just thinking of all the packages I'd ripped open, all the beautiful paper carefully labeled with my name, unsettled my stomach. I appreciated the thought our friends had put into picking out my gifts, but the idea of dealing with all the new stuff overwhelmed me. I sighed.

"Rhonda?" Concern laced Greg's voice.

Suddenly the steps seemed impossible to climb as the next week stretched before me, a depressing runway into another year. Just the thought of starting over made tears burn against my eyes. I turned to look at him as I asked, "What are you doing for New Year's?"

Frowning, he left his post by the car to stand in front of me. "What's going on, Jellybean? You're not yourself. Is it the breakup with Kevin, or is something else going on?" One gloved hand reached out, hovering in the space between us, stopping just shy of my arm.

I didn't pull away, but I didn't close the distance either as annoyance flashed through me. "I'm tired of people assuming my life ended when my relationship with Kevin did. Or apologizing for it. 'I'm so sorry to hear about your breakup!'" I rolled my eyes. "There's nothing to be sorry for. I knew exactly what I was doing then, and I haven't regretted it for a moment." Truth rang through my statement, echoing in the silence between us. Yet my words fell short. I really didn't regret breaking up with Kevin, but it didn't change the fact that I was floundering.

I'd been raised my entire life for one job—to marry someone wealthy, and accept my place on that pedestal, visible for everyone's admiration and scrutiny. The thing about pedestals was they were only built for one. And it was hard to get down on your own.

Greg cleared his throat, looking like he might apologize.

But that was the opposite of what I needed, so I repeated my question, more firmly, "What are you doing for New Year's?"

He sighed. "I was thinking of going home. It's been a while, and my sister's having this big New Year's wedding…"

My jaw dropped. "Wait. You haven't said if you're going to your sister's wedding yet? It's only a week away!"

As he always did when he was uncomfortable, he adjusted his hat. "It's not that simple. I don't have a date, for one. And if I show up by myself, my family will try to set me up with every single girl there."

I practically felt him shudder, and my wheels started spinning. "Take me." The words tumbled out of my mouth before I could think twice.

"What?" His hat nearly flew off his head, the way his eyebrows shot up. He scoffed. "Yeah, right."

The more I thought about it, the more perfect the idea sounded. "Why not? No one knows me other than your uncle." I shrugged. "Sure, they've probably heard of me, but that just makes you sound better." My last name carried weight in all the right circles. "No one has to know you're my driver, unless you want them to. I've got nothing going on and I desperately need a change of scenery. Where is this wedding?" Images of warm, tropical places floated through my head.

"Marquette."

Those two syllables shut down any vacation fantasies I had. "In the middle of winter?" Michigan's upper peninsula was harsh at the best of times, but during the winter, it was simply brutal. I frowned. "*That's* where you grew up? No wonder you're so grumpy."

A noise escaped from him, part snort, part grunt. "So, you *don't* want to go?" He folded his arms, staring at me with those unnerving gray eyes.

He was still taller than me, even though I stood on the step above him. "I didn't say that." The very thought of spending New Year's here threatened to send me into a panic.

"Then you want to come?"

This time I didn't hesitate. "Yes."

"And you'll go as my date?" Skepticism laced every word.

"Yes." My stomach flipped at the idea.

A slow smile spread across Greg's handsome face. "Rhonda Elgin going out with the chauffeur. What are you going to tell your parents?"

His words punctured a hole in the carefully erected barrier I'd placed my teenage fantasies in. There had been a time when not a day went by without me dreaming of that very thing, but he'd never known. *Except for that one unfortunate incident.*

I swallowed, fighting to keep the tremor out of my voice. "Unless you plan to announce it to them, I doubt they'll find out. Especially since they're out of the country." With a quick glance at the limo, I said, "Could you please put the presents on the dining room table? I'll sort through them later. Text me the details about the trip." I started up the steps, then I paused.

Greg was bent over the open trunk.

"And Greg?"

That handsome head poked around the side.

"I mean it, I actually want details." Not vague suggestions. I needed actual concrete plans to figure out what I should bring. I waited until he nodded to finish climbing the steps.

* * * *

Upstairs, I snitched a few jellybeans from the package before changing out of my dress. My shoes came off next as I rummaged for comfy clothes. It was a relief to let my hair down.

Then my phone started pinging. And it didn't stop. *What the hell?* I hurried over, wondering what the emergency was.

It was Greg, texting me every possible detail he had, mostly copies of messages from his sister. I trotted downstairs to find him leaning against the counter, behind the tower of presents on the dining room table.

His smirk grew as I scowled. "Was that enough details?"

"You seriously want to leave the day after tomorrow?"

When he shrugged, his uniform jacket bunched up around his waist, and he tugged it down with a sharp motion. "If we're doing this, we're all in. I haven't been home in a while, so it'll be a big to-do. I'll be in it for the whole nine yards—the bachelor party, rehearsal dinner, and, of course, the wedding." He paused. "All or nothing."

I digested the information, a far cry from the easy getaway I'd imagined.

He arched an eyebrow. "And, as you so politely pointed out, I should let my sister know sooner than later."

His challenging stare lingered on me, and I felt naked without my formal wear.

He stepped closer, an earnestness coming over him. "Rhonda, I know it's a lot. And its short notice, but once I started thinking about going with you… I really want to. It'll be great to see everyone again. My sister will die outright of happiness, an Elgin attending her wedding!" His throat bobbed. "This might be overstepping, but I think it'd be good for you to get out of here."

Silence hung between us as I digested his words, the sincerity of his request taking me aback. *He wants me to go?* My heart skipped a beat.

"We're all worried about you, Avery and Derek especially. You've lost weight." He scanned my length, a frown tightening his mouth. "You hardly go anywhere. You don't talk to anyone."

Wow, I know Greg and Derek are close, but this is a whole new level. Is that Avery's doing? Unease sat in me that he was paying such close attention without me even knowing it. I didn't know what to do with his scrutiny. I swallowed hard, glancing at the floor.

"Come with me." His tone softened, almost begging me. "My family will love you, and I promise you won't be bored. What do you say, Jellybean?"

My eyes flicked back to his. When I took in that pleading smile, I simply couldn't say no.

* * * *

Two days later, a horn honked outside while I scrambled to find my other Jimmy Choo. *I just had it.* Three quick raps on the door let me know it was Greg. He always knocked the same way.

"It's open," I called, ducking under the table.

The annoying squeak of the front door sounded, once then twice. Countless repairmen had been fired and given bad Yelp reviews for not fixing that ridiculous noise.

"Your hinges are too tight."

My head slammed against the underside of the table, and I grit my teeth against the pain as I backed out as gracefully as I could.

Greg grinned down at me, one black Jimmy Choo dangling from his finger. "Missing something?"

Rubbing my head wouldn't do anything except mess up my hair, and yelling at Greg wasn't going to make either of us feel any better. So I choked back my annoyance, giving him a tight smile before biting out a clipped, "Thank you."

When I reached for my shoe, he offered his hand. I took it, my breath hitching at the warm touch. Usually his gloves formed a barrier between us, and I blurted out, "You're not wearing your uniform." The moment the words left my lips I wished I could take them back. I bit my lip. "I, um..." I sagged into the nearest chair. "I'm sorry, that sounded idiotic. I haven't had the best morning, and I'm running on no caffeine." Our gazes collided as I lifted my chin, relieved at the understanding in his.

Instead of handing me my shoe, he knelt in front of me. *What's he doing?* He gestured to my stocking-clad foot and softly asked, "May I?"

I nodded, still unsure.

One side of his mouth tipped up. His bare hand grasped my ankle ever so gently, reminding me of the night of the gala when he'd untangled me from my dress. Except now I couldn't breathe, each brush of his fingers sending jolts of electricity up my calf. Then he slid my shoe onto my foot, buckling the dainty strap like he'd done it a million times. "All right, Jellybean, now you're ready to go to the ball."

When he offered me his hand, I wasn't positive I was steady enough to stand, especially in the wake of that dimpled grin.

About the Author

Maren Jenner lives in Michigan with her supportive husband and spunky daughter. She loves writing, and when she's not working on her next book, she's got her nose in a different one. Her summers are spent on any lake she can visit, but the beaches of Lake Michigan are her favorite.

The Cupcake Standard is her debut novel, though she's been writing for as long as she can remember. It's always been a dream to become a full time author. Her dreams wouldn't be possible without the love and support of her family and friends.

Maren loves to hear from readers. You can find her contact information, website details and author profile page at https://www.totallybound.com

Home of Erotic Romance

Sign up for our newsletter and find out about all our romance book releases, eBook sales and promotions, sneak peeks and FREE romance books!

www.ingramcontent.com/pod-product-compliance
Lightning Source LLC
Chambersburg PA
CBHW022143010726
47493CB00002B/323